Aaron lifted her off her feet and hard against him.

"Is this a good idea?" Mel's voice wavered.

"You can tell me no." He lowered his mouth, stopping a millimeter shy of kissing her.

In the deepest recesses of her mind, a small voice shouted a warning to be careful. This was inviting danger.

She didn't listen. Aaron smelled too delicious and felt too good for her to stop now.

"I've missed you, Mel." He brushed his lips across hers, the touch softer than a butterfly's wings.

The words she'd longed to hear. Aaron had never said them before, in this or any context. Missing her implied he thought about her when they were apart. Hadn't she just ripped the rug out from under him with her pregnancy announcement? Yet, he admitted to missing her.

This wasn't just a matter of growing feelings. There had to be more.

COUNTRY LEGACY

THE LAWMAN'S FAMILY

NEW YORK TIMES BESTSELLING AUTHOR

Cathy McDavid

&

USA TODAY BESTSELLING AUTHOR

Mary Leo

2 Heartfelt Stories

A Baby for the Deputy
and *A Baby for the Sheriff*

HARLEQUIN

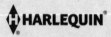 **HARLEQUIN®**

Recycling programs
for this product may
not exist in your area.

ISBN-13: 978-1-335-44883-5

The Lawman's Family

Copyright © 2022 by Harlequin Enterprises ULC

A Baby for the Deputy
First published in 2017. This edition published in 2022.
Copyright © 2017 by Cathy McDavid

A Baby for the Sheriff
First published in 2017. This edition published in 2022.
Copyright © 2017 by Mary Leo

This edition published by arrangement with Harlequin Books S.A.

For questions and comments about the quality of this book,
please contact us at CustomerService@Harlequin.com.

Harlequin Enterprises ULC
22 Adelaide St. West, 41st Floor
Toronto, Ontario M5H 4E3, Canada
www.Harlequin.com

Printed in U.S.A.

CONTENTS

Since 2006, *New York Times* bestselling author
Cathy McDavid has been happily penning
contemporary Westerns for Harlequin. Every day,
she gets to write about handsome cowboys riding
the range or busting a bronc. It's a tough job, but
she's willing to make the sacrifice. Cathy shares her
Arizona home with her own real-life sweetheart and a
trio of odd pets. Her grown twins have left to embark
on lives of their own, and she couldn't be prouder of
their accomplishments.

Books by Cathy McDavid

Harlequin Heartwarming

Wishing Well Springs

The Cowboy's Holiday Bride
How to Marry a Cowboy

The Sweetheart Ranch

A Cowboy's Christmas Proposal
The Cowboy's Perfect Match
The Cowboy's Christmas Baby
Her Cowboy Sweetheart

Visit the Author Profile page at
Harlequin.com for more titles.

A BABY FOR
THE DEPUTY

Cathy McDavid

To the lovely and dedicated members
of Cathy's Crew—thanks for being part of
my street team and helping me get the
word out. You're the best!

Chapter 1

Sensing danger, Melody Hartman quickly straightened and scrambled out of the way. A split second later, the horse's rear hoof sliced the air in the exact spot where Mel's head had just been.

She pretended to wipe sweat from her brow. "Whew. That was close."

"Sorry." The horse's owner, a tall, trim woman in her fifties, tugged on the bay's halter. "This fellow has a temper. I should have warned you."

"It's okay." Mel relaxed her grip on the surgical scissors she held and let out a sigh, grateful her instincts had once again paid off. "Not my first near miss."

The truth was, Mel encountered far closer calls on a regular basis. As recently as this morning, she'd been knocked to the ground by a potbellied pig, narrowly missing the steely prongs of a pitchfork. Last week, she'd been stomped on by an eighteen-hundred-pound bull, miraculously escaping with only minor cuts and contusions. An infected cat scratch recently sent her to the emergency medical clinic.

Such was the daily life of Mustang Valley's sole resident veterinarian. Dangers and difficulties aside, she wouldn't trade her job for the world. Mel was living her dream. Quite literally. She'd wanted to be a veterinarian for as long as she could remember, and buying Doc Palmer's practice when he retired a few months ago had turned that dream into reality.

"Think you should give him more tranquilizers?" the woman asked, shielding her eyes from the glaring Arizona sun.

They were at Powell Ranch, the largest and oldest horse operation in the area. The woman was one of many people who boarded their horses there and made use of the riding facilities.

Mel shook her head. "I don't want him so sleepy he lays down on us. The wound's right between his gaskin and stifle. He could pull on the flesh and inflict more damage."

The bay was tied to a post at the far end of the outdoor stalls. He'd gotten into a scuffle with his neighbor, a shaggy and even more temperamental pony, who'd retaliated by biting the bay and leaving two gaping holes on his left rear leg. Unfortunately, the injury went unnoticed for a couple of days—the horse's owner had been out of town. By the time she discovered the wound, it was inflamed, infected and just plain nasty.

Seeing the bay's eyes drift close, Mel decided to make another attempt at removing the necrotic tissue. The procedure didn't hurt the horse. He'd kicked at Mel more out of anger than pain. Also, just like some people, he wasn't a good patient.

"Hold him steady," Mel told the woman as she quickly snipped away with the scissors. Finishing that task, she cleansed the wound again and applied a liberal glob of medicated ointment.

"Are you going to stitch him up?" the woman asked, peering around the bay's head.

Mel continued to assess the wound. "I don't think so. The edges are too ragged for sutures to hold. Better we stick to a strict antibiotic regiment. You know how to give injections?"

"Me? I'm an old pro."

Many livestock owners, especially those in rural areas, were capable of doctoring their animals to some degree. Vets were consulted for only the more serious cases.

"Good. I'll leave you enough penicillin and syringes for two weeks. He's going to need twice daily injections." Mel ran her hand gingerly down the bay's leg. "No sense bandaging the wound, either. It won't hold."

"He'd just chew it off," the woman said with a resigned sigh.

Mel started to pack her case. Before closing it, she handed the woman her jar of salve. "Cleanse the wound at the same time you give him the injections and apply this. Call me if he's not showing any improvement or the wound becomes reinfected."

"Thanks for coming out on such short notice."

"No problem."

Mel carried her case to her truck while the woman returned the sleepy horse to his stall. Setting the case on the ground, she leaned against the hood and stifled a yawn. The bay wasn't the only one who was tired. Mel had been up and hard at it since five this morning, nearly nine hours ago, with no break.

As she opened the storage compartment on her truck, she was struck with a sudden wave of nausea and light-headedness. Hugging her middle, she waited for the sensation to pass, hoping she hadn't caught that flu bug going around.

Tomorrow was a big day. She, her two sisters and her new stepmom were throwing a huge sixtieth birthday party for her dad at the Cowboy Up Café where her older sister worked. They still had a lot to do, and the last thing Mel needed was to be under the weather.

Fortunately, the nausea passed, and the next instant, Mel felt perfectly fine. That was…strange.

She might have thought more about it if not for a black SUV turning the corner of the horse barn, distracting her. The writing and logo emblazoned on each side identified the vehicle as belonging to the Maricopa County Sheriff's Department. Three deputies were assigned to Mustang Valley and its nearest neighbor, Rio Verde. They were often spotted patrolling the streets, parked in front of people's homes or, like today, at one of the ranches.

The driver's door opened, and a pair of familiar leather cowboy boots hit the ground, followed by long legs clad in dark brown slacks and a khaki uniform shirt. Mel's heart gave a flutter as it always did upon seeing this particular deputy, and she promptly forgot all about stowing her case.

As she watched, he walked slowly, yet deliberately, toward her. She imagined a twinkle in the vivid blue eyes he hid behind aviator sunglasses. Recalled how the bristles of his five-o'clock shadow tickled her palm when she cradled his cheek.

"Dr. Hartman." He nodded in greeting.

Pushing aside her long braid, a silly, nervous habit she wished she could break, she smiled with more reservation than if they were alone. "Afternoon, Deputy Travers."

"Is Ethan nearby? I was told I might find him with you."

"Actually, he's over there." She indicated the row of outdoor stalls. "At least, he was earlier."

"Thanks." He tugged on the brim of his felt cowboy hat, hesitated briefly and then continued on.

A stranger might not realize they were well acquainted, and, to be honest, they preferred it that way. For the last year and a half, Aaron Travers and his family had lived in Mustang Valley, moving here when he transferred from the Phoenix Police Department. He and Mel occasionally ran into each other, as everyone ran into one another sooner or later in a small town.

There were also those encounters that weren't accidental. But she and Aaron didn't talk about them. Not with anyone else.

Once he'd passed and her heart rate slowed, she returned to stowing her supplies. The sensation of awareness he'd left in his wake wound through her, interfering with her ability to concentrate.

Bam! Another wave of nausea hit Mel, and she swallowed, willing her queasy stomach to settle. By some miracle, it did. A moment later she was fine, as if she hadn't been nauseous at all.

She'd just finished preparing her invoice for the horse owner when Ethan Powell and Aaron—make that Deputy Travers—approached.

"Mel," Ethan said, "do you have a minute? Aaron has some questions for you."

"Sure." She set down her invoice pad. "How can I help, Deputy?"

"Last night, three horses went missing from the Sanford place."

Mel drew back in alarm. "You're kidding!"

"It's the third incident this month," Aaron said. "I'm pretty sure we're dealing with rustlers."

"I can't believe it."

The first missing horses had been considered a fluke. A few even claimed they'd escaped their pasture and joined a wild herd often spotted near the Salt River. Then, after a second group of horses disappeared, people took notice. But horse rustling? That seemed like something out of the Old West. Not modern day.

"Why?" she asked, still grappling with the news. "None of the horses were particularly valuable. Mostly ranch stock."

"Slaughter?"

Mel's off-and-on sensitive stomach gave a lurch. She regularly dealt with the death of animals, many of the circumstances heartbreaking. As a result, she'd learned to cope. Still, the idea of horses being stolen for the purpose of profiting from their slaughter sickened her.

"Aaron's visiting all the area ranch owners," Ethan said. "Seeing if they've noticed anything suspicious in recent months and asking them to check with their employees."

"What can I do?" Mel asked Aaron.

"You travel the valley on a regular basis," he said. "Just keep your eyes and ears open. Contact the station if you spot anything out of the ordinary. Unfamiliar vehicles parked where they don't belong. Strangers lingering or asking unusual questions. Don't worry that you're being overly paranoid."

"Of course," Mel said. "Absolutely."

"I appreciate it."

After another nod, he and Ethan wandered a short distance away, continuing their conversation. Mel studied them before returning to her invoice. She'd give it to the horse owner on her way out. After checking her schedule, she phoned her next customer and gave him a heads-up on her impending arrival.

She was about to climb into the truck when Aaron unexpectedly appeared in her peripheral vision. She turned, her hand resting on the door. "Hi."

"Are you okay?"

"I'm fine. Why?" She automatically glanced about to see if they were being observed. Another nervous habit.

"You look pale."

"Do I?" Mel touched her face, only to let her hand drop. "I got up early. And," she added, suddenly recalling, "I missed lunch."

"You work too hard."

It was true. She did. But she had no choice. Not if she expected to make her monthly payments to Doc Palmer.

"Speaking of which, I'd better go. I have another appointment." She smiled, wished for just a moment they were alone and started to slide in behind the steering wheel. She didn't suggest calling him later. Chitchatting on the phone wasn't something they did.

Aaron's next words stopped her. "See you tomorrow. At the party."

"You're going?" That was a surprise. Mel had reviewed the guest list last night and knew his name wasn't on it.

"Dolores invited us. She and Nancy are in the same Bunko group."

"Right. I forgot."

"You don't mind?"

Mel dismissed his concerns with a nonchalant wave. "Dad'll be glad to have you there. All of you."

By all of you, Mel meant Aaron's almost three-year-old daughter and his mother-in-law, Nancy, who'd lived with him and his daughter since the death of Aaron's wife.

Granted, their arrangement might seem a bit unconventional to some, but apparently it worked. Nancy's late daughter had been her only child. Watching her granddaughter during the day, sharing Aaron's home, allowed her to stay connected while also providing him with a trustworthy and devoted caregiver. At least, that was how he'd explained it to Mel.

All at once, Ethan returned from wherever it was he'd gone and hailed Aaron.

"Go on," Mel told him, and hopped in her truck. "I'm running late as it is."

"Do me a favor. Eat and get some rest." Before she could start the ignition, he placed a hand on her shoulder and squeezed gently.

She wanted to be mad. He was breaking their strictest rule. Except it was hard to be mad when her shoulder tingled deliciously at his touch and continued to even after he'd moved off.

Mel shut the truck door and drove away, almost forgetting to drop off her invoice with the horse owner on her way out.

Reaching the end of the long drive leading down the mountain from the ranch, she stopped and let the truck idle. Since she and Aaron had begun seeing each other, they'd both worried how people, like Nancy for instance, might be hurt. It was yet another reason for the two of them to keep their relationship casual and private.

Lately, however, Mel worried about her vulnerable heart. She hadn't counted on her feelings for Aaron growing and did her best to hide it from him.

She let out a long sigh. What had seemed so simple at first was slowly becoming complicated. Aaron and his family attending her father's party, and his mother-in-law developing a friendship with Mel's stepmom certainly wasn't helping matters. Neither was her upset stomach, which gave another lurch.

Nerves. And stress. Those had to be the reasons. Mel refused to consider anything else.

Aaron was making his third trip of the day to the Sanford place. The first time he'd arrived at 6:20 a.m. in response to the 9-1-1 call. He'd returned at 9:50 a.m. when Ken Sanford, Sr. called to say he'd discovered fresh tire tracks behind their far pasture—no one had driven the dirt road since before the last rains.

Now, Aaron was heading to the ranch for another look around, planning to focus on the cut fence where the thieves had entered the property. When his cop's gut told him to persist, he usually did. There was always the chance he'd missed something during his previous inspections.

Horse rustling. Who'd have guessed he'd be investigating a crime of that nature in this day and age? A search of records at the station revealed the last such incident committed in Mustang Valley had been in the 1930s. Wow.

Aaron observed every detail as he drove, despite frequently traveling this road. He couldn't help himself—too many years on the force. That didn't stop the other half of his brain from wandering. Specifically to Mel. Not that he didn't always think of her when they weren't together.

She'd looked unwell earlier, and that bothered him. He understood the lines of fatigue on her pretty oval face. With her demanding schedule, that wasn't uncommon. Rather, it was the lack of color in her cheeks and slowness of her steps concerning him.

She was almost always happy and vivacious—a ball of energy contained inside a petite package. Those qualities more than her sparkling brown eyes and curvy figure were what caused him to notice her two winters ago at the community's Holly Daze Festival.

After that, it was hard not to keep noticing her and, eventually, talk to her. Just being in her proximity breathed new life into parts of Aaron's heart and soul he'd thought forever darkened.

Dangerous feelings and ones he shouldn't have. Not if he wanted the life he'd scraped together for him and his daughter, Kaylee, to remain calm, quiet and stable. Emphasis on the last word. That was why he'd quit the Phoenix Police Department and taken the less demanding job of deputy sheriff.

His phone abruptly rang. The personal one he kept in his vehicle, strictly for family and close friends. Snatching it from the cubby, he glimpsed his sister's name and photo on the display. The picture of her and Kaylee was one of his favorites, taken during his sister's last visit.

"Hey, Pickle."

She groaned expansively. No secret, she hated the childhood nickname. Which was why Aaron insisted on using it.

"What's up?" he asked.

"Bad time to call?"

Hearing Joanna's voice immediately thrust him back in time to their family's rural home in Queen Creek and their life together growing up. She'd moved to Seattle a year ago, and he missed her terribly. She'd been his rock, his staunchest supporter and his sounding board during the many difficult months Aaron's wife was ill and every day since she'd died.

"I'm on the road," he said. "Have about ten minutes."

"Don't tell me." Joanna laughed, the sound rich and vibrant. "A rancher let his hound dog run loose, and it got in with the lady down the street's King Charles spaniel."

He pretended to be affronted. "Believe it or not, there's real crime in Mustang Valley."

"Riiiiiight." She drew the single word out over three syllables.

"We've had a recent rash of horse thefts."

"No fooling? That actually sounds serious."

"I'm on my way now to talk to the third victim."

"Do you have any leads?"

"Not yet. I've been interviewing the locals." Most people didn't realize that 90 percent of good detective work was questioning potential witnesses.

"Locals like Mel?"

Aaron paused, not wanting to give his sister any

ideas. "She's a regular at most of the ranches in the valley and might run across something."

"How you two doing?"

"We're not dating."

"Hey, hey," Joanna protested. "Don't get mad. I think what you and Mel have is great. More couples should be as open-minded as you two."

"Yeah." Except, what Aaron and Mel had didn't feel open-minded to him.

"Something wrong?" Joanna asked.

"I don't know." He blew out a long breath. "Lately, I've been thinking she deserves more than casual hook-ups."

"Did she say so?"

"No."

"Are *you* tired of the arrangement?"

"Yes, but not in the way you think."

Joanna gave a delighted gasp. "You love her."

He gave a start and steadied his free hand on the steering wheel. "I wouldn't say that." Not yet, anyway. "I like her. A lot."

"Well, you should like the person you're sleeping with."

"Am I being a jerk? Taking her for granted?" It was the opinion he'd recently formed of himself.

"Come on. You and Mel have an arrangement. A good, sensible arrangement that works. Neither of you are ready or in a position for all the demands of a committed relationship. Yet, you're human, and human beings require intimacy. You and she have come up with a creative solution. You get together a couple times a month for a few discreet hours of adult pleasure. No strings attached. It's perfect."

"Spoken like a psychology major."

"Spoken like a feminist," she said, correcting him. "I wish I could find someone with your progressive attitude. Beats being single."

His sister was the only person Aaron had told about his and Mel's secret arrangement, and there were days he wished he hadn't.

Cripes, what was wrong with him? There was nothing sordid or dirty or wrong about what he and Mel did. She was completely on board. In fact, she'd been the one to originally suggest it. Yes, in a roundabout way, but not so subtle that Aaron hadn't understood and, after a long, emotional tug-of-war with himself, agreed.

She was beautiful and smart and as sexy as hell. When they were alone, she displayed the kind of passion he'd always hoped to find in a woman. Which only increased the guilt eating away at him. He could and did tell himself he wasn't being disloyal to Robin. She'd been gone nearly three years.

His heart argued differently, insisting he was dishonoring his late wife's memory. Aaron's mother-in-law would agree.

"Mel should be with a guy who can offer her more," he said to Joanna. "A guy who's emotionally free."

"If that was what she wanted, she'd give you the boot."

"Sometimes, I wish she would." Then he could stop wanting what he couldn't have and beating himself up over it.

"You're worried about Nancy," Joanna said, "and you shouldn't be."

"If she ever found out—"

"What? She'd leave? Go home to Ohio?"

"I don't want that. She loves Kaylee, and Kaylee loves her."

"If Nancy left, that would be her choice and her mistake to make."

Aaron rubbed his suddenly throbbing forehead. His arrangement with Mel was supposed to be without strings and without angst, yet it wasn't. In hindsight, they'd been silly and stupid.

He had, anyway. Truthfully, Aaron wasn't entirely sure how Mel felt about him. She didn't talk about it. Ever. And she didn't encourage him to, either.

"You're single," Joanna continued. "It's not fair that Nancy expects you to remain that way for the rest of your life."

"Isn't it?"

"You aren't betraying Robin."

"I made a promise to her," he bit out.

"To never fall in love again?"

"To devote myself to Kaylee. I owe Robin that much. She gave up her life for our daughter."

Joanna's voice softened. "You couldn't save her, Aaron. No one could. At best, she might have lived a few more months. And you probably wouldn't have had Kaylee. A lot of people, me included, think she made the right decision."

That didn't lessen his loss, relieve his guilt or diminish his hurt.

A few weeks after learning she was pregnant, Robin began having severe headaches that over-the-counter pain relievers wouldn't touch. Two weeks later, she was seeing a specialist and undergoing all manner of tests. Aaron would never forget sitting in the doctor's office and hearing the diagnosis: inoperable brain tumor. And then hearing the prognosis: terminal.

Robin refused any treatment that might have extended her life because it would harm the baby. At thirty-four weeks pregnant, she'd delivered a small but healthy baby girl. Unfortunately, it was too late for her. The treatments she'd previously refused had no effect on her rapidly growing tumor, and she lost the battle when Kaylee was just a few weeks old.

Robin's wish to be a mother had been fulfilled and, in the process, she'd given Aaron a last precious gift. He would do nothing to jeopardize Kaylee's safety and happiness.

"Why don't you talk to Mel," Joanna suggested. "If you're having doubts."

"Or, I could just end things."

"You could. Except that isn't what you want."

Should he tell his sister what he really wanted was to date Mel and not just sleep with her? No, Joanna would have a field day with that one, and Aaron wasn't in the mood.

"Pickle, can I call you later? I'm almost at my next stop." Not entirely a lie; the Sanfords were less than a mile down the road.

"Tomorrow. I've got plans later," she added with a teasing tone.

"Have fun."

"Oh, I intend to." She laughed again.

Aaron disconnected, his thoughts a jumble. He really did like Mel and hated the thought of ending things. But he was being grossly unfair to her. She may think she preferred whatever this was they had, but deep down, she was a forever and ever kind of gal. Aaron wasn't fooled for one minute.

A quarter mile up the road, he spied an older model pickup and rusty horse trailer pulled off to the south side of the road. The truck hood was up, signaling trouble, and someone sat in the driver's seat.

He slowed, determining the driver to be a young woman. As he passed, she rolled down her window and waved at him. Aaron executed a swift U-turn and parked behind the trailer. A reddish-brown tail hung out over the rear gate and swished aimlessly.

Before getting out, he radioed the station, then proceeded with caution all the while making mental notes. The situation didn't appear dangerous, but he took nothing for granted.

Nearing the driver's door, he realized the young woman was on the phone.

"Good afternoon." He looked her over. "Having some trouble?"

"I broke down. The engine light came on and then smoke started coming out from under the hood."

"License and registration, please."

"Have I done something wrong?" Her voice quavered.

"Just routine."

Producing the required documents, she passed them through the open window, still clutching her phone. Aaron decided she must have maintained an open line as a precaution. Smart move. She wasn't very old, maybe not even out of high school, and pretty, even with her torn jeans, faded tank top and ratty old ball cap. Add to that her disabled vehicle, and she was a potential sitting duck.

Aaron reviewed the documents, noting the eighteen-year-old's name and home address of Flagstaff. He compared her face to the tiny picture. Something about her struck a familiar chord, but he couldn't quite put his finger on it.

"Be right back." In his vehicle, he ran her name and license plate. Nothing significant came back. What had he expected?

Returning to her truck, he handed over the documents. "You're a long ways from home."

"I'm staying with my…with friends in Mustang Valley."

"Are they on their way to help you?"

"Uh…no. I wasn't able to reach them."

"I see." Aaron suspected she was coloring the truth and didn't know why. "Do you have a roadside assistance service?"

"I don't think so."

"What about your parents?"

"My mom can't help."

"Because she's in Flagstaff," Aaron stated.

"Yeah. And at work. I'm not supposed to call her unless it's an emergency."

"This might qualify."

The girl, Samantha, according to her driver's license, shook her head. "I'm not calling. She's busy."

"And your friends aren't available?"

In response, her mouth firmed to a thin line.

There was definitely more going on than she was telling him, and he didn't trust her. Nonetheless, she'd broken no laws and was in distress. Not to mention her truck and trailer were a potential hazard and the horse would need water soon. Aaron had a duty to help her.

"Sit tight," he said, and walked to the front of the

truck where he inspected the engine. Heat wafted off
in waves, and it made a soft hissing sound. The smoke
she'd claimed to see was probably steam.

A moment later, she disobeyed his order and joined
him, anxiously watching as if he might sabotage the
engine rather than repair it.

"You have an old rag I can use?"

"In the, uh, trailer."

"I'll wait."

She didn't take long.

Aaron rolled up his sleeves and, using the rag to re-
move the radiator cap, inspected the water level. No
surprise, the radiator was bone dry.

"You might have a leak," he told her. "You should get
this serviced right away. There's an auto shop in town.
Conroy's. Ask your friends, they'll tell you where he is."

"Okay."

Would she do it? She wouldn't get far otherwise.

After filling her radiator with water from the five-
gallon jug he carried in the back of his SUV for just
this reason, he had her try to start the truck. Luck was
on her side, and it turned right over, chugging like an
old man having a coughing fit. She definitely needed
to see Conroy.

Leaning her head out the window, she removed her
ball cap. "Thanks for your help."

Aaron slammed the hood closed and, wiping his
hands on the rag, started for his vehicle. "You be careful, you hear?" He stopped and flashed her a smile.

She didn't return it.

Reaching his SUV, he sat behind the wheel and waited
for her to pull ahead. Once she had, he radioed in, giving an update and advising the other deputies to keep a

lookout for her. That accomplished, he executed a second U-turn and made for the Sanford place.

Even though the girl's name and license plate had checked out, he couldn't stop thinking about her. She was exactly what Aaron had warned Mel to watch for: a stranger in an unfamiliar vehicle. The idea that a slip of a girl was involved with horse rustlers seemed preposterous. Appearances, however, were deceiving and something thieves might use to their advantage.

Turning onto the Sanford's private road, he recalled the young woman removing her ball cap and nearly slammed on the brakes. That was it! The reason she'd looked familiar to him. Her physical description was almost an exact duplicate of Mel's. Blond hair. Brown eyes. Five foot two in her boots. They even had a similar small cleft in their chins.

What were the odds of that?

Chapter 2

"Over here. Another three feet. Wait. No. Up against the wall." Frankie Hartman barked orders in her customary bossy voice.

Mel exchanged looks with her younger sister, Ronnie. As if on cue, they both rolled their eyes and shuffled the table to the exact spot their older sister wanted. Which, it turned out, wasn't so exact.

"Centered beneath the window." Frankie motioned with her hands to demonstrate.

After two more shuffles with the table, Mel and Ronnie were released from their task and instructed to undertake another. There was still a lot to do before the party started at six, including all the decorating.

Mel had brought streamers, a banner, party favors, confetti and a case of champagne. Ronnie's job had been to create a photo collage depicting their father's life from birth to now. Frankie brought the barbecued beef, a family favorite and her specialty dish.

The owner of the Cowboy Up Café, and Frankie's employer, had been kind enough to let them use the covered outdoor patio free of charge. With its built-in misting system, the patio was reasonably comfortable even in ninety-plus-degree temperatures.

The sisters were grateful. With several dozen people expected to attend, they'd definitely needed a large venue, equipped to feed so many mouths. And as if the location wasn't perfect enough, the owner was giving them a discount on the side dishes and beverages.

"Napkins!" Frankie ripped open packages as if the success of the party depended on guests being able to wipe barbecue sauce off their faces and hands.

Mel and Ronnie took their sister's theatrics in stride. Besides being the oldest of the Hartman sisters and a single mother, she was the Cowboy Up Café's head waitress and self-appointed organizer of their dad's party. She'd also stepped in—to the best of her twelve-year-old ability—when the sisters' mother had died over twenty years ago in a horse riding accident. "We're here," a high-pitched voice trilled. "Sorry we're late."

Mel's stepmom was accompanied by two very excited little girls: Frankie's twin daughters.

"We got balloons," Paige announced.

"And string," Sienna added, holding up her booty.

They were dressed alike in matching shorts and tees but were as different as night and day in personalities and features. Tiny, fair-haired Paige took after the Hartmans while tall, doe-eyed Sienna resembled her father, who wasn't and had never been in the picture.

"You wait until Mommy can help," Frankie called

from the chair on which she stood, hanging the Happy Birthday banner with Ronnie's assistance.

Mel went over to the girls and scooped them both into her arms. They squirmed and giggled and squealed, loving the attention while pretending not to.

"Let us go," they protested.

"Kisses first."

The girls gleefully obliged.

"Can I help?" Mel asked. Blowing up balloons and taping them to the backs of chairs sounded more fun than laboriously writing out name tags.

"No scissors," Dolores admonished.

Mel relieved her stepmom of the plastic sack and small helium tank she'd carried in. "Does that apply to me, too?"

"Depends. They're sharp." Dolores wagged a finger at her. "Can I trust you?"

"We'll be careful." Mel winked at the girls and then led them to one of the tables where they set up a balloon inflation station.

"Me first," Paige insisted.

Mel distributed a package of colorful balloons to each girl while keeping the scissors for herself. "Remember to share and take turns."

Ha! Like that was going to happen.

Of course, the pair was more trouble than help, but that didn't matter. They were having a blast. Mel, too.

As luck would have it, Dolores excelled at writing name tags, and between the four of them, the room quickly took shape. Then again, they were old pros, having done this before. Most recently, they'd organized a wedding reception—for Ray Hartman and his new bride.

Ronnie came to stand beside Mel, having finished with bringing in extra chairs from the storeroom. "This is going to sound terrible."

"What?" Mel asked.

"Is it wrong to miss Mom today?"

"No. Of course not. It's Dad's birthday. A milestone birthday."

"I mean, Dolores is wonderful. I adore her."

"Me, too." Mel didn't think there was a more perfect stepmom around.

Ronnie linked arms with her. "Sometimes, I have trouble remembering Mom. I hate that."

"We were young. Don't feel bad. It happens." Mel surveyed the room. "I think she'd approve of this party. I also think she'd like Dolores."

"She'd be proud of us," Ronnie said with conviction. "And of how Dad always supported us. You know the date of their anniversary was one of the numbers Dad used for his lottery tickets."

Mel laughed. "And to think we gave him such grief for buying tickets every week like clockwork."

"None of us ever thought he'd win."

But, then, he had. Last winter. The amount of the jackpot wasn't staggering, about two hundred thousand dollars after taxes. But for the Hartmans, it was a fortune.

Livestock foremen didn't typically earn a lot. Mel's father gave all he had to his daughters, providing a comfortable, if modest, home and the basic necessities. After he won, he'd divided the money equally between the four of them, using his share to pay for his wedding to Dolores and their honeymoon.

"I almost refused the money," Mel said.

Ronnie drew back. "Me, too."

"He didn't tell me that."

"Because he wanted us to take the money. And, frankly, we needed it. You couldn't have bought Doc Palmer's practice otherwise."

"Probably not."

Shortly after the elderly veterinarian announced his retirement, he'd approached Mel about buying his practice. She'd had to tell him no at first. Calling him the following month had been a dream come true.

"And forget Frankie buying that new house," Ronnie said. "It wouldn't have happened."

"True."

Frankie had been desperate to move out of their dad's place. What new bride wanted to share her home with a stepdaughter and two rambunctious stepgranddaughters? Frankie had used the money from their dad for a down payment on a cute house in town and some new furniture.

"Mom would be really happy for us."

Ronnie sighed contentedly. "She did always call us her fairy princesses."

If not for a lack of handsome suitors, Mel thought, she and her sisters were living fairy-tale existences.

Did Aaron count? Not at the moment. She didn't let herself imagine "someday" and what the future might hold for them if circumstances changed. Her energies were best focused on making the monthly payments to Doc Palmer and all those pesky necessities like food, clothes, repaying college loans and rent on the house she shared with Ronnie.

The simple and straightforward arrangement she had with Aaron was enough for both of them. At least, that

was what Mel repeatedly told herself. Every time she
caught herself falling a little harder for him, she remembered that he wasn't ready or able to fall for her.

Her nieces came bounding back from showing off to
their mother, balloons bobbing in the air behind them
as if filled with jumping beans and not helium. Ronnie
warned them to be careful, her tone a decent imitation
of Frankie's. Dolores chatted amiably while putting the
finishing touches on the centerpieces.

Soon, they'd leave for their respective homes to
change and freshen up before the party. In Frankie's
case, she'd pack the barbecued beef for transport and
arrive early to start warming it.

Mel stepped forward, intending to gather the balloon
supplies, when all at once her stomach lurched and the
floor seemed to ripple beneath her feet.

Convinced she was about to embarrass herself, she
muttered, "Be right back," to Ronnie and speed-walked
across the patio to the café's main building.

By sheer force of will, she made it to the empty restroom and one of the stalls before losing her lunch. Waiting a few moments to be on the safe side, she slowly
rose, the sensation of weakness persisting.

She felt her forehead. No fever. Or sore throat or
runny nose. Other than intermittent nausea, she exhib-
ited no other symptoms of the flu bug.

What was wrong with her?

Was it possible…? Could she be…?

No. She and Aaron had always been careful about
using protection. Mel could not be pregnant.

Nonetheless, she counted backward. How many days
since her last period? The answer sent a spear of alarm

slicing through her. How had she not realized she was late? She wasn't *that* busy.

Oh, God! Mel sucked in air, unable to catch her breath. Her skin burned as if she did indeed have a fever.

What would she do if she was pregnant? How would Aaron react? Would he be angry? Disappointed? Blame her? Accuse her of trapping him?

She stumbled out of the stall toward the row of sinks along the wall. Turning on a spigot, she splashed her face with cool water. It didn't alleviate the panic building inside her. Staring at her worried reflection in the mirror only worsened things.

Drying her face with paper towels from the dispenser, she told herself not to cry. There could be any number of reasons she was late and nauseous. Working ridiculous hours, skipping meals and not getting enough sleep, to name a few. Plus, Mel had a history of being irregular. No sense freaking out until she knew for sure.

With a whoosh, the restroom door flew open and Dolores breezed in. Seeing Mel, she stopped midstep.

"Are you okay?"

"I think I have a touch of the flu."

"Oh, no. I'd hate for you to miss the party, but maybe you should stay home and get some rest. You look awful."

Mel tried to wave off her stepmom's concern, only to rush to the stall she'd vacated minutes earlier. When she finally emerged, shaky but in one piece, it was to find Dolores waiting, arms crossed and brows raised.

"How far along are you?"

Mel's knees, already wobbly, threatened to give out. "What?"

"I have three children of my own. I'm very familiar

with morning sickness, even when it comes in the afternoon or evening."

Mel started to object. Dolores's kind expression changed her mind. The older woman wasn't her mother. But she was Mel's friend and, she hoped, a confidant.

"Please don't say anything to anyone. Especially Dad. Until I know for sure."

"Then it's possible?"

"We've been careful."

"I was, too. Both the second and third times." Dolores reached for Mel and gave her a quick but warm hug. "Does the father know?"

Again, Mel thought of Aaron. How would he take the news? When would be the best time to tell him? "No. Not yet."

"Do you love him?"

Mel had expected Dolores to ask the name of the father. This question left her nearly as shaken as the bout of nausea had.

Unable to answer, Mel mumbled an excuse and hurried past Dolores. It was one thing to contemplate her changing feelings for Aaron. Another thing altogether to voice them aloud.

Mel gave herself a figurative pat on the back for surviving the past few hours. Shortly after escaping the restroom and Dolores, she'd returned to the patio and been immediately recruited to hang paper lanterns. Thank you, Frankie. After that, they'd all gone home to change clothes and then returned before the party started.

Mel didn't typically procrastinate. It wasn't her style. But her father's birthday just wasn't the time for dealing with potentially huge problems. Like, for instance, a missed period. Not even with someone as compassionate as Dolores.

Seeing the party went off without a hitch, celebrating with her family, those were her priorities. Tomorrow, she'd purchase the home pregnancy test—in Scottsdale where no one knew her—and hopefully eliminate one potential reason for her nausea.

Now *that* was Mel's style. Every move was calculated in advance and every contingency explored. She liked it that way. Order and purpose equaled confidence and a sense of security.

If she turned out to be pregnant, a highly unlikely probability, she'd talk to Aaron and together they'd devise a new plan using the same equation. A plan that didn't throw both their lives into complete and utter chaos.

"Here's my girl!"

The next instant, Mel was swept up in a fierce embrace.

"Dad!" She giggled and squirmed, not unlike her nieces.

"Thank you for the party," he said, releasing her.

"I can't take the credit. It was Frankie's idea, and she did most of the heavy lifting. But you can thank me for not allowing any Over the Hill and Grim Reaper party favors."

"She couldn't have pulled it off without your help."

"I'm glad you're pleased."

His gaze traveled the room. "Who knew I had this many friends?"

His daughters, for one. Mel's dad had lived and worked in the valley for over thirty-five years. He was liked, if not loved, by many.

Not all the guests had arrived. Most noticeably absent was Theo McGraw, Ray Hartman's boss and owner of The Small Change Ranch. Mel hoped the older gentleman would make it. He suffered from Parkinson's disease, and some days were harder than others.

Also absent, and of more concern to Mel, was Aaron and his family. Perhaps he'd gotten called away on a last-minute emergency. Or, something had happened to his daughter. Mel tried not to obsess, which also wasn't her style. But lately, he was constantly on her mind.

"You're being modest." She patted her father's generous beer belly. That, and his gray beard, had made him the perfect choice to play Santa Claus at his granddaughters' preschool. "You have lots of friends."

"I'm a fortunate man."

She noticed him watching Dolores. He often did, and the look in his eyes softened as if the mere sight of her melted his heart.

Someday, maybe someone would look at Mel like that. Welcome her home after a hard day at work. Slip into bed with her and wind his arms around her. Someone who didn't cling to the memory of his late wife.

Oh, God! Had she really just thought that? Mel was ashamed of herself. She wasn't normally shallow and unkind. Naturally, Aaron grieved his late wife. It had taken her father years to get over her mother's death.

A group of nearby guests burst out in raucous greeting, distracting her. The source of the commotion became quickly apparent. Aaron, his mother-in-law, Nancy, and daughter, Kaylee, had finally arrived.

A grinning Aaron held Kaylee in his arms, balancing her against his broad chest. The shy little girl buried her face in his shirt when one too many people tugged on her silky curls or pinched her chin. Aaron patted her back with his strong hand and, bit by bit, Kaylee's face emerged.

Aaron could do that. Make a person feel safe and sheltered. Mel had experienced it firsthand.

"Hey, there, birthday boy." One of her father's buddies hailed him. "Get over here before all the barbecued beef is gone."

"See you later, honey."

"Enjoy yourself," Mel said to his retreating back, her attention remaining riveted on Aaron.

Eventually, their eyes locked. That was the usual outcome when someone stared long enough. She should step away. Engage the Powells or other clients of hers in conversation. Help Frankie with the food or Dolores with hosting duties.

She and Aaron had agreed not to draw attention to themselves in public, and here she was doing exactly that. Except, she didn't break eye contact and neither did he. The connection Mel had been feeling lately intensified more and more until it practically sizzled.

Was it the same for him? If so, he gave no indication.

Mel's nieces skipped over to Aaron and Kaylee, high on sugar from fruit punch and blobs of icing swiped from the birthday cake.

"Kaylee, play with us," Paige pleaded with her friend. "We have balloons and bubbles and prizes."

The little girl's features lit up like a ray of sunshine after a storm, and she insisted her father put her down.

Aaron relented, holding her hand as if not quite ready to part with her. Mel was close enough to hear him say, "Don't go far, okay?"

"Okay, Daddy," she parroted in her sweet angel voice.

Mel's nieces immediately grabbed her, and the preschool buddies scampered off, disappearing from sight.

"Are you sure she'll be all right?" Nancy asked Aaron, ready to follow the girls.

Aaron waylaid her by saying gently, "She'll be fine. Frankie Hartman is right there."

The creases permanently etched into Nancy's forehead deepened. "I'm going to get some punch."

By sheer coincidence, or not, the punch bowl was located within a few feet of the game area where the girls were playing. If Aaron realized that, and he probably did, he chose not to address it.

Mel admired him for picking his battles. Nancy could be formidable. A self-defense mechanism, no doubt, from losing her only child at a young age.

Funny that Nancy and Dolores had become close. Then again, Dolores was the nurturing kind, taking the lost and lonely into her care. Hadn't she done that with Mel's father and, a few hours ago in the restroom, with Mel?

What if she was pregnant? Mel had tried hard to keep the thought at bay, but it crept back every few minutes, shouting, "You can't ignore me," in her ear.

As if sensing her distress—was he that tuned in to her?—Aaron glanced her way again. Confused and emotionally overwhelmed, Mel turned and snuck away in search of a quiet place.

Five minutes. That was all she needed. Time enough to collect herself and calm her frayed nerves.

Heading outside the café, she skirted the corner to an old hitching post that was still used today for customers arriving by single horse rather than two hundred of them beneath the hood.

Leaning her forearms on the thick railing, she let the warm breeze blow over her. A thin crescent moon hung in the sky above the mountains, waiting for dusk to fall and the stars to come out. Faint strains of piped-in music drifted to her from the patio.

"Hiding?"

Hearing Aaron's voice, Mel jumped.

"Are you okay?" He strolled over to her, his eyes roaming her face. "What's wrong?"

Did he have to look as good in jeans and a cowboy shirt as he did in his uniform? "Just tired. It's been a long week."

"You need to take better care of yourself." He raised his hand and rubbed a knuckle along her jawline. The tender gesture nearly undid her.

It wasn't like him to break the rules. Her, either. No intimacies away from the motel where they typically met. Boundaries were to be respected.

But, then, she remembered she was two weeks late.

"Aaron." She suddenly wanted to confess everything. The fact she was late. Her increasing feelings for him. Her constant confusion.

Wasn't that what couples did? Communicate?

Except, they weren't a couple. They were sex buddies. At her suggestion and insistence.

"What?" he prodded.

"Nothing." She pushed off the hitching post. "We should get back to the party."

At that moment, an older pickup truck going too fast pulled into the parking lot, its tires squealing. Aaron tracked its slightly slower progress to the back row and the only available spaces.

"Someone you know?" Mel asked.

"If it's who I think it is, I ran into her yesterday." He was no longer Aaron but Deputy Travers. "Do you recognize the truck?"

She shook her head. "I don't think so."

Just then, she heard the truck door slam and watched a young, slim woman navigate the parked vehicles, purpose in her stride. Rather than enter the café through the main entrance, she went directly to the outdoor patio.

"Maybe she's someone's plus one," Mel mused.

"I'll be back," Aaron said, barely acknowledging her.

She'd seen this determination before when he was on the job. Did this stranger have something to do with the horse thefts?

"Wait!" She trotted after him, refusing to be excluded.

She reached the patio moments after Aaron. The young woman stood near the food tables, searching the room. Cupping her hands to her mouth, she shouted, "Where's Ray Hartman? I need to talk to him."

For a wild second, Mel thought the young woman was delivering a singing telegram. Except, she didn't wear a costume. Unless one counted that ratty old ball cap.

"I'm Ray." Mel's father, beaming as if he, too, was expecting a birthday surprise, emerged from the crowd, a heaping plate of food in his hands.

"Do you recognize me?"

"'Fraid not."

"I'm Samantha Egherman." She glared at him. "Your daughter. I'm here for my share of the lottery money."

Bursts of laughter vied with gasps of disbelief.

"Who's that?" someone asked.

"She said she's Ray's daughter," another answered. "Is this someone's idea of a joke?"

Mel was convinced she'd misheard the young woman. Then, like everyone else in the room, she looked at her father. His expression wasn't one of surprise but rather guilt and resignation.

This couldn't be happening. Samantha Egherman? Mel had never heard the name before.

Her ears started ringing, the sound increasing in volume until it blocked out everything else.

His daughter? That made no sense.

Slowly, Mel's father set his plate on the nearest table. Facing the young woman, he said, "Samantha," as if testing her name.

In that instant, Mel knew the outrageous claim was true. She had a half sister. More than that, her father had apparently known and hadn't told anyone.

Chapter 3

Aaron and the other partygoers watched the train wreck unfolding before them with a mixture of surprise, embarrassment and sympathy for those involved. And, of course, morbid fascination. Ray repeating the young woman's name was the equivalent of two locomotives colliding. Mel's startled cry of distress was the first piece of wreckage flying.

Worried by the unsteady way in which she swayed, Aaron pushed past several people to reach her.

"I got you," he said, grasping her elbow.

"I don't believe it." She lifted her face to his. "I don't want to believe it."

Well, who would? Discovering you had an eighteen-year-old sibling wasn't typically on anyone's bucket list.

"Are you okay? You're shaking."

"Okay? You've got to be kidding." She gave a brittle laugh and then bit back a sob.

"I'm happy to see you, Samantha," Ray said. "Finally. I've been waiting a long time."

The young woman glared at him. "Look. All I want is my money. Then I'll get out of here."

Her money? Aaron thought she had some nerve. Make that a *lot* of nerve. Ray had bought the winning ticket. The money was his to gift to whomever he chose.

"Is she scamming Dad?" Mel obviously didn't see the resemblance between her and Samantha that Aaron had noticed yesterday.

"Just wait." He increased his hold on her. "Give them a minute."

Mel briefly resisted before relenting, which probably had more to do with Frankie's warning glance than Aaron's advice.

"Why don't you have some supper?" Ray offered Samantha a smile. "You must be hungry. Then we'll go home. Continue this discussion in private."

"I don't want any food," she said, her voice tight.

"All right then." He turned and addressed the entire room. "Thank you everyone for coming and making this birthday special. Please stay and enjoy all this great food. My...daughter—" he glanced at Samantha "—and I are leaving."

After that, Aaron couldn't stop Mel from rushing to join them. Her sisters, Frankie and Ronnie, beat her there.

"Dad," Mel said, "you don't have to do this. You have no proof she's who she says she is."

"I'm sorry."

Aaron wasn't sure which of his daughters Ray was apologizing to and what for.

"Is it true?" Frankie demanded. "Is she our sister?"

Ray's smile faltered. "We'll talk about this at home."

"Yes, it's true," Samantha insisted.

"Oh, God." Frankie blinked rapidly as if that could halt the tears filling her eyes.

"I know you." Ronnie nudged Mel aside and pointed at Samantha. "I've seen you compete. You're a barrel racer. A national junior rodeo champion. You turned professional this year."

Being recognized visibly upset Samantha. She didn't let it faze her, however, and rallied by raising her chin. "I know you, too."

From the rodeo circuit or as her long-lost sister?

Ronnie must have wondered the same thing, for she asked, "Why didn't you say something to me when we met before?"

Samantha's answer was to raise her chin another notch.

People continued to gawk and whisper behind the shields of their hands. A few respectfully inched away. The gaps they left were instantly filled.

Aaron debated whether to don his deputy hat and clear the room or allow things to play out. He wasn't on duty, no crime had been committed and no one was in immediate danger. Unless Mel's fragile state counted.

He took a step forward. The hell with this being the Hartmans' crisis to handle. Mel needed a friend, and he was that first and foremost.

His next step was blocked by Nancy, who held Kaylee's hand in a death grip. "Let's go home, Aaron."

"Not yet." He wasn't leaving without talking to Mel.

"Kaylee's upset."

He glanced down at his daughter, who stared over

her shoulder at Mel's nieces, a forlorn expression on her face. If she was upset, it was at having to abandon her friends.

It was on the tip of his tongue to chide Nancy for overdramatizing things. Instead, he nodded at their neighbors who were gathering their things.

"There's Geo and Leslie," he said. "Why don't you ask them for a ride home?"

Nancy frowned, not liking the idea. "What about you?"

"I'll be home soon." Aaron bent and gathered Kaylee close. "I love you, jelly bean."

"I wanna stay, Daddy."

"You'll see your friends at preschool on Monday."

Kaylee pouted. In another minute, she'd be whining. In two minutes, she'd be crying.

"I'll be home in time to tuck you in." Aaron straightened. He'd been ready to promise, then stopped himself. With the demands of his job, he couldn't always be where he wanted, when he wanted, and he hated disappointing Kaylee.

Except, this was personal and not work related. He didn't have to stay.

"Will you tell me a story about Mommy?" she pleaded.

Guilt pricked at him. "Of course."

Nancy wasn't the sole keeper of Robin's memories. Aaron's stories tended to be less eloquently spun than Nancy's, but they were told from the heart. He made sure Kaylee knew how much she'd been adored by Robin and how much Robin had been adored by him.

"Bye, Daddy."

Aaron watched his daughter and Nancy until the

patio door closed behind them. By then, thankfully, more guests had left, their tongues wagging, Aaron was sure. A few kindly individuals began clearing tables and packing food. No one had heeded Ray's invitation to stay.

Mel, her sisters and Ray stood shoulder to shoulder, presenting a united front. Samantha, for her part, didn't flinch. She either had a lot of nerve or was desperate.

Because he couldn't just stand around doing nothing, he grabbed a heavy-duty plastic bag and began collecting trash. When Mel noticed him, he mouthed, *You okay?*

She shrugged limply. Her red-rimmed eyes indicated she'd been crying or trying hard not to.

He wished he could comfort her. Wrap his arms around her. Without conscious effort, he pictured them lying nestled softly together in the aftermath of making love. In those moments, he let himself imagine a life beyond stolen evenings here and there. Unfortunately, the fantasy always vanished the instant he set foot inside his house.

It did now, too, as Samantha continued causing a scene.

"Fine," she spat out. "I'll follow you in my truck." She made for the door, her boots clomping on the concrete floor.

A chagrined Ray hurried after her. He was either escaping the wrath of his wife and daughters or attempting to head off disaster. Perhaps a little of both.

"Are we just going to let them leave?" Mel demanded of her sisters.

"Hell, no," Ronnie and Frankie chorused.

"Maybe you should give them some time alone," Dolores said.

The three sisters blinked at her in disbelief.

She crossed her arms. "I'm serious. And you know I don't usually put my foot down. Ten minutes, then you can go. For now, let's finish cleaning up."

"What about the girls?" Frankie asked, more to herself than anyone else. "I can't just leave them, and I don't want to take them. For obvious reasons."

All eyes fell to Dolores, who gave an expansive huff.

"Thank you," Frankie said, taking the huff as agreement to help.

"We're not excluding you." Mel at least sounded apologetic for all of them taking terrible advantage of Dolores.

"Meet you at the house," Dolores said. "And tell your father to leave me the car. He can catch a ride with one of you three."

Frankie called after her. "Bring the leftover barbecued beef home. Everything else can be stored in the restaurant cooler."

Dolores stopped midstep. "Anything else?"

"Um…no."

Aaron gave Dolores a lot of credit. She was coping very well with a difficult and awkward turn of events no one had seen coming. She also wasn't protesting when Mel and her sisters took advantage of her generosity. He hoped they let Dolores know how much they appreciated her.

One by one, people were leaving. He supposed he should hit the road as well—except his legs disobeyed his brain and took him in the direction of Mel. She'd already had a rough time tonight and appeared to have a rougher time in store.

When he neared, she actually brightened as if glad to see him.

"Call me if you need anything," he said in a low voice. "I don't care how late it is."

"Thanks for staying. You didn't have to."

"I wanted to." Glancing around first to make sure they weren't being watched—everyone's attention remained elsewhere—he brushed her hand. "I'm here for you, Mel."

When he would have walked away, she quickly touched his arm. "That means a lot to me."

More stolen moments. They were fast becoming not enough.

Outside, the parking lot was considerably less full than earlier. As Aaron crossed it, raised voices drew his attention. In the back row, Samantha stood beside her junkyard truck, its hood raised. Ray was with her, and the two of them argued bitterly.

Aaron hesitated, reminding himself yet again that this was none of his business. If only the law-enforcement officer in him didn't view the situation differently.

Uttering a low groan of frustration, he changed direction. Mel would probably be mad at him for interfering, but Aaron didn't feel he had any other choice. Here was a powder keg on the verge of exploding if ever he saw one.

"Is there a problem?" Aaron asked.

Samantha's laser-beam glance said *butt out*.

Ray, on the other hand, responded with relief. "Aaron.

Samantha's radiator is leaking and her truck won't start. I offered to help."

What Ray left out, but Aaron had picked up on, was that Samantha refused any assistance.

Aaron inspected the engine, Samantha peering over his shoulder. "I'm assuming you didn't drop by Conroy's."

"I would if I had the money," she snapped.

Luckily, Aaron had refilled his water jug the previous night. "My vehicle's parked over there. Be right back."

"I'll pay for the repairs." Ray reached in his pocket for his wallet.

"You got forty thousand dollars in there?" Samantha asked. "Because I figure that's my share. Two hundred thousand dollars split five ways."

Aaron wasn't surprised Samantha knew the amount Ray had won. He'd chosen not to remain anonymous, an option given to winners. As a result, an article had appeared in the local paper, and he'd been interviewed by several TV stations, during which he'd stated his plans for the money. Links to both had made the social media rounds.

In five minutes of online searching, Samantha would have found out everything. Which indicated she'd known about Ray and her sisters or someone else did and told her. Her mother, for instance?

That still didn't explain why she felt entitled to a share of the winnings. Perhaps Mel had been close to the truth when she accused Samantha of scamming her father. If not that, then something else. Aaron hadn't trusted Samantha from the moment they'd met.

He also didn't believe her motives were entirely bad or selfish. She struck him more like a scared kid. He knew from both professional and personal experience fear could drive a person to behave in ways they normally wouldn't.

"I'll give you what's left of the money," Ray said to her.

"How much is that?"

"Let's start with the truck repairs."

By the time Aaron returned with the water jug, Mel and her sisters were flying across the parking lot, bags and containers jostling at their sides. Aaron couldn't help thinking here came the disaster Ray had attempted to head off.

"What's going on?" Frankie demanded, out of breath.

Samantha responded as she had before by going stonily silent.

"Nothing." Ray moved toward the young woman as if to shield her.

It didn't go unnoticed, judging by Mel's widening eyes and Ronnie's narrowing ones.

"You should have told us." Tears roughened Frankie's voice. "We had a right to know."

"Not here," Ray said. "We'll talk at home."

That triggered a loud debate among all the Hartmans. Aaron heard the words "betrayal" and "lied to" uttered more than once.

"Excuse me." He squeezed past Mel with the heavy water jug. Ray had already removed the radiator cap. Using his pocket flashlight, Aaron verified that the radiator was once again bone dry.

Mel appeared beside him. "You're helping her?"

"I'm assisting a stranded motorist by filling her radiator with water. Not taking sides."

"Sorry. This is tough." She swallowed and looked around. "As you can see, we're all a bit rattled."

"Go slow. Try not to make judgments or rush to conclusions. Give your dad and Samantha each a chance to tell their story."

Mel glanced over at the others, several feet away, and lowered her voice. "I'm not sure who to be angrier at."

"What you're feeling is natural. But it's important you keep listening no matter what."

"You sound like you've been through this before."

"I worked on the Phoenix police force for eleven years and responded to my share of domestic dispute calls."

"Is that what we're having? A domestic dispute?"

He bent, unscrewed the cap on the water jug and lifted it up to the truck. "You're a family with a problem."

"That's putting it mildly." She watched him as he filled the radiator.

Finishing, he set the jug down and called to Samantha. "Jump in there and give it a try."

The young woman fled to the truck cab as if she couldn't get away from the Hartmans fast enough and shoved the key into the ignition. The engine sputtered twice, then started.

"She really does need to get that radiator leak fixed," Aaron said to Ray.

"I'll make sure of it."

Aaron wasn't the least bit disappointed this gathering was over. His part in it, anyway. Soon, he'd be home and telling Kaylee another story about her mother.

"You two are on a first-name basis?" Mel asked.

"I met her yesterday when her truck broke down on the side of the road."

"And you didn't tell me?"

"There was nothing to tell at the time."

"You're right, you're right. I'm sorry." She scrubbed her face with her hands and groaned. "What a mess. I didn't mean to take it out on you."

"I've been subjected to far worse."

"On those domestic dispute calls?"

He was glad to see her mouth curve in the beginnings of a smile and leaned closer. "How you feeling? Stomach still bothering you?"

"Frankly, I forgot about it in all the, um, excitement, shall we say."

Only a few inches separated them. Aaron shifted his weight, closing the distance to almost nothing. If they were alone, and oh how he wished they were, he'd gather her into his arms and kiss her over and over until he'd driven every thought of their respective families from their minds.

"What's going on here?"

They sprang apart, separated by Ray's voice and the surprise lacing it. Turning, they found not only Ray but Mel's sisters staring at them.

"Dammit," Aaron said under his breath. This was his fault. He should have been more careful. He and Mel had been getting laxer and laxer lately.

"Dad," she started, then faltered.

They were spared from having to explain whatever it was her family thought they saw when Samantha's truck suddenly quit running. Her attempts to start it again resulted in a horrible grinding sound.

"Shut it off," Aaron hollered, afraid continued effort might result in severe damage.

Samantha scrambled out of the truck. Her mouth was

set in an identical stern line Aaron had seen all three Hartman sisters wearing earlier. He was beginning to think looks weren't the only quality they had in common.

By now, evening had given way to night. Above their heads, the parking lot lights flickered and crackled with an electrical hum. A few daring nighttime insects ventured down from the lights. One had the nerve to tangle in Samantha's hair.

She swatted at it furiously. "What now?"

"I'll call Conroy's in the morning," Ray said. "He'll send the tow truck. You can leave your truck here. No one will bother it."

"And in the meantime?"

"Where are you staying?"

Samantha hesitated, wilting a little under the pressure of being scrutinized. "The inn."

Morning Side Inn, like a lot of establishments in the community, was horse friendly. Behind the main building, the owners had constructed a corral and dirt RV lot for guests to use during their stay, which explained what Samantha had done with her horse and trailer.

The inn was also expensive. If she couldn't afford to pay for her truck repairs, she certainly couldn't afford to stay at the inn for long.

"I can drop you off there later tonight," Ray said. "Once we've finished talking." He fished his keys from his pocket. "Let's meet at the house. Samantha, you can ride with me and Dolores." He turned in a circle and frowned, suddenly realizing his wife had been missing all along.

"No way am I riding with you," Samantha stated frimly. "I'll walk to the inn. It's not far from here."

"I think we should talk tonight," Ray insisted. "The sooner the better."

She scrunched her mouth to the side, debating what to do. Suddenly, she pointed at Aaron. "I'll ride with him."

Reactions ranged from surprise to displeasure to resistance. Aaron didn't blame them. He'd already intruded enough on what was a private matter. Besides, someone else needed him more. "I can't take you. My daughter's expecting me home any minute."

"What if I drive you?" Frankie asked Samantha.

The young woman raised her chin like before. "If he doesn't take me, I'm not going."

Aaron had witnessed this same stubbornness in Mel, usually when she refused to give up on a sick or injured animal. Also, the one time he'd broached the subject of them dating like a regular couple.

She'd insisted what they had suited them both. Why complicate matters? Lately, he'd been thinking he should have argued more. She deserved better than what they had, even if she didn't believe so. And he had started wanting more, even if he refused to admit it.

Their gazes briefly connected, and he wondered if she also ever reconsidered their arrangement.

"This is probably best handled by your family," Aaron said to Samantha.

"They're not my family," she contradicted him. "I already have one. My mom and dad and two brothers."

Again, everyone except Ray seemed taken aback by the news, eyes widening and jaws going slack. What other secrets was he keeping?

Mel was the first to speak. "Maybe you should drive her to Dad's house. We certainly can't keep standing here all night." Before Aaron could refuse, she added, "I'll go with you."

No one brought up the obvious. As deputy sheriff, Aaron was familiar with the town and didn't need directions. Could Mel be trying to find time alone with him? As alone as they could be with another person sitting three feet away.

That wasn't why Aaron ultimately agreed to drive Samantha. It was the scared look on her face. She was a kid in trouble, though no one else apparently saw it. If his daughter ever needed help, he hoped a responsible and trustworthy person like himself stepped in.

An unofficial vote was taken, and Aaron found himself in his SUV with Mel in the front, Samantha in the back and a heavy silence surrounding them. Guess he'd been wrong about Mel's motives.

"Take a left," she instructed when they reached the parking lot exit. "Turn east onto Harvest Street."

Traffic was never heavy in Mustang Valley, with the exception of holidays when the whole town came out to celebrate. With each occasional vehicle passing them in the opposite direction, the interior of the SUV was illuminated by oncoming headlights.

Aaron caught quick glimpses of Mel's profile. She was just as scared as Samantha. He also understood why—her entire life was changing—and was glad he'd come along for her, too.

Chapter 4

The Hartman home was about four miles past where the paved road leading out of town ended and the dirt road began. Mel's parents had built it soon after her father accepted a head wrangler position at The Small Change Ranch, using the entirety of their meager savings for construction. The house was a short distance from the ranch and until recently, her father had ridden to work every day.

He told people the reason he quit was because his favorite horse had been retired and put to pasture, not that his arthritis had worsened. Mel didn't have the heart to dispute him. Her father was a proud man.

"What about your friends?" Aaron asked Samantha, glancing again in the rearview mirror. Mel noticed he'd been doing that a lot during the drive.

"What about them?" Samantha said tersely.

"Are they expecting you tonight?"

"No."

"Have you called them?"

Samantha gave another terse reply and slouched into her seat.

Mel frowned. Really? Aaron was attempting chit-chat? And who were these supposed friends of Samantha's anyway?

"What if they're worried?" Aaron asked.

"You always this nosy?"

"Comes with the job."

Gauging by her tone, Samantha didn't like Aaron better than Mel or the rest of them. So why insist on him driving her?

The two had another brief exchange, and Mel's irritation escalated. Perhaps because Aaron had obviously learned details about Samantha and Mel knew nothing. None of them did. Except her father. He'd known her name, at least. And that she existed. He was certainly on good terms with Samantha's mother. Or, had been at one time.

A sister. Mel had *another* sister. She silently did the math. Her dad and Samantha's mom must have met one, no, two years after Mel's mother died.

Pain burned inside her chest. Plenty of people would defend her father, saying he hadn't been married when he and Samantha's mom met and that two years was a reasonable period to mourn before entering into a new relationship.

Only it didn't feel reasonable to Mel. The man she remembered had been devastated to his very core, blaming himself for a freak riding accident he couldn't have prevented even if he was there when it happened. Afterward, Mel's father could barely drag himself out of the house to buy groceries or take the girls to a school function. He'd gone to work every day only because he'd needed to support his family—what remained of it.

Date? Engage in dinner conversation? Laugh? Have sex? It was beyond Mel's ability to take in, and she hugged her middle.

"Cold?" Aaron asked, already adjusting the air conditioning.

"I'm fine."

She quietly fumed. Why hadn't her father told them about Samantha? It made no sense. Having a child with another woman was a big deal. Life altering. Did he think they'd never find out or not care if they did?

"Why now?" The words erupted from her, and she twisted in her seat to confront Samantha. "Why pick today of all days to suddenly show up?"

"Does it matter?" Samantha stared out the passenger window.

"You crashed my dad's birthday party and demanded forty thousand dollars. I'd say I'm owed an explanation. All of us are."

Samantha's head snapped around. "You haven't wanted an explanation for eighteen years. I could ask you, why now?"

"Wait just a minute. I had no idea—"

"And that's my fault?"

Mel opened her mouth to protest, realized the futility of it and instead swung back around, her tenuous hold on her temper threatening to break. She did not like this person. This stranger. This interloper.

"He's not the great guy you think he is," Samantha said.

"How do we even know you're his daughter? You could be making the whole thing up."

"Did he act like I was making it up?"

Mel wanted to scream. This could not be happening. It had to be a mistake. A terrible joke gone horribly wrong.

The next instant, Aaron's hand reached across the console for hers.

"Relax," he said softly. "There's no use getting upset."

She should have shaken him off and would have if not for the warmth flowing through her and the knotted muscles in her neck slowly loosening. Damn him for sensing what she needed, which at the moment was a nonjudgmental friend in her corner.

Opening her fist, she linked her fingers with his, marveling at this tiny intimacy. For the first time away from the motel, they were holding hands, and she had to admit, the sensation was nice. It was also something she could get used to if she let herself.

"You two together?" Samantha asked from behind them.

Mel snatched her hand away, the remark hitting much too close to home for her liking. "It's not like that. We're just friends."

"Right."

Mel imagined Samantha rolling her eyes.

Aaron grinned and shrugged, not the least bit bothered.

If only Mel could be as unconcerned as him. But she couldn't. Not when she secretly, sort of, wanted to take their relationship to the next level. Or was that back a level since most couples began by dating, not sleeping together whenever the time was right and they felt like it.

Her hand drifted to her belly. Could she be pregnant? If yes, their relationship might jump ahead two or three levels overnight.

She remembered her plan to purchase a home pregnancy test tomorrow. Well, so much for that. With Samantha's appearance and her outrageous demand, the day, and entire weekend, had taken a crazy turn. She'd be lucky to get to the store by Tuesday.

One good thing, she hadn't felt nauseous for a while now. Perhaps it was the flu after all.

Without being told, Aaron turned the SUV onto the road leading to her father's house.

"I've been here before," he said in response to Mel's raised brows. "Your house, too."

"Make the rounds a lot?"

"I like to keep tabs on certain people."

Did he? "Is that also part of the job?"

His response was a smile.

What did that mean? That he personally watched out for her and her family? Why, for heaven's sake? Sure, he cared for her, but not like that.

"How much farther?" Samantha demanded with growing impatience.

"Not long."

Beyond the next rise, the front porch light on the Hartman house came into view. Aaron increased his speed slightly, and the SUV bumped over several potholes carved into the road.

Mel's stomach abruptly lurched. Well, so much for thinking she'd recovered. Leaning back, she closed her eyes and hoped she didn't throw up in the SUV.

"You all right?" Aaron let up on the gas, slowing the vehicle.

"Just nerves."

"It wasn't nerves yesterday."

She sent him a sideways glance, silently warning him to drop the subject. Thankfully, he did.

A few minutes later, they pulled into the driveway, and Aaron parked to the side in order to let Mel's father pass them. He and her sisters had been following close behind the entire drive.

Mel thrust open her door, more than ready to get out. She was less enthusiastic about what lay ahead.

"Thanks again." She attempted a feeble smile. "For everything." There'd be no more hand holding for her and Aaron. Not tonight and not with Samantha watching.

"Call me later," he said, repeating his earlier request.

"I will." A phone call that had nothing to do with arranging an evening at the motel. Their first of that sort, Mel mused.

Realizing Samantha hadn't moved, she said, "We're here," then waited, feeling like she'd stated the obvious.

Samantha chewed on her lower lip, not moving. Mel wanted to ask what was wrong. After making a huge scene at the café, she couldn't believe Samantha had suddenly developed cold feet.

"I'm not going inside." Samantha hitched her chin at Aaron. "Not without him."

"No!" Mel managed to get out, a second ahead of Aaron.

"Samantha," he said, "it's getting late. I have to go home to my daughter."

By now, Mel's sisters had disappeared into the house. Her father waited beside the open garage door.

Samantha spoke so quietly, Mel wasn't sure she'd heard correctly.

"Please. You're the only person I know here." After a beat, she added, "You helped me before."

Aaron considered briefly, ultimately relenting and unbuckling his seat belt. "Only for a few minutes."

"That's not a good idea." Mel was thinking of her family's reaction.

"She's young and all alone."

Apparently, Mel's corner wasn't the only one Aaron was in. He'd taken a position in Samantha's, too. Mel was torn between being furious at him and touched by his concern.

Samantha's shoulders slumped with relief. So, she did have cold feet after all. Hard to believe after the brazen way she'd confronted them at the party.

Aaron got out of the SUV, followed by Samantha. He waited for Mel to join them before heading into the garage. She made a point of walking on his other side and slightly in front. This was her family. Their house. She would lead.

"You need something, Deputy?" her father asked when they neared.

Samantha cut in before Aaron could respond. "He stays or I leave."

Aaron lifted a shoulder in apology. "I promise to keep my mouth shut and any opinions to myself."

Mel's father didn't look happy. She found it hard to sympathize despite defending him earlier. He was in large part responsible for this mess.

Samantha hung close to Aaron as the four of them paraded single file through the laundry room, along the short connecting hall and into the kitchen where Frankie and Ronnie waited. They, too, showed surprise and displeasure at seeing Aaron.

"What's he doing here?" Frankie glowered accusingly.

Mel's father dropped his phone, wallet and keys on the counter. "Samantha invited him."

"Do we need a mediator?"

Rather than reply, he addressed the group. "Anyone want a cold drink before we get started?"

Mel thought she might want a stiff drink but decided that wasn't a good idea.

"I'll get them." She recruited Ronnie to help. When her sister wasn't looking, she grabbed a couple of the peppermint candies her father kept in the drawer for his frequent indigestion.

The moment Aaron was finished with his phone call to his mother-in-law, letting her know he'd be late, people began sitting at the dining-room table. The area was separated from the kitchen by a long breakfast bar and a trio of oak bar stools. Frankie switched on the overhead light. The normally cozy glow did nothing to improve their collective serious mood.

Aaron waited for Samantha to pick a seat at the end of the table before pulling out the chair beside her. Since he'd been invited by Samantha, it was natural he'd sit beside her. That was what Mel told herself, anyway.

By the time Mel finished distributing glasses of ice water, Ronnie had already claimed a seat. That left one empty chair, which just happened to be on Aaron's other side.

All attention was focused on her when she sat. Her *and* Aaron. Eventually, she'd have to answer their unspoken questions. Like what was going on between them and for how long?

Not tonight, however. For in the next instant, everyone's gaze turned to Samantha.

Aaron couldn't remember when he'd last felt this out of place. Maybe in the attorney's office when Robin, her head partially shaved from a recent medical procedure, had insisted they update their living trust and her medical directive. Or when he'd told Nancy he was taking a job in Mustang Valley.

It wasn't just the invisible daggers being fired at him from all directions or the furious expressions on every Hartman face. Nor was it being dragged into the middle of a family dispute. Aaron had dealt with plenty of those during his law-enforcement career.

What made him uncomfortable was the fact that, in this particular dispute, he was a participant. An unwilling one, and only by association with Samantha, but a participant nonetheless.

Maybe he should leave after all. Forget Samantha needing an ally. But Mel looking ready to fall apart at the seams kept him rooted to his chair.

Guessing from her stiff posture and refusal to acknowledge him, she didn't appreciate his assistance. Hopefully later, when she'd calmed down, she would see he'd been trying to help.

Please don't take long, he thought, certain it would. Messes like this one, almost twenty years in the making, required more than a single evening of discussion to resolve.

For one brief second, he considered locating Mel's fingers beneath the table and folding them inside his. He came to his senses at the precise moment Frankie's searing gaze elevated to nuclear.

Great. What effect was this going to have on their daughters' friendship? None, he hoped.

Aaron suffered another pang of guilt—he'd lost track of how many tonight. Poor Kaylee. That she always forgave him when he came home late and missed story time was a minor miracle and one he didn't take for granted.

Ray finally broke the silence, chuckling nervously. "Where to start?"

His glance traveled to each of his daughters, one after the other, lighting last on Samantha. If he was hoping to promote a camaraderie among them, they were having none of it.

"I met Samantha's mother... I guess it was a couple years after your mom died. I accidentally stepped on her foot while picking out tomato plants in the garden department at the Home Warehouse Store. She asked for my advice on which was the best variety to grow in patio pots."

"Carrie Anne," Samantha said, her voice bowstring tight. "Her name is Carrie Anne."

"Yes. Of course. Carrie Anne."

It seemed Ray had the ability to slight all of his daughters without trying hard.

Drawing in a deep breath, he continued wreaking more emotional havoc with his story.

"We got to talking and before we knew it, an announcement came on the speakers that the store was closing. I asked her, Carrie Anne, to go for coffee with me, convinced she'd turn me down. I was, am, older than her, and she was so pretty. Plus, I was out of practice. When she said yes, I nearly lost my nerve. But she laughed at my jokes and smiled at me like she was interested in what I had to say."

All of them, Aaron included, sat spellbound. Did Mel and her sisters wonder what quality Carrie Anne had possessed, other than looks, that turned their grief-stricken father into a flirt who asked random women he met in the garden department out for coffee?

"We didn't date long." Ray avoided making eye contact with anyone. "A few months. I wasn't ready to commit and neither was she, for that matter. She'd just broken up with her boyfriend and was feeling insecure about herself. Eventually, we came to our senses and parted ways. No hard feelings. She called me four months later to tell me she was pregnant and intended to have the baby."

Beside him, Aaron heard Mel suck in air through clenched teeth. He was thinking Carrie Anne had duped Ray a little by waiting so long to break the news and denying him any say in the matter. Was Mel thinking that, as well?

"Carrie Anne was very sensible about the whole thing," Ray said. "I offered to get married, but she'd hear none of it. She insisted I'd proposed out of duty and was still grieving my wife, and that you girls were in no emotional state to accept a stepmother, much less a new baby sibling. I went along, for her sake and mine. I didn't want her missing out on the opportunity to meet the right guy.

"Turns out, I was right. Carrie Anne eventually reconciled with her boyfriend. After they got married, he asked to adopt Samantha. They were in love. Planned on having children. I thought it made sense."

Samantha didn't contradict Ray, which gave Aaron reason to believe the story was true.

"Did you love her?" Mel asked in a quiet voice. "Carrie Anne?"

Ray grimaced. "Whatever I say, I'm going to sound like a jerk."

Aaron related. He struggled with the same thing when it came to him and Mel and defining his feelings for her.

Did she notice the similarities between their situation and her father and Carrie Anne's and appreciate the irony? Both he and Ray grieved late wives and were reluctant to commit. Both had children who would be affected by and possibly resent their father's new relationship.

"If Carrie Anne and I had met a few years later," Ray said, "if she hadn't been in love with another man, who can say what might have been? But things were what they were, and I'm convinced they worked out for the best."

"Best for whom?" Samantha asked.

"Your mother seems happy. She always indicated to me that you were, too."

"You've spoken to Carrie Anne?" Mel's voice cracked.

"Periodically. She's kept me updated."

Samantha glowered at him. "You didn't speak to me."

"That was your mother and father's choice. Didn't she tell you?"

"She said you didn't want any contact with me."

"Really?" Ray looked surprised. "She told me you didn't want any contact with me."

Samantha stiffened, obviously not liking this revelation.

Ray addressed Mel and her sisters. "Carrie Anne and her husband decided when Sam was sixteen, she'd be informed about me and given my phone number to call if she wanted. Until then, Sam was raised believing Carrie Anne's husband was her father."

"How could you have agreed to that?" Mel flushed in outrage. "She was your child."

"I had my hands full raising you girls. You were my priority. Sam had a mother."

"Not so full you couldn't find time to date."

"I get that you're mad, honey. But I didn't go out with Carrie Anne to hurt you. I was lonely and sad. Try to understand."

"Why would I contact you?" Samantha apparently wasn't finished throwing punches. "You didn't want me when my mom got pregnant and left her to raise me alone. Just to get out of paying child support."

Aaron doubted Ray was required to pay anything as he'd waived his parental rights.

"Now, that's not true," Ray said, shocking everyone. "I gave your mother money every year up until a few months ago when you turned eighteen. I have the canceled checks to prove it."

"Why would she lie to me?" Samantha shook her head in confusion. "That makes no sense."

"Why not?" Mel said. "She lied to you about your real father."

"Enough." Ray sent Mel a warning look.

To Samantha, he said, "You'll have to ask your mother about that."

She thrust back in her chair, an angry scowl on her face. Aaron suspected more and more that Samantha was on the outs with her parents, particularly her mother.

Ray studied the young woman, his expression changing as if seeing her for the first time, which wasn't far from the truth. "Is that why you refused to talk to me? Because of the child support?"

"You didn't want me," she repeated with considerably less conviction.

"Honestly, Sam. You had a much better life with your parents than you would have had with me. It's not that I don't love you—"

"Do you?"

"I could. I *will* love you once we get to know each other." Ray paused, seeming to search for what to say. "I did as much right by you as your mother would allow me and, honestly, as much as I was capable of at the time."

Samantha's expression changed, and she suddenly appeared younger than her eighteen years.

"I'd like to get to know you now," Ray said. "If you're willing. Broke my heart two years ago when you refused to call."

"Forgive me if I'm still a little confused." Mel peered around Aaron at Samantha. "Your mother wasn't honest with you. She hid your real father from you and conveniently forgot to mention he paid child support. And instead of connecting with him when you had the chance, getting his side of the story, you blamed him for abandoning you. Now, you show up out of the blue, demanding money that you have no right to. My mind is boggled."

"He gave you each a share. Why not me? I'm his biological daughter."

"But not his legal daughter."

Mel's harsh but true reply visibly rippled among the others at the table.

"What did your mother have to say about you coming here?" Ray asked.

Samantha was slow to respond. "She…doesn't know."

As Aaron had expected.

"And don't call her." Samantha pointed at Ray.

"Because she wouldn't approve?" Mel asked.

Ray jumped quickly to Samantha's defense. "Give the girl a break."

"Dad! She's being unreasonable. And thinking only of herself. This isn't your fault. Not all your fault, anyway. She's out of line."

"I need the money." Samantha ignored Mel, addressing Ray instead. "You owe me."

He blew out a long breath. "The fact is, most of the money's been spent."

Samantha's eyes widened. "Already? I don't believe you."

Two hundred thousand dollars might seem like a huge sum. But in Aaron's experience of dealing with a catastrophic illness and premature birth of a baby, it could be spent in a week. Thank goodness for health insurance.

"I could try to scrape together a few thousand dollars," Ray offered.

"That's not enough." Samantha's pout returned. "I need more. A lot more."

"Why? For what?"

"Big John." Samantha promptly burst into racking sobs.

Frankie sprang up and put a comforting arm around the young woman's shoulders.

Mel, on the other hand, must've reached her limit. Pushing away from the table, she left through the Arcadia door that lead to the patio. Aaron thought there might have been tears in her eyes.

Ronnie returned to the kitchen for another round of ice water while Ray stared off into space.

Aaron debated for several seconds before getting up and following Mel outside. The hell with what anyone thought of them.

He found her sitting in one of the lawn chairs, her back to him. At his approach, she glanced up, then quickly looked away.

"Mind if I join you?"

She acquiesced with a sigh.

Aaron took that as a yes and dropped into the chair next to hers.

Mel needed no prompting, her words coming out in a rush. "I get it. She's young and a victim of circumstances beyond her control. Her parents, my dad included, made some crummy decisions. She deserves our sympathy and understanding. But that doesn't stop me from being mad. At her. At Dad. At Carrie Anne whatever-her-last-name-is."

"You have good reason. Your dad lied to you."

Mel let her face fall into her hands. "How could he?"

"Be honest. Would you and your sisters have accepted a stepmom and baby sister?"

Her head popped up. "I love Dolores."

"You're an adult. What about when you were ten?"

"Twelve. I'd have been twelve at the time."

"Would you have accepted Carrie Anne and Samantha then?"

"Well, we'll never know, will we? Because I wasn't given the opportunity."

He let her stew in silence for a few minutes.

Eventually, she said, "I don't have any money to give her even if I wanted to. I used it all to purchase my vet practice."

"That problem is your dad's to solve. Not yours."

"Do you think he didn't give her a share because he'd have had to explain it to me and Frankie and Ronnie?"

Aaron shook his head. "If I were to venture a guess, I'd say he already gave far more financially to Samantha than he was obligated to."

"Hmm." Mel let that sink in. "Sorry I was short with you earlier."

"I didn't notice." He smiled.

"I realized you weren't taking her side."

"It's a tough situation. Tempers are bound to flare."

"You've done nothing but try to help."

"I told you before, Mel, you can count on me."

Because her hands were clasped in her lap, Aaron rested a hand on her knee. After a moment, she closed her eyes.

"We should talk."

"I agree," Aaron said.

"In a day or two."

"Let me know when. I'll make myself available."

They had plenty to say to each other. His hand on her knee was evidence of that.

The door suddenly slid open, and Frankie stuck her head out. Mel pulled her knee away, but Aaron didn't think her concern was necessary. Frankie probably hadn't seen anything in the darkness.

"Dolores just got here with the girls," she said. "And I have an idea for what to do about Samantha. So, get in here now, you two." She ducked back inside.

Aaron rose first and assisted Mel to her feet. They didn't immediately separate.

"I'm sorry you got caught up in all this," she said softly.

"Don't worry about it."

The wedge of light shining from the door provided just enough light for him to see the regret in her eyes and something else. Something he couldn't pinpoint.

"What's happening with us?" she whispered.

Frankie hollered at them from inside the house, preventing Aaron from answering. Not that he knew what to say.

Chapter 5

"Her horse is injured," Frankie said, nodding at Samantha. "A torn ligament. That's why she wants the money. Not for herself."

Mel didn't see the logic. Wasn't wanting money for one's horse the same as wanting it for oneself? Frankie didn't usually split hairs, which Mel took to mean her sister sympathized with Samantha.

She studied the table. The family had resumed their former seats, with the exception of Mel's father. Dolores now occupied his chair, and he stood behind her, his hands resting on her shoulders. She periodically glanced up at him with love and support. Her father, as usual, returned her affection.

Mel increased her scrutiny. Strange that Dolores didn't appear upset or shocked to learn her husband had a daughter from a previous affair or even that the daughter suddenly showed up. If anything, she was…

He'd told her! Dammit. Nothing else made sense.

Mel didn't like the anger rising inside her but was unable to stop it. How could her father have confided in his new wife and not in his own daughters? The ones most affected.

Frankie settled more comfortably into her chair, preparing to lead the discussion. Mel tried not to be angry at her, either, just because she "had an idea what to do" and wasn't furious like Mel.

The girls were in the spare room, tucked into bed for the night but probably giggling. They'd stay over, with Frankie returning for them in the morning. Dolores had furnished the spare room with their various grandchildren specifically in mind.

"When did the injury happen?" Mel asked Samantha.

"Six weeks ago."

She encountered these type of injuries on a regular basis. "It's not the end of the world. I'm sure your vet recommended a treatment course."

"Two vets," Samantha clarified. "The first one said I should pasture Big John for six months. The second said I could bring him along sooner but to take it slow."

Both schools of thoughts had their merits. Which one was best depended on the nature of the tear and the horse. In Mel's opinion, the treatment of a torn ligament, even a small tear, shouldn't be rushed or else the horse risked permanent injury.

"Samantha's trying to qualify for the National Finals Rodeo," Ronnie said. "Her horse is…was her best chance. Without him, she'll have to quit competing."

"Can't she use another horse? Borrow one?" Mel didn't see the problem. "She must have friends who are barrel racers."

"There isn't one available," Ronnie said. "Not from a friend and not of the caliber she'd need to consistently win."

"Ah." That explained the demand for money. "She wants to buy a new horse."

"Not exactly," Ronnie admitted.

Mel's younger sister would identify with Samantha's problem. She'd come close to qualifying for the NFR herself more than once in her barrel-racing career, always falling just short. Retiring from the circuit without a NFR championship to her name was her biggest regret.

A bell went off inside Mel's head, and the last several minutes started to make sense. "You want me to treat her horse."

"You're a good vet," Frankie said.

"And no better than those other two, I'm sure."

"You haven't examined the horse. Maybe you should hold off until you have."

"It's July. She has, what? Four months left to qualify? No horse is going to sufficiently recover from a torn ligament before then. And does it really matter? How close are you to qualifying, anyway?"

Samantha shrugged. "I can do it. If I start competing again in the next few weeks."

"And win," Mel added. "On an unfamiliar horse."

She knew a little about barrel racing from watching Ronnie compete through the years. It was an arduous sport that required skill, talent, drive and a perfect partnership between horse and rider. Also, sufficient resources. Barrel racing wasn't cheap. Ronnie had worked part-time during high school to help their father pay her expenses. After graduation, she'd worked full-time, with half her salary going toward competing.

Surely another reason Samantha wanted the money. To pay her hefty costs.

"It's always sad when an animal is injured," Mel said, "and I feel for you. But, there's no money left from Dad's winnings and not much I can do for you that your own vets haven't."

"Can or will?" Samantha asked, her voice sharpening.

"I'm not a miracle worker, and I won't be held responsible if your horse ends up permanently lame."

She snuck a peek at Aaron beside her. Did he think she was being too hard on Samantha? He'd grown up with horses and these days enjoyed recreational riding, but he wasn't a hard-core enthusiast like everyone in Mel's family.

His expression revealed nothing other than mild curiosity. Mel wanted to think she cared little about his opinion and was taken aback by how much she did. If they were alone, she'd ask him what she should do.

"I think we can help Samantha," Frankie said. "She deserves it after all. She's missed out on a relationship with Dad and us her whole life."

"Did you not hear the same story I did?" Mel asked. "She *chose* not to have a relationship with him, *and us*, these last two years."

"She was hurt."

"And she's not the only one." Mel hated that she was on the verge of tears. "I'm not trying to be mean. Really. But you can't make us responsible for her mom and our dad's screwup. How is that fair?"

Frankie wore the same struggling-to-be-patient face she frequently did with her daughters. "How is it fair that Samantha suffer when we can help her? Won't you at least examine her horse?"

Mel's father spoke for the first time since they'd resumed the meeting. "You're angry. Who wouldn't be? I should have told you girls about Samantha a long time ago. Whenever the right moment arose, I came up with an excuse. Eventually, I stopped looking for moments."

"That's not a good enough reason, Dad." Mel shook her head. "It's actually a pretty bad one."

"You girls loved your mother so much." Sorrow filled his eyes. "I didn't want you to hate me."

"So, instead, you were grossly unfair to Samantha."

Had Mel just defended Samantha? More likely, she was just angry at her father.

She stared across the table, not recognizing the man standing there. Her father, the one who'd raised her, had been kind and good and loving and honest. He didn't deceive people, regardless of the reason.

Yet, he had. For more than eighteen years. How could Frankie and Ronnie not feel the same bitterness and disappointment she did?

Mel tamped down her emotions and faced Frankie.

"Don't make me out to be a terrible person just because I'm upset. I think we can all agree Dad hiding the fact he had a daughter with another woman is hard to understand and difficult to forgive."

"You don't want me, either," Samantha ground out.

Mel groaned in frustration. Was everyone intentionally taking what came out of her mouth the wrong way? "That's not what I said."

"You implied it."

Had she? Mel rubbed her throbbing forehead. This discussion was gaining momentum and going entirely in the wrong direction.

"You've known about us for a while. My sisters and

I only just learned about you less than two hours ago. We deserve a break. Some time to adjust."

"I agree," Frankie said. "Which is another good reason for what I'm going suggest. Not only can we help Samantha, we'll have a chance to get better acquainted with her and her with us."

She made it sound like a meet the teacher night at school.

"Dad, Ronnie, Samantha and I talked while you were outside with Aaron, and we're in agreement."

Mel doubted she was going to like what came next. "I'm all ears."

"Okay." Frankie squared her shoulders. "Here's the plan in a nutshell. Starting tomorrow, Samantha will stay with me. In exchange for room and board, she'll help around the house. Maybe, if things go well, she can watch the girls when I'm at work. Take them to and pick them up from preschool."

"She's going to remain in Mustang Valley?" Mel asked.

"You'll treat her horse. At no cost."

"It's not the money. I already said, there's no way the horse can improve sufficiently to compete in time for Nationals."

"Ronnie will let Samantha use one of her horses in the meantime."

Mel had to swallow her shock. Ronnie had purchased those two horses with the money from their father in the hopes of selling them for a profit. She was sacrificing a lot.

"Lastly, Dad will cover Samantha's competition costs and see to it that she gets to and from the rodeos." Frankie finished with a satisfied smile.

Everyone looked at Mel and waited, as if the entire success of this harebrained scheme depended on her.

"I can't stop any of you from doing what you want."

Frankie's smile faltered. "Are you saying you won't treat the horse?"

"I'd like to sleep on it."

"Come on, Mel. You're being stubborn."

"She's not," Dolores said, contributing for the first time. "It's a reasonable request. You're the ones who are out of line, expecting her to agree on the spot."

Mel sent her stepmom a grateful look.

Dolores began gathering water glasses, signaling the end of the meeting.

"There's still a lot to discuss," Frankie objected.

"I'd like to go home." Mel was tired, the most tired she'd been in weeks. Months. "It's been a long day."

As the last word escaped, she realized she didn't have a vehicle here. She'd driven with Ronnie to the café and with Aaron from there to her father's. Her truck was at home. Son of a—

"I can drop you off." Aaron checked his watch. "I need to leave myself."

She couldn't ride with him. What would her family say? They were already suspicious. Then again, with the way she felt now, the heck with her family and what they thought.

"Fine."

"Samantha?" Aaron asked. "You want to come with us?"

"I'll take her," Mel's father volunteered. This time, Samantha didn't refuse. "Frankie and Ronnie, you can ride with us and pick up your vehicles. The Morning Side Inn is right down the road from the café."

Mel's house was a ten-minute drive at most from her father's. She and Aaron spent the first eight minutes in silence. But Mel couldn't keep quiet after that.

"Do you think I'm being unreasonable?"

"Not at all."

He sounded genuine, which relieved her greatly, then brought her to tears. "I don't know what's wrong with me." She wiped at her damp eyes.

"You've had a rough day, and you're not feeling well."

Oh, yeah, thought Mel. That, too. She'd momentarily forgotten about her pregnancy-like symptoms.

"Don't be so hard on yourself."

Aaron didn't walk her to the door, not that she'd expected him to. But, before she got out of his SUV, he did take her hand and raised it to his lips for a lingering kiss.

"Good night, Mel." He met her eyes across the darkness.

"Um, night." She reclaimed her hand.

In a half-daze, she hurried up the walk to her house, thinking Aaron kissing her hand was the most romantic gesture any guy had ever made.

Oh, yeah. They really did need to talk.

Unless there was an emergency that couldn't possibly wait, Mel took Sundays off. It was her one full day of rest and relaxation and, normally, she relished it, sleeping in until seven or even later.

But today, she'd gotten up early and wandered the empty house, too restless and nervous to stay in one place long. Last night's events were on her mind, though not as prominently as her possible pregnancy. Still no period. Off and on nausea. Overwhelming tiredness.

Ready to cry at the drop of a hat. It was getting harder and harder to ignore the signs.

Thankfully, Mel had the place to herself. Ronnie had left at daybreak for Powell Ranch to ready her two barrel-racing horses. Samantha would meet her there after breakfast and, together, they'd choose the right horse for her.

Grabbing a second cup of coffee, which wasn't helping her anxiety—she tried not to think how bad caffeine was for a baby—Mel padded outside to the shaded patio.

She had always loved the backyard. It was her main reason for choosing this house over the other available rentals in town. To her right was a perfect view of the McDowell Mountains and Pinnacle Peak. To her left, and beyond the neighbors' houses, stretched endless desert. The fenced yard, with its see-through rails, allowed her to view both to her heart's content.

She'd always thought that someday, when her schedule allowed it, she'd adopt a rescue dog or two. The yard was designed for romping and playing, and she missed having pets. The yard was also custom-made for children. A family was also in her "someday" plans, along with a caring and devoted husband.

It seemed, however, she might be having children sooner than expected. One, at least. And no caring and devoted husband.

Mel leaned back in the wicker lounge chair and closed her eyes. Later today, regardless of what happened, she'd drive to Scottsdale and buy an early-pregnancy test. Then, she could concentrate on Aaron and their evolving relationship, which seemed bound to change whether she was pregnant or not. Equally pressing was Samantha, and Frankie's plan for the entire Hartman clan to help out their surprise half sister.

Mel decided assessing her priorities was a good stepping-off place. Naturally, her practice topped the list. It was more than a job or a salary to Mel. It was her dream. Her passion. Her reason for eagerly embracing each day. Her goal was to be as successful as her predecessor, if not more so, and a valuable part of the community.

When she did eventually have a family of her own, she'd need to be able to help support them, if not be the sole provider. Her father had taught Mel independence and the value of hard work. He'd also taught her the importance of honesty.

Him hiding a huge secret all these years didn't cause her to question his lessons. But it did force her to view him differently and, to a lesser degree, herself, as well.

Which brought her right back to her potential pregnancy and the need to buy a home pregnancy test. Perhaps because she lost her mother at a young age, perhaps because she witnessed the miracle of new life on a weekly basis with her job, keeping a baby was the only option for Mel.

Sitting alone on her back patio, watching a glorious sun peeking out from above her neighbors' roofs, Mel couldn't help but feel optimistic. Even if Aaron didn't want their child, her mind and her heart were made up. Granted, there would be obstacles to overcome and challenges to face. But a baby? A beautiful, tiny being brought into this world by her? Mel would fall head over heels at first sight.

She definitely wouldn't fall head over heels for a man who didn't want their child. The next instant, she dismissed the notion. For one, her pregnancy had yet to be confirmed. Two, she had no clue of Aaron's feelings on the subject, since she hadn't told him. Three, he had a daughter whom he adored and cherished. The man was a natural born father. She doubted the accidental circumstances of their child's birth, if there even was a child, would change him.

Before meeting Aaron, Mel had never approached sex casually. She did date, a couple guys semiseriously. Frankie accused her of being afraid to commit, a hang-up from losing their mother. There might be a sliver of truth to that. Mel tended to believe she simply hadn't fallen in love.

After meeting Aaron, she had tried to convince herself she was capable of remaining emotionally uninvolved. How wrong she'd been. Worse, she'd set herself up for being hurt by growing fonder and fonder of a man who couldn't have been clearer about his unavailability.

What should she say to him if she was indeed pregnant? Give him an out? Amicably part ways? Admit the truth about her feelings for him?

She recalled the previous evening when he'd dropped her off and kissed the back of her hand. How sweet was that? And romantic. There was also his kindness toward Samantha—which was touching, and now that Mel wasn't smack-dab in the middle of a tense family discussion, she could admit it.

Oh, Samantha. What to do about her? The abrupt change in direction her mind took dampened Mel's spirits.

Frankie appeared ready to accept the young woman as a member of the family. Then again, Frankie was the motherly type. She'd looked out for Mel and Ronnie after their mother died and, these days, was fiercely protective of her own daughters. She regularly took in stray dogs and cats, finding them good homes and keeping them if she couldn't. Ronnie's willingness to help Samantha was likely due to their shared interest in barrel racing.

Mel had decided at some point she'd at least examine the horse. There'd be no harm in it, and the exam would get Frankie off Mel's back. Plus, she was curious about the horse's injury and the prognosis. Beyond that, she'd make no commitment.

Hearing a noise, she turned to see the door leading to the patio open and Dolores step outside.

"You're up."

"Morning," Mel said. "What brings you by?"

Dolores's appearance wasn't out of the ordinary. Mel and Ronnie had a tendency to leave their doors unlocked when they were home, a habit formed from small-town living and family members who frequently dropped by unexpectedly.

"I brought you something." Dolores held up a small paper sack.

"What's that?"

She came over, sat on the other lounge chair and passed the sack to Mel. "See for yourself."

Mel sat up, opened the sack, peered in and read the label on the box. She arched a brow at her stepmom. "A home pregnancy test?"

"Stopped at the market on my way over."

"Get any snide comments?"

Dolores laughed. "Like I care."

"Thank you."

Mel didn't take Dolores's purchasing the pregnancy test as interfering in something that was none of her business. She truly appreciated having the older woman's advice and help.

"You could take it now," Dolores suggested.

Mel swallowed, her throat suddenly dry. Now that the moment was upon her, she hesitated. There were so many uncertainties, not the least of which was Aaron's feelings for her.

"The instructions recommend seeing a doctor to verify the results."

Mel glanced up from staring at the package. "You read them?"

"I've taken the test before. Though it's been a long while."

Gathering her courage, Mel rose from the chair and headed into the house, Dolores following close behind.

"Do you want me to stay or leave?"

"Stay," Mel said without reservation. She might need a shoulder to lean on.

In her bedroom, she read and reread the instructions, her anxiety escalating with each paragraph. She was actually doing this, taking a home pregnancy test. Focusing became difficult, and the printing on the leaflet blurred. Finally, when she felt ready, she took the testing wand with her into the adjoining bathroom. After that, it was a matter of waiting the longest three minutes of her life.

Determined not to peek until the required time had passed, Mel placed the testing wand on the bathroom counter, set the timer on her phone and returned to her bedroom where she proceeded to pace and stare at her phone and struggle to contain her racing thoughts. Finally, three minutes became two, and Mel stared as the numbers changed.

Would Aaron be angry if she was pregnant? She'd assured him she was taking the Pill. What if he thought she'd tricked him?

Mel pressed a palm to her warm cheek, taking another spin around the room. What? Still one minute to go?

Unknotting and reknotting the belt on her bathrobe, she scooped up a pile of dirty laundry she'd left on the floor the previous night and tossed it in the hamper sitting near the bathroom door.

Her gaze went to the testing wand sitting on the counter. Mel swallowed a startled cry. Even from this distance, she could see the results. Lunging forward, she grabbed the wand.

Her spaghetti legs took her only as far as the bed where she plopped down. Her breath came fast, and her heart beat a hundred miles a minute as relief washed over her. Now that the results of the pregnancy test were literally in her hands, she was able to admit what she'd wanted all along but was afraid to say.

A soft knock interrupted her. Dolores stood in the doorway, her expression expectant. "Well?"

Mel waved the wand, happiness filling her as she erupted in a wide grin. "It's positive. I'm pregnant."

Chapter 6

At the kitchen sink, Mel turned on the water and poured the remains of her coffee down the drain. That, she decided, had been her last official taste of caffeine for the next seven-and-a-half months, or thereabouts. She'd learn her exact due date when she saw her doctor, hopefully this week.

Mel wrote herself a note to call him first thing tomorrow morning, not that she'd need reminding. If the doctor was booked and couldn't see her right away, she'd visit the medical clinic in town. Just to verify her pregnancy and obtain prenatal vitamins.

Oddly enough, from the moment she took the test, she'd felt physically fine. Not the least bit nauseous or fatigued. If anything, she was bursting with energy.

"What are you doing?" Dolores asked.

Mel paused from rummaging through the kitchen

cupboard. "Looking for the herbal tea Ronnie bought last winter when she had the flu."

"Since when do you drink herbal tea?"

"Since I quit caffeine."

Dolores sat at the kitchen table, texting her oldest son who lived in Louisiana. She also regularly Skyped with her other son and daughter.

Mel had to laugh. Her father barely understood the workings of his phone while Dolores was an expert.

Finding the tea at last, Mel heated a cup in the microwave, then sat down next to her stepmom.

Putting her phone aside, Dolores asked, "Does Aaron know about the baby?"

Mel jerked, almost spilling her tea. "Who told?"

"It's not hard to figure out. You two have been pretty cozy of late."

"What about Dad?"

"Don't worry. I haven't said anything. But he's not stupid. Neither are your sisters."

"I'll tell them. Eventually."

"They've seen you and Aaron being cozy, too. So far, they think you're just flirting."

Mel should've seen this coming, probably had but chose to turn a blind eye.

"I thought you might have told him last night when he took you home," Dolores said.

"My mind was otherwise occupied."

"Be careful you don't wait too long."

"We have tentative plans to talk soon." Mel sipped at her tea, which was more of a distraction than a restorative beverage. "Speaking of Dad, how is he this morning?"

"You could call him."

Mel had considered it earlier then changed her mind. "I'm not ready."

"He's worried about you and your sisters. He's convinced you hate him."

"Of course I don't. But I'm mad and with good reason."

"You're changing the subject," Dolores scolded. "We were discussing you and Aaron and the baby."

"Family first. Aaron next. I can only deal with one problem at a time."

Her stepmom released a heavy sigh. "A huge upheaval isn't what I expected two months into my marriage."

"You knew, didn't you? About Samantha?"

She was slow to respond. "Yes."

"Dammit!" Mel let her hand fall hard to the table. "He told you but not us. That hurts."

"For the record, I disagreed with him. It's the only fight we've ever had. I conceded because the story of Sam was his to tell and didn't directly concern me. But secrets don't generally stay secrets forever, and I worried that you and your sisters would find it hard to forgive him when you did find out. I take no satisfaction in being right."

Mel appreciated the other woman's honesty and that she saw Mel's side. Her father had found a special lady the day he met Dolores, which was, of all places, on an internet dating website for seniors. Mel had been amused by it all, Ronnie, embarrassed. Their father meeting women online! Frankie had been the most encouraging. Similar to how she was the one welcoming Samantha and enlisting the entire family to help her.

When the sisters finally met Dolores, they'd liked

her from the start and not only because of her sweet nature and fun personality. Their father had been alone for too many years. Even after the sisters were grown and on their own, he'd remained a bachelor. The only new "ladies" to enter his life were Frankie's daughters.

Mel had quit suggesting he "get out more," or "find someone interesting." Little had she known he'd already done that years ago with Samantha's mother.

"Do you think I'm being unreasonable?"

Mel had asked Aaron the same question last night. As with him, she was genuinely curious in the answer.

Dolores studied her. "You are going to examine Samantha's horse, aren't you?"

"Yeah. I guess."

"Then, no, you're not being unreasonable. As far as being angry at your father, I'd be shocked if you weren't."

"Frankie and Ronnie don't act mad."

"Maybe not on the surface. Underneath, I'd bet they're fuming, too. You and Samantha are the only ones letting your true feelings show, and I say, bully for you."

"What's your opinion of Frankie's plan?"

"When your father won the lottery, I mentioned Samantha and that he might want to consider giving her a small share. He was, and still is, hurt that she refused contact with him when she turned sixteen. I suggested he put a sum aside in a bank account in case he changed his mind later on. He didn't. He was afraid there wouldn't be enough for you girls to get what you wanted and for us to go on an expensive honeymoon."

"Is that really the reason?"

"Who am I to argue?" She shrugged. "The money

was his to spend as he wished. Just like telling you about Sam was his story to tell. Not mine."

Sam. Mel had heard her father address Samantha by the nickname last night. Then, like now, a sharp pain pierced her chest right next to her heart.

Francine, Melody and Rhonda. Those were the names appearing on her and her sisters' birth certificates. The shortened, slightly masculine versions, Frankie, Mel and Ronnie, had been bestowed on them by their father. Until last night, Mel had thought that made her and her sisters special. Did he also choose Samantha's name?

Mel swallowed, hoping to dull the pain. "You still didn't tell me what you think of Frankie's plan."

Dolores hesitated. "As long as you're all in agreement, it's a good one."

"Really?"

"Sam's related to us, a part of the family, whether we like it or not and whether we accept it or not."

"That doesn't obligate Frankie, Ronnie and me to give her money we don't have anymore."

"I agree. But if you girls don't agree to help Sam, your dad will have to mortgage the house or cash in some of his retirement."

Mad as Mel was at him, she didn't want him to put a strain on his finances or deplete his 401(k). Dolores had a decent job as an insurance rep and her own retirement account, but she shouldn't have to give Samantha money, either.

"Like Frankie suggested last night, working together to help Sam would be a good way for all of you to get to know her."

Mel looked away. "What if I don't want to get to know her?"

"She's collateral damage," Dolores said, "just like you and your sisters. She didn't ask for what happened to her. Can you imagine being sixteen and finding out the man you thought was your father is, in fact, your adoptive father? That had to be rough."

"What's wrong with her mother anyway? Why doesn't she help Samantha?"

"Maybe she did and the lottery money's just an excuse."

Mel drew back. "For what?"

"Sam could finally be ready to meet you all and wasn't sure how to go about it."

"There are better ways. Like picking up the phone and making a call."

"She's eighteen. Probably not very experienced in handling difficult situations."

Mel made a face. "I think she's spoiled."

"I'm not excusing what she did. Just offering one possible explanation."

"Hmm." Mel would have to ponder that for a little while. "Would I be considered uncooperative if I insisted on a few stipulations before I agree to go along with Frankie's plan?"

"Not by me. What are they?"

"One really. I think we should take this week by week, if not day by day. Should me or anyone want out, we can withdraw with no hard feelings and no scorn from the others."

"You want that in writing?"

Mel laughed. "Not a bad idea. I'll draft a rough agreement."

"Need help?."

"I was kidding."

"I'm not." Dolores shrugged. "You all should at least discuss a flexible set of rules. This isn't easy. I admire you for putting aside your personal feelings."

"No guarantee they'll stay there."

Dolores leaned in closer. "Now, about the baby."

"I'm going to wait to tell Aaron until after I've been to the doctor. Just in case." Sage Powell, Mel's friend and client's wife, had recently miscarried very early in her pregnancy. They were just now trying again.

"You're going to keep the baby then?"

"Absolutely."

"And if Aaron doesn't want another child?"

"I'll let him off the hook."

"Oh, Mel. Is that really wise? Being a single mother is hard. Just ask Frankie. She could really use child support payments, not to mention a helping hand with the girls' care."

Mel reconsidered. "I'll accept Aaron's help if he offers. But I won't force him to take any responsibility. Or acknowledge the baby if he doesn't want to."

"Are you serious? Not acknowledge the baby?" Dolores looked stricken. "In the first place, Mustang Valley is a small town. He's going to run into you and his child. Frequently. In the second place, you can see how that plan didn't work out at all for your father and Sam's mother. He needs to step up, and you need to let him."

"I won't wreck his life."

"Who's to say you would?"

Mel rested her elbow on the table and propped up her chin with her hand. "His wife sacrificed months of her life in order to have their baby. If not a year. He carries a lot of guilt."

"I can imagine."

"He loves Kaylee more than anything and promised Nancy a home with them as long as she wanted one. She'll be devastated when she learns about the baby and think Aaron is betraying her daughter."

"Aaron's still a young man. What is he, thirty-two?

"Thirty-three." Mel would be thirty herself in a few months.

"It's reasonable to expect he'd eventually meet someone new and have more children."

"I don't think Nancy's ready for him to move on, and he's not ready to set wider boundaries or push her away." Mel didn't like the hoarse quality in her voice. "She's your friend. Is she as needy as she appears?"

"She does rely on Kaylee and Aaron to fill the void Robin left. Obviously, too much."

"Yet another reason for me not to pressure him."

"That doesn't change the responsibility he has to you and the baby," Dolores insisted. "Think hard before you let him off the hook."

"This wasn't his fault."

"Or yours. It takes two to make a baby."

Mel didn't answer.

"Have faith in him. He deserves a chance."

Whether intentional or not, Dolores had hit the nail on the head. Mel's nagging doubts didn't allow her to believe in a possible future with Aaron. "I'm the one who insisted on a no-strings-attached relationship. He's playing entirely by my rules."

"Which you now regret."

"Only because I'm pregnant."

Dolores smiled. "Only because you're falling for him."

Mel's shoulders sagged. "So much for modern relationships. They're apparently not for me."

Her cell phone rang. She pushed back from the table and hurried to the bedroom to answer it before the call went to voice mail. She got there just in time.

Seeing the familiar number, she answered with a breathy, "Hello, Cara."

"Sorry to bother you on a Sunday morning."

"No problem. Is something wrong?"

Cara Dempsey was the owner and manager of the mustang sanctuary, a local refuge for neglected, displaced and unadoptable mustangs. There were usually two hundred or more formerly wild mustangs residing in the sanctuary at any given time. Mel made regular trips, donating her services. When forced to charge, she always gave Cara and the sanctuary a deep discount.

"We had five head go missing last night," Cara said. "From the maternity pasture."

"Oh, my God!" Another horse theft. Less than a week after the last one. "Did you call the authorities?"

"Yes. Right away." Cara sobbed. "Four of the mares were pregnant. The fifth was a new mother. Her foal is three weeks old. I'm worried about the little guy. I tried bottle-feeding him, but he refuses."

Mel felt a tug on her heart. Losing a foal was always devastating. Losing one who wasted away because it missed its mother, even worse.

"If you don't have an empty stall in the horse stables, clear one and put him there. I'll meet you in an hour."

As soon as Dolores heard about the call, she left, promising to update Mel's dad on the horse theft. He'd probably want to head to The Small Change where the sanctuary was located even though it technically wasn't his responsibility.

Mel showered and dressed in record time, mentally inventorying what supplies she'd need to care for the foal and which techniques she'd employ to encourage it to eat.

Going outside to inspect her truck, she swore when she discovered she was low on mare's formula. Once on the road, she called the owner of Mustang Valley Feed and Supply Depot. Normally, the store wasn't open on Sundays, but the owner made an exception and promised Mel that his niece and assistant manager would meet her there.

She hung up, refusing to let herself wonder if Aaron would be at The Small Change when she arrived, investigating the horse theft—and hoping he'd be there just the same.

"I wanna come with you, Daddy." Kaylee peered up at Aaron, her huge blue eyes, so like her mother's, pleading with him.

"Sorry, sweetie." It tore at him, having to leave her again, especially after he'd gotten home too late last night to read to her.

"I don't understand why you have to go out again," Nancy said.

She and Kaylee were lingering over Sunday breakfast. That had been Aaron's plan as well, along with taking Kaylee to the park in town before it got too hot outside. Those plans went by the wayside twenty minutes ago, when he received a call about a horse theft at the mustang sanctuary.

Normally, he might let Shonda, the deputy on duty,

handle things on her own. But she was new to the job and a rookie to boot. On top of that, she didn't have a lot of experience with livestock, none before taking this job. Eduardo, the other deputy, had requested the day off to visit his ailing grandmother in Apache Junction and wasn't available. That left only Aaron.

"I won't be long. I'm just checking on Shonda. Ninety minutes tops." He lifted his hand and smoothed Kaylee's curls, also just like her mother's. "We'll go to the park when I get back."

Nancy made the pinched face she always did when Aaron disappointed her or his daughter. "It'll be a hundred degrees by then."

"How about I take the two of you to the new aquarium and butterfly exhibit?" He'd been saving that trip for Kaylee's third birthday next month. Now, he'd have to come up with something else.

"Yay!" Kaylee bounced in her chair.

"You spoil her too much," Nancy admonished.

"And you don't?" Aaron grinned good-naturedly, attempting to lighten his mother-in-law's mood.

"That's a grandmother's prerogative." Her features softened as they always did when she looked at Kaylee. "But we'll let you off the hook this time."

Aaron hadn't expected anything less. One thing he and Nancy had in common was spoiling Kaylee whenever possible.

A kiss and hug for Kaylee, a goodbye to Nancy and Aaron was out the door and on his way to the mustang sanctuary. Radioing Shonda, he learned the deputy was with Cara Dempsey in the ranch office housed in a building adjacent to the horse stables.

The Small Change Ranch, home to the sanctuary,

was one of the larger cattle operations in the valley, running over two thousand head. Advances in technology during the last fifty years had impacted how cattle were raised. One aspect, however, remained the same. Ranch hands still utilized horses for much of the work. In addition to the various barns, The Small Change boasted a state-of-the-art, air-conditioned horse stable and numerous pastures, including the one exclusive to pregnant and nursing mares, and where the latest horse theft had occurred.

Aaron aimed his SUV in the direction of the ranch office. Spying Mel's pickup parked in front of the stables, he executed a sharp right. Shonda and Cara could wait a few more minutes. Having discovered Mel at the ranch changed his priorities.

He spotted her immediately upon entering the stables. She stood in a horse stall, the sixth from the end, her back to him and bent over something. He started to call her name, only to reconsider and instead walk quietly down the aisle.

She was holding a bottle to a young foal's mouth and encouraging him to drink. At her feet sat a black rubber bucket and her medical case. The foal didn't act interested in the bottle and kept trying to pull away, bobbing his head vigorously. Mel made escape difficult by locking one arm around the foal's neck and putting herself between him and the stall door.

"Come on," she cooed, pushing the nipple into the foal's mouth. "You can do this. Aren't you even a little hungry?"

The foal abruptly jerked and almost broke free.

"Pretty please?" Her voice had become strained.

"You need fluids or you'll get dehydrated. We can't let that happen. Trust me, the outcome isn't good."

Aaron watched Mel, unable to take his eyes off her. He'd seen her treat animals before, that was nothing out of the ordinary, and witnessed the enormity of her caring. Never had he seen her with such a young patient or sensed her deep emotional involvement.

Veterinary medicine wasn't just a job to her. It was her way of making the world a tiny bit better for everyone else. Kind of like how law enforcement wasn't just a job to him.

The revelation gave Aaron pause. He and Mel were more alike than he'd realized.

With each jerk of the foal's head, Mel's long braid swayed like a pendulum. He liked her no fuss hairstyle and thought it suited her. He liked better undoing her braid and running his fingers through the long blond strands, marveling at their glossy sheen.

From this angle, her shapely curves were accentuated and inspired thoughts having nothing to do with work and everything to do with stolen hours alone together in the dark. He pictured her head fitting perfectly into the crook of his shoulder when they snuggled as if their bodies were custom-made for just that purpose.

The twinge of guilt came right on schedule. Not so much from his thoughts dishonoring Robin's memory but from disregarding the promise he'd made to put Kaylee and his family first.

All at once, Mel glanced up and, for a moment, they stared at each other. Aaron because he liked looking at her. A lot.

"I didn't expect to see you today," she finally said,

shaking off the spell they were under. "I thought your deputy was investigating the horse theft."

"I'm backing her up."

The foal suddenly slipped from Mel's grasp and scurried to the far corner of the stall. She didn't go after him. Setting the bottle down, she rubbed the small of her back, which had to ache from maintaining such an awkward position.

"She's in the ranch office talking to Cara, if you're looking for her."

"I know." Aaron closed the distance to the stall and leaned a forearm on the door. "I talked to her earlier."

"Then why are you here?" She looked around, indicating the horse stables.

He grinned. "To see you. And I'm glad I did."

She actually glanced shyly away. In that instant, he became even more smitten—which meant he was treading further and further into forbidden territory.

To distract himself, Aaron nodded at the foal. With a coat the color of tarnished gold, a wide white blaze down the center of his face and four perfectly matched white stockings, he was striking to say the least. "That's a nice looking colt. What happened to the mother? Is she sick?"

"She's gone. She's one of the missing horses."

Aaron swore softly, cursing the horse thieves.

"I'm worried we're going to lose him." Mel sighed wearily. "He won't eat."

"You'll figure this out. He's not going to die."

"No, he's not." She straightened. "I still have a trick or two up my sleeve."

"Like what?" He was truly interested. Aaron had

grown up around horses, though his family hadn't raised any from birth.

"There's milk pellets. According to Cara, he's been eating a little solid food. But he's still going to need the complete nutrition of mare's milk. I checked around, and there aren't any lactating mares available to foster him. But there are several tame burros in the sanctuary that could serve as a companion. A large part of this guy's problem is he misses his mother. His chances of improving increase if he can bond with another horse. Or something close to a horse."

"If you want some help," he said, "let me know."

She searched his face. "Seriously?"

"I wouldn't have offered if I wasn't serious."

"Thank you."

Aaron had to look twice. Were those tears in her eyes? "It's no big deal. Really."

"What's your mother-in-law going to say if we're seen together?"

"I'd like to say I don't care."

"Except you do." Mel wiped off the bottle with a towel and returned it to her medical case.

"Helping you with the foal is business. Not personal."

"Of course. So why would Nancy care?"

"Okay." Aaron could have kicked himself. "That didn't come out right."

"You think?" Mel's movements were stiff and jerky as she collected the bucket and closed her medical case.

"I'm sorry."

She nodded, her mouth drawn into a thin, tight line. "I put you on the spot. That wasn't fair."

Aaron should probably leave before he shoved his

other foot in his mouth. Only he didn't. "Things settle down with the family yet?"

Her answer came slowly. "I haven't talked to my dad or sisters since last night. And before you say anything, I will. I needed to handle this emergency first."

"You consider Frankie's plan at all?"

"And some other things." She pushed her hair back from her face. "I didn't sleep much last night."

He just then noticed the dark circles beneath her eyes and reached for her across the stall door. Too quick for him, she retreated a step, her no-touching message broadcasted loud and clear.

Should he tell her he was finding it harder and harder to resist her? Probably not. She'd been the one to set the rules, it was true, but he'd agreed to them, as much for his personal situation as hers.

Robin had made him swear he'd be open to finding someone new someday. At the time, when she'd been lying in a hospital bed, he couldn't conceive of loving again. Lately, with Mel, the prospects didn't seem completely impossible.

The pull between them was definitely growing stronger and stronger. But his home life, of which Nancy was a big part, remained unchanged. He'd made commitments to her, too, and Aaron didn't like going back on his word. Even something as small as missing reading time with Kaylee bothered him.

"You're an easy person to like, Mel." It was the closest he could come to expressing his feelings.

She stared, her features stricken.

Aaron wanted to kick himself. Once again, his remark had hurt her rather than ease her unhappiness or uncertainty.

"Let's meet tonight." At her arch glance, he added, "For that talk. Nothing else."

After a moment, she relented. "Is six o'clock too early?"

"Can we make it seven? I'm taking Kaylee to that new aquarium and butterfly exhibit this afternoon."

The briefest of smiles touched Mel's face. "That should be fun."

Aaron thought it might be more fun if Mel went with them. He didn't dare ask her, though. That was guaranteed to make a muddy situation muddier. He set the fantasy aside, along with the other ones he'd recently been having about him and Mel going to dinner and a movie rather than hiding out in a room at the motel.

"I'd better head to the office. Check in with Shonda and see how the investigation is progressing."

"And I need to track down a good companion burro."

Mel bent to retrieve her case, then abruptly straightened, her hand clasped to her middle, her eyes squeezed shut and her lower lip caught between her teeth.

"You okay?" Aaron pushed through the stall door.

She held up a hand. "Stay back."

Ignoring her, he hurried to her side.

"Please." She spun sideways. "I'm going to be sick."

She barely made it to the corner opposite where the foal stood watching them with wide eyes before leaning over and vomiting.

Aaron waited a minute for her to recover. She was breathing hard, as if she'd just run a hundred-yard dash. Averting her head, she wiped her mouth with her forearm, kicking dirt to cover the mess at her feet.

Her acute embarrassment tangible, he said, "Don't

worry. I have a young daughter. I see throw up and a whole lot worse on a regular basis."

She exhaled slowly. Sweat lined her brow, from the heat and the exertion. "You haven't seen my throw up."

"You should call your doctor. This has been going on for days."

"I'm planning on it. Tomorrow."

"I could drive you."

What little color remained in her cheeks promptly drained. "No, that's all right. I can manage."

Before he could say more, she doubled over and vomited again. This, he decided, was getting serious.

"Go home, Mel. Forget about the burro. You're sick."

"No, I'm not." She wiped at her mouth again.

"Do I have to toss you over my shoulder and kidnap you?"

"You'd better be joking."

"I'm not, Mel. You're really worrying me."

Drawing in a long breath, she blurted, "I'm pregnant. I was going to tell you tonight, but there's no point in waiting."

Pregnant? Aaron struggled to absorb the news, but his mind kept throwing up barriers.

"You're…on the Pill," he stammered.

"It obviously failed."

Her tone implied she was mad, though Aaron wasn't sure at what. Him or the situation.

A beep, a crackle and then a distorted version of Shonda's voice erupted from his radio. "Aaron. Are you here yet? We're waiting on you. Over."

He responded automatically, pressing the button on the transmitter clipped to his shirtfront. "Be right there."

To Mel, he said, "I don't want to go."

"I understand. You're here on official business. I should have waited to tell you."

"I don't know how long I'll be tied up with the investigation. Then I have plans with Kaylee. Can this wait until tonight?"

"Sure." She stared at him. If she was attempting to gauge his reaction, he didn't think she was getting much other than surprise and disbelief.

What did she expect? She had just pulled the rug out from under him.

He knew he should reassure her. Tell her everything would be okay. That they'd figure this out, and she could rely on him.

All he could muster at the moment was, "All right. See you then."

He could only guess at the depths of her disappointment in him.

Chapter 7

Mel waited until she reached the four-way stop before grabbing her phone off the passenger seat and reading the text. It was from Aaron, as she'd suspected.

#22 Be there shortly

He was giving her the number for their room at the Desert Oasis Motel. This was the extent of their texts, a room number and a few token words.

Returning her phone to the passenger seat, she accelerated though the quiet rural intersection and continued on the road toward Rio Verde. For some ridiculous reason, she thought Aaron might say something different tonight. Like, *hurry up, can't wait to see you* or *I've missed you* followed by a heart emoji.

She was being stupid. Ten hours ago she'd delivered

the bombshell of the century. Did she really think the subtle changes she'd noticed in him lately would carry over to a text when he was probably still reeling?

Neither would tonight be a typical hookup. No falling into bed after a few minutes of small talk.

On the plus side, her morning sickness had all but disappeared since this morning's disastrous encounter in the horse stall.

An hour researching online, as well as reading pamphlets a nurse at the medical clinic had provided that afternoon, had taught Mel this particular pregnancy symptom often came and went. With luck, her stomach would behave. Hard to have a conversation when one person was bent over the toilet.

She didn't return Aaron's text and not because it was unsafe to do so while driving. She simply didn't know what to say. Her usual reply of *On my way* seemed trite under the circumstances.

Aaron's SUV was easy to spot in the small parking area behind the motel. He hadn't driven his official sheriff's department vehicle. Too risky. What if someone spotted him? Rather, he drove his personal SUV, a smaller, "friendlier" and completely unremarkable version that garnered no attention.

Mel parked in the next space over, noting the child's car seat through the window. She was struck with a sudden pang. Would he have a second car seat for their baby? Or, not want anything to do with Mel anymore?

Her father had given up all parental rights to Samantha without a single objection. Aaron could easily want that too. He already had a family, one he'd sacrificed a great deal for. A baby and baby mama on the side could endanger their security.

A heavy lump formed in the pit of her stomach that had nothing to do with the physical aspects of her pregnancy and everything to do with her emotional state. She could well be facing motherhood alone. Not the future she'd envisioned for herself.

Standing in front of the door to room 22, she raised her hand to knock, then paused, a sense of indecency heating her cheeks. She hadn't been embarrassed since the first time she and Aaron came here. They'd met in the lobby, and she'd been convinced the clerk pegged them right off the bat as having an affair.

By their third rendezvous at the motel, Mel hadn't cared about proprieties. She and Aaron weren't doing anything wrong. So why, then, had those old feelings suddenly resurfaced?

She fought the urge to turn and flee. Aaron was expecting her. And besides, they really did need to talk.

Rapping soundly on the door, she waited, every nerve in her body stretched to its limit. He answered almost immediately, as if he'd been standing directly on the other side of the door.

"Hi." The smile he flashed paled in comparison to its usual brilliance.

Mel worried it was a bad sign. "Sorry I'm late."

She entered the room when he swung the door wide and gave a cursory glance around. The two dozen rooms at the small motel were identically furnished and decorated. Realizing she and Aaron had occupied over half of them, she nearly laughed. From tension, not because she found the idea funny.

He didn't pull her into a hug or kiss her, which was how most of their evenings together started and ended.

It was a definite highlight of their time together and one she usually looked forward to.

"You want some water?" He came prepared with two chilled bottles, which now sat on the spindly legged desk.

"Thanks." She might need an outlet for her pent-up energy. Sipping water would serve the purpose.

After a moment, he planted himself in the equally spindly chair, his long jeans-clad legs fighting for space in the cramped area between the desk and the bed. "How's the foal doing?"

Apparently, they *were* going to start with small talk.

"Putting the burro in with him hasn't helped." She sighed dejectedly. "He did finally drink milk from a bucket and nibbled on a few pellets."

"You think he'll make it?"

"Too early to say. The next few days, few hours, really, are critical. Cara's keeping an eye on him."

"You'll pull him through."

Aaron had said something similar to her this morning, and it pleased her that his confidence hadn't wavered in light of recent events.

"I hope."

Silence followed. Sipping at her water, Mel perched on the bed. The mattress, as hard as an ironing board, barely budged. On past evenings, when their moods were lighter, they'd joked about the motel's lousy accommodations.

"Who wants to start?" she asked, forcing a smile.

"How about you, seeing as you have the most at stake?"

Did she? Mel tended to disagree. Unless he *was* planning on leaving her to raise the baby alone.

"I went to the medical clinic in town today and had

the pregnancy confirmed." Since early pregnancy tests could be wrong, and there was a lot riding on their talk tonight, she'd decided to make absolutely sure by visiting the clinic. "I'm calling my regular doctor tomorrow for an appointment."

"Want me to drive you?"

His offer initially took her aback. She hadn't thought about him going with her. Then again, he'd probably accompanied his late wife on all her appointments, considering she'd spent the majority of her pregnancy battling a brain tumor.

"That's not necessary," Mel said. "Maybe when I'm further along."

"How far are you?"

"Five weeks, give or take." She hesitated, her certainty waning. "You do believe me when I say this was entirely an accident?"

"Of course."

"Really?" Doubts still plagued her.

"Mel, I know you pretty well. We've been seeing each other for over eight months. You're not a liar. The Pill can fail. It did with Robin."

"Oh!" He hadn't mentioned that before. "I always had the impression you and she were trying for a baby."

"We were when we had Kaylee. The year before, Robin conceived while on the Pill. Unfortunately, she miscarried. I always wondered if she was so determined to have Kaylee because she'd lost one baby."

Mel had no idea what she would do if she were terminally ill. Maybe the same as Robin. Oddly enough, the thought made her feel a tiny connection to Aaron's late wife. While disconcerting, it was also comforting in a way.

"Since this wasn't what either of us planned," Mel

began, "I completely understand if you want no part of the baby."

He stared at her. "You're kidding."

"Actually, no."

"I'm the baby's father, Mel. Trust me, I'll be an involved father."

He sounded completely committed. Not a trace of hesitancy or uncertainty colored his voice.

Mel wanted to be glad. Relieved. Aaron was willing to step up. But something held her back.

"I just wanted to put it out there. I have no expectations."

"You should," he said. "High expectations. And I promise to meet them. I was thrown today when you told me, and I apologize for that. Please don't think too badly of me."

"I didn't. Honestly. You were caught off guard."

"It was a lot to process. But I've been thinking about you, about us, all day."

As she looked at him, her hesitancy wavered. Aaron was the kind of man Mel had always dreamed of meeting—someday, when she was ready to settle down. His intentions were clearly good.

"I suppose we have a decision or two to make."

"Let's not try to figure everything out tonight," he said. "We have time."

She thought it interesting that he hadn't asked her if she wanted the baby or not. Had he assumed or—and this was irksome if true—did he know her as well as he'd claimed?

"I'm going to support you," he continued, "financially and in every way you need."

"What about your family? Will you tell them?"

"Yes. Eventually."

She supposed Aaron had a valid reason to wait. She wasn't very far along and, as she'd learned tonight, his late wife had miscarried.

"What about you?" he asked. "Telling anyone?"

"Dolores knows, but only because she found me being sick in the café restroom and figured it out. But she won't say anything until I'm ready."

"You sure? Not even your dad?"

"I trust Dolores."

"That says a lot about her character. You must be close."

His remark prompted Mel to stop and think. "I guess we are."

"I'm glad. You can use a friend right now. Someone besides me."

Mel studied him, noting the rugged good looks and strong physique that had first attracted her. He appeared capable of taking down the burliest of criminal offenders. Yet, she'd seen his gentler side many times, with her and, from a distance, with his daughter.

"Are you my friend, Aaron?"

"I'd like to think so." He sat up, causing the old chair to creak. "More, if you'll let me."

What was he implying?

Nothing, apparently, for he continued with, "We're having a baby together. Better for everyone involved if we get along."

"Yeah. Right." She sighed. "How is Nancy going to take the news?"

"Honestly?" he asked.

"That's the only answer I'm interested in."

"Probably not great."

While putting her vet practice first had been Mel's

reason for keeping their relationship status casual, Nancy's hold on Aaron was the driving force behind his. Mel disliked being harsh. He had lost the woman he loved. But it was as if Nancy didn't want him moving on. She fanned his guilt over Robin's death, keeping the flame alive and burning bright.

"She has to expect you're going to meet someone eventually." For a moment, Mel thought Aaron might confess that he already had. It didn't happen.

"She's been good to me and Kaylee since Robin died."

Mel didn't press the issue. She had no right. He was entitled to tell Nancy in his own time and in his own way.

"What about you?" Aaron asked. "Not your family but your job. Having a baby is going to interfere in a big way with your work schedule."

"You're right. I'll have to make some changes. But other single mothers manage." She was thinking of her older sister. "I will, too."

"No rush. You have a lot on your plate at the moment."

He didn't ask the obvious question, for which she was glad. How did she expect to simultaneously build her practice and raise a child? Perhaps he, like Mel, believed she didn't have to choose and could succeed at both.

"I want this baby," she said, admitting out loud what was in her heart.

His response was an ear-to-ear grin. "I can tell. I'm excited, too."

"You are?"

"It was hard being happy when Kaylee was born. Don't get me wrong, I wanted her. But I was losing Robin. She was dying by degrees, and each day was a challenge. This time, with you, I can celebrate. Pass out cigars. Laugh when the guys make jokes."

His admission struck a tender chord in Mel's heart. If she hadn't thought him perfect before, she did now. Managing to keep her distance was getting harder and harder.

They spent the next thirty minutes discussing less pressing matters. It seemed not all of Aaron's memories of Robin's pregnancy were sad. He had some humorous and sweet stories to tell, too.

Any other night, they would have made love. Tonight, however, they were there to talk, and it was Aaron who suggested they get a move on as they both had early mornings.

He walked with her to her truck. "Good night, Mel. Drive safely."

"You, too. I'll let you know about the doctor's appointment."

Assuming a parting kiss was unlikely, she reached for her door handle—and was caught off guard when his arm captured her by the waist.

"Aaron! What—"

He lifted her off her feet and hard against him.

"Is this a good idea?" Her voice wavered. The message earlier had been hands-off.

"You can tell me no." He lowered his mouth, stopping a millimeter shy of kissing her. "Otherwise, hang on."

Hang on? Like to his shoulders? Weak in the knees, she decided maybe she'd better. Just as a precaution.

In the deepest recesses of her mind, a small voice shouted a warning to be careful. This was inviting danger.

She didn't listen. Aaron smelled too delicious and felt too good for her to stop now.

"I've missed you, Mel." He brushed his lips across hers, their touch softer than a butterfly's wings.

The words she'd longed to hear. Aaron had never said them before, in this or any context. Missing her implied he thought about her when they were apart. Hadn't she just ripped the rug out from under him with her pregnancy announcement? Yet, he admitted to missing her.

This wasn't just a matter of growing feelings. There had to be more.

Any other thoughts, coherent or scattered or wildly improbable, were banished when Aaron's mouth covered hers. He didn't have to demand a response from her, she willingly offered. Clutching the fabric of his shirt in her fingers, she dragged him backward until they stumbled into her truck, and she was pinned between two hard and unyielding surfaces.

Yes. At last. This was what she'd been wanting, needing, craving all night. Letting go and throwing caution to the wind, she lost herself in the kiss.

Wait—that wasn't it at all. She *found* herself. And she wanted to stay. Indefinitely.

Eventually, and too soon for her liking, they slowly broke apart. Just as well. They might have gone a little too far. Their immediate future was up in the air still, and intimacy tended to confuse situations.

But when Mel peered up at Aaron, he wore a grin. Not a satisfied one and not a sexy one. It was…happy. How was that possible when they'd just made a big mistake?

"I'd better go," he said, as reluctant to release her as he'd been to end their kiss.

Rendered speechless, Mel could only nod. With a last, lovely caress to her cheek, he walked away. She stared after him for several seconds before climbing into her truck and starting the engine.

At the first stop, Mel touched a hand to her cheek and then a finger to her lips, reliving the sensation of Aaron's hand and mouth. Unless she was mistaken, he had kissed her as if he wanted her with every fiber of his being. And she had wanted him with the same intensity.

Wrong and dangerous as it was, she hoped they'd make another mistake again soon.

Mel commended herself for arriving at Frankie's house only—she checked the dash clock—thirty-six minutes late. It had been a crazy busy day with two unscheduled emergencies. Thirty-six minutes late was a pretty impressive accomplishment in her opinion.

Four days had passed since she and Aaron met up at the motel and shared their incredible kiss. Four days when Mel had a thousand and one important things to contemplate—like her pregnancy and the doctor visit, which had gone well. Aaron telling his mother-in-law and her reaction. Mel telling her family. The latest developments with Samantha.

Yet, unbelievably, Mel was most occupied with the kiss, constantly reliving every vivid detail and analyzing every tiny aspect from beginning to end. It probably meant nothing. She and Aaron had often kissed. No reason to go overboard just because her toes continued to tingle even now.

Her phone beeped, alerting her to a text message. Mel quit breathing. Was it Aaron? They'd been communicating daily, mostly about how she felt, the results of her doctor visit, the young foal's condition and what, if any, progress had been made on the horse thefts. But it was always by phone call. Their last text had been the one on Sunday containing the inn room number.

She checked, saw Frankie's name and told herself she was glad. Talking to Aaron would only confuse her more.

Frankie's text asked how much longer Mel was going to be. Apparently, her older sister didn't look out her front window much or she'd see Mel's truck sitting there. Then again, she might be in the backyard with Samantha.

Mel answered "Here," then retrieved her medical case from the locked compartment. As expected, Frankie and Samantha were with Mel's newest patient— Samantha's horse.

Entering through the side gate, Mel crossed the large, grassy backyard. Frankie had purchased the country-style house, with its half-acre corral and minibarn especially for her daughters. She'd yet to acquire a pony or small horse for them, still in the process of getting settled after the move. Which meant that Samantha's horse, a long-legged, muscular brown and white paint, had the place to himself.

Judging from his loose-limbed stance and idly swishing tail, he liked his new surroundings. Same for his owner. Samantha chatted amiably with Frankie, the defiance in her eyes absent for once.

"There you are." Frankie spotted Mel and threw her arms up in exasperation. "Finally. It's after three."

Samantha didn't issue a greeting. She stood beside her horse, perhaps shielding him from danger or taking comfort from him. Mel wasn't sure which. Big John, his lead rope dangling from the fence, shook his head in annoyance at the dozen pesky flies attempting to land.

Mel hadn't changed her opinion of the horse's condition; it would require months of rest and physical therapy for a full recovery. But she did believe he'd eventually compete again and had told Samantha as much.

That, and Ronnie allowing Samantha to use her expensive barrel-racing horse, were likely responsible for the young woman's improved attitude. And possibly Frankie's mothering too. She did have the magic touch.

"Jeez, Mom," Mel teased, "I'm not that late." She set her case down near the horse and opened it, revealing an assortment of equipment and supplies.

Frankie's daughters played nearby, wearing bathing suits and darting in and out of the water sprinkler. They were having so much fun, laughing and squealing, they hadn't seen Mel.

She wiped sweat off her forehead with the back of her hand. Tempted to join her nieces in the water, she asked Samantha, "How's he doing today?"

"No better."

"Rehabilitation takes time. You have to be patient."

"I'm walking him twice a day like you said."

"That's good." Mel conducted her examination, quizzing Samantha about the horse and his symptoms.

"And I'm taking him to Powell Ranch tomorrow to work him in the round pen there."

"Don't they usually charge for that?"

Powell Ranch, where Ronnie had her barrel-racing school, offered several levels of service to their customers. Mel doubted Samantha could afford the most basic one.

"They're letting me use some of the facilities in exchange for cleaning stalls and exercising horses."

"It was Ronnie's idea," Frankie interjected. "That way, Samantha can train with Ronnie's other students."

Training under Ronnie's supervision. Using her best horse. Living with Frankie. Helping with chores and babysitting her daughters.

Mel marveled at how both her sisters had so readily accepted Samantha. Unless they were just making the best of the situation, which was what Aaron had suggested when they spoke yesterday.

"That's great." Mel was slow to respond.

"She registered for the barrel-racing competition this weekend in Rio Verde," Frankie said.

Mel had heard. Like with bull riding, bronc busting and calf roping, barrel racers often organized nonsanctioned events in order that both the riders and horses could practice as much as possible.

"Dad's driving her." Frankie looked pleased. "And covering the entry fees. We're all going."

Mel continued manipulating Big John's injured leg, gauging his sensitivity to pain. "We?"

"The girls and me. Dad. Dolores. Ronnie, naturally. And you?" she added with a hopeful smile.

"I'm working."

"All day? It doesn't start till early evening."

"She doesn't have to go," Samantha said sulkily.

Mel stifled her temper, irked at being made to feel guilty. "I'll do my best."

One of the girls squealed in anger and took a swing at her sister, fortunately missing by a good foot. Something must have gone wrong during their playing. Frankie rushed over to separate them and make peace.

Mel noticed Samantha watching, a tender expression on her face as if she actually cared about the girls.

Who, now that Mel thought about it, were Samantha's nieces. Mel remembered the mention of two younger brothers. Did Samantha miss them? They must be older than the girls.

The next moment, Samantha returned her attention to Big John. Ignoring Mel, she rubbed the broad space between his eyes and cooed softly. Big John responded by lowering his head, pressing his nose into her arm and blowing contentedly.

Liking young children. Loving her horse. Samantha apparently possessed a gentler side. Mel had been like that when she was younger.

That wasn't the only similarity she'd observed between the two of them. Though, to Mel's dismay, she might have more in common with Samantha's mother Carrie Anne. Both had unexpectedly gotten pregnant by a man who still grieved his late wife, and both were reluctant to commit to that man.

Mel reached into her medical case for liniment and leg wraps. Bandaging Big John's leg protected it from further injury, and the liniment improved flexibility. Mel was trying many different methods to help the horse, including exercising and stretches designed to strengthen his leg.

"Can I help?" Samantha asked.

"Um, sure." Mel pointed. "Hand me that square of cotton padding.

Samantha did as instructed and then watched Mel closely as if trying to absorb everything she did.

"You interested in veterinary medicine?"

"I'm interested in taking care of Big John," she answered.

Good enough, thought Mel. "He's a nice horse. Strong.

Spirited. Clearly attached to you. I can see why you're upset he's hurt."

"He's all I've got." Samantha continued to stroke the horse's broad face. "I'd do anything for him."

Like demand money from a biological father she hadn't met before?

"What about your family in Flagstaff?"

Samantha didn't answer. Okay, apparently, Aaron was right. She was on the outs with her parents. Maybe they didn't approve of her choices or disliked her boyfriend. What eighteen-year-old wasn't on the outs with his or her parents at some time?

"I'm really grateful to Ronnie and Frankie." After a long pause, Samantha said, "And you."

Mel almost laughed. "That wasn't so hard, was it?"

Samantha became suddenly preoccupied with Big John. Mel let her be, focusing instead on the horse's leg. Overall, she was satisfied with his improvement, slow though it was.

"Rodeoing is my only shot to make anything of myself."

Mel glanced over her shoulder at Samantha. "I doubt that. You're smart. And pretty capable from what I've seen, no insult intended. I'm sure you have more than one shot. What about college?"

"I'm not going. I don't care what my parents say."

Ah. School was the reason for the falling out. Had they talked since Samantha came to Mustang Valley? Samantha hadn't taken the news of her mother's lies well. Their original rift could have possibly, and understandably, widened.

"I loved college," Mel said, choosing not to ask about

Samantha's mother. "But it's not for everyone. Given the choice, what would you do?"

"Barrel race. What I'm doing now."

Ronnie had made a career of rodeoing. It could be done.

"You'll have to work really hard."

"I'm tough."

This time, Mel did laugh. "No kidding."

Did she actually admire the young woman? When had that happened? Must be her maternal instincts kicking in, messing with her thinking.

"Look, I know you're mad at me..." Samantha stopped there, leaving the sentence unfinished.

"I am." Mel stood. "What you did wasn't right. Demanding money." She braced her hands on her hips. "But, you were lied to by your parents, and, trust me, I understand how you feel." She had yet to look her father in the eyes since learning his giant secret. "And because my sisters believe you deserve a break, I'm willing to help."

"Okay."

"Okay?" Mel waited.

"Thank you."

A little better. She had no idea why, but she said, "If you'd like to come with me sometime on a call, I wouldn't object. I'm going to need a hand in the coming weeks. With some of the heavier work."

"Help you?" Samantha brightened. "You're offering me a job?"

"No. I can't afford to pay you. Consider it a trade for treating Big John."

Her enthusiasm didn't wane. "When? Tomorrow?"

"Don't you have to watch the girls and train with Ronnie?"

"Frankie doesn't go in to work until noon, and practice starts at 7:00—p.m.," she clarified.

"I'll be by at 6:00 to pick you up—a.m."

Samantha didn't say much else, but Mel caught her smiling to herself and almost tripped on her case. While not a carbon copy, Samantha did have many of the Hartman characteristics, reminding Mel of Ronnie when she was younger. Or, she swallowed, herself.

How could she have missed the resemblance?

"That was nice of you." Frankie had snuck up behind Mel.

"I'm probably going to regret it."

"No, you're not."

They both turned when Aaron's family SUV pulled into the driveway. Mel's heart rate immediately skyrocketed. What was he doing here? He must have spotted her truck while driving by and stopped to talk. She finger combed her hair, scolded herself for caring and let her hand drop.

"Ah!" Frankie said. "Right on time."

"What?" Mel blinked.

"Aaron. He brought Kaylee over for dinner and a playdate with the girls."

Really? They'd just talked a couple hours ago, and he hadn't mentioned a playdate. Not that he was required to inform her of his schedule. But he'd known she was going to be here.

"What's wrong with you?" Squinting, Frankie shielded her eyes from the sun. "You look funny."

"Nothing." Mel turned away.

Childish though it might be, she was a bit hurt. Aaron hadn't dropped by to see her but rather her sister and nieces. Apparently, she was the only one affected by their kiss.

Chapter 8

"Wait." Aaron sprinted toward Mel. "Put that down. Better yet, give it to me." He relieved her of the bucket of water, ignoring her protest. "It's too heavy for you."

"I'm not frail and helpless."

"You need to be careful. Don't take any chances. It's hot as blue blazes out here."

"And you're overreacting."

He was, he'd admit to it. "Comes with the territory. I worried a lot about…" He stopped, closed his mouth and started again. "You have to be careful during the first few months."

She turned, her gaze roving his face. He expected her to snap at him. Instead, she said, "That's sweet."

Mel never failed to amaze him. "So, I didn't mess up?"

"You're bound to compare my pregnancy to Robin's.

You wouldn't be human if you didn't." The barest of smiles appeared.

Aaron thought about kissing her, a frequent preoccupation lately. First thing in the morning, last thing at night, during work, while pumping gas, images assailed him. He used to look forward to their get-togethers. Now, all he thought about was the last time they'd made love and how much he missed her.

"Who do you compare me to, Mel?"

She had mentioned a few past boyfriends. None that had seemed serious or lasted for more than a year.

"No one. My problem, lately anyway, is comparing you and me to other people."

"Who?" He was curious.

"I hate to admit this." She winced and drew in a breath. "My dad and Samantha's mom."

"Huh." He could see how she'd come to that conclusion.

"Yeah, I feel the same way. Unsettling, isn't it?"

Aaron set down the bucket. This would require some mulling over.

The girls squealing and giggling a short distance away had him glancing around for Kaylee. He should be checking on her, not leave her supervision entirely up to Frankie. Bad parenting on his part. Then again, the second Kaylee had seen her little friends darting in and out of the water sprinkler, she'd run toward them, forgetting her father existed.

"Do you think she's suspicious of us?" Mel asked.

"Kaylee? Absolutely not. She's too young."

"Very funny. I was referring to Frankie."

"Ah. Well, possibly. We haven't been keeping very low profiles lately."

Us. We. He liked them using those terms when describing each other.

"No, we haven't," she agreed.

"When they find out we're having a baby, they'll know why we've been talking."

Frowning, she went back to cleaning her medical equipment in the bucket of water, sponging the implements with soapy water and rinsing them in a second bucket of clean water.

Aaron could have kicked himself for being an idiot. "Let me rephrase. We are having a baby, it's true, but that's not all there is between us."

"I'm equally guilty of sending mixed signals. Because I'm confused about how I feel." She stopped scrubbing. "You confuse me, Aaron."

"I understand. That kiss the other night..." He chuckled. "It surprised me, too."

"You think it was a mistake?"

"Oh, hell no!"

"But it does make things a little messy." She resumed scrubbing.

Is that what she thought? Aaron didn't dispute her. But messy or not, he'd kiss her again in a heartbeat.

"The thing with my family—" she dried her hands "—they can go a little overboard. Interfering and calling it helping. Except for Dolores," Mel amended. "She manages to help without interfering. They should take lessons from her."

Aaron thought of his sister and parents, how they were five hundred miles away and he only got to see them once or twice a year. He'd love some interference disguised as helping.

"You're lucky to have your family close by. We can all

use help now and then. I'm here today because Frankie's daughters are a lot more fun than I am, according to my daughter."

"She loves you."

"And I love her. Doesn't make me everything she needs. Children benefit from having friends their own age." He groaned and clasped his forehead. "I believe I just quoted my mother-in-law. You have my permission to throw me out on my backside."

Mel finished putting away her equipment. Aaron had the feeling she expected, or hoped, he'd say something else. What, he wasn't sure.

Samantha spared him from the continuing silence by returning from taking her horse to his stall in the minibarn.

"See you tomorrow morning," she called to Mel before joining Frankie and the girls. A moment later, she waved and headed into the house.

"What's going on tomorrow morning?" Aaron asked.

Mel shut and locked her case. "She's going with me on a couple of calls."

"Wow." Aaron gasped and grabbed a fistful of his shirtfront, pretending to have a heart attack. "Call 9-1-1."

"Very funny."

"You can't deny it's unexpected."

"Tell me about it." She gave a small laugh. "I barely recognize myself anymore."

"You're dealing with everything pretty well, if you ask me."

"Or, I'm hiding my head in the sand and praying my troubles will disappear. I'm not sure which."

Joking aside, she was saying more than she realized.

Beneath her brave front, she was worried and scared and uncertain. Like him. He wanted to, *needed* to, do something to let her know he cared and that their connection was deepening. Something more than carrying heavy buckets.

He moved closer.

"Frankie's looking," Mel warned.

"Have dinner with me tonight."

"What?"

"Doesn't have to be fancy. But I want to take you out, Mel."

"Have you lost your mind?"

"We have to start making plans sometime," he said. "Why not over dinner?"

"Are we making plans or going on a date?"

"Both. Couples combine the two all the time."

She narrowed her gaze at him.

"Come on," he pressed.

"Maybe."

"Otherwise, we'll have to wait until Sunday." And it would be harder for him to get away. He tried to spend free weekends with Kaylee, and Nancy would question any change in those plans.

This, however, was important and worth risking any repercussions from Nancy.

"Where?" Mel asked.

"Wherever you want. Rio Verde. Scottsdale. Fountain Hills."

She took a long moment to respond. "Vito's Old Country."

The Italian family eatery in Rio Verde. He'd taken Kaylee there once, and she'd made a terrible mess with her spaghetti. Aaron had tipped the server extra and apologized on the way out. Would they recognize him and remember?

"Sounds good. What time?"

"Not too late." Mel checked her phone. "I have an early-morning appointment. A goat with an ear infection."

"Six thirty okay? I'd like to give Kaylee another hour at least to play with her friends."

He'd also have plenty of time to shower and change and sit with Kaylee while she ate supper.

"I'll meet you there," Mel said.

"No way. This is a date, remember? I'll pick you up."

She relented with a nod and a huff he thought might have just been for show. "I'd better hurry. Who knows what's clean in my closet."

A dress, please, Aaron thought. As much as he liked her in jeans—her curvy figure did them justice—he really wanted her to wear the dress he'd seen her in last month at the community potluck. The tiny straps and low-cut back had shown off lots of lovely bare skin.

"Daddy!" Kaylee squealed. "I want my towel."

It was right where she'd left it, folded on the lawn chair. But Kaylee was notorious for having short-term memory loss.

"Hang on a sec, kiddo."

When he swung back around, Mel was already carrying a load toward the driveway where her truck was parked. If Aaron went after her, there'd be no hiding their relationship from Frankie. From the entire Hartman clan, really, because Mel's sister would report what she'd seen at the first available opportunity.

Then again, Aaron and Mel weren't doing anything wrong.

He hesitated for a good ten seconds before grabbing her medical case and sprinting after her. Even at a distance, he could sense the heat of Frankie's stare boring a hole in his back. Too late now.

Mel sat beside Aaron in his family SUV as they traveled the road to Rio Verde and Vito's Old Country. A dozen concerns flitted through her head, circling like hawks and making it hard for her to concentrate.

This was a bad idea. What if they ran into someone they knew at the restaurant? Thank goodness Ronnie was still practicing with Samantha when Aaron had arrived at the house to pick up Mel. This wasn't a date, she told herself, merely a strategy meeting.

Uh-huh. As if she'd wear a yellow dress and three-inch heels to a meeting. And speaking of heels, this pair was killing her. She could already feel the sharp pinch in her toes and heels.

That was what she got for always wearing boots or going barefoot. Maybe she'd kick her shoes off under the table once they were seated.

"Sorry." She turned to Aaron. "What did you say?"

He lowered the volume on the radio, as if that was the problem. "I hear the stuffed eggplant is really good."

"I figured you for a beef man."

"I'll have you know, I'm a person of varied tastes."

He would have to grin and trigger that stupid chain reaction inside her, starting with the catch in her throat and ending with the tingle that reached all the way to her toes. He would also have to wear a turquoise cowboy shirt that matched his vivid blue eyes. Perhaps if she looked out the window...

"What's your favorite Italian dish?" he asked, sounding an awful lot like they really were on a date.

She abandoned the window to face him. It wasn't as if she hadn't seen the local landscape a few hundred, make that a thousand, times.

"Linguini. With cream sauce. And caprese salad. But I like to try new dishes, too."

"You drink wine? When you're not pregnant, that is."

"On occasion. Chianti with Italian."

What did they usually talk about when they were together? Clearly not favorite foods or dining out. She tried to think. They'd discussed their personal situations, specifically why they couldn't date. A little bit about their pasts. Growing up in Mustang Valley and Queen Creek respectively.

Nothing meaningful, not that one's wine of choice was particularly meaningful. But there was something nice about casual conversation. Just like a regular couple.

At the restaurant, Aaron parked. Mel reached for her door handle, intending to open it.

"Hold on. I'll get that."

"You don't have to."

"I want to."

Pleased by this show of gallantry, she sat until he came around the SUV to her side and opened the door. Men in these parts tended to treat her like one of them. Especially when she was trudging through cow manure.

"Thanks." She accepted the hand he extended.

At the hostess station, she learned he'd called ahead and made a reservation. For a booth. There was a candle in the center of the table and dim lighting.

Not special. She noticed all the tables had candles.

Yet, Mel felt special all the same, proving she was a secret romantic.

"I thought this was a family restaurant."

Aaron remained standing until she'd slid into the booth. "It is."

She surveyed the large room, observing mostly couples but also several parents with their children, and decided her imagination was working overtime.

Soon enough, the server left them alone, their drink and appetizer order in hand. Iced tea for Aaron, plain water for Mel and a caprese salad to share.

"What made you decide to become a vet?" he asked after their drinks arrived.

"No big secret there. I grew up in a ranching community."

"That's not an answer."

She sat back against the vinyl seat. "We had a bunch of barn cats when I was a kid. A house cat, too, but also all these half-feral ones. A mama birthed a litter of kittens in the hay trough and then a week later disappeared. I was about ten or eleven. Not long after my mom died. Dad was going to humanely euthanize the kittens. What other choice did he have? I carried on until he let me bottle raise the litter. It was a lot of work. Like 24/7 work. Luckily, it was during summer when I didn't have school."

"Did the kittens survive?"

"Yes. To everyone's surprise, including mine." She laughed softly, then sobered. "I loved it. I'd been utterly miserable and missing my mom. Suddenly, I was less miserable. Of course, Dad made me find homes for the entire litter and a few of the barn cats."

"Unexpected deaths. They're rough." Aaron covered

her hand with his. Despite their size and strength, his touch was gentle and caring.

Two decades had passed, but Mel remembered every detail from those months following her mother's death. "She went riding alone all the time. She was an expert horsewoman. For whatever reason, on that ride, the horse spooked or slipped, and she fell. Hit her head on the only rock within eight feet in any direction. When the horse came galloping home without my mom, Dad figured she wasn't far behind. Two hours later, he went out looking for her. Four hours later, he reported her missing, and the authorities sent out a search party." Mel lowered her voice. "They found her the next morning. The medical examiner's report said she'd died instantly."

"I'm sure you heard this before," Aaron squeezed her fingers, "but at least she didn't suffer."

"I'm sorry that Robin did. Truly. It must have been horrible for you. But at least you got to say goodbye to her. My mom's last words to me were, 'clean your room or we aren't going out for pizza tonight.'"

"Robin's last words were, 'it's on the bathroom shelf.'"

"What was?"

He shrugged. "I don't know. She was on high doses of pain meds, fighting a massive brain tumor and in and out of consciousness. That didn't stop me from tearing the bathroom apart after she died, searching for some secret item she left behind for me."

"That's a sad story." Mel's heart ached for him.

He released her hand when the server arrived with their salad and didn't attempt to take it again. Mel picked up her fork. Aaron, too.

"She constantly worried I'd be killed in the line of duty. Neither of us figured on her dying first. We thought we'd be together until we were old and feeble and living in a nursing home."

He spoke with such tenderness and love, Mel couldn't help being affected. They must have been incredibly happy together. Had the kind of relationship her dad did with Dolores. The kind she dreamed of but didn't think possible.

"What made you choose law enforcement?"

The agony he clearly still felt over Robin's death receded a little. "No cute story, I'm afraid. When I started college, I majored in marketing."

"A salesman! You?"

"My dad's in the business. I took a class on introduction to criminal justice just for fun and because I needed some extra credits. Next thing I knew, I'd changed over to the Police Academy Preparation Program."

Mel didn't ask what had brought him to Mustang Valley. She already knew he'd wanted a less dangerous job for Kaylee's sake.

"Did you ever have any close calls when you worked for the Phoenix Police Department?" The salad was delicious. Mel, however, only picked at it.

"A few."

"Been shot at?"

"Yeah." He paused as if to reflect. "My partner took a bullet my first year on the force. A flesh wound. He was back on the job a month later. Six months after that, his wife divorced him. Said she couldn't take the stress."

"Robin must've been a very strong person."

"I'm convinced another reason she fought so hard to have Kaylee was she didn't want both of us to die. If I was left with a child to raise, she thought—hoped, I'm sure—I might take a less dangerous position or quit law enforcement altogether." He glanced up as their entrées arrived. "Mustang Valley's just the right speed for me. Quiet. Close-knit. Low crime rate."

Normally, Mel would savor her first bite of linguini. Their somber discussion had taken away the enjoyment of their beautifully prepared food.

Then again, there was something uplifting in sharing how they'd both learned to cope with loss.

"Speaking of crime," she said, "any new developments with the horse rustling?"

"Nothing so far. I'm going to the barrel-racing event this coming weekend at the Silver Spur Arena."

"Really? Why?"

"Wherever horse people gather, there's bound to be talk. I thought I might learn something of interest. And it'll be fun for Kaylee."

"We're going, too. Samantha's competing."

"I heard." His voice took on an intimate quality.

Was her being at the event part of his reason for going?

"Not sure how much information I'll get," he said, "but I have to try. The thieves are from this area, I'm sure of it, or at least in partnership with someone who is."

"Someone like whom?"

Aaron stabbed at his stuffed eggplant. "This person, if there is one, would have pretty intimate knowledge of the horse setups around the valley."

She laughed. "You're describing me."

"Maybe I should check you out. Thoroughly." His eyes darkened and dipped to her neck, igniting that stupid chain reaction again.

"Maybe you should."

Was she actually flirting? This was crazy. They hadn't even flirted when they first met.

She recalled Aaron speaking about his late wife and the expression on his face when he did. Her mood immediately sank.

Flirting was one thing. Love, another. He'd had that once with Robin, his obvious soul mate. Mel couldn't expect anything remotely close to that, and wishing for it would only bring her pain.

What would it be like to be loved by Aaron? Robin's life had been cut short, but she'd been one incredibly lucky woman to have been the object of Aaron's adoration.

Mel set down her fork. Who was she fooling? No way could she compete with Robin's memory. The best possible circumstances were she and Aaron getting along, him being a great date and them united in giving their child a wonderful upbringing.

"I'm going to take care of you and the baby, Mel."

Shoot. He must have guessed her thoughts. She wasn't always guarded with her emotions.

"You don't have to take care of me, Aaron. I'm quite capable of supporting myself and the baby."

He shook his head. "You're not really going to pull the old independent woman act?"

"Yes," she conceded. "I'll accept your help and support. We can share custody. Swap weeks when the baby's a little older."

"Is that what you want?"

His sincerity momentarily threw her, prompting her to answer in kind. "Honestly, I always figured I'd be married when I started a family."

And in love, she silently added. *The way you were in love with Robin.*

"We can talk about that. Down the road."

Memories of her father saying he'd offered to marry Carrie Anne flashed in her head. He might have done the right thing according to some, but Mel wanted more than a husband who proposed simply out of duty and not love.

"No rush. Lots of couples raise their child together without being married."

After that, Mel and Aaron never quite regained the fun, flirty camaraderie from earlier. For the rest of the meal, they discussed Kaylee, Mel's nieces, Mel's progress with Samantha's horse and how the orphan foal wasn't doing as well as Mel would have liked.

In the parking lot, Aaron took her arm, just as she'd expected. That didn't stop her from enjoying the feel of his strong fingers on her skin, the heady scent of his aftershave and the occasional bump and brush of his body against hers. She was reminded of the many times she'd lain beside him, her leg draped over his and her fingertips drawing patterns on his bare chest.

At his SUV, he opened the passenger door, repeating his chivalry from earlier. She was about to climb in when he caught her by the wrist and tugged her into his embrace.

Ignoring the other patrons returning to their vehicles, she met Aaron's stare, searching his eyes for the look she'd seen when he talked about Robin. It wasn't there. The hunger burning in them, however, did give her a sensual thrill, and she involuntarily arched into him.

All right, not involuntarily. She very much wanted his arms circling her waist and drawing her close. She also wanted him to kiss her. Wildly and without restraint, like the other night.

When he threaded his fingers into her hair, she leaned her head back. When he nuzzled her ear, she sighed. When his lips skimmed the column of her neck, she moaned softly. When he whispered her name, she melted.

Finally, thankfully, his mouth found hers and took it possessively. Pressing her against the SUV, he trapped her between the rear door and the long length of him. As his tongue swept into her mouth, she relished in the familiar, exciting taste of him.

Aaron certainly knew how to kiss. Hard and demanding. Gentle and coaxing. She took what he offered and gave in return. Of their own volition, her hands worked their way up his back to his shoulders. There, they gripped the hard muscles and brought him closer—if that was possible. When he would have broken off the kiss, Mel refused to release him. Not until she was fully satisfied.

By the time they were in his SUV and driving toward her house, Mel was almost sorry they weren't going to the motel instead. It wasn't very far.

Chapter 9

Aaron wasn't disappointed he and Mel had skipped the motel tonight. Okay, that wasn't entirely accurate. But he hadn't wanted her thinking sex was the only thing between them. Besides, he'd enjoyed their interplay during dinner, and the kiss in the parking lot afterward had tested the limits of his willpower.

Whatever was changing between them, and he still wasn't able to define it, had affected every aspect of their relationship, including intimacy.

Could be he was more disappointed about not going to the motel than he first thought. She'd looked so pretty tonight, her hair loose around her shoulders rather than twisted into her usual braid. Her skin aglow in the candlelight. Her mouth full and wide and impossible not to kiss.

Pregnancy certainly agreed with her. Then again,

it might be those changing feelings affecting how he perceived her.

Pulling into the garage, Aaron jangled his keys as he walked into the house, his steps light, his mood elevated.

Kaylee was awake, something immediately apparent when he entered the kitchen.

"Hey, kiddo. Why aren't you in bed?" She should have been asleep an hour ago.

"I had a bad dream." She sat at the table, a glass of milk and half an English muffin in front of her.

"That's not good." He sat beside her and tweaked her nose.

Her silly giggle washed over him, elevating his mood even higher.

There was probably no bad dream. Kaylee used that as an excuse whenever she had trouble falling asleep or woke up after a short time. The excuse worked better on her grandmother than Aaron, landing her a little extra attention.

Speaking of which…

"Where's Gramma?" Aaron stole a sip of her milk.

"On the phone."

"Really?" She didn't usually leave Kaylee alone for any length of time. And it was late for a phone call.

"Tell me a story about Mama?" Kaylee pleaded when she was done eating.

"You got it."

He scooped her into his arms and carried her down the hall to her bedroom, passing Nancy's room as he did. The older woman sat on her bed, her phone glued to her ear. Seeing him, alarm flashed across her face.

He tilted his head at Kaylee's room, indicating he was putting her to bed.

"Gramma must have an important call," he said, drawing the sheet up to Kaylee's neck and dropping down beside her.

She snuggled with a well-worn and well-loved stuffed bear, and he began telling one of her favorite stories about how Robin broke the news to him that she was pregnant.

"When I got home from work, there was a big teddy bear sitting on the counter with a pink pacifier tied to the bow around its neck." He poked the stuffed bear's stomach.

"Why pink?"

"Because she wanted a little girl."

"Were you surprised?" Kaylee gazed up at him, her expression so reminiscent of Robin's.

"Very surprised."

The story took five more minutes to finish. Kaylee wouldn't allow Aaron to skip a single part, despite having memorized every word. When he was done, he stood and kissed her on the forehead.

"Go to sleep now. I love you."

"Love you too, Daddy." She curled her fingers into the shape of a heart and held them to her chest.

He left the door partially open behind him and headed toward the kitchen, planning to shut off the lights before going to bed himself. Shonda was expecting him tomorrow morning at the crack of dawn.

He found Nancy sitting at the table, nursing a cup of tea and wearing a scowl. Strange, she usually retired early herself.

"You're still up," he said.

"We need to talk." Her clipped tone put him on the defensive.

"What's wrong?"

"Sit down."

Aaron tolerated a lot from Nancy, including her often short temper and surliness, because she adored Kaylee, was a wonderful grandmother and helped him enormously with daycare. He also understood he was the closest target when it came to venting her heartache over the loss of her only child.

Not that she blamed him or held him responsible for Robin's brain tumor. If anything, Aaron had fought hard to extend Robin's life. Nancy's grief was simply overwhelming and beyond her abilities to cope with most days.

But she was making progress, if slow. No one had celebrated more than Aaron when she joined the Bunko group. If she wouldn't attend counseling or support groups, at least she was getting out once in a while and making friends.

"That was Winnie Hensley on the phone." She paused, apparently waiting for him to make a connection. "From church."

"Okay."

"She and her husband were at Vito's Old Country tonight, having dinner."

Aaron said nothing as the pieces fell into place.

"She saw you," Nancy accused.

He refused to volunteer any information. There was a big difference between seeing him and Mel sitting together in a booth and them kissing in the parking lot.

"Why didn't she say hi?" he asked, feigning mild interest.

"You were occupied. Having dinner with Melody Hartman."

"I see." Tiring, he cut to the chase. "Before I get upset, why don't you just say what's on your mind?"

"You were on a date with another woman."

"I was on a date with *a* woman. Not *another*."

Nancy became flustered. "H-how could you?"

He was glad her friend Winnie missed seeing Aaron and Mel's scorching kiss and that Nancy hadn't learned about their evenings at the motel. "Mel and I are friends."

"Winnie said you looked pretty cozy."

He considered insisting the dinner was strictly business. Mel *was* helping him with the horse thefts. Instead, he came clean.

There was a reason he'd been careless lately about hiding his relationship with Mel. The fact was, he'd grown weary of sneaking around and suspected Mel had, too. He subconsciously, and possibly consciously, felt ready to go public, even before Mel got pregnant.

Time to start preparing Nancy. "We were on a date," he admitted.

"Oh, no." Her face crumpled, and she swallowed a sob. "I don't believe it."

Out of respect for her distress, he gentled his tone. "It's been three years, Nancy. Even Robin would expect me to start dating again."

"But Melody Hartman?" Nancy made a face.

He was slightly offended. No, a lot offended. "Mel's a great gal."

"She may be great, but she's isn't very…ladylike."

What worse insult had Nancy been about to utter? And if she'd seen Mel in that sundress and sexy sandals, the last thing she'd be calling her was unladylike.

Comparisons were bound to happen, and Nancy was comparing Mel to Robin. He decided not to get upset about it and try a different approach instead.

"You like Dolores. And you're always saying how nice Frankie is when we go to the café. I'm sure you'd like Mel, too, if you got to know her."

Nancy's eyes widened in alarm. "Is there a reason I need to? How serious is this?"

Aaron changed his mind. This wasn't the right moment to tell her about the baby. "I will always love Robin and miss her. She's the mother of my child, and that won't ever change. But chances are, I'll eventually meet someone new and possibly marry again. You need to accept that."

"She sacrificed months of her life for Kaylee. And you promised her to always put Kaylee first. Above everything and anyone else."

"I do put Kaylee first."

"What about when you work late?"

"My job provides a decent roof over her head, food on the table and a roomful of toys. I call that making her a priority."

"Instead of being home with her, you went on a date."

Aaron had spent almost the entire day with Kaylee. Even so, the invisible dagger Nancy thrust hit its mark.

He had made a commitment to cherish and honor Robin's memory. Promised to put Kaylee first. Told Nancy she was a welcomed and valued member of his family for as long as she wanted.

On the other hand, Mel was pregnant, and he had an obligation to her, too, as well as their baby.

When had things become so complicated? Why had he let them? What had he been thinking, sleeping with

Mel when he wasn't willing to do right by her? Aaron didn't have a high opinion of himself at the moment.

Remembering how she'd looked at dinner and the sparks that had flared between them when they'd kissed was part of the answer. She was hard to resist. But, perhaps he should. For the time being, anyway. At least until Nancy became more accustomed to the idea.

He got up from the table.

"Where are you going?" she demanded. "We're not done talking."

"I have to be up at five."

"What about Melody Hartman?"

He pushed in his chair. "I'm going to keep seeing her."

"Have you considered Kaylee? She may not accept a woman in her life who isn't her mother."

"She's young. Mel's nieces are her friends." Aaron stopped at the doorway, thinking Kaylee would like Mel and just might love having a baby brother or sister.

"She'll forget about Robin."

That, Aaron suspected, was the real reason for Nancy's objections.

"I won't let her," he said with utmost sincerity. "And neither will you."

Eyes clear and bright. Ears pricked forward. Attentive and alert. No fever. No lameness. No swelling or tenderness. The horse, a sleek and muscular roan with proved speed and agility, was the epitome of health.

"He's ready to rock and roll," Mel said, finishing her routine exam.

Samantha's worried expression eased a tiny fraction. After Big John's injury, she'd probably always fret before a competition. And this particular horse belonged to Ronnie, not Samantha. A lot of responsibility and yet another reason for her to be chewing her nails to the quick.

"You'll do great," Mel assured her. "You were flying at practice last night."

She'd had a vet call near Powell Ranch and decided to drop by and observe the practice. That was the excuse she told herself, anyway, not admitting to a much-needed distraction from her many problems.

Despite her pregnancy being confirmed for almost two weeks now, she'd yet to do anything about it other than visit her doctor, purchase prenatal vitamins, struggle with bras that were becoming tight and painful, and discover plain crackers and ginger ale helped with the morning sickness.

Sure, she and Aaron talked daily, and he'd been adamant about providing for the baby. But no specifics had been decided, and she wasn't telling her family until at least a basic plan was in place.

"I'm still getting used to him." Samantha absently groomed the horse, running a thick brush over his flank. "He thinks and reacts differently than Big John."

She'd gone twice with Mel this week on calls, and Mel had heard the entire lowdown on the horse to the smallest detail.

Ronnie appeared from behind the trailer, stared long and hard at Samantha and said, "Shouldn't you have saddled up by now?"

"Yeah. Mel was just examining the horse."

"It's hot. You'd better take him to the water trough for a drink."

"I will. Give me a minute, okay?"

It wasn't *what* they said as much as the *way* they spoke to each other that had Mel paying close attention. The friction was undeniable and uncomfortable and apparently brand-new.

Had something happened between yesterday and today that set them off? A difference of opinion, perhaps? Could be stress, Mel supposed. Ronnie's temper always flared before a competition, though she wasn't the one climbing into the saddle today.

Later, perhaps, when she and Ronnie were alone, she'd ask what was going on. Then, Ronnie would probably ask her the same question and bring up Aaron. Not what she needed at the moment.

Returning from stowing her medical case in her truck, she grabbed the bridle hanging from a hook on the side of the trailer and handed it to Samantha. The young woman had finished saddling the horse, triple checking the cinch and adjusting the length of the stirrups. Only the bridle remained. And herself.

She'd yet to fix her hair and change into nice boots and her fancy show chaps. The competition wasn't an official rodeo event, but that didn't change the fact competitors were expected to adhere to a certain dress code. Horses, too. This roan's coat shone, and he wore tack decorated with gleaming silver conchos.

"You're going to get dirty," Mel said when the horse bumped his nose against Samantha's clean dress shirt sleeve. "Let me."

She bridled the horse while Samantha braided her hair, tied it with a ribbon and applied makeup, using the truck's side mirror to view her handiwork. Mel was struck with a sudden sentimental pang. How many times had she seen Ronnie do the same thing before an event?

Glancing about, she searched for her errant sister. Apparently, she'd left to help another student prepare.

The person she did spot was Aaron, carrying his young daughter and accompanied by his mother-in-law. They made a charming picture, Dad, daughter and grandmother.

Mel's hands suddenly went still and only the horse bobbing his head prompted her to finish her task. She automatically buckled the bridle and straightened the reins, her mind wandering and wondering where she and her child would fit into that picture.

At the entrance to the bleachers, Aaron parted from Kaylee and her grandmother. He then went off to join a group of local ranchers gathered at the arena fence. What was it he'd said? Whenever horse folk gathered, they talked, and worthwhile leads could come from the most unexpected sources.

"Thanks," Samantha said, appearing beside Mel.

"Sure." Mel realized she'd just been standing there, staring. Patting the horse's neck was a poor cover-up, but she did it anyway. "No problem."

"This is the first time I've ever competed when my parents weren't here to watch me." Samantha's voice broke.

"I'm sure they'd like to be here." *And would be if they knew about it.*

Without asking, Mel took the paper entrant number and motioned for Samantha to turn around. She pinned the square, with the Mustang Valley Feed and Supply Depot name and logo printed in bold letters, to Samantha's back, thinking again how often she'd done the same for Ronnie.

When she finished, Samantha suddenly threw herself at Mel, practically knocking her off balance. While not ready to call her "sister," Mel returned the hug with genuine emotion. Without her parents there, Samantha was obviously in need of a friend.

"I'll be rooting for you from the stands," Mel said, extracting herself.

"Can I go to work with you on Monday?"

"We'll see."

"Frankie's off that day. She won't need me to baby-sit."

Not for the first time, Mel considered Samantha helping her more as her pregnancy advanced. She'd wait and see, however. Samantha might patch things up with her parents and leave Mustang Valley.

"I'll see you after the event." She patted Samantha's shoulder. "Good luck."

Samantha's group was the last to go and included those individuals competing on a professional level. The first group, comprised ages twelve and under, was always popular with the crowd. The youngsters might be small in size and less experienced, but they were incredibly daring and talented.

Stopping at the refreshment stand for a cold soda, Mel wandered toward the bleachers. She'd spotted her dad and Dolores earlier and went in search of them again.

Zigzagging through the crowd, she almost ran smack into Aaron. He'd left the group of ranchers and retrieved Kaylee from her grandmother. The pair stood before her, Aaron as startled to see Mel as she was to see him.

"Hi." She fumbled with her hands. "You're here."

He simply grinned.

"What's so funny?"

"I'm just happy to see you."

Was he? Then why hadn't he asked her out again? He'd had plenty of opportunities.

"How's the investigation coming?"

"Nothing good yet." He shifted Kaylee to his other side. The little girl wore a neon pink cap and purple shorts and looked absolutely adorable. "But the evening's young."

A truck with the feed store logo on the side drove past them, its loud engine momentarily preventing conversation. Neighboring businesses were often recruited to sponsor community events, and the feed store could always be counted on to pay for an advertising banner as well as participant numbers.

Once the truck had passed, Mel said, "Well, um, take care," certain she sounded awkward and confused.

"Do you mind?" Aaron abruptly thrust Kaylee at her. "Guillermo's here, and I'd like to talk to him."

Mel gasped, automatically holding out her arms to accept the little girl. "Wait!"

Too late. Aaron was gone, jogging off toward the man Mel recognized as a grain rep who worked the area. She understood Aaron's haste. The man got around and sold to most of the ranches in Mustang Valley. He also had a tendency to swear a blue streak. Not the sort of language appropriate for a three-year-old, and Aaron probably hadn't wanted Kaylee to hear that.

Of course, she started to cry.

"Hey, there," Mel said, bouncing Kaylee. "You remember me? I'm Paige and Sienna's aunt."

That earned her a wary stare. Okay, Kaylee wasn't a baby. Maybe Mel was better off entertaining her rather than rocking her. It wasn't as if she lacked experience with preschoolers.

Which reminded her, where were Frankie and Mel's nieces? Just when Mel needed them most, as a playmate for Kaylee, they were MIA.

"Come on," she said. "Let's go look at some of the pretty horses."

She set Kaylee down, and together they walked over to the arena fence. Mel wanted to stick close by should Aaron come looking for them. Some of the competitors were warming up in the arena, walking, trotting or slow loping their horses to loosen muscles and acclimate them to the commotion.

"See the white horse over there?" Mel received another stare from Kaylee and sighed. "I don't blame you." She took Kaylee's hand. "I would be unhappy if my dad left me with a stranger."

Not that Mel was exactly a stranger. She was intimately acquainted with Kaylee's father and carrying the girl's baby brother or sister.

What a sobering thought. Mel glanced down, studying the girl. Under different circumstances, she might have been Kaylee's stepmom. They were certainly going to be better acquainted in the future. However Mel and Aaron worked out the custody agreement, their child would eventually be spending time at his house with him and Kaylee.

Also with Nancy, Kaylee's grandmother. An even more sobering thought.

"I like the tan horse with the white stockings. See?" Mel pointed.

Kaylee actually looked.

"He reminds me of the baby horse I'm taking care of. He's really cute. Like you."

At last, Kaylee responded with a tentative smile.

"Maybe your dad will bring you out to see the baby horse. I could ask him."

The little girl nodded.

Success! Mel felt a rush of pleasure. She wanted to be on good terms with Aaron's daughter.

For whatever reason, the thought brought a lump to her throat. She blamed pregnancy hormones. It also might have to do with Kaylee and Mel being kindred spirits—they both had or would have a surprise half sibling. Both their families had suffered a great loss with the death of a loved one. And, for the moment, they'd both been abandoned by Aaron.

All right, abandoned was too strong a word. Aaron was returning for Kaylee any minute. And he hadn't exactly abandoned Mel, either. Rather, he'd been taking some necessary alone time this past week to sort things out. At least, she wanted to believe that was his reason for not suggesting a second date.

Drat. Tears? Really? She wiped angrily at her eyes.

"Are you sad?" Kaylee asked.

"No, no." She patted the girl's head, oddly soothed by the soft texture of her silky curls. "I'm fine."

"What are you doing with her!"

At the brusque question, Mel and Kaylee both turned. Nancy stood there, holding two drinks and a box of popcorn.

"Gramma!" Kaylee hurried to Nancy, arms outstretched. "I'm thirsty."

"Where's Aaron?" Bristling, Nancy handed Kaylee a juice box.

"He's over there talking to the grain rep." Mel refused to be intimidated. "He asked me to watch Kaylee."

"Why didn't he wait for me?"

"He was in a hurry."

Kaylee didn't appear to notice the tension or didn't care. She was busy emptying her juice box as fast as possible.

"Gramma, look at the horse." The one with the white stockings happened to be trotting by them, delighting Kaylee. "I want to go riding."

"You can't today, darling."

Everything about Nancy changed when she addressed her granddaughter. Her voice, her expression, her manner, all softened around the edges. Mel was almost convinced that between her obvious love for Kaylee and Dolores being her friend, Nancy had a nice side. But, as the saying goes, she spoke too soon.

"I need to talk to you." Nancy's glance, tender a moment ago, cooled. "As long as you're here. And if you don't mind."

Mel breathed deeply to calm he nerves. She'd never been alone with Nancy before. They'd conversed only once, briefly at her dad's birthday party when Dolores introduced them and before Samantha's big scene.

"Um, sure. About anything in particular?" Mel shifted, praying Nancy had a sick pet and wanted free medical advice. She knew better, however. This had to do with Aaron.

"I've enjoyed playing Bunko with your stepmother and her friends."

They moved toward the fence, following Kaylee who wanted a closer look at the horses.

"Dolores's group is a great bunch of ladies."

"They are. They've made me feel welcome." Nancy rested a fond hand on the top of Kaylee's head.

Mel had been doing the same thing a few minutes ago. Didn't mean she felt a connection to the other woman. If anything, the opposite was true. Mel wasn't sure she'd ever be able to warm up to Nancy. She would try, though. For Aaron's sake and their baby's.

"I admit," Nancy continued, "it was hard when we first moved here."

"I can imagine."

"Robin had passed just six months earlier."

"I'm very sorry for your loss." Mel wasn't sure what else to say or where this conversation was going. Nancy didn't keep her waiting.

"She and Aaron were so much in love. And I'm not simply saying that because Robin…because they didn't get to spend their entire lives together. They were happy. Ecstatic, really. A bright, beautiful future ahead of them." She paused. "No one expected Robin to get sick."

Mel did sympathize. "It was like that when my mom died. One day, she was there. The next day, she wasn't."

Nancy considered Mel's remark, her hand still resting on Kaylee's head. "Yes. Very tragic. You would understand. Loving someone so very much, then losing them. Each of us handles grief differently, and we don't always act in our best interests or that of others."

Mel immediately thought of her father and his involvement with Carrie Anne.

"Aaron's duty lies with Kaylee," Nancy said. "She's the most important person in his life. He will never let Robin down or dishonor her memory by doing something he'd regret. It's what I respect and admire the most about him. What everyone does." She narrowed her gaze at Mel. "As I'm sure you do, too."

Nancy clearly knew, or at least suspected, that Mel

and Aaron were involved. And she was issuing a not-so-subtle warning for Mel to stay away.

She should be annoyed, possibly offended, only she wasn't.

Nothing like having someone hold up a mirror to your face. Mel could suddenly see herself through Nancy's eyes and didn't like the person staring back at her. Reasonably, rationally, she could argue that Aaron was free to date. That wouldn't alleviate Nancy's pain or make what Mel and Aaron were doing right.

"My family's waiting for me," she said, excusing herself. "Bye, Kaylee." She waved. "See you soon."

Nancy wore a satisfied smile. "Nice talking to you."

A minute later, and out of Nancy's eyesight, Mel stopped, her heart racing. With trembling fingers, she pulled out her cell phone and texted Aaron, letting him know Kaylee was with her grandmother.

After he responded, she texted back that she wanted to get together later that week when they were both free. She didn't add they simply could not continue in this limbo state any longer. She'd save that discussion for when they met.

Chapter 10

The crowd broke into applause as the rider finished her run, crossing in front of the electronic timer at a full gallop. The young woman, close to Samantha in age, slowed her horse to a trot, then to a walk. Circling to the left, she listened for her results to be announced. The spectators quieted, also listening.

"Sixteen-point-five."

Frowning, the young woman turned her horse toward the exit gate and rode through.

"She cut that last barrel too wide," Frankie said. "Lost a good half a second on her time. She's in fourth place."

Half a second? Mel shook her head. Hard to believe the first four places were separated by tenths of a second. That was true, however, with a lot of sports. One had only to watch the Olympics.

"We aren't even halfway through the class." Mel

fanned herself with the paper number an earlier competitor from the junior class had left behind and wished she'd worn a hat with a wider brim.

Samantha was one of the last competitors to go, which could be to her advantage. She'd have the opportunity to study the other riders and possibly modify her strategy.

"Dad and Dolores still down there?" Mel switched the paper number to her other hand, using it as a shield against the blinding glare of the setting sun. Last she'd seen her parents, they were with Samantha and Ronnie, offering help and moral support and most likely getting in the way.

"Grandpa said he would buy us ice cream." Paige bounced up and down in the bleachers, enjoying the noise it made. Other nearby people, not so much.

"He will." Frankie rested a hand on her daughter's knee, silently encouraging her to stop.

"I'm bored," Sienna complained, also getting a pat from her mother.

The twin girls sat, one on each side of Frankie, with Mel beside Sienna. They were growing increasingly restless and tired of hearing their mother say, "Be good." They wanted to play with their friend Kaylee, but the little girl's grandmother had vetoed that idea with an "It's not safe," even though Frankie had volunteered to supervise. Mel supposed she was the real reason behind Nancy's refusal.

She caught a glimpse of grandmother and granddaughter from the corner of her eye, then risked a longer look. They were seated a few rows down and over from Mel, close enough for Kaylee to see her young friends, but too far to interact. During one of those times Kaylee had snuck a peek, Mel summoned the courage to wave. She'd received a tiny wave in return, just enough to make her smile.

The next instant, Nancy had glanced backward, and Mel quickly lowered her hand. It had been a stupid idea to begin with. She might win over Kaylee eventually, but Nancy was another story.

While Frankie attempted to entertain the twins with one of the emergency toys she always stashed in her purse, Mel scanned the crowd for Aaron. He'd been busy chatting up as many people as possible. Mel knew this because she'd been keeping tabs on him. He'd apparently been keeping tabs on her, as well. More than once, their gazes had connected.

"Thanks for helping with Samantha," Frankie said. "It means a lot to her."

Mel abandoned her efforts to locate Aaron. "To be honest, I didn't do it for Samantha. I did it for you."

"Yeah, I know. She still appreciates it. As do I."

The girls were enthralled by a handheld game and not paying attention to the grown-ups.

"What changed your mind?" Frankie asked. "You never told me."

"Nothing. I simply reconsidered."

"Ha, ha, ha."

"It wasn't a joke."

"Come on," Frankie insisted. "Something's been bothering you lately."

"A half sister we had no idea existed showing up out of the blue isn't enough to bother me?"

"Since before then. You've been preoccupied for the last month or two."

If anyone would understand Mel's situation besides

Dolores, it was her older sister. She'd given birth to and raised twin girls without ever telling their father and slaved at the café in order to give them a decent home. All without any help. Other than the lottery money, that was, and every cent of her share had gone into the purchase of her house.

She was the definition of independent single mother. Mel could learn a lot from her. And Frankie would appreciate Mel's uncertainty regarding Aaron's feelings for her, having been through a similar situation with her ex-boyfriend.

"I...um..." Mel struggled. "Have some news."

"What? Tell me."

"Okay. Relax. This isn't easy." She checked on the girls, who had switched places in order to sit together and play. "I'm..." She gestured with her hand, showing a rounded belly.

Frankie's eyes nearly popped out of her head. "No kidding! You're—"

"Shh." Mel's glance cut to the girls and the couple on the other side who were clients of Ronnie's. "I've only told three people so far. Well, two. Dolores sort of figured it out."

"The father is one of those people, I hope."

"Yeah," she reluctantly admitted.

"Who is he? And when did you start dating? Is he from out of town?" She gasped. "Did you meet at that seminar?"

"No. He's, ah—"

"I can't believe you were flirting with Aaron the other day, and you're pregnant with another man's baby."

Frankie was one of the smartest people Mel had ever

met. Yet, she certainly wasn't using all of her brain cells today. Mel sighed expansively.

"I *was* flirting with the father."

"Aaron! Seriously?"

"Not so loud."

"Holy cow. This is unbelievable." Frankie took a moment to assimilate the news. "What are you going to do?" she finally asked in a half whisper.

"I only recently found out. We're still in the figuring-out phase. Plus, he hasn't told Nancy yet. Though, she suspects we've been seeing each other and isn't happy. She gave me a less than subtle stay-away warning earlier."

"Here?"

"Right before the barrel racing started."

"Ooh. Not cool." Frankie helped the girls figure out the next step to the game. "What did you do?"

"Nothing much. Let her talk. I truly understand where she's coming from. Aaron told me from the start he wasn't ready for a committed relationship, and neither am I."

"Uh, excuse me, Mel. You're having a…" She mimicked Mel's big belly gesture. "That's a commitment. A big one. He needs to step up. Financially, if anything."

Mel must have misunderstood her sister. "I'm surprised to hear you say that. You didn't tell—" She caught herself before mentioning Spence's name. "You-know-who."

"No, I didn't."

An odd note penetrated Frankie's voice. One Mel hadn't heard before.

"Do you regret not telling him?"

"Constantly." Frankie nodded at her girls. "Every time I look at them."

"Then why not call him?"

"It's complicated."

Mel snorted. "Tell me."

"You-know-who is completely untrustworthy. Nothing like Aaron. Now there's someone with a great job. A daughter he loves. Roots to the community. Responsible, reliable, a family man. Look how he puts up with Nancy."

"I hear she's not that bad. Dolores likes her, and Kaylee adores her."

"Dolores likes everyone, and Kaylee's her granddaughter. But we were talking about Aaron, not Nancy. He's a great guy. He'll be good to you and the baby. Take care of you both."

Mel noticed Frankie hadn't mentioned love. Was her sister's heart that hardened? Granted, Spence had hurt her. In Mel's opinion, that didn't justify her not telling him about the girls. But the decision was her sister's to make, not Mel's. And she was expecting the same treatment from Frankie and the rest of her family—being allowed to choose her own path without criticism or interference. She'd settle for no less.

"I can give you the name and number of my attorney if you want," Frankie said.

"Since when do you have an attorney?"

"He's mostly on standby. But he has given me some pretty good advice if you-know-who ever contacts me."

"Did he advise you to tell you-know-who about you-know-what?"

"He might have mentioned it. But, again, we're talking about you. Not me. Aaron can and should pay you child support."

"He's already offered."

"That's good."

Frankie tapped her girls' shoulders and motioned to the arena, telling them to watch. Mel noticed that Samantha had mounted her horse and was waiting by the gate for her turn.

"Duty and responsibility are very high on Aaron's list."

"I'm actually surprised he hasn't proposed," Frankie said. "He just strikes me as an old-fashioned kind of guy."

Mel pictured Aaron's expression when he talked about his late wife at dinner. How she wanted her future husband to look at her the same way.

"I wouldn't accept."

"How far along are you, anyway?"

"About seven weeks."

"A lot can change between now and the big day."

Mel supposed her sister was right. Much had changed already.

"You could do a lot worse than Aaron."

Again, Mel snorted. "You make it sound like I won third prize in a contest."

"I'm just saying, you might want to think hard about latching on to him. If you don't, some other woman will. He's too good-looking. And then there's that uniform." Frankie nudged Mel and gave her a wink. "That's what did it for you, right?"

They managed to drop the subject, for which Mel was infinitely glad, when Samantha took her run at the barrels. Her performance was practically flawless and at the speed of light. Her time put her in first place, a position she held through the remainder of the event. Mel and Frankie clapped and whooped loudly when her name was announced at the end, and she was presented with her prize.

While the entire family gathered at the horse trailer, Mel considered the similarities between her situation and Samantha's mother with a fresh eye.

Had she been unfair to her father? He wasn't so different from Aaron. Grieving the loss of a late wife and reluctant to introduce a new romantic interest to his family for fear of their negative reaction.

Watching him unsaddle the horse and issue instructions to Samantha, just like he'd done when Mel and her sisters were younger, a small dam broke inside her. The next moment, she went to him, determined to make amends. To her delight, he greeted her with an affectionate smile.

"There's my pretty Melody."

"And there's my handsome dad." She stood on tiptoes and kissed his cheek.

Chuckling, he rubbed the spot. "What's that for?"

"Just cuz."

She half expected him to mention their minor tiff. Instead, he gave her a big squeeze. "I love you, hon."

Suddenly, Mel wanted to tell him about the baby. This was big. Life changing. Her father was too important not to include him. Maybe this wasn't the best time or place, but she decided to follow her heart.

"Hey." She took his arm. "Come walk with me."

"What's up?"

"I have something to share with you. If you have a second."

"For you, always."

"You have to promise to keep this a secret," she said when they were far enough away not to be overheard. "Except for Dolores. She knows already."

"Knows what?"

Mel stopped to look her father in the face and take

his hand in hers. "I'm pregnant. And I'm very happy about it, so please don't worry."

"That's like asking the sun not to shine." He hung his head, more in confusion than disappointment. Like everyone else, he'd had no idea she was involved with anyone. "Who's the father?"

"Promise me you won't talk to him."

"Is he going to do right by you?"

"If you mean, is he going to pay child support and help raise our child, then yes."

"But not marry you."

"I don't want to get married, Dad. My choice."

"Then why did you…you… Dammit, Mel, why'd you sleep with him?"

"We were careful."

"Apparently not careful enough. And you still didn't say who he is."

"Please, Dad." She fought back a sudden surge of emotion. "I really need your support now. Not to make things harder on me."

He inhaled deeply. "Fine, fine. I won't shove my fist into his face. Promise," he added when she glowered at him.

"It's Aaron," she admitted softly.

"Aaron!"

"Shh. Not so loud." Mel glanced around, worried they'd been heard.

"And here I was just starting to like him."

"No reason you shouldn't. He's a great guy. And I think he'll be a good dad."

"Can't be all that great if he won't—"

"Dad!" Mel rolled her eyes.

"I'm looking out for you."

"And I don't want that to ever change. But you have to let me, let Aaron and me, decide what's best for us."

"Your sister Frankie didn't marry Spence."

"This is different," Mel insisted. "She never told Spence she was pregnant. Aaron knows and will be an involved father."

"I still don't like it."

"I get that." She gave his generous waist a squeeze. "I wouldn't have you any other way."

During their walk back to rejoin the family, she reminded him to keep quiet until Aaron had a chance to tell Nancy and Kaylee. Mustang Valley was a small enough community that word traveled. And while he wasn't happy about her single state, she had no doubt whatsoever he'd be just as wonderful of a grandfather to her child as he was to her sister Frankie's daughters.

Once the horse was finally loaded and the equipment stowed, the family collectively agreed to meet back at Mel's dad's house for pizza and a dip in the pool. If the girls got tired, they could always sleep in the spare room.

Mel strolled along with them to the parking lot where they went their separate ways. Rounding the row of parked vehicles, she spotted her truck—and the tall, lanky figure in boots and jeans leaning on the hood.

"I was hoping to find you," Aaron said when she neared, his sexy grin in full force. "Got a minute?"

"Be strong," she murmured, only to have her feet disobey her instructions and hurry toward him.

Aaron and Mel wandered leisurely across the quickly emptying parking area. On impulse, he took her hand and when she didn't object, linked their fingers.

By now, the sun had long set. Parking-lot lights cast inky shadows that moved and shifted every few feet.

"Where's Kaylee and Nancy?" she asked.

"Driving home. We came separately in case I was called away."

"Do you do that a lot? Take separate vehicles?"

"Not really. Today was a special circumstance." He didn't mention the arrangement had worked out in his favor. Otherwise, he and Mel wouldn't be together now.

"By the way." She sent him a sidelong glance. "Where are we going?"

She'd accepted his request to accompany him without question. But apparently her trust had limits for he was sensing some hesitancy. He tried to put her at ease with a smile.

"I made, oh, let's call it, dinner plans."

"What kind of plans?" Suspicion crept into her voice.

"Come on. Take a chance." Aaron led her to his SUV, opened the rear compartment and removed a small, personal-size ice chest. Flipping open the top, he produced two cold cans of soda and two foil-wrapped sandwiches.

Letting her choose a soda—she picked orange—he handed her a sandwich.

Mel lifted a corner of the foil and raised her brows. "Peanut butter and jelly?"

"The best the snack bar had to offer."

"I see."

He wasn't deterred by her disdain. "It's late. You must be hungry. Especially since you skipped lunch."

"What makes you think that?"

"I know more about you than you realize. For instance, you get busy and forget to eat."

"I happened to have had an apple and protein bar for lunch today."

"That's all? Next time, add a big glass of milk. Starving isn't good for the baby." He perched on the SUV's rear compartment and then patted the spot beside him. "Sit. Take a load off."

She ducked her head and plunked down beside him, carefully arranging herself so only their knees touched.

"I'm supposed to be having pizza at Dad's."

"Consider this an appetizer."

"Only because you're right. I am hungry." She ripped open the foil and bit into the sandwich.

If he'd known he could bribe her with peanut butter and jelly, he'd have done it sooner.

Swallowing, she asked, "Make any progress on the horse thefts today?"

"I learned there's a new ranch hand at Dos Estrellas. He was hired on about the same time as the first horse theft."

Mel's interest was visibly piqued. "You think he's responsible?"

"Not really."

"How can you say that for certain?"

"I can't." Aaron polished off his sandwich with a swig of soda. "Except I doubt someone brand-new to the valley could pull off a series of sophisticated horse thefts that clearly require familiarity with the area. Especially a kid barely out of high school."

"He could be working with someone local. You said so yourself."

"Yeah. Maybe."

"Or he's savvier than you're giving him credit for."

Aaron laughed. "You missed your calling, Mel. You'd

make a good detective. But you're right. I shouldn't discount the kid just because he's young and not the sharpest tack in the box."

"I wish there was something more I could do. I'd hate for another foal to lose his mama."

"Your little guy improving?"

"I thought he might have turned a corner, but then he barely ate today." She sighed. "He's literally going to die of loneliness if I can't come up with a miracle."

"Being orphaned is never easy on youngsters."

"I'm sorry." Mel's face fell. "That was thoughtless of me."

"Kaylee was just a few weeks old when Robin died. She doesn't remember her mother."

"She knows she doesn't have one. How can she not? All her friends do. The loss is there and may grow greater as she gets older."

"Nancy's wonderful with her. She really tries hard to fill the void."

"Anyone can see she adores Kaylee. I have a great respect for her."

"Look, about her confronting you earlier."

Mel blinked in surprise. "She told you?"

"A friend of hers saw us the other night at Vito's. Nancy's still sore."

"Is that why you haven't suggested getting together again?"

"Partly," he admitted.

Mel resumed eating her sandwich. "I figured it was something like that."

"Nancy can be a little pushy."

"She was actually very civil."

"But she got her point across, I bet."

"It's a valid point. She wants to protect Kaylee. And to protect Robin's memory."

"You aren't a threat to either, Mel."

She sought his gaze and held it for a long moment. "Aren't I?"

She was right. He'd been fooling himself all along, thinking he had a handle on his emotions. The proof he'd lost control was right here, staring him in the face and waiting for an answer.

"I shouldn't have left Kaylee with you. I apologize."

Mel turned away, perhaps to hide her disappointment in him. She'd bared her heart, gone out on a limb, and he hadn't had the decency to acknowledge her, much less open up in return. What was wrong with him? Why couldn't he admit he cared for her?

"I'm glad you did," she said. "Kaylee's a beautiful little girl. You're a lucky man."

"I am." He raised his hand to Mel's cheek, attempting to show her by his actions what he couldn't muster the courage to say. "In more ways than one."

She tilted her head away from his hand.

"Mel. I…" Dammit. Could he screw up any worse?

"I thought at Vito's, when we kissed, you might have feelings for me." She faltered. "Only then, you were distant. I understand now that might only be because of Nancy. But you should've said something."

"You're right." He balled up the foil from his sandwich and flung it into the ice chest. "I won't lie, coming to terms with having a baby, figuring out where we stand, it's not easy. For any of us. I'm doing my best."

"You have plenty of reason to be reluctant. That's not what frustrates me. You run hot and cold, Aaron. What am I supposed to think?"

Aaron took his time responding. "It's not that I've sworn off meeting someone special again or having more children. I just wasn't expecting it this soon."

"It's the same for me," Mel said softly. "I want children. Figured on having several. Someday. With a man who loves me."

The stab, intentional or not, hurt. Aaron wanted to be that man, but first, he had to break the ties holding him to his past. Guilt kept preventing him.

"Have you told anyone about the baby besides Dolores?" he asked.

"Frankie."

"Was she happy for you?"

"Not really. Sort of." Mel made a face. "She was kind of funny. But she'll be supportive. She's a single mother, too."

Single mother. Mel was telling him in no uncertain terms she planned on raising their child alone.

"Also my dad," she added.

That took him aback. "How'd he handle it?"

"He'll be fine. And he promised not to shove his fist in your face."

"Oh, boy."

"I'm joking. He likes you. But he is worried about me."

"I would expect nothing else."

Aaron should be relieved, except he wasn't. Did Mel's family believe he wouldn't step up and take responsibility? Did she? He'd let her down. Multiple times. Who could blame her for not having faith in him? Add to that what Nancy had said to her today, and Mel's worst fears had probably been confirmed.

What he needed to do was reassure her. Words

weren't his strong suit, as the last few minutes had demonstrated. There must be another way.

The answer was obvious and one Aaron should have thought of before. He started to speak, only to shut his mouth. This wasn't the time or place. Later, after he'd put some effort into preparing, he'd show Mel just how willing he was to step up.

"Samantha won today," Mel said. "Did you see?"

"Not her run. But I heard her name announced."

"There's a rodeo next weekend in Show Low. She's going."

"You, too?"

Mel shook her head. "Dad, Dolores and Ronnie will. I can't afford another day off."

"You need your rest," he reminded her.

"Did you see how hard we worked today? Helping Samantha compete is no vacation."

"How's her horse? Any improvement?" Aaron cleaned up their trash and the soda cans.

"It's a slow recovery. The tear was bad. She hopes he'll be well enough by the National Finals in December. I don't see that happening."

"She did win on your sister's horse."

"This competition was good practice for her and that horse. But Nationals is on a whole different level. Show Low will be make or break for her."

"Spoken like a big sister." Aaron worried he might have prodded a sore spot.

Evidently not, for Mel said, "She's not a bad kid. Just a bit mixed up. Like the rest of us, I suppose. Dolores thinks Samantha used the lottery money as an excuse to get to know us. I didn't agree with her at first. Now, I think she's right."

"It does make sense." Aaron rested a hand on Mel's thigh, half waiting for her to smack it away.

Instead, she inched closer. He tried not to jump to any conclusions. Not easy. He very much liked the conclusions he was forming.

"Sam and I have a lot in common," Mel said, appearing unaware of Aaron's inner turmoil. "Have you ever noticed?"

Wait. Sam? Did Mel realize she'd called Samantha by the same nickname her father used? Those things in common must have formed a bond between them.

"I haven't. But I'm hoping you'll tell me."

"Her mom, Carrie Anne, she got involved with a man who wasn't emotionally available. That man being my dad."

"And you think I'm emotionally unavailable."

"Please." Mel turned to him, her eyes brimming with emotion. "I didn't mean that in a bad way. I'm simply trying to make sense of everything that's been happening lately."

"Me, too."

She touched his hand, her fingers light and warm and sending tiny shock waves along his skin. "Somehow, we went from having this easy, comfortable relationship to one that's complicated and confusing. I'm not sure how that happened." She let out an uneven breath. "But I believe it's about more than just the baby."

Ah. Those feelings for her he wasn't ready to admit to having.

"I don't disagree with you." He pulled her nearer, securing her in the crook of his arm. "Whatever happens, we'll figure out a solution together. Trust me."

She nodded, swallowing before she spoke. "You're right."

Not that Aaron ever had much success in resisting Mel, but in that moment, she was so lovely and so vulnerable, resisting her wasn't an option.

"Aaron?" Her whispered question fell against his lips. "Are we only making things worse?"

He had to be honest with her. "I'd like to say no."

Convinced she'd pull away, he was elated when she raised her mouth to meet his.

Mel had called their relationship easy and comfortable. For Aaron, it had also been exciting and passionate. He believed Mel felt the same. Her eager response to his kiss certainly indicated as much.

Craving more contact, he drew her onto his lap. She came willingly, making him acutely aware of her enticing curves and firing his need.

Hooking a hand behind her knees, he repositioned her, the part of him most aware of her instantly responding. Mel slid her arms around his neck, parted her lips and kissed him with an intensity matched only by the summer heat.

In moments like this one, Aaron wasn't confused. In fact, he knew precisely what he wanted, and she was sitting in his lap.

One minute stretched into two. Two became five. The need driving Aaron grew, quickly approaching the point of no return.

Slowly, regretfully, he ended the kiss. "That was…" If he kept talking, he'd blabber like a fool.

Mel's arms fell away from him, and she cleared her throat. "We may have gotten carried away."

Aaron waited for his pounding heart to slow. "I'm not complaining."

"Me neither." And, yet, she stood, her damp shirt clinging to her skin and accentuating her hourglass shape. Grabbing her sunglasses, she moved away from him. "My family's waiting for me at Dad's."

"Right." Aaron also stood, not yet over the effects of their kiss. "If I hurry, I can tuck Kaylee into bed."

The parking area had completely emptied while they'd eaten and talked and done things bordering on indecent.

He took a chance and said, "Why don't we meet at the motel tomorrow?" That would allow him time to put his idea in motion.

"It hasn't been two weeks."

She couldn't be serious. Their usual routine had long gone by the wayside.

"I can't wait that long," he said.

She hesitated. "I'm not sure I'm ready to, you know, resume…"

"Just talk. Nothing more." Aaron tensed. This was the closest he'd come to making an admission. Did she not see that? "We can wait till later in the week if you want."

"Tomorrow's fine." She abruptly walked away, sending him a last, lingering glance over her shoulder. "Bye, Aaron."

He watched her until she reached her truck. Grabbing his cowboy hat and plunking it on his head, he shut the rear door of the SUV, all the while whistling to himself.

She hadn't exactly said yes. Then again, she hadn't exactly said no. Aaron was betting on the latter and would be at the motel tomorrow. Neither wild horses nor an irate mother-in-law would keep him away.

Chapter 11

Aaron was waiting for Mel in the parking area behind the motel. She spotted his SUV the moment she rounded the building. He must have seen her, too, for the driver's door opened, and he stepped out, cowboy boots and long legs first. He probably had no idea how great he looked. Aaron didn't spend any time trying to make an impression. He just did, naturally.

She briefly wondered why he chose the parking lot and not the room to wait for her. She was fifteen minutes late; he must've checked in already. His last text had said, "I'm here."

The space beside him was empty, and Mel parked there.

"Sorry I took so long. I was with the foal and lost track of time."

Aaron drew her into a quick, warm hug, catching her completely off guard. They didn't do that. Not in public.

"Is he okay?"

She needed a second to find her voice "I was worried he might have caught a respiratory infection, though he's not running a fever. I drew some blood to send to the lab tomorrow, just as a precaution."

"I'm glad you're here." He reached for her hand.

It was becoming a habit, this hand-holding. One she was growing to like. "Were you worried I wasn't coming?"

"Well, you were vague last night."

After that kiss they'd shared? How could he have had any doubts? That he did was interesting and, possibly, telling. Mel would revisit this recent development later at home.

"You check in already?" she asked.

He produced a key—an actual key, no plastic key cards at this motel. "Room 11."

Inside, he removed his wallet and two phones, tossing them onto the dresser. "I forgot water. Guess I was distracted."

"By work?" *Or thoughts of me?*

He stopped, letting his eyes roam over her. "That, too."

Mel's cheeks warmed. She reminded herself they were here to talk. Not tear each other's clothes off.

Aaron went to the dresser where a plastic ice bucket sat next to the coffeemaker. "Is tap water okay? I'll get some ice from the machine outside the lobby."

"I'm not picky."

She didn't offer to go with him. A minute alone would do her good. She'd been anxious about seeing Aaron since their make-out session in the rear of his SUV after the barrel-racing competition. There had been something so...so...regular-old-couple about it.

A sudden thought panicked her. What if she alone felt that way? Aaron's doubts about her showing up tonight indicated otherwise, but her confidence waned. She could be misreading him. She had before.

"Be right back." Aaron shut the door behind him.

Mel went to the window, parted the curtains and watched him disappear down the walkway. Exhaling slowly, she let the curtain drop back into place and returned to the dresser where she set her purse. Aaron's phone ringing startled her.

She glanced down, recognizing the blue phone as his personal one. Because he'd laid the phone with the screen down, she couldn't see who was calling. Nancy? Was Kaylee all right? Perhaps she should go after him. The ringing stopped and was eventually followed by a ping signaling a voice-mail message had been left.

Mel paced the room until Aaron returned twenty minutes later. Okay, really only five.

"You got a call while you were gone," she said the instant he entered the room. "On your personal phone."

Handing her the ice bucket, he picked up the phone and swiped a finger across the screen. "It's my sister."

Mel was aware Aaron's sister knew about her and Aaron's arrangement. "Go ahead and call her back if you want."

"I won't be long."

While he listened to the voice-mail message, Mel removed two tumblers from the tray and added ice. Taking the glasses to the sink, she filled them with water. By then, Aaron was engrossed in conversation.

"Tell her I'll call tomorrow." After a pause, he said, "I can't tonight… Because I'm busy." Another pause. "Yeah, something like that."

Mel thought she might have heard a laugh coming from the phone and suffered a twinge of embarrassment.

"Love you, too, Pickle. Talk to you later." He disconnected, returning the phone to the dresser. "Mom's sick."

"Not seriously, I hope."

"Sounds like a bad summer cold. I'll call tomorrow."

"I'm sure she'll appreciate that." Mel just had to ask. "You call your sister Pickle?"

"A nickname from when we were kids. She hates it."

"Who wouldn't?"

Mel chewed her lip. She'd officially run out of excuses. With sex off the table, only conversation remained. This, she realized, would be the second time they'd come to the motel and refrained. In fact, they hadn't slept together since before she found out she was pregnant.

"Here's your water."

Before he could take the glass she offered, Mel's knees went boneless and her field of vision narrowed. The glass tumbler suddenly seemed to weigh twenty pounds and slipped from her fingers.

"Hey, hold on there!" Aaron materialized beside her. Taking her arm, he walked her across a floating room and eased her onto the side of the bed. "You okay?"

"Yeah." Mel closed her eyes, fighting the wave of dizziness and encroaching darkness. "No. I feel strange."

"Put your head between your legs."

She did. After a minute or so, the dizziness receded. As it did, she noticed Aaron had sat beside her, his arm securely around her shoulders.

"Careful," he warned when she tried to raise her head. "Go slow."

"I feel silly."

"Stop it." He rubbed her back, his palm making large circles. "Have you fainted before?"

"Not since I was six and the nurse gave me a shot."

"It's not uncommon. Especially in the first trimester. Your blood pressure could have spiked."

Had Robin fainted? Mel didn't ask.

"Here. Have some water." Aaron got up and retrieved her tumbler from the dresser. It was then Mel saw his tumbler on the floor, ice cubes spilled and laying atop a spreading wet spot.

"Did I do that?"

"It's just water. No harm done. The carpet will dry."

She rubbed her head, though the mild throbbing had mostly receded.

"Did you have dinner?" Aaron came back from the bathroom with a towel, which he used to blot the water.

"Yes. A chicken quesadilla and a salad, if you must know."

"Good girl."

He surprised Mel by arranging the pillows against the headboard and insisting she sit back and stretch out her legs.

"I'm fine. Really." She smiled. This was the most relaxed they'd been all evening.

"The dizziness usually doesn't last. Still, you might mention it to your doctor at your next visit. In fact, I insist you do if this happens again."

"Are you going to come with me and make sure I do?" she half joked.

"I'd like to. If you don't mind."

He was serious. And so sweet. She almost said yes. "What will Nancy say?"

"I'm telling her about the baby this week."

"That's not what I asked."

"Isn't it?"

He grinned, and the resulting zing winding through Mel had nothing to do with her earlier dizziness.

It didn't require a genius. Aaron's good looks were what had initially attracted Mel. But what kept her meeting him every two weeks for the last eight, no, nine, months was his *straightness*, for lack of a better word.

Simply put, Aaron was a straight up guy. What one saw was what one got. He was also straightforward. No beating around the bush. And he was a straight arrow. He held himself to high standards and did his best to adhere to those standards. Their affair might be his one and only fall from his pedestal. Ever.

He actually reminded Mel of her father, and not just because they had both lost a wife and wound up having a baby with a woman they didn't marry. They shared many good, admirable traits that had probably enhanced his attractiveness.

"You look serious," Aaron said. He still sat beside her on the bed. "What's wrong?"

"I was thinking about my dad." Not a lie, though not entirely accurate.

He laughed and tucked a loose strand of hair behind her ear. Another sweet gesture. "Not what I expected you to say."

"I was unfair to him when Samantha first showed up. Not that I agree with his decision to waive his parental rights. I've learned a lot these last couple weeks. People deal with grief differently. If seeing Carrie Anne helped him through a difficult time, then where's the harm? Again, other than their truly terrible choices regarding Samantha." Mel touched her belly. "I'll never understand that."

"They're a lot like us."

"Kind of. Only you aren't walking away from our child."

"And you're not insisting I do."

"Does that make us better than Dad and Carrie Anne? Samantha has a good life, even if she's currently at odds with her parents. Despite our best efforts, things could turn out badly for our child."

"I'm not going to let that happen, Mel."

There he was, taking her hand again.

"I apologized to Dad yesterday, before I told him about the baby."

"And the rest of your family?"

"I'm getting to them one by one." She gave him a look. "How about we make a pact? You tell Nancy this week, and I'll tell the rest of my family." She extended her hand for him to shake.

"Deal." He folded her fingers inside his. "I'd like to speak to them, too, if you don't mind."

That took her aback. "Why?"

"I want them to know I'm not abandoning you, and I won't be waiving my rights. Not for anything."

"I'm glad. I'd like our child to grow up with you loving him or her the way you love Kaylee."

"I already do." He raised her hand to his lips, brushed them lightly over her knuckles. "I'm not unhappy at the prospect of spending the next twenty years with you. And not just because of the baby."

In that instant, she knew what she felt for Aaron had gone far past affection and attraction. If he didn't reciprocate, she was heading straight for heartache.

She should get off the bed. Leave. Run away. Before she did something stupid. Something she couldn't take back.

Only Mel stayed put, studying their clasped hands. They'd been flirting a lot lately. He'd given her a hug outside. They'd kissed as if they couldn't get enough of each other. His feelings for her *must* be deepening.

Maybe if she let him know in no uncertain terms she was ready to go from casual to committed, he'd tell her that was what he wanted, too.

Only one way to find out, right?

Mel reached up and cradled Aaron's cheek, brought his mouth to hers.

He resisted.

Mel withdrew, mortified. Clearly, she'd made a mistake. He didn't want her. Not like that.

He brought her gaze back to his and stopped her from looking away when she tried. "Mel, listen. I can't let you start anything you aren't prepared to finish. I want you too much."

Excitement spiraled through her. Hot. Electric. Powerful.

It wasn't enough, however. She needed more.

"This isn't just sex for me, Aaron. Not anymore."

"Me neither." Taking her by the shoulders, he lowered his mouth to hers. "I couldn't bear to hurt you. If there's any chance of that happening, tell me to go, and I will."

"Stay."

Mel leaned back against the pillows, bringing him with her. This time, he didn't resist.

This wasn't what Aaron had planned when he suggested meeting Mel at the motel tonight. Kissing her.

Holding her in his arms. Needing her to cling to him and cry his name as he entered her.

No. He'd wanted to talk. And to ask her...

She nipped at his ear, and his mind shut down.

Mel could do that. Make him forget everything, including his own name.

"Wait." She sat up and wriggled back a bit.

He groaned. Had she come to her senses? It seemed yes, which was probably for the best.

"Give me a minute to recover," he grumbled.

"I'll give you two seconds to prepare."

"Huh?"

In one quick, efficient move, she removed her shirt, slipping it over her head and flinging it onto the floor.

"There."

Aaron stared, lost in the sight before him. She was gorgeous. Her normally satiny skin glowed. And her breasts, rounded to begin with, spilled from the tops of her turquoise bra.

He couldn't keep from touching her and reveled in her low, dreamy sigh when he slid the straps down, taking care to smooth his hand over the silky curve of her exposed shoulders.

She leaned forward, reached behind her and unfastened the hooks. The bra instantly fell away, freeing her and revealing every stunning inch of her.

His throat went bone-dry.

"Are you sure about this? You were feeling faint earlier."

"Don't worry. I'm not getting up." Letting the bra fall onto the floor, she scooted over, making more room for him on the bed. "I'm planning on staying in bed for the next hour at least." When he didn't move, she sent him a seductive smile. "That is, if you'll join me."

Her playful tone and manner reminded him of how they'd been before they found out about the baby, as if the past few stress-filled weeks hadn't happened. Aaron struggled to hold back, determined not to climb all over her like some inexperienced teenager. No matter what, they were going slow—until going slow was no longer possible.

He kicked off his boots, which hit the floor with a thud, landing in the vicinity of her bra. Next, he stood and divested himself of his shirt, jeans and the remainder of his clothes. Mel watched, her eyes never straying. He, in turn, watched her. By the time he removed his underwear, he was hard and ready.

Rather than fall onto the bed beside her, he reached for her sandals and slipped them off. Her toes were painted with a bright blue polish. Cute. When she ran her toes in a swirly pattern down the length of his chest to his stomach, then lower, he was thinking blue was his new favorite color.

Her shorts were next. The sound of fabric against skin when they glided over her hips nearly did him in. Finally, Mel lay naked in front of him, the dainty scrap of fabric she dared to call her panties dangling from his fingers.

Lying there, completely unabashed, she took his breath away. And his ability to move. The panties, as light as a feather, drifted to the floor.

Curling onto her side, she drew circles on the hideous floral bedspread. "You're wasting time, cowboy."

Nothing sexier than a direct woman.

Aaron lay down beside her and scooped her into

his arms. When she made a small sound of protest, he froze. "You all right?"

"I'm a little tender." She indicated her breasts.

Concerned, he drew back. "We should stop."

"Absolutely not."

"You're in pain."

She pushed him down onto his back and swung a leg over his middle. "I won't be if I'm on top."

Before he could answer, she straddled him and braced her arms on each side of his head. Those magnificent, if tender, breasts were within kissing distance. On her face, she wore a wicked smile.

"See? I knew we could find a solution."

No reason for him to worry. She seemed completely recovered from her fainting spell.

"Make love to me, Aaron."

Make love. Not have sex. Not hook up. Not fool around. Had either of them ever said "made love" before? Aaron didn't think so.

"I have every intention of doing that and more." He skimmed his palms down her back, over her smooth, rounded hips and along her thighs.

"More? I'm intrigued. Describe this *more* to me." She rocked back and forth. Side to side.

He sucked in a sharp breath. "I'd rather show you."

Grabbing the backs of her knees, he moved her legs until she was poised in the perfect position. When she reached for him, he told her to wait.

"There's more. Remember?"

She pressed her forehead to his and murmured, "Quit teasing me."

Aaron proceeded to make good on his promise. Dragging her mouth down for a kiss, he slipped his hand between her legs, excited as always to find her ready for him.

He'd made a point from the very beginning to learn what she liked. Which way, how much pressure to apply, where her most sensitive spots were, when to go faster, when to let her take the lead. That last one was the most important for it almost always guaranteed her satisfaction.

He had no problem giving up control. *His* satisfaction was also something Mel liked, and she had a talent for finding new and different ways to excite him. And herself.

"Like that," she whispered when he entered her. "Don't stop."

Aaron didn't. Not until they were both covered in sweat and completely sated.

She fell forward and buried her head in his neck, a low moan escaping. He kissed her cheek and temple and that place behind her ear, noticing the faint flowery scent of her shampoo.

"Aaron?"

"Mmm?"

"That was..." She moaned again.

"I'll say."

Eventually, when their strength returned, she rolled off him and onto the mattress. He groaned, from the rush of cool air and the abrupt loss of contact, not his aching muscles.

"I've missed you."

She propped herself up on an elbow and peered at him. "Me, or the sex? Because we just saw each other yesterday."

"I've missed the closeness."

"We were pretty close in your SUV yesterday, as I recall."

"I'm not good at expressing myself." He chuckled and tweaked her cheek. "And you don't make it any easier."

She rolled over onto her back, her smile flatlining.

"Did I say something wrong?"

"If I ask you a question, will you answer honestly?"

He levered himself up, to look at her and also to assure her he was taking this conversation seriously. "Absolutely."

"You said you liked the idea of spending the next twenty years with me raising our child."

"I did. I can't wait."

"How do you want to spend those twenty years? Have you given it any thought?"

"Actually, I have." He spoke slowly, fearing he might say the wrong thing or that he hadn't understood her question. Was she referring to the sex? To them and the baby? Maybe he shouldn't have said twenty years.

She stared at the ceiling as if avoiding him. This was going from bad to worse.

"Look at me, Mel."

She faced him, her eyes filled with sadness. When had her mood changed and why?

"I'm sorry," she said.

"For what?"

"I put you on the spot again. That wasn't fair."

"After what just happened between us, which, let's admit was mind-blowing, it's more than fair. We deserve to know where we stand with each other."

"I agree. So, tell me, where do I stand?"

Shit. This wasn't going the way Aaron had planned. But it would have to do.

Pointing a finger at her, he said, "Hold that thought."

"You're kidding." She didn't sound amused.

Aaron sat up and reached for his jeans on the floor. From the front pocket, he pulled out a small velvet jewelry box.

This morning, he'd gone into Scottsdale and made a purchase. Taking Kaylee with him, he'd let her help pick out the ring, though he hadn't told her who it was for and why. A stop for ice-cream cones had secured a promise from her not to tell her grandmother or anyone else.

Straightening, he held out the box to Mel, opening the lid to display the object inside. "I was saving this for later. Thought I might get down on one knee. The whole nine yards." He grinned, more than a little pleased with himself. "Mel, will you—"

"No." She snatched the bedsheet with one hand and covered herself. She held up her other hand as if to ward him off. "Don't."

"I'm asking you to—"

"I know *what* you're asking. What I want to know is *why*?"

He frowned. "Why I want to marry you?"

"It's a reasonable question, Aaron."

He supposed it was. He hadn't made any flowery speeches or broken down with unrestrained emotion. Hadn't given her reason to believe no one in the world mattered more to him than she did and that he couldn't spend another day without her by his side. He hadn't said he loved her.

When he tried, the words stuck in his throat. Not just because of Robin or any sense of loyalty to her. And not because Mel wasn't someone he *could* love. Eventually. She'd be a wonderful wife and partner, and a great stepmom to Kaylee.

But that wasn't what she'd want to hear, either.

Aaron closed his eyes. He took admissions of love very seriously and believed Mel did, too. She'd instantly dismiss empty platitudes or insincere declarations, rightfully tossing them back in his face.

"I like the idea of us marrying and raising our family together. You're someone I want to be with. Someone I clearly care for. I think I can make you happy. I know you'll make me happy."

She shook her head, and when she spoke, tears clogged her voice.

"Not good enough."

"Mel. Please."

She climbed out of bed and went straight for her clothes. Shoving her arms into the sleeves of her shirt, she quickly dressed.

"Mel. Hang on." Aaron found his underwear among the remaining scattered clothes and stepped into them. "Where are you going?"

"Home. To check on the foal. Frankie's. I'm not sure."

"Wait." Pocketing the ring box, he finished dressing. "We're not done talking."

"I think we are." She began gathering her things. Purse. Cell phone. Sandals.

Aaron realized he had less than twenty seconds to change Mel's mind and stop her from leaving. Whatever he said next, it had to be good.

Chapter 12

I love you. You are every woman I've ever desired rolled into one. Marry me and make me the happiest man alive.

Or, words to that effect. Mel wasn't particular. As long as Aaron mentioned love and looked at her with a besotted expression on his face.

The same besotted expression he wore when he talked about his late wife.

Mel refused to be an afterthought or a consequence of duty or a means of avoiding a messy custody battle. She'd rather raise her child alone and without a red cent from him.

"I botched the proposal." Aaron reached around and prevented her hand from opening the door.

She didn't think he'd forcibly detain her. He wasn't the type.

"I could have done a better job."

"You think?" Okay, she was being snippy. But when did proposing become a job?

Mel frowned. Why was she not hightailing it to her truck? She supposed some part of her wanted to hear what Aaron had to say. Feel that he recognized and understood how much he'd hurt her.

"Let me try again," he said.

She turned, thinking he couldn't be serious. "You're asking for a do over?"

He continued as if he hadn't heard her. "I want to give you and our child the best home possible. Is that wrong?"

"Being married is no guarantee."

"Call me old-fashioned. I like the idea of a traditional family."

Kudos to Frankie, she'd pegged Aaron 100 percent.

Something her father had said the night Samantha showed up suddenly came to Mel. He'd proposed to Carrie Anne out of duty. Not love. Aaron's reasons for proposing to Mel were too similar, wounding her even greater.

She stole her sister's favorite quote, more resolved than ever to stand her ground. "One happy parent is better than two miserable parents."

"What if we aren't miserable?"

"Marriage is hard. Even for couples in love." More wise words from Frankie.

"Kaylee likes you," Aaron said, trying a different tactic.

"And I like her," Mel said. "But what about Nancy? Would she be part of our *traditional family*?"

"I doubt she'd stay with us. She'll probably get a place of her own nearby."

"You doubt it? Does that mean you won't ask her to leave?"

He waited a fraction too long before answering. "I will."

"If it comes to that. But you'd rather not. Which makes me out to be a bitch. Nicely done, Aaron."

It was silly for them to continue standing at the door. Mel, however, wasn't budging. Aaron needed to think she might flee any second.

"You're right," he admitted. "Nancy would be crushed, and I'd hate hurting her."

"But not me?"

"Yes, you." Everything about him screamed defeat. From his untucked shirt to his shoeless feet and mussed hair. "I didn't think this through before I went and bought the ring."

She didn't tell him the ring and his spontaneous purchase of it was the only romantic part in all this wretchedness. The solitaire diamond nestled in a circle of smaller diamonds was beautiful and exactly the kind of ring Mel would have picked out herself.

"I really do understand your loyalty to Nancy," she said. "She's an important part of Kaylee's life. Of your life. I would have always respected that and accommodated her."

"Would have?"

A sharp pain speared Mel's chest. The effect of having her heart broken.

How could she have not realized the enormity of her feelings for Aaron? Fear of rejection, most likely. So what did she do? She walked the wobbly limb of baring souls all by her lonesome. Gee, and look where it got her.

"I'll accept child support," she said. "Only because I won't deprive our child. And you can see him or her as much as you want. We'll come up with a reasonable schedule that works for both of us."

"Dammit, Mel."

"I think I'm being very accommodating."

"Except now I'm feeling cornered."

Was he not listening to a thing she said? "None of this is my fault."

"That's not entirely true."

She stiffened. "If you're feeling cornered, it's because you painted yourself into one by proposing."

"You're the one who insisted on dissecting my remark about twenty years."

"Dissecting? *Dissecting?* Excuse me for trying to understand your intentions."

"Are you sure you weren't trying to force me to—"

"That's it. This discussion is officially over."

He struggled for composure. "Sorry. Wrong word choice."

Not that excuse again. "Goodbye, Aaron."

"I'm upset. You're upset." He put a hand on her arm. "Let's meet tomorrow, after we've both had a chance to cool off."

If not for the fact he didn't seem to realize how much he'd hurt her, she'd agree. "I can't. I'm busy."

"Then when are you free?"

She took a breath and reached for the doorknob. "I'll let you know."

"I hate that things have come to this point." Regret filled his eyes.

"It was bound to happen. We made a mistake. We thought we could sleep together, no strings attached.

Without falling for each other. Then, despite developing feelings anyway, despite this baby being a very big string attaching us, we kept trying to play by the old rules."

"Have you fallen for me?"

How like a guy to hear only one thing.

"That doesn't matter now. We got in over our heads. Way over." She had to hurry before her worst nightmare came true, and she started crying. She was already on the verge. "You want to do right by me and the baby. I want a man who loves me the way you loved Robin." There, she'd said it.

"Give me time."

"Time? This isn't some TV sitcom where the star finally falls for the quirky neighbor after three seasons. You either love somebody or you don't."

Their conversation had circled an empty track for the last time. Even if Aaron dropped to his knees and begged her, she wouldn't marry him.

She wrenched opened the door.

He must've decided any further pleas would fall on deaf ears because he didn't stop her.

As she crossed the threshold, she felt the faintest of brushes on her arm. It might have been Aaron's hand. Or, the air conditioning turning on.

She half walked, half ran down the path. Her blinking truck lights, normally welcoming, seemed to mock her.

Mel swore when the key wouldn't fit in the ignition. After several frustrating failed attempts, she stopped, inhaled and tried again, willing her fingers to cease their trembling. If she didn't get out of here soon, Aaron would come walking around the corner.

Finally, thank God, the key went in, and she started for home. At the last minute, Mel changed her mind and headed to Frankie's house. She needed to talk to someone, and she'd rather that someone already know about Aaron and the baby.

She must've looked terrible for Frankie uttered, "Are you okay?" the moment she opened the door.

The emotion Mel had been holding in for the last twenty minutes burst free. Sobbing, she threw herself at her sister.

Frankie gasped. "Is the baby all right?"

"Aaron and I broke up."

"I thought you weren't dating."

"Not funny."

"Who's joking?"

Patting Mel's back, she maneuvered them to the couch. At this hour, the girls were fast asleep. Mel and Frankie could talk privately.

"Sit. I'll make us some hot tea."

How like her older sister, convinced tea was the universal cure for whatever ailed a person.

"I don't want any."

"All right." She reclined against the cushions. "Tell me what happened."

"He proposed."

"I thought you said you broke up."

"We did. He had a ring. I told him no before he could finish. And to answer the question I see burning in your eyes, he doesn't love me."

"Are you sure? He did propose."

Mel recalled Aaron's expression when he'd produced the ring box. He'd been wearing a goofy, didn't-I-do-good grin like her nieces did when they made a macaroni-and-construction-paper Christmas ornaments.

"I'm sure," Mel said.

"He was willing to do the right thing. That counts for a lot. It shows he's a decent guy."

"He is a decent guy. But me being pregnant isn't reason enough to get married."

"You have to consider your child."

"I am. Lots of single parents raise happy and healthy kids. Look at you."

"Maybe I'm not the best role model. Children do need a father."

Mel started crying again. "I want my husband to be in love with me."

"We all want that, honey. But I'm not sure it's possible."

"What's wrong with us?" Mel lamented.

"Bad timing, I guess. Bad choices."

"I think if I had met Aaron a couple years from now, we'd be dating."

"Possibly. But what good does playing that kind of game accomplish? Other than making yourself feel worse?"

Her sister was right.

"I really wanted things to work out with Aaron. I've never admitted that before. Not to myself, not to anyone."

Frankie put an arm around Mel. "Are you in love with him?"

"I might be. Yes, a little. I think so." She sniffed. "Not that it matters. I screwed up."

"Been there, done that." Frankie's tone had the ring of personal experience.

"I shouldn't have gotten mad."

"He hurt you. Anger is a natural defense."

"What am I going to do?"

"About what?" Frankie asked. "The baby? Aaron? The fact you're clearly in love with him?"

"All of the above?"

Frankie became instantly pragmatic. It was how she dealt with life's blows. She'd done it when Samantha appeared at their father's birthday party and when Spence left, forcing her to raise their two daughters on her own.

"About the baby, you and Aaron will talk. Once you've had some time to think. About Aaron, you'll get along with him because it's best for everyone involved. About being in love with him, he'll own a small piece of your heart forever."

"Like his late wife owns a small piece of his," Mel said glumly.

"Look. If you're not going to marry him, then hire my attorney and get yourself an airtight custody agreement. You don't want him taking your baby from you."

Was that what Frankie feared? Spence returning and wanting custody of their daughters?

"Aaron wouldn't do that."

"A legal contract will make sure he doesn't."

What strength Mel had left seeped slowly out of her. She'd just turned down a proposal from a wonderful man any woman would be thrilled to marry. She still believed her reasons were good, but doubts were starting to creep in and take hold.

She stood. "I should get home."

"Are you okay to drive?"

"I'll be fine."

Frankie walked her to the door. "Call me anytime. Day or night. I don't care." They hugged. "Love you, honey."

Mel went outside. Once removed from Frankie's calming influence, her anger returned. Not at Aaron but at herself. She'd walked eyes wide open into a situation that couldn't possibly end well. Stupid, stupid, stupid.

Starting tomorrow, she was making a new plan, one based entirely on logic and without emotion. One that made her baby a priority. And she'd stick to the plan, come hell or high water. No breaking the rules just because some sexy cowboy came along who turned her head and awakened her long slumbering libido.

She'd learned her lesson, thank you very much. Love was for dreamers and people with their heads in the clouds.

Not her. Not again.

Aaron had only been to Dos Estrellas Ranch once before, and it wasn't on business. Though he didn't know the Dempseys well, he'd been invited to the wedding reception for Josh, the oldest of the three brothers who owned the ranch, and Cara, the manager of the mustang sanctuary.

Of course, half the town had been invited to the reception. He supposed no one wanted to exclude the local deputy.

This time the reason for his visit was official. He'd just completed a lengthy interview with Mike O'Donnald, the young, newly hired ranch hand who'd come under suspicion related to the recent spate of horse thefts.

Initially, Aaron had dismissed the kid as an unlikely suspect. But, then, he'd heard a second rumor and was compelled to follow up. After nearly two hours, he was leaving the ranch with the same opinion as before. Mike wasn't their man. Or, teenager in this case. Besides his alibis checking out, he simply didn't strike Aaron as the type to steal horses. An aw-shucks personality like his couldn't be faked.

Aaron tended to blame the rumors on folks being scared enough to point fingers without thinking. Mike was new to the community and had admitted when hired at Dos Estrellas that his dad was currently in prison, serving time for stealing a car.

The interview had been Aaron's last call in what had turned out to be a long, grueling day. Shortly after coming on duty, he'd been dispatched to break up two neighbors exchanging verbal blows over the placement of a fence. He'd hardly finished with them when he was summoned to the local market to arrest a shoplifter—who turned out to be a scared seven-year-old unable to stop crying. Before going to Dos Estrellas, he'd written three tickets for illegally parked cars. In this heat, no one wanted to walk one block farther than necessary.

Being busy wasn't all bad. It did give him a few minutes reprieve here and there from thinking about Mel.

Damn, he missed her. More than two weeks had passed since their night at the motel when they'd gone from making incredible love, to his rejected marriage proposal, to ending things completely and not seeing each other at all.

They kept in regular contact though. He made sure she was eating right, getting enough rest and that she knew without a doubt he'd help in whatever way she needed. He'd asked to tag along at her next doctor appointment, and she'd agreed, if hesitantly.

Their conversations were always polite and sometimes bordered on nice. Aaron wondered if someone else was in the room during those calls. Like her sisters or Dolores.

As he cruised the road from the ranch to town, tired, grouchy and hungry, he tried to pinpoint exactly when

Mel had gotten under his skin, though that hardly described his feelings for her. Not right away, for sure. He'd been too cautious to let anyone in, too convinced he was making a mistake.

What had Mel said about falling in love? You either did or you didn't.

To him, she was like an addiction that started out as an occasional indulgence. Before long, he couldn't go a day without seeing or hearing from her.

Was that love? Aaron didn't know. The only woman he'd loved was Robin, and their relationship had taken an entirely different course than his and Mel's.

Aaron rubbed his temple. He'd been nursing a headache off and on for days. Sixteen days to be precise.

A chime from his personal cell phone distracted him. He was startled, then alarmed, to see Frankie's number. Was she calling about Mel?

"Hi, Frankie," he said with forced calm. Mel's sister knew the story. By now, her entire family had been told about her pregnancy and former relationship with Aaron. He had no idea what they thought, not having talked to them since his falling out with Mel. "What's up?"

"Just wondering if you're busy tomorrow. The girls have been begging me to invite Kaylee over for another playdate. Thought I'd give you a call and ask if you're free."

"We are. And I'm sure Kaylee would love to come over. What time and what can I bring?"

"Kid snacks, if you're inclined. And be sure Kaylee doesn't forget her swimsuit. Also, there's something else…"

Forget being calm. "Is it Mel? Tell me."

"No, she's fine. Stubborn. What else is new?"

Interesting. This was the first time Frankie had dropped a hint of how she felt about Mel and Aaron's breakup.

"We recently took in a stray puppy," Frankie said. "About three months old. He's really cute and super-friendly, if a bit excitable. Perfect size for a kid. Half Chihuahua and half terrier. Kaylee always loves playing with the animals when she comes over. I thought she might want a dog of her own."

Aaron liked pets. Robin had owned a clownish yellow Lab when they married. Unable to care for a dog and a brand-new baby in the wake of Robin's death, Aaron had given the dog to his parents, who still owned him.

He always thought of getting another pet when Kaylee was older. A puppy might make a perfect early birthday present.

"Sure."

"Really?" Frankie's voice rose with delight.

"We could use a positive change in the house."

"I'm sorry." There was no need to ask what or who she was referring to.

"Me, too."

They discussed a few more playdate details before disconnecting. Aaron contemplated how he'd break the news of the puppy to Nancy. She might not be too pleased, having to watch a puppy while he was at work. But she'd liked Robin's Lab and would do anything for Kaylee, so maybe he was anticipating a problem where there wasn't one.

Passing through the center of town, Aaron decided to stop at the feed store. They stocked a small inventory of pet supplies, including dog and cat food. Might be a good idea to have a bag of puppy chow on hand before tomorrow.

A bell over the door announced his arrival. Glancing at the wall clock, the face of which advertised a popular grain supplier, he calculated he had about fifteen minutes before closing time.

"Howdy." He nodded at the assistant manager behind the counter, trying to recall her name.

"Be right with you."

She was waiting on another customer. The middle-aged man in dusty boots and an old T-shirt leaned casually against the counter, giving the impression he was a frequent and welcome visitor to the store. But Aaron immediately picked up a negative vibe from him, which could be because he and the manager had been caught socializing when she should be working.

"Where's the dog food?" Aaron asked.

"First aisle on the left." Her smile appeared strained.

Aaron didn't think much of it. Uniforms intimidated some people, even innocent ones.

Looking over the available supply of puppy chow, Aaron selected a small bag, along with matching water and food bowls. He and Kaylee could make a trip later in the week to the pet-supply store in Scottsdale for a collar and leash and anything else they needed.

Did Mel treat small animals? Should he ask her to give the puppy its vaccinations and a checkup?

By the time Aaron carried his purchases to the counter, the other man had left. The assistant manager stared out the large window, but not at her friend. Ray Hartman had arrived and was climbing out of his truck.

The assistant manager shot Aaron a glance. Evidently, she and the entire town now knew about Mel and Aaron. The assistant manager must be worried he and Ray were going to have a showdown.

Aaron didn't duck and he didn't hide. He was going to be a part of Mel's life for a very long time. He intended to get along with each and every member of her family.

Setting the puppy chow and dishes on the counter, he reached for his wallet. While the assistant manager checked him out, Ray entered the store. He spotted Aaron immediately.

Glancing at Aaron's purchases, he smiled. "I thought you might be here on a call. Apparently not."

"It seems Kaylee is getting a new puppy courtesy of Frankie."

"Ah. That one." He shook his head. "Always rescuing some stray."

Not only was their exchange civil, it was downright sociable.

The assistant manager completed the transaction and handed Aaron his change and receipt. "Thanks for coming in."

He grabbed his purchases and, rather than leave, walked over to Ray, who was reading the notices on the bulletin board. "I'm not sure what Mel has told you, sir."

His smile returned. "She's having a baby. I'm going to be a grandfather again. And you're the dad."

That about summed it up. "I wanted you to know, I'm going to support the baby and share in raising him or her." He considered mentioning to Ray that he'd proposed but decided against it.

"Mighty admirable of you."

Aaron almost asked Ray to repeat himself. Had he heard correctly? It sounded as if the older man wasn't angry. Hard to believe. If Aaron was confronting the father of his precious daughter's baby, he'd have a few choice words to say if nothing else.

"You aren't leaving Mel in the lurch," Ray said. "I give you credit for that. Wish I'd done the same with Samantha." Ray held out his hand for Aaron to shake. "We're going to see a lot of each other from now on. No reason we can't get along."

"I couldn't agree more, sir." Aaron accepted Ray's hand, impressed by the older man's firm grip.

"I figure any man Mel takes a liking to can't be all bad."

Aaron chuckled mirthlessly. "Did take a liking to."

"Did. Does." Ray gave Aaron a clap on the shoulder. "I'd best finish my shopping before the store closes. Dolores has dinner waiting for me."

The assistant manager seemed relieved when Aaron left.

He barely noticed, unable to get the encounter with Ray out of his head. The man's attitude was unexpected. But what had Aaron replaying the scene over and over in his head was Ray's remark about Mel.

Did...*does*? Was it possible she still cared? And how did Aaron find out?

Chapter 13

Kaylee greeted Aaron the second he walked through the door, crashing into him and hugging his knees.

"Daddy, Daddy!"

He lifted her into his arms, and she rewarded him with a wet, sticky kiss on the cheek. Not that he minded.

"You're home," Nancy said from the kitchen. She stood at the counter, cutting up tomatoes for a salad. She and Kaylee usually ate earlier, and Aaron had leftovers.

"I have a surprise for you." Aaron tickled Kaylee's neck before putting her down. "Two, actually."

"What? Tell me."

"Paige and Sienna's mom invited you over tomorrow. After lunch."

"Yay!" Kaylee jumped up and down in excitement. She'd just seen her little friends at preschool that day. Apparently, that wasn't enough time together.

"And, if you want, she has a puppy for us!"

Kaylee's face brightened as if she'd swallowed a ray of sunshine. "A puppy! For me?"

"We have to see him first, then decide if we want him."

Kaylee had already made up her mind for she ran to her grandmother and shouted, "Gramma, I'm getting a puppy."

"I heard." Nancy wiped her hands on a dish towel, and then tossed the towel onto the counter. "Shouldn't we talk about this first?"

"Okay." Aaron went over to the table, pulled out a chair and sat. A plate and silverware was already set out for him. "Let's talk."

He'd mostly made up his mind. But letting Nancy have a say in the decision might improve her willingness to cooperate.

"A puppy requires a tremendous amount of attention." She joined him at the table.

"I know I'm asking a lot from you. I'll help as much as possible. And Kaylee can take on some responsibility."

Nancy looked skeptical. "A three-year-old?"

Aaron inhaled slowly. Getting mad would gain nothing. "Please, Nancy. I'd really like to get her this puppy. She could use a boost. We've all been a little out of sorts lately."

"We? I'd say you're the only one in a bad mood."

"Daddy," Kaylee interrupted. "Can the puppy sleep in my room?"

"Sure. But you'll have to make a bed for him."

Kaylee hurried off, presumably to her room to construct a puppy bed. Just as well. Aaron preferred she not hear his conversation with Nancy.

"I didn't realize my mood was affecting everyone." He'd been trying hard to put forth a pleasant—if not happy—face.

"Don't get me wrong," Nancy said. "I'm glad you aren't seeing that woman anymore."

That woman? Her tone rubbed him the wrong way. "Her name is Mel."

Nancy ignored his remark. "Are you sure taking Kaylee tomorrow is a good idea? What if she's there again?"

She? Aaron was definitely getting tired of this. "Just in case I wasn't clear earlier, you should know I really care about Mel. She's more than a friend."

"I see." Nancy drew herself up. "I wonder what Robin would have thought of her?"

"She was one of the most practical, and generous, people I've ever met. She told me before she died that she wanted me to be open to finding someone new someday."

"Is Mel that someone new?"

She might have been. Regretfully, Aaron had blown his chances with her before finding out.

"She's important to me. And she's going to remain important for a long, long time."

He was yet to tell Nancy about Mel's pregnancy. Yes, he should have done so before now, but he hadn't wanted to deal with her reaction. Not while he was still coping, apparently poorly, with his and Mel's breakup.

"She's having a baby. My baby." Aaron spoke quickly, as if that would soften the blow. "I'm going to be an involved parent, and Kaylee will be an involved sister."

Nancy went stone still. For a full minute.

"I understand you're upset," Aaron finally said.

"Actually, I don't think you understand me at all."

She stood and clasped her hands, but not before he noticed the tremor. "I'll need a few weeks."

"For what?"

"To move out."

"Sit down, Nancy," Aaron said gently. "You're not moving."

"Clearly, you've started a new life and don't need me."

He had always given Nancy a lot of leeway, making allowances for her immeasurable grief. But this threat to move, like all her previous threats, was a way of manipulating him. He'd let her get away with it for too long, choosing the path of least resistance instead of standing up to her.

Not anymore.

"Forget it," he said. "I've changed my mind. Go on and move if that's what you want."

She stared at him, the bluster draining from her like air escaping a punctured inner tube.

"I won't stop you," he continued. "Kaylee will be heartbroken, of course, but you need to do what you need to do."

"You can't be serious."

"I'm not abandoning Mel and our baby. If you're unable to accept that, or can't bear the thought of it, then I'll respect your wish to leave. You're always welcome to visit and stay as long as you like."

"What will you do with Kaylee? Who will watch her?"

"I'll figure something out. Hire a babysitter. Enroll her in day care."

Nancy slowly lowered herself into her seat.

After a moment, Aaron said with a smile, "That's better."

"I'm not sure what you're insinuating."

"Nancy, you're part of this family. An important, irreplaceable part. And not just because you watch Kaylee while I'm at work. You're her grandmother. Her one real connection, besides me, to her mother. Don't let your anger at me rob Kaylee of your love and guidance."

"What happens to me if you do…find someone new? Or, decide you want to marry Mel Hartman? Another woman isn't going to want her husband's former mother-in-law living with them."

This, Aaron suspected, was the real reason Nancy clung to the past and insisted he did, too. She was scared that, with Robin gone, and without Aaron and Kaylee, she'd lose her place in the world and never find it again.

His anger and frustration at her vanished. "If whoever this woman turns out to be can't accept you, then maybe she's not the right person for me."

"You say that now."

"There may come a day when you move out and have your own home. Not just because it's more comfortable for me. But because you're ready. I really hope that home is near Kaylee and me."

Blinking away a tear, she rose. "I'd better get your dinner on the table. You must be hungry."

This time, Aaron didn't stop her.

Nancy wasn't the demonstrative type. She didn't hug. She didn't make emotional declarations. In her subtle way, she was accepting what Aaron said and apologizing to him. It was, perhaps, her first step in facing a future that didn't revolve entirely around him and Kaylee.

If only he and Mel had been able to resolve their problems so easily. How different their last evening at the motel would have gone. He might be sitting across from her instead of Nancy, talking about a puppy for their brand new family.

He wasn't done trying with Mel, not after what Ray had said in the feed store. The problem was she'd yet to give any indication the wall she'd erected to keep him at bay could be breached. Until then, Aaron didn't stand a chance.

His personal cell phone went off, startling him. The ringtone identified the caller as Mel, giving him an even greater start. Pushing back from the table, he dived for the phone on the counter.

"Hi." He strove to sound casual. "What's going on?"

"I'm at The Small Change," she blurted. "With the orphan foal. Something's going on here. I think the horse thieves are back. I noticed a strange truck and trailer cutting across the back of the outbuildings toward the gate."

"Where does the gate lead?"

"To the cattle-grazing sections. But the mustang sanctuary is there, too."

Aaron glanced at the kitchen clock. It was past seven thirty and well into dusk. Night would be falling soon. Mel didn't need to be at the stables in the dark and with potentially dangerous individuals in the vicinity.

"You get out of there, you hear me?" Aaron all but shouted into the phone.

"I can't. The foal's sick. He must've ingested some moldy hay or pellets. I'm really worried about him."

"His life isn't worth yours, Mel. If the thieves are there and they think you've spotted them, you could be in real trouble."

"Aaron—"

He cut her off. "Get in your truck, lock the doors and crouch down. Don't go anywhere. If they see your lights, they'll figure out they've been spotted. Do it now, Mel," he insisted before she could object.

"All right."

"That's my girl."

Aaron briefly wondered how the truck had driven past the ranch house without being observed. They must have entered the ranch from a side road.

"I'll call you on my way there." His voice cracked, and he quickly cleared his throat to cover it. "Keep your phone with you at all times."

He hoped she'd say something about missing him or wanting him to stay safe before hanging up. She didn't.

"Where are you off to?" Nancy called after him as he headed for the door. "Your dinner's ready."

"There's a possible horse theft in progress at The Small Change."

He said no more. Nancy wouldn't have heard him anyway for he was halfway out the door.

Protocol may or may not have warranted him turning on the siren and breaking every speed law on the way to the ranch. After radioing the station and requesting backup, he dialed Shonda and Eduardo. Despite being off duty, they both promised to be ready within minutes. Because Eduardo was more familiar with the towns-folk, Aaron ordered him to track down Theo McGraw, the owner of The Small Change, or Theo's daughter. And of course, Cara Dempsey, manager of the mustang sanctuary. He told Eduardo to have her meet him at the gate leading to the pastures in order to unlock it.

Lastly, he instructed Eduardo to very clearly warn Josh Dempsey, Cara's notoriously hotheaded husband, to stay away. This was police business; they didn't need civilians interfering. Well-intentioned or not.

When he finished, he called Mel again. She didn't answer and after five rings, her voice-mail greeting sounded. Swearing, and accelerating on the open road, he tried again. Still no answer. He'd have thrown the phone onto the floor in frustration, but he needed it handy in case she called him back.

Was her battery dead or had something happened to her? Pounding a fist on the steering wheel, he turned sharply onto the dirt road leading to The Small Change. The SUV's wheels sprayed a shower of dirt into the air.

What a fool he'd been to let her go. He should have run after her at the inn, refusing to take no for an answer. Convince her he truly wanted to marry her, not just fulfill an obligation. Swept her off her feet. Treated her the way she deserved to be treated. Wooed her and charmed her and demonstrated through words and actions that they were meant to be together. That she was the one he'd been waiting for. The one who mattered more than anyone else.

Would she have believed him? Aaron vowed he'd move heaven and earth to show her when this was all over and prayed he had the chance.

Flying past the ranch house, he silenced his siren and drove to the horse stables. Mel's truck was there. Dark. Still. Empty. As badly as he wanted to catch the horse thieves, he wouldn't move onward without making sure she was safe. His SUV idling, he hopped out and jogged toward her truck.

Mel's head popped up before he reached the driver's door, and she lowered her window. "I'm okay."

He stood there long enough to catch his breath and whisper a soft, "Thank you."

She opened the door.

"You're not coming with me," he barked, correctly reading her intent.

"I could—"

"No way."

"Then hurry, Aaron. Catch the bad guys."

He turned to go. At the last second, he changed his mind. Caressing her cheek through the open window, he said, "Wait for me. I'll be back."

"Be careful," was all she said.

Maybe Aaron should have brought Mel along after all. No sooner was he driving behind the outbuildings than he realized he had no clue where the gate to the pastures was located. Almost immediately, a pair of zigzagging headlights came toward him. Suspecting it was Cara Dempsey, he slowed to a stop.

She motioned for him to follow, and Aaron noticed she had a passenger. Her husband, Josh. They apparently hadn't heeded Eduardo's warning for Josh to stay away.

At the end of the corral, Cara stopped. She and Josh both exited the Jeep. By the time Aaron neared, Josh was inserting a key into the padlock.

"Don't think you're going after them by yourself," the tall, lanky man said.

Aaron figured there was no sense fighting him. "Cara stays behind. If not, I'll arrest you both for interfering with an investigation."

"Got it."

The padlock released, and the chain securing the gate fell away. Josh swung open the gate just as Cara came around to grab it, her long black hair swinging in the breeze. Josh had probably tasked her with shutting the gate behind them.

"If you don't hear from us in the next twenty minutes," Aaron told her, "call the sheriff's office in Rio Verde." He passed her a card.

"Will do." She looked worried and not at all happy her husband was going with Aaron.

The two men jumped into Aaron's SUV and took off. Josh gave directions, his voice clipped. By now, darkness had fallen. Aaron phoned Eduardo and Shonda for updates as he navigated the narrow, winding dirt road. Eduardo reported that Theo McGraw was in the hospital after a bad fall, and his family was at his side.

"These guys are either incredibly brave or incredibly stupid," Josh said. "Attempting a second theft at the same ranch they hit last time."

"They probably learned the McGraws weren't home." Another reason to believe the thieves had access to inside information.

Landscape, illuminated by moonlight, flew by as they traveled the two miles to the sanctuary. Aaron grew impatient when their progress was impeded by having to stop and unlock two more gates separating the cattle grazing sections from the sanctuary. Josh indicated a knocked-over post and tangled barbed wire while unlocking the third gate. "They cut the fences. There's going to be chaos tomorrow."

Escaping cattle was a problem. It was also the least of Aaron's concerns.

Over the next rise, the sanctuary appeared.

Aaron instantly spotted the barely visible outline of a truck and trailer parked along the fence. He'd cut his headlights a mile back to avoid detection. Now, he slowed his speed, hoping the thieves didn't see them until it was too late.

Luck, unfortunately, wasn't on their side. All at once, the thieves executed a one-eighty and pulled away, the truck tires spinning. They, too, had cut their headlights.

"Dammit," Aaron grumbled and went after them, hitting the gas and going as fast as he dared.

To Josh he said, "Did they get any horses?"

"I can't tell."

Hauling the trailer, even empty, slowed the thieves enough that Aaron was able to catch up. According to the last transmission on the radio, Eduardo, Shonda and three backup units from the Scottsdale Police Department were en route with an ETA of five minutes.

"Don't let them get away," Josh said, pounding his closed fist on the dash.

"I'm trying."

The driver of the truck was obviously no stranger to these hills.

"Where does this road lead?" Aaron asked.

"To the north, it connects with a county maintenance road," Josh said. He'd been making phone calls to Theo McGraw's family and Ray Hartman, putting them on the alert about the loose cattle. "To the south, it dead-ends at the base of the mountain."

Aaron radioed in the information, stating that he and his approaching backup should attempt to force the thieves toward the mountain. He then flipped on his siren and flashing lights.

In the distance, he spotted a fast-moving storm of white, red and blue lights from what had to be at least five emergency vehicles. A helicopter suddenly materialized from behind the mountain, its spotlight cutting a path across ground below.

The cavalry had officially arrived.

Attempting to escape, the truck and trailer veered off the dirt road, bouncing wildly over the rough terrain. Aaron and the emergency vehicles changed course.

Big mistake on the thieves' part. Traveling too fast, they hit a ditch and lost control.

The truck tilted high on its two right wheels and hung suspended in midair for several precarious heartbeats. Only the weight of the trailer prevented it from rolling. Coming down hard, the truck made a loud crashing sound, then sat, heaving and groaning like a wounded animal.

Within seconds, the thieves were surrounded on all sides by six vehicles, including Aaron's, and above by the helicopter. Two more emergency vehicles could be seen in the distance, one of them Shonda's.

Aaron grabbed his transmitter and activated the loudspeaker. "This is the Maricopa County Sheriff's Department. Remain where you are." He then reached for where his rifle was stored. No telling if these men were armed or what they might do.

He stared hard at Josh, rifle in hand. "Do not get out of this vehicle under any circumstances."

The other man's jaw visibly clenched, but he stayed put.

Taking the suspects into custody was almost anticlimactic. The pair emerged from their vehicle, arms in the air, averting their gazes from the blinding glare of numerous flashlights and headlights. The helicopter's spotlight was trained on them as well.

Aaron and Eduardo quickly subdued and cuffed them. Both were belligerent when Aaron recited their rights. Both refused to give any information, with the taller one swearing profusely and telling the shorter one to, "Shut your mouth," as they were separated and loaded into the backs of police vehicles for the drive to Scottsdale.

It was only then that Aaron recognized the taller man.

He'd seen him in the feed store not two hours earlier, standing at the counter, chatting up the assistant manager.

Bells went off in Aaron's head. The feed store! It was a place where horse folk gathered and conversed, where announcements were posted on the bulletin board and where supplies were purchased and questions asked of the staff.

It was a place where someone intent on stealing horses might obtain all the information necessary to carry out their thefts. Especially if they had an accomplice, either a knowing or unknowing one.

By now, the two remaining vehicles had showed up. A half dozen uniformed law-enforcement officers surrounded the truck. Two more were searching the empty trailer. The sound of voices combined with radio transmissions and the choppy hum of the exiting helicopter to create a noisy din. Whatever horses had been in the area were long gone, retreating to an out of sight corner of the sanctuary.

"Eduardo." Aaron hailed his fellow deputy. "I'm leaving. You're in charge."

"Where are you going?"

"Following up a lead. And I need to hurry before word of this spreads."

"Got it."

Cara was still waiting at the first gate when Aaron dropped off Josh. Fully intending to track down the assistant manager, he took a few minutes to stop at the horse stables.

Mel wasn't in her truck where he'd told her to remain. Figured. He found her in the horse stall with the foal, bent over her small patient. Also figured.

"You aren't good at following orders."

She glanced up at him. "I saw the helicopter leaving and assumed the coast was clear."

"He doing any better?" Aaron moved toward the stall.

"Not at all." Sadness filled her voice. "It's been one thing after another with this poor little guy. I'm completely out of options. It's up to him now. He either decides to fight and live, or he gives up."

Aaron didn't have to be an expert to see the foal was at death's door. His eyes were listless, his coat dull, his ribs protruded and he hung his head low as if it were too heavy for his neck.

"I'm sorry to hear that."

"I take it you caught the bad guys?" Mel asked.

"They're being transported now and should spend at least one night in jail, courtesy of the county, before being arraigned."

"I'm glad."

She looked up from the foal and for the first time that night, smiled. "You did good, Aaron."

He stared at her, struck utterly speechless. Her worry over the foal accentuated her features and gave her a soft, glowing beauty. Aaron was enamored. Captivated. Charmed. In love.

The realization stunned him. He *was* in love with Mel and had been for some time.

She met his gaze, and the spark he often sensed between them crackled. She must feel the same. What else could account for the longing in her eyes?

The radio attached to his collar went off, reminding him that duty called. "I have to leave." Tear himself away was more accurate. "I'm following up on a lead."

"Okay. Be careful." When he didn't move, she asked, "Something wrong?"

Nothing he could tell her. Not right now. Later, if all went well.

"Do you happen to know the name of the assistant manager at the feed store?"

"It's Gail. Why?"

"She may have a connection to the horse thefts."

Mel gasped softly. "I don't believe it. She's always been so nice and helpful to me."

"I'm not saying she's involved, Only that she may know something useful to the investigation. I saw her and one of the thieves talking at the store earlier." Aaron took out the small pad and pen he always carried. "What's her last name?"

"Saunders. Her uncle owns the store. I have his number if you need it."

"That would help. Yes."

"I also know where she lives. It's not far from my house."

"Can you give me the address?"

"I'll do better than that. I'll show you."

"Not a chance, Mel. This is official business."

"And I'm someone with information who can assist with a case that's very important to me. To this whole town."

"I get that. But I'm not changing my mind."

She reluctantly relented and recited the address.

Radioing Shonda, Aaron instructed the rookie deputy to meet him at Gail's house. While he didn't anticipate trouble, it was always better to have backup.

"Go home and get some sleep," he told Mel when he was done.

"I will. In a while. I don't want to leave Cracker Jack alone."

"Cracker Jack?"

"He needed a name."

Because Mel didn't want the foal to die without one.

"I'll come back to check on you when I'm done," he said.

"You don't have to, Aaron." She hugged the foal's neck and then straightened.

Seeing the sorrow in her eyes, he wanted to kiss her. And would have if he thought she'd welcome it.

"Yes, I do," he said. If only to tell her how he felt.

Leaving her was hard and required all his willpower. But from the moment he walked out of the stables, his entire attention became focused on his job.

Approaching Gail's house, he noted the lights were on, which Aaron hoped meant she was home. A call to Shonda confirmed she was two minutes away. He parked along the curb and waited for her.

The moment Gail answered the door and saw him and Shonda, she burst into sobs. "Oh, God. I'm sorry. It's not my fault. I was played."

All right. Not just a source of information. She was involved.

"Ms. Saunders," Aaron said, "I'm going to need you to come with me to the station for questioning in connection with a series of horse thefts in the area."

"Am I under arrest?" she squeaked.

"No, ma'am." *Not yet.*

After more tears, she went in search of her purse and to make sure the cat had food, Aaron and Shonda accompanying her. She didn't ask to take her own vehicle. Rather she agreed to let Aaron drive her, which he hoped signaled her willingness to cooperate.

Aaron left her in the back seat to confer with Shonda and instruct her to follow him and Gail to the station.

The other deputy sighed. "I would have never pegged her as the type to associate with criminals. I feel strangely let down."

"Probably why she was able to pull it off. The least likely suspect."

Gail didn't say much during the fifteen-mile trip to the nearest Sheriff's office. Aaron anticipated pulling an all-nighter and phoned Nancy to let her know. She didn't sound as mad as she usually did. Perhaps they were making progress.

Four hours later, the chief deputy released him. Gail had confessed, even telling them where in the mountains the horse thieves had constructed a makeshift horse camp.

Aaron drove straight to the horse stables at The Small Change. Mel's truck wasn't there. No surprise. It was the middle of the night, and she'd no doubt gone home for some much-needed sleep.

That didn't stop the insecurities from assailing him. Weeks—if not months—late, he'd finally admitted to loving Mel. Only she was nowhere around to hear his declaration, and, at this hour, he didn't dare call or go beating on her front door.

He may well have lost her, and it would serve him right. Aaron had only himself to blame.

Chapter 14

Mel had been with Cracker Jack since 5:00 a.m.—two long, grueling hours ago. Ronnie had offered to call and reschedule all her appointments for the day, freeing up Mel to tend the foal.

On the outside, she maintained her composure. Inside, she was a wreck. The steps she'd taken were merely prolonging the inevitable. Cracker Jack had another day at the most. Possibly less.

"Please, please, sweetheart," she cooed, and scratched the foal between his ears. "Don't quit on me. If you would just try to stand."

Lying hastened his organs shutting down. Mel had already seen the beginning signs.

He did no more than slowly blink his unfocused eyes.

Within the last hour, his breathing had become labored, exhibiting an ominous, gravelly quality. Intravenously replacing the fluids lost due to his intestinal

A Baby for the Deputy

infection made no difference. The most Mel could—
and possibly should—do was make him comfortable.

The giant lump lodged in her throat burned as if she'd
swallowed a hot stone. This was highly unusual for her.
Sure, she'd wept before when a patient didn't survive. Mel
wasn't unfeeling. This time, her despair knew no bounds.

She could fault pregnancy hormones, but to blame
them entirely would be a lie. Mel suffered because she
hadn't healed from losing Aaron. She might never heal.
Then what? Find a new line of work?

"You look plumb tuckered out."

"Hi, Dad." Mel pushed to her feet from where she
knelt beside the foal, her bones aching and ready to snap
in two. She didn't bother trying to smile.

"You're here early. Pull an all-nighter?"

"I went home around midnight."

"And returned at five, I was told."

"This is an emergency."

"Mel, you have to take care of yourself. Think of
the baby."

"I'm planning on napping in the bunkhouse later, if
no one minds."

"You really should go home. Wearing yourself out
won't save that foal. Nature's going to take its course
regardless of what anyone does."

Mel bent and retrieved the thermos of coffee resting
in the open medical case. "Want some? It's just decaf
but at least it's hot."

"Decaf's great. Dolores has me cutting back to one
cup of regular coffee a day." He gave his head a dejected
shake. "She's torturing me."

"She loves you."

"For no good reason I can fathom. Did Samantha tell

you she entered the Richland County Fair Rodeo next week? Theo's giving me a couple days off."

"No, and good for her."

Mel's youngest sister now had two wins under her belt, a first and a third place. She'd stopped helping Mel as much, focusing on training with Ronnie and babysitting Frankie's girls. Mel was happy for the teenager, though she'd have to find someone else to assist her. Or cut back on her practice—the least favorable option, as far as she was concerned.

Aaron wouldn't agree. He'd been nagging her a lot recently about working less. She supposed she should be glad they were talking and that he cared enough to nag. She might have to break down and hire part-time help to quiet him.

She stretched and rubbed the small of her back. "Been a long twenty-four hours."

"Heard you helped with rounding up those good-for-nothing horse thieves," her father said. "Lots of happy people today."

"They're not convicted yet."

"They will be. Caught red-handed from what Josh says."

"I'm just glad it's over." No more foals left motherless.

"How's Aaron?" Her father glanced around. "Thought he might be here."

So had Mel. "In bed, probably. He had a longer night than any of us."

What would it be like waking up next to him? They'd never experienced that and likely wouldn't. For a moment before he left to talk to Gail, Mel had sensed a change in him and hope flared—only to have it extinguished.

Why was it she and Aaron seemed destined to always be on the wrong track at different times? Now, permanently.

"It's a shame things didn't work out between you and him," her father said. "He's a good man."

"Guess it wasn't meant to be."

"Don't reckon you'd patch things up, given the chance?"

Yes.

"I'm not sure that's what he wants." Mel glanced down at Cracker Jack. There had been no change in the last five minutes.

"Nancy's coming to dinner this week. You mind?"

Her father's offhand remark got her attention. "No. Why would I?"

"Could be awkward."

"She and Dolores are friends."

"Nancy knows about the baby. She mentioned it when she and Dolores were on the phone last night."

So, Aaron had finally told her. "Really."

"Dolores said she acted like she didn't mind. But here's the interesting part. She mentioned a duplex apartment one of their Bunko ladies has for rent."

"Oh." That surprised Mel.

Was Nancy moving out to give Aaron space for when the baby came or because they'd fought over Mel? She was curious, though uncertain if she should ask.

The foal suddenly made a pathetic wuffling sound. Mel bent and petted his neck, noting his hide was losing its elasticity.

"I wish there was more I could do."

"Have you tried giving him honey?" her father asked.

"Yes. Twice." Mel didn't usually subscribe to home remedies. This time, however, she'd been desperate.

"What about salt? They say if you rub the inside of

a foal's mouth with salt, it'll make him thirsty and encourage him to drink."

Mel studied Cracker Jack. He was lying on his side in the soft sawdust bedding. She looked closer to make sure his narrow chest was expanding and contracting. "I'm not sure he's strong enough to drink anymore."

"Might be time to let him go."

She knew her father was right; she just didn't have the willpower to walk away. Mel vowed if he started to suffer, she would make the difficult decision all vets dreaded.

"How did Theo take the news of the horse thieves' capture?" Small talk kept her spirits from sinking any lower.

"Blames himself for not being here."

The Small Change owner was still in the hospital, receiving treatment for his fall, though he was expected to be released before the coming weekend.

"That's ridiculous," Mel said.

"Of course it is."

"You talk to Gail's uncle? How's he doing?"

"He's devastated, naturally. Can't believe she betrayed him and the ranchers. He'd have sold the store years ago if not for her. She's his right hand. Or was. Almost like a daughter to him."

"I can't imagine what he's feeling."

Then again, maybe she could. A little, anyway. Mel had felt betrayed when she learned about Samantha and Carrie Anne. Eventually, she'd come to understand and forgive her father. She had Aaron to thank for that valuable lesson.

Seems one good thing had come out of their relationship. Two, counting the baby.

Her father started to speak, only to pause. His cell phone must've been on vibrate for he removed it from his pocket and answered with a robust, "Ray Hartman speaking."

She watched his expression change by degrees as he listened, going from interest to shock to excitement.

"Right," he said, grinning broadly. "Be there as soon as I can."

"What's going on?" Mel asked.

"The horse thieves had a makeshift holding camp on the east side of the mountain, about a mile from Javelina Crossing. Gail told the authorities all about it."

"I know. Aaron left me a text message."

According to Gail, when the thieves stole enough horses to fill a stock trailer, they would transport them to a slaughterhouse across the state line that didn't ask a lot of questions. Mel was appalled. She was also shocked that someone she dealt with on a regular basis and had liked was involved.

"Well, believe it or not," her dad said, "Game and Fish rangers were able to locate the holding camp. Five horses are there."

The number screamed at Mel. "Five?"

"All mares. Could be they're the pregnant ones stolen from the maternity pasture."

Cracker Jack's dam might be among them!

"The rangers are sending me directions. I'm headed out there now with a truck and trailer."

Mel scrambled to collect her equipment. "I'm coming with you!"

"'Fraid not, honey."

"The mares might require medical attention," she insisted.

"Which you'll give them the moment I return. But, for now, you're needed here." He entered the stall and took her by the shoulders. "You keep that foal alive for a couple more hours. You hear me?"

His words fired Mel's determination. She could do

it. She could keep Cracker Jack alive. She refused to entertain the thought of anything else.

"Hurry, Dad."

He left, and Mel wasted no time tending to her patient. The wait was excruciating. Thirty minutes later, Samantha unexpectedly showed up.

"Can I help?" she asked.

"I thought you were babysitting."

"Nancy's watching the girls."

Would wonders never cease?

Mel gave her sister a look. "Did Dad send you?"

"He called and told me what happened. Coming here was my idea."

The teenager's sincerity touched Mel, making refusing her impossible. Besides, she'd recently grown fond of having her youngest sibling tagging along.

"You don't by chance have a box of salt," she asked.

Samantha looked at her strangely. "Salt?"

"It's Dad's idea. Run to the ranch house and ask whoever's there if we can borrow some. I think I saw the housekeeper's car pull in a little while ago."

Mel and Samantha kept up a constant conversation with Cracker Jack, assuring him that his mother was on her way, even though Mel didn't know for sure. Calls to her father went straight to voice mail, but that was expected, considering he was at the base of the mountain.

Finally, at long last, Mel heard the rumble and clang of a heavily loaded livestock trailer. Samantha ran down the aisle, returning moments later to report the good news.

"It's them! They're here."

Mel bent and, cradling Cracker Jack's small head between her hands, she kissed his warm nose. "Stay with us, sweetheart."

As if he understood, the foal opened his eyes and

blew out a weak breath that felt like the brush of dandelion fluff on Mel's face.

She couldn't wait. Together, she and Samantha left the stall and went out to where her father had parked the truck and trailer in front of the stables. The doors of the truck flew open and several ranch hands spilled out, along with her father.

That wasn't what had Mel's undivided attention, however. She stared at the SUV with the official logo on the side parked behind the trailer. The one with the driver behind the steering wheel wearing a familiar dark Stetson and aviator sunglasses.

Aaron was halfway out of the SUV when Mel reached him. Her riotously pounding heart made speaking difficult, and she needed a moment to recover.

"Wh-what are you doing here?" she managed.

"I went with the Game and Fish rangers to retrieve the horses. They're considered live evidence and will be held in a secure facility until the trial is finished, if there is a trial."

"Did the thieves confess?"

"No. I wouldn't be surprised if they eventually accepted a plea agreement. Gail's statement is pretty damning."

"Will she get in trouble?" Mel was thinking of the feed store owner.

"Her confession and willingness to testify will go a long way in reducing her charges."

"I still can't believe she was involved."

"According to her, she wasn't in on it from the beginning. She genuinely believed Monty Schartz—he's one of the two perpetrators—was romantically interested in her and that his questions about her job and the goings-on in town were because he cared."

In her early forties, living alone, divorced for over fifteen years, no children. It was easy for Mel to see how Gail might have been taken advantage of by a man pretending to like her.

"Eventually," Aaron said, "she figured out what was going on."

"Why didn't she turn this Monty and his partner in?"

"She claimed by then she was afraid of him and what he might do to her."

"Poor Gail. She must have felt vulnerable and in over her head."

Aaron had been in deputy mode since arriving. Now, his expression softened around the edges as he met her gaze. "I can't say much more. This is a pending investigation."

"I understand." Throwing caution to the wind, she touched his arm. "You must be exhausted."

Lines of tension marred his handsome face, and weariness showed in his eyes when he removed his aviators.

For a long minute, they simply stood there. Mel willed him to say the words she yearned to hear. The ones that would erase all her doubts and allow her to reveal what was in her heart.

"Mel. I—"

He was cut off when one of the ranch hands lowered the rear gate on the trailer with a metallic bang. Inside the trailer, the restless horses stomped and shifted and kicked. The nearest one lifted her head high and whinnied shrilly. In the enclosed space, the sound was deafening.

Samantha hopped onto the trailer's running board and peeked inside. Ignoring their father's warning to be careful, she reached her arm through the opening and petted one of the mares.

"I'd better help with the unloading," Mel said.

"Right." Aaron put on his sunglasses and returned to his SUV. Standing by the open driver's door, he spoke into his radio.

Mel sighed, wishing she knew what he'd been about to say to her.

The first mare backed out of the large trailer and down the ramp, spinning around the instant her hooves made contact with the ground. A ranch hand grabbed hold of her lead rope before she could get away.

Mel quickly assessed the mare. She wasn't Cracker Jack's dam. And other than a few nicks and cuts and a thick layer of dirt, she appeared to be in good shape. The ranch hand led her off to the maternity corral for a long drink of water and all the hay she could eat.

The next three mares looked much the same and were equally excited to be home. By the time the last mare was unloaded, Mel was at her wit's end. But with a shiny copper coat, four matching white stockings and a rounded udder hanging low, there was little doubt Cracker Jack and his mama were about to be reunited.

Jerking hard on the lead rope, the mare gave Mel's father a difficult time.

"I'll take her, Dad."

"You sure? She's a handful."

"She's just looking for her baby."

He passed her the lead rope. "I'll be by once we get these other girls settled in. Cara's already waiting. Called me three times."

Mel started walking toward the stables. As she rounded the corner, she glanced back to see her father shaking hands with Aaron. He must be thanking Aaron for the help. At the last second, they broke into laughter. When had they become so chummy?

The impatient mare practically dragged Mel along as they entered the stables.

"I know." Mel held the mare to a walk when she would've trotted ahead. "I'm in a rush, too."

"Mind if I come?"

Hearing Aaron's voice behind her had Mel stopping in her tracks, much to the mare's consternation. Mel had expected him to leave, but he hadn't. Instead, he'd come after her. Ran, apparently. She warned herself not to make more of this than there was.

"Wouldn't you rather go home?" she asked. "Kaylee must be waiting."

"What, and miss the big reunion?" He caught up with her, and together with the mare they started for the stall.

She shoved her disappointment aside. He'd been concerned about the foal. Not her.

As they neared the stall, Mel fervently hoped the mare hadn't been returned only to see her baby die. She must have suddenly smelled the foal for she broke free of Mel's grip and charged ahead the last twenty feet, ramming her large, broad body into the stall door. Nickering loudly, she pranced in place and anxiously bobbed her head.

Mel and Aaron hurried. Hearing a feeble greeting from inside the stall, she nearly let out a sigh. Cracker Jack was still alive and recognized his mama.

"Be careful," Aaron warned when Mel squeezed in front of the mare.

Opening the stall door, she tripped while getting out of the way before the mare rushed in, whinnying more softly now. Stopping in front of Cracker Jack, she lowered her head and sniffed him. He tried to rise, only his weak legs refused to support him.

"Are you okay?" Aaron pulled Mel aside, though she was no longer in any danger.

"Fine." She'd bumped her elbow on the stall door but hardly noticed the slight sting. She was too worried about Cracker Jack.

Concern flashed in Aaron's eyes, and he held her arm. "What about the baby?"

"Really, I'm fine. I just lost my balance for a second."

"You should get checked out by a doctor."

"And you're overreacting."

"I'm insisting. Visit the clinic at least," he said. "I'll go with you."

He was being ridiculous. And adorable. She considered visiting the clinic if only to spend more time with him.

Cracker Jack suddenly positioned his front feet beneath him and struggled to rise. Falling back with a grunt, he blew out an exhausted breath. His mother nudged him with her warm nose.

"He can't stand without help." Breaking away from Aaron, Mel went into the stall.

He followed her in. "Careful. She might kick or bite you."

It was good advice. The mare's instincts were to protect her baby. Help could be perceived as a threat.

Aaron's concerns turned out to be unfounded. The mare allowed Mel to lift Cracker Jack to a standing position. With Aaron supporting the foal's hind end, she pushed his nose toward his mama's udder and waited.

Despite being separated for several weeks, the mare still had milk, though it might take several days for her to produce enough to meet Cracker Jack's needs.

Unfortunately, he was too weak to latch on, try as he might.

"Come on, sweetheart," Mel coaxed.

"What if he won't eat?" Aaron asked.

Mel continued nudging Cracker Jack. "Then I'll see if he'll drink from a bucket or bottle. Now that he's with his mama, there's a chance he'll fight. He's already more alert and responsive."

The mare swung her large head around and nuzzled Cracker Jack, ignoring Aaron. The next moment, the foal summoned all his strength and finally latched on.

"He's nursing!" Mel exclaimed.

Aaron grinned. "Well, I'll be."

Cracker Jack let go a couple minutes later. Completely depleted, he lay back down, his mama standing guard. Mel didn't complain. Emotional nourishment was just as important as physical nourishment.

She quickly poured what manufactured mare's milk remained from earlier into a shallow pan and set it under Cracker Jack's nose. He drank about a cup. Not much, but more than Mel could have dreamed possible two hours ago. She'd try again once the foal had rested.

"You're crying," Aaron said softly.

"Am I?" She wiped at her cheeks with the back of her hand.

He came over to her. Tilting her chin up, he brushed away her tears with the pad of his thumb. "He's going to be all right."

"He still has a long road ahead, but I think he'll make it."

"Like us." Aaron's eyes roved over her face as if drinking in every detail.

"Aaron…"

He didn't let her finish. Drawing her into the aisle, he pulled her close. "When I was here last night, watching you with the foal, I realized something." He lowered his head until his mouth was inches from hers. "Something important."

"What?" Her pulse beat faster.

"I love you, Mel."

"You do?" She wanted to throw herself into his arms, but she resisted, requiring more from him than a declaration. "What changed your mind?"

"I'm pretty sure I've been falling for you since the moment we met. I was just too stupid to admit it. And too scared."

"Of Nancy?"

"Hardly." He laughed. "She's indomitable, but I'm tougher." He put an arm around her waist, anchoring her to him. "I was afraid that what I was feeling was fleeting. Or that you couldn't possibly love me in return."

"You're right." The wall she'd erected around her heart to shield herself from hurt crumbled to pieces. "You are stupid."

"Trust me." He brushed his lips across hers. "I've smartened up considerably in the last day. The next time I propose, I'll do such an incredible job, there's no way you'll say no."

"Next time?"

"I want to marry you, Mel. Not because it's the right thing for our baby, though it is, but because I love you and can't stand the thought of not spending every day for the rest of my life with you."

She very much liked the sound of that.

He kissed her then, delicately and tenderly. "First, however, we date. Then, after we've gotten to know each other, we'll get ready for the baby."

"You don't say?"

He'd suggested dating before, but Mel hadn't been ready. The last two miserable weeks had her reconsidering. The last few minutes had her changing her mind completely.

She mustered her courage and stared into his eyes. There, shining bright and true, was the love she'd been wanting and waiting for her whole life.

"I love you, too." There, she'd said it.

"Are you free tonight?"

She smiled, joy filling her to bursting. "Are you asking me out?"

"I'm starting with asking you out. I may work up to more as the night goes on. Keep in mind, I still have a ring."

Mel didn't hesitate. "Yes, I'm free." And she'd say yes to anything else he suggested.

His lips met hers then, making silent promises for tonight and the wonderful, beautiful future in store for them. Whatever problems they faced, and there were many, Mel was confident she and Aaron would overcome them. They were a family now—Mel, Aaron, Kaylee and the baby.

How silly Mel had been to resist a committed relationship. As she and Aaron kissed and kissed, unable to get enough of each other, Mel couldn't imagine anything better than joining her life with his, forever and ever.

* * * * *

USA TODAY bestselling author **Mary Leo** grew up
in south Chicago in the tangle of a big Italian family.
She's worked in Hollywood, Las Vegas and Silicon
Valley. Currently she lives in Las Vegas with her
husband, author Terry Watkins, and their sweet
kitty, Sophie. Visit her website at maryleo.com.

Books by Mary Leo

Harlequin Western Romance

A Cowboy in Her Arms
A Cowboy to Kiss

Harlequin American Romance

Falling for the Cowboy
Aiming for the Cowboy
Christmas with the Rancher
Her Favorite Cowboy
A Christmas Wedding for the Cowboy

Visit the Author Profile page at
Harlequin.com for more titles.

A BABY FOR THE SHERIFF

Mary Leo

For darling Elena, who contacts me every day to see how I'm doing, who surprises me with thoughtful gifts and who is a constant delight.

And for my son, Rich, who fell in love with her.

Chapter 1

The wine was poured. The fire burned bright in the hearth. Doctor Coco Grant, the town's vet, had painted her toenails, donned extra makeup, chosen her most seductive underwear—the blush lace panties and bra she'd bought anticipating this moment—slipped into her sexiest black dress and even shaved her legs.

All of it done in preparation for her date with Russ Knightly, the potential new mayor of Briggs, Idaho, and one of the most sought-after eligible bachelors for a hundred miles. At thirty-three, he would be the youngest mayor of Briggs, and the one man in the entire county whom Coco had lusted over for the past five years while he dated several other women. One of them he'd even proposed to. Fortunately for Coco, that engagement didn't last more than a few weeks.

Now it was Coco's turn…the woman he was meant

to be with, the woman he would love like no other, the woman for whom he was about to fulfill all her sexual fantasies in one hot night, and the woman she hoped would one day be referred to as Doctor Coco Knightly, the mayor's wife. Her family, especially her brother, Carson, admired Russ. Carson had been sponsored by the Knightly Endowment for the Preservation of Western Culture when he had first started competing as a bronc rider in local rodeos.

Coco had been smitten ever since Russ, and a few other cowboys, rescued a small herd of wild horses trapped up in the Teton Mountains. Russ had risked his life to go up there and lead those animals out, under severe avalanche warnings for the area.

Ever since that moment, she thought Russ Knightly was a kindred spirit who loved and respected animals as much as she did. He was simply the bravest man alive, or at least the bravest man in Briggs, next to her brother and her dad, of course.

"I've been thinking about you all day," Russ said as he walked backward to her bedroom, pulling her along with one hand, the other caressing his glass of expensive scotch, a scotch that Coco had ordered online just for this occasion, a fifteen-year-old scotch she knew he would love.

"Me, too," she told him as she eagerly followed him, aroused by the mere idea of what was about to happen in her once lonely bedroom.

She and Russ had been dating for almost two months, thanks to an official introduction by her brother, but because of her schedule and his mayoral campaign, they hadn't found the time to take their relationship to the next level.

Tonight, they would break through all those levels with pure lust, pure sex and pure seduction. At twenty-nine, Coco hadn't really experienced a lot of sex, especially not the kind that Russ Knightly was noted for. She'd been too busy with her studies, volunteering and dreaming about Russ to care much about dating other guys.

But all that was in her past now. Tonight the floodgates were open, and each time he touched her a fire ignited that she didn't want to put out anytime soon.

Heck, Coco had even locked her little dog, Punky, a Yorkshire terrier, in the bathroom. For some reason she couldn't understand, Punky didn't seem to like Russ, and growled whenever he came close to Coco.

Well, there would be none of that tonight.

Tonight Coco and Russ would be so close they might need the Jaws of Life to pull them apart.

"I have plans for you, baby, plans for your body," he muttered in a deep voice.

She loved it when he called her *baby*.

"What kind of plans?" she teased, loving how he made her feel all tingly.

"Dirty plans that will make you blush whenever you think about our first night."

"I'm already blushing," she demurely said. "And I have my own plans."

That was a complete fabrication. The only plans she'd had that day were how to foal a breached horse and what kind of drugs she would administer to Helen Granger's horse, Tater, for the infection in his right front femur.

Russ stopped, pulled her in tight and kissed her. Although Coco's mind sometimes drifted whenever they kissed, she felt certain once they were in bed together her focus would laser in on the task at hand—not that making love to Russ was a task. What she meant was, once they were in bed together, nothing else would matter and she'd be able to surrender to the moment.

Of course it would be that way, she told herself. He was the man she wanted to be with forever. The man she'd dreamed about, longed for and pictured as the father of her children.

Russ Knightly was her man, her guy, her Mr. Right.

As he pulled her in tighter and she felt the bulge of his manhood press against her body, her heart raced, and suddenly all she could think of was how this was finally going to happen. She was going to make love with her dream man. Life couldn't get any better if it had been scripted.

Until the doorbell rang for her animal clinic downstairs. She'd only recently, in the last eight months, finished construction on the two-thousand-foot expansion. She'd had proper ventilation installed, added to the reception area and incorporated two large pens for the livestock she inevitably took in. She'd been thinking of hiring another doctor to help out, but so far, she hadn't made the time to begin the search…a fact she now found herself regretting.

Russ kept his lips pressed to hers as if he hadn't heard it.

"I… I, um, I should get that," she mumbled while his lips stuck to hers.

"Not tonight. Whoever it is will go away."

The bell rang again.

"Or not," she said, trying to disengage from him. It

felt as though his lips were glued to hers and she couldn't unstick them.

"I…really…need…to…get…that."

He finally stepped back and Coco swore their lips popped apart. "You're not seriously going to leave me here like this while you answer the door."

He nodded down toward the bulge in his pants, which for some odd reason was no longer doing it for her. Not when she knew someone's animal could be in crisis.

"I'm sorry," she said, slipping out from his embrace, "but as much as I would like to, I can't ignore the bell. It wouldn't be right. If someone's trudged through all that snow and cold, I have no choice but to at least answer the door."

He glanced at his watch. "It's ten o'clock at night. Nobody just brings over their sick animal at this time of night without calling first."

"All the more reason why I need to get that. It's probably an emergency."

Coco ran a hand through her hair, placed her wineglass on the table and turned to dash down the stairs to answer the door.

The bell rang again.

"Persistent, aren't they?" he said, sounding resentful.

She turned back to him. "I'll only be a minute. I'm sure it's something minor and I'll be able to fix it in no time."

But Coco wasn't so sure. Usually whenever her doorbell rang this late, someone was leaving behind an unwanted or sick pet they could no longer care for. She flipped on the light switch in the stairwell and through the glass on the top half of the door caught the shadow of a woman wearing a puffy coat and hood as she walked away.

"Oh, shoot," she said aloud, knowing full well it was a drop-off. She already had a piglet named Jimmy, two baby goats, one puppy, two persnickety calico kittens, an adult tortoise named Tortie and two temperamental baby llamas taking shelter in her clinic. She'd find homes for all of them eventually, but at the moment, the farm animals were illegal within city limits, and if Sheriff Jet Wilson—who did everything by the book— learned about them, he'd issue her another fine on top of the last two she couldn't afford to pay. She'd spent all her savings on the expansion.

When she arrived at the bottom of the stairs, she grabbed the gray sweater that hung on a hook next to the door and slipped it on. Whatever was waiting for her on the other side of that door was more than likely going to require her standing out in the cold for a minute or two before she could wrangle it inside.

Good thing she still wore her shoes, albeit three-inch heels, but shoes nonetheless.

"Okay, what do we have this time?" she asked as she swung open the door expecting another goat or llama or...

Sheriff Jet Wilson fought his way back to the jail. The official white SUV, with the Briggs Sheriff's Department logo emblazoned on the two front doors, was fishtailing at almost every turn. The snow was piling up fast now, and driving was nearing impossible. Benny Snoots, the town's one and only official snowplow driver, worked as fast as he could, but the snow was just too much for him.

Russ Knightly, a man Jet Wilson didn't much like, promised two more snowplows if he was elected mayor, and on a night like this, Jet considered giving him his vote...or not.

If, on the other hand, Mayor Sally Hickman won again, Jet would make sure at least one more snow-plow was on her agenda, and if it wasn't, he promised himself he'd take up the cause himself and add plow-ing capability to the front of the SUV.

When he finally pulled up in front of the small jail-house, he parked curbside and got out. His very first step encased his cowboy boots in so much snow that it slipped inside his boots and made a mess of his nice warm woolen socks. He grabbed the bags of food that he'd picked up at Sammy's Smokehouse off the back seat, slammed the doors shut and headed for the front of the jail. None of the townsfolk knew he was living at the jail these days and no one needed to know.

A water pipe had burst in his apartment earlier that week, and until his landlord could get it fixed and re-pair the damage to the floor and the wall, Jet didn't have anywhere else to go...at least nowhere he could afford. All the rooms in this town were too pricey for him and, well, he didn't want to impose on what few friends he had.

Being relatively new to Briggs, having lived there for less than two years, making friends had been tough. Especially since he'd ticked off Russ Knightly, who seemed to be a big deal in town, next to Carson Grant, the town's one and only rodeo hero. Jet admired Car-son, and had met him a few times, but Russ was an-other story entirely. He hadn't meant to make him mad, but the guy had been doing seventy-five in a fifty-five-mile zone, had a taillight out and was missing his front license plate when Jet had pulled him over. Idaho required two license plates, no matter what kind of vehicle you drove, and besides, the guy had way too much attitude for Jet's liking.

Little had Jet known that Russ seemed to pull all the important strings in town, and in the state, for that matter, and when you were merely a small-town sheriff, those strings could get pretty tight.

In the end, his violations had somehow been dismissed, and Jet had ended up the bad guy.

Of course, at the moment, Jet didn't give a hoot. The jail suited him just fine, thank you very much. The bed in the cell was comfortable enough, and rarely used, so he thought he'd break it in for a few days.

He swung open the heavy front door, hit the light switch, slipped out of his bulky parka and cowboy hat, tugged off his boots and his wet socks, sat down at his desk inside his small office and tore open the bags of delicious-smelling barbecue. His mouth instantly watered in anticipation. He hadn't eaten all day, and his stomach had started aching about three hours ago from lack of food. The pungent smells filled the room as Jet cracked open a can of beer and took a long pull.

He was in for the night, and it felt good to finally be free of all responsibilities. He took a big bite of one of the beef ribs, ripping the meat off the bone with his teeth, groaned his delight and walked over to put his wet socks on the old radiator under the bank of windows so they could dry. All the blinds were closed, so no one could see him, not that there was anyone out there looking on a night like this. Still it gave him comfort to be hidden from view for a while. He walked back to the desk, took another big bite and was just about to sit down and settle in when the phone rang…his phone, in his pocket. The phone that he kept private, and only a handful of people had the number.

That phone rang.

The jailhouse phone had an all-night service for any emergency calls, but that wasn't ringing.

He felt the sigh that seemed to come up from his bare feet before he heard it expel from his throat as he pulled his phone out of his pocket and checked the screen.

Doctor Coco Grant's name lit up the black screen along with the picture he'd taken of her in front of her illegal goat pen inside her clinic.

Part of him didn't want to answer, but he knew if she was calling this late at night, it must be important.

Frankly, he didn't want to hear about "important" right now, not in the middle of what had to be the best barbecue ribs Sammy had ever created.

He chewed and swallowed.

"Hello," he reluctantly said into his phone.

"Hi, Sheriff. Sorry to bother you this late, but I've got a situation over here that requires your attention."

He glanced up at the large clock above the front door knowing perfectly well that whatever it was that required his attention would take him at least another hour or more and it was already going on ten thirty.

"Can I give it my attention over the phone? It's pretty nasty out there tonight, and it's late. Besides, if someone left you another goat or any other farm animal, there's nothing either one of us can do about it tonight."

"It's not a goat, Sheriff. It's a baby."

As he took another bite of a rib, sauce dripped down his fingers and landed on his shirt and lap—bright red sauce that stained everything it touched. He cursed under his breath as he tried to wipe it up.

"You don't have to get nasty about it," she said in his ear.

"No. I wasn't talking to you. It's just that… Look, let's call a truce for tonight. I don't care what kind of illegal baby critter someone left you. We can deal with it another time, just not right now."

"If you don't want to do your job, fine, but you should know it's not a critter of any kind this time. It's a baby, as in a human baby. A little girl named Lily. She's about two weeks old from what I can tell and in desperate need of a diaper change, which I think I can do with an old T-shirt. But some real diapers would be nice. And some formula, and a new outfit, cause she soiled this one and wrapping her in something of mine isn't a real option."

He didn't know what to say or how to respond. He'd never dealt with an abandoned baby before. He'd have to read up on it, or at the very least call someone over in Boise to give him a quick rundown of protocol.

"Hello. Hello. Hello. Are you there?" she said, sounding agitated.

He finally took a breath. "Did you say a baby girl?"

"Yes. An infant, and from what I can tell, the only note we have is written on the back of a restaurant receipt from Sammy's Smokehouse with Lily's name on it and nothing else."

He stood, raking a hand through his hair while trying to gather his thoughts. Then he said, "I'll be right over."

"Why is she crying so much?" Russ asked for the umpteenth time as he awkwardly held baby Lily by her head and butt, flying her back and forth like he was getting ready to propel her through the air. "Is she sick? Maybe she's got something really wrong with her?"

"Or maybe it's the way you're holding her. Haven't you held a baby before?"

Coco walked over and took Lily, carefully folding the baby into her arms. At once, Lily calmed down as Coco gently spoke to her and naturally bounced with each step, trying to soothe the fretful child.

"There has to be something wrong with her. She smells horrible. I don't want to get too close, what with all the events I have coming up in the next week. I can't afford to be sick."

He was right about the events, at least five that she knew of, and three of them she would be attending alongside him.

So no, he couldn't get sick, but she really didn't think that baby Lily had anything physically wrong with her other than needing a diaper change and maybe a bottle.

Coco knew how to treat and care for animals, but what she knew about babies couldn't fill one page. She was going on instinct here, and what she'd seen her sisters do. Sure, she'd held their babies, but she'd never changed a diaper nor had she ever had to soothe the little darlings or feed them. She'd successfully avoided all of that...up until now.

"She's a baby. Babies poop and pee. It's not her fault she smells. She just needs her diaper changed."

"Can you do that?" His forehead furrowed as if the mere thought of changing a diaper made him nauseous.

"I could if I had a diaper or even an old T-shirt or a dishcloth, but I don't think I own any safety pins. We'll just have to bear it until the sheriff gets here with supplies."

"Well, you can at least strip her down and clean her up, then maybe wrap her in a clean blanket."

From the tortured look on Russ's face, Coco thought she should do just that, or what was left of her date night might end right now.

"Okay. Let me see what I can put together," she reassured him. "Not that I wanted to call him in the first place—we could have simply called Child Welfare or the hospital or anyone other than Sheriff Wilson...even his deputy would have been better. There's no telling what that man might do with a baby."

"Don't be ridiculous. He'll do what he's been trained to do with an abandoned baby...whatever that is."

"You know how that man is with the animals that get left on my doorstep. I'm still paying the fines for keeping some of them longer than the city will allow. If it were up to him, he'd turn them all over to the animal shelter in Idaho Falls, where they'd be put down if no one claimed them in seventy-two hours, sooner if they're overcrowded. The man has no heart."

"He's just doing his job, as I'm sure he will with Billy."

"Her name is Lily. Why can't you remember that?"

"I don't know. Does it really matter? She can't understand me."

Lily let out a blood-curdling wail.

"I actually think she can. Or at least she doesn't like the tone of your voice."

Coco pulled the baby in tighter.

"Okay. Okay," he whispered. "Is this better?"

Coco bounced Lily and she quieted down. The little darling seemed to like motion, so Coco kept it going.

"Yes, thank you."

Coco walked to her bedroom with Lily fussing on Coco's shoulder, but she seemed to want to calm herself. She squeaked and cooed instead of wailing, a definite improvement. Once inside her bedroom, Coco contemplated putting Lily down on her bed, the bed she'd bought new silky sheets for, and sprayed with perfume, and surrounded with candlelight. The bed she and Russ would make love on until her body ached and she cried out for more.

The bedroom that had been set up for sin.

That bedroom where she now flipped the switch for the overhead light and blew out the candles…at least for now.

She carefully laid squirming baby Lily down on the scented bed while trying to soothe her with soft-spoken words, which weren't working. She walked to her bathroom and prepared a couple warm washcloths and then brought along a couple fluffy clean towels—new towels that she'd also picked up for the shower she and Russ would take together after hours of making love.

So much for all her sexy plans.

Of course, the night was still relatively young. Anything could happen.

Placing one towel under Lily and keeping one handy to wrap her in, Coco began to undress the little sweetheart, who had stopped fussing when Coco started singing the first song that came into her head, "Happy Birthday."

"I'd offer to help," Russ said, coming up behind her, "but I'm horrible with kids, especially babies. Plus, I don't know the first thing about changing a diaper."

"And you think I do?" Coco said as she gently wiped off Lily's soiled bottom. Russ made a few disgusted grunts and turned away.

Coco knew enough from birthing livestock to keep hold of Lily's arms while she cleaned her. Newborns of any kind liked to be touched and held whenever something else was happening to them. This one little action seemed to soothe her, exactly like it soothed a foal.

"You're a woman," Russ announced as if that fact had any relevance in this situation.

"What's that supposed to mean?"

"It's in your DNA. Besides, you deal with babies all the time."

"There's a big difference between a puppy or a foal and a little baby girl, an abandoned baby girl. Poor sweetheart doesn't know what to think…do you, sweet Lily?"

Lily made a couple complaints, but then settled when Coco began singing "Happy Birthday" again.

"Where's that sheriff? He should've been here by now." Russ walked up behind Coco and ran his hands down her body. Normally a great sensation, and a real turn-on, but not while Coco was trying to clean up baby poop. "We need to pick up where we left off."

She moved away from him, leaning in closer to Lily, who was now nice and clean and smelling of new baby, a delightful scent if there ever was one.

"I don't know if that's possible tonight, Russ. The mood has sort of been broken."

Coco swaddled Lily as best she could inside the soft white towel, then picked her up, cradling her tight against her chest, her little rosebud mouth suckling the air.

"Not really. I know how we can get it back again."

"How?"

He leaned in and kissed her with one of those sin-

ful kisses that might have brought her to her knees…
if it wasn't for the warm trickle of liquid that now ran
down between her breasts.

Sheriff Wilson wasn't about to drive over to Dr.
Grant's clinic without all the supplies she'd asked for,
and then some. He'd taken care of enough babies in his
life to know exactly what she needed. Plus, he knew
enough about the system to know that the chances of his
being able to drop off a baby with the appropriate authorities at this time of night, with all this snow, were slim to
none. After he'd changed out of his uniform into more
casual wear, he'd made a few phone calls, and the only
words of encouragement he'd gotten were *keep her warm*.

Driving down Main Street was proving to be a challenge, despite his being the only actual vehicle on the
road. Even Travis Granger, who maneuvered his red
sleigh and Clydesdales, picking up any stranded pedes-
trians, was having a time of it. The two men nodded to
each other as they passed, silently acknowledging that
Briggs was in for it tonight.

By the time Sheriff Wilson tried to pull his SUV
curbside on Main Street, then trudge up to the glass
front door of Whipple's One Stop and push on the bell
that rang inside the Whipple apartment upstairs, he
felt the tension intensify in his neck and shoulders. Jet
braced himself for what was sure to be the third degree
from Cindy Whipple, proprietor and one of the biggest
town gossips. Not only was she a gossip, but she had
town radar and could usually figure out what someone
was trying desperately to hide. She had the uncanny
ability to guess exactly what was going on before anyone could tell her the truth.

A sweet woman with a heart of gold, but she couldn't keep a secret if God came down and asked her personally.

Within moments, a soft light came on inside the store, illuminating the frozen-food section located in the back. Jet and Cindy locked eyes for a moment before she disappeared behind the produce shelves.

When the glass door finally swung open, bells chiming overhead, Cindy Whipple greeted him wearing a fuzzy red robe and matching slippers. Her short white hair stuck out in strange angles, as if she'd just come out of a windstorm, and her horn-rimmed glasses were askew on her wizened face. But her lips were perfectly smeared with red lipstick. Ms. Whipple never went out in public without her bright red lipstick in place. And, apparently, that went for answering the door late at night.

"Sheriff Wilson! What in blazes are you doing out here so late? Did somebody die? Is there a big accident somewhere and you need medical supplies? Because I can give you a deal you won't believe."

"No, nothing like that, but is it possible that you could open your store for me? I know it's late, ma'am, but I would really appreciate getting a few things."

"I take it this is some kind of emergency, or you wouldn't be standing here. Are you going to tell me what happened or is it a secret?"

He decided to play along. "Yes, it's a secret, and I can't tell anyone about it. Not even you."

"Me? I'm Fort Knox," she said with a chuckle.

If only that were true.

"Good, because I'm depending on you not to ask me any questions. I promised I wouldn't say a word."

"Absolutely. Not one question. Not a word. My lips are sealed." She slipped two fingers across her pursed lips, as if she was zipping them up. "Now, what do you need?"

He was hoping he could get out of there without giving her any details. At this point, that was about all he could hope for.

"Baby formula, newborn diapers, a few of those onesies, some undershirts, a couple baby bottles, nipples, a little knit hat and blankets, lots of those small baby blankets," he told her all in one breath. "Oh, and baby wipes, several containers of baby wipes."

Her eyes went wide, and she straightened up her glasses. "Now, why on earth are you in here buying up baby supplies?"

"You promised no questions. I'm depending on you."

"But…"

He tilted his head and gave her a look.

She took a step back and let out a big sigh. "Okay, okay." Then she quickly went about gathering up all the supplies, placing them on the counter.

After a moment she yelled from across the store, "A boy or girl?"

"Why would that matter?" He knew she was fishing.

"Just want to know if I should pick up blue or pink blankets and onesies."

"Yellow or green will work."

"Fine!" she said, but he could tell this secret thing was killing her.

Soon, the counter was littered with baby things. Fortunately, Jet knew enough about newborns to know they didn't need rattles, teething toys or the high chair she'd stuck next to the counter.

In the end, he managed to get exactly what he needed, even picking up a thermal onesie suitable for winter weather and some sort of soft travel bassinet Cindy had sung the praises of. He'd have gotten a car seat as well, but it wasn't sized for an infant. Other than that, Whipple's One Stop truly had everything he needed for baby Lily.

He was just about to compliment Cindy Whipple when she interrupted. "I've thought about the expectant moms in town, and I've accounted for all of them. I think it's someone from out of town. Am I right?"

"I can't say," Jet told her, swallowing his praise.

"Is it one of our teens? Some poor girl who has managed to keep her pregnancy a secret, even from her parents? I bet it's Roseland Cooper, or maybe Jennifer Wells…or maybe it's not either of them. I bet it's one of them Century sisters, maybe Bess or Dani. Them girls always were wild…no mother to raise 'em and a dad who didn't value nothin' but his next drink. Just because they're of age now doesn't mean they've got a lick of common sense. Neither one of 'em could settle. Always movin' 'round the country."

Jet knew the Century sisters well, especially Dani Century, but he didn't want to think about her now. That was over a long time ago, and bringing up her name only reminded him of a time in his life he didn't want to relive, especially not tonight.

"They don't live here anymore, Mrs. Whipple. They both headed out months ago."

"Oh, that's right. Time gets away from me," she said as she bagged everything. "You're not going to tell me, are you?"

"I can't, remember?"

"But it's a baby. Nobody can hide a baby…unless…" She sucked in air and put her hand over her mouth.

"Unless what? Mrs. Whipple? What are you thinking?"

She leaned in closer over the counter, and whispered, "Some out-of-towner abandoned a baby at the jail, didn't they? And your deputy is caring for it right now while you're in here getting supplies. Child Welfare can't do nothing about it in all this snow, and the road to the hospital is probably closed by now, so you're stuck. I bet that's it. You can tell me. My lips are sealed. Fort Knox."

But Jet didn't answer. Instead he picked up the two overflowing bags wondering how on earth Cindy Whipple could have gotten so close to the truth. The woman had a sixth sense about these things, and if Jet hung around any longer he was sure she'd figure out the baby's name, gender and, even worse, that the baby was abandoned on Doctor Grant's doorstep.

As he walked out of the store, he contemplated hiring Mrs. Whipple as a special investigator. Not that he ever could or would, but having her work with him seemed a lot smarter than having her working against him…of that he had no doubt.

Chapter 2

"Are we ever happy to see you," Russ Knightly said as he opened the front door to Coco's private residence above her clinic. The door to her clinic sat right next to her private apartment door, but despite the sign above it that touted Paws & Tails Animal Clinic, the sheriff knew her patrons managed to get the two doors confused, just as he had the first time he'd stopped by. They looked exactly alike but for the sign, which, in his opinion, should have been placed on the door itself.

Russ's clothes looked disheveled and he wore a harried look on his cover-model face, as if the normally cavalier mayoral candidate had reached his breaking point. Even his habitually groomed dark hair was tousled.

Jet could only think of one question: Why was *he* here?

The shock of seeing Russ standing in Doctor Grant's doorway instead of Doctor Grant herself threw Sheriff

Wilson off his game for a moment. Of all the men in this town, Russ Knightly was the last person he ever thought he'd see anywhere near Coco Grant. For one thing, he'd thought she was a smart woman…but unless there was a really good reason for this lunkhead to be answering her door at this time of night, Jet had sorely misjudged Coco's common sense.

"I got a call from Doctor Grant, but if you're already here, I'll just drop these off with you." He shoved the bag of baby things into Russ's hands, and placed a bigger bag of diapers and baby wipes just inside the doorway. "I'll be on my way before the snow gets any deeper."

Then he turned to go, angry that he'd been used as an errand boy.

"No. Wait. Aren't you going to take the baby?"

The sheriff turned back around, detecting a hint of angst in Russ's normally brazen voice. "Can't. There's nobody to care for her tonight."

Jet proceeded down the three front steps off the wide porch, until Russ called to him again. The man had actually followed him, carrying both bags of baby things. Did Russ really think he was going to stop him from leaving?

"Well, we certainly can't take care of it. We're not authorized, but I know for a fact that you are. It's your duty as town sheriff to take custody of this baby."

Jet hesitated at the bottom of the steps on the snowy sidewalk and contemplated his options. According to the local newspaper, the *Teton Valley Gazette*, Russ Knightly was beating Mayor Sally Hickman by ten points. If he became mayor, he could make Jet's life miserable, and even replace him if he so chose.

Despite all his complaints, Sheriff Jet Wilson loved

his job and didn't want to start over again in some other town...at least not yet.

"You're right about that, Mr. Knightly. I must have been mistaken. I thought you and Doctor Grant wanted to keep that poor, destitute, abandoned child overnight, which would be fine, according to the law, as long as I approved it. Which I do."

"Well, don't, because we do not want to keep the baby overnight. We want you to take her. Coco... I mean, Doctor Grant, and I have other plans."

Jet got it loud and clear. This charming snake and Doctor Grant were in a relationship. Russ might as well have sucker punched him right in the jaw. It would have made more sense than this tawdry relationship.

As much as it pained Jet, he walked back up the three steps, past Russ Knightly, then began walking up the flight of stairs to the doctor's private residence, an apartment he'd never seen before, but had thought about many times.

"You could have carried some of this stuff, ya know," Russ complained behind Jet as the two men made their way up the steps.

"I sure could have," Jet said, offering no excuse, listening to Russ grunt as he tried to maneuver the steep stairs.

Jet's guilt kicked in and he was about to turn back around and grab one of the bags from Russ when the door opened to Doctor Grant's apartment.

She looked absolutely gorgeous, almost beatific, as if she was no longer human, but rather an angel that had come down from heaven. It was all there in her smile, a radiant, joyful smile not really intended for Jet, but coming from deep within her.

Seeing the doctor standing in the doorway, with that tiny baby cradled in her arms, wearing a beautiful black dress that hugged all her curves, her short-cropped, almost black hair hugging her face, showing off that lovely long neck of hers, earrings gently dusting her bare shoulders and the low light from her apartment bathing her body in its warm glow, took Jet's breath away. Her steel blue eyes seemed brighter, her lips fuller, and that chiseled nose set everything off making her look regal. Doctor Coco Grant always stood up straight, proud of her six-foot height, which Jet loved considering he cleared six foot four easy.

No woman had ever had that kind of impact on him before. The world might as well have stopped spinning.

For the first time in his adult life, he knew what it meant to be tongue-tied. It was all he could do to keep from blabbing like a schoolboy.

"Thanks for coming out, Sheriff. I know it's late, but we didn't know what else to do," the angel said, her voice low and enthralling.

"I…um…"

"Excuse me," Russ said from just behind Jet, then nudged him out of the way. "But this stuff is heavy."

That knocked Jet back into reality…the reality of an abandoned baby cuddled up against Doctor Grant, with bare shoulders exposed to the cold of the stairway.

Jet cleared his tight throat. "Not a problem," he told Doctor Grant. "I picked up a few things on my way over."

"More like the whole store," Russ muttered.

All of a sudden, the baby started wailing. Jet figured it was the grating sound of Russ's voice that set her off.

Smart baby, Jet thought.

"Why don't you let me get some clothes on that little

darlin' while you make her a bottle. We can talk about how you found her after we get her settled," Jet said.

From the look on Doctor Grant's face, he could tell she hadn't expected him to know much about babies.

"Are you sure?" she tentatively asked. "Because, I mean…"

But Jet had already taken the tiny bundle wrapped in a fuzzy white towel into his arms. She felt as light as a feather as he spoke to her in a soothing voice and gently rocked her. At once the wailing turned into tiny whimpers.

"How'd you do that?" Coco asked, but Jet wasn't in the mood to answer her question. Instead he asked one of his own.

"Any bruises on the child?"

He walked past her and into the spacious apartment and immediately noticed all the lit candles on just about every flat surface in the large rooms, plus the open bottles of wine and scotch on the dining table that still held the remnants of what had to be a romantic dinner for two. A large bouquet of roses, undoubtedly a gift from her shining knight, sat in a clear glass vase in the center of the table.

Sheriff Jet Wilson could only imagine the disruption this little girl must have caused. He did a mental snicker.

"None that I could see," the doctor answered using her official voice. "She looks well cared for, and she's the appropriate size and weight for a two-week-old infant. I looked it up online."

"That's good. Now, where can I change her?"

"In my bedroom, down the hall on your right."

Jet picked one of the bags of essentials that Russ had dropped on the floor and went off to make little baby Lily a bit more comfortable in this uncomfortable situation.

"Can one of you please bring in the other bag?" Jet asked, not turning back around. He assumed Russ would carry in the bulky bag, and the less he saw and spoke to that man, the better.

Just last week he thought he'd seen Russ locking lips with a petite blonde woman over in Jackson Hole, Wyoming, a town less than thirty minutes from Briggs. Jet had been there for a meeting with law enforcement officials when he spotted Russ through a restaurant window cozying up with a woman Jet had never seen before. And from the way they'd been eyeing each other, Jet had assumed they were an item.

Apparently he'd been wrong.

Apparently Russ Knightly liked to spread his affections around.

"You wouldn't be taken in by that kind of behavior, would you, Lily?"

She blinked and pushed her spindly legs out from under the towel. He could tell she didn't particularly like that heavy towel over her. Jet put her down on the bed, opened the box of diapers, pulled one out and quickly slipped it under Lily's bottom and fastened it. Then he grabbed a white side-snap undershirt and slipped that on her. She at once looked much more comfortable and happy.

"There, now you can relieve yourself at will, and no one will be the wiser."

Her little arms reached up as she let out a soft wail. "Aw, sweet cakes, don't be cryin'. We're gonna fix you up with a bottle, and I promise you, you'll be well taken care of. No need to make a fuss."

As he soothed Lily, his mind wandered back to Russ and Jackson Hole, pondering whether or not the good doctor knew about the other woman or, for that matter, if the other woman knew about Doctor Grant.

And if both women knew, were they okay with it?

Call him old-fashioned, but in Jet's world, a relationship consisted of two people who only had eyes for each other.

Unfortunately, so far, those kinds of old-fashioned ideas hadn't panned out so well. He kept falling for the wrong women, but *dang it*, after his last broken heart, he'd promised himself he would never do that again.

Until the next time.

"Seems like you've got it covered," Doctor Grant said from behind him, her statement confusing him for a moment.

"Yes... I mean...you are referring to baby Lily, right?"

She came around and sat on the edge of the bed, facing him. Her forehead mirrored her confusion. "What else would I be referring to?"

He needed to change the subject, and fast, as he slipped Lily into a warm, long-sleeved, bunny-covered sleeper gown and zipped it closed. "Is that bottle coming soon?"

She nodded. "Right here," she said. "I can feed her." She held out her arms, but Jet was reluctant to give Lily up. Instead, he gently picked her up and cradled her in his arms. She felt warm and delicate against his chest, and he had to get over the thought that she might break if he held her too tight. It had been a while, a long while, since he'd held a two-week-old baby, but he had no problem remembering exactly what to do.

"Just point me to a comfortable chair, and we'll be fine."

"You want to feed Lily?"

"Sure," he told her, swiping the bottle, testing the

heat of the formula on the inside of his wrist, then gently enticing Lily to take it. She fussed, and wouldn't suckle no matter how he tried to encourage her. "Maybe she's used to her mama's breast, and this won't work. If that's true, we really have a problem."

He glanced over at Doctor Grant, whose breasts just happened to be at eye level and looking quite tempting spilling over that low-cut neckline.

"Well, don't look at me," she said, immediately standing.

"I wasn't looking… I mean… I couldn't help but see…" He stopped and took a deep breath, slowly letting it out. "I only meant this could be a real problem if she doesn't take the bottle."

Jet kept trying, but Lily kept making a face and crying. He could feel the tension building down the back of his neck and in his shoulders. He never even considered that she wouldn't take a bottle, and now he felt foolish for being so naive.

"You brought two kinds of bottles. Maybe she'll take the other one. It's worth a try," Doctor Grant said.

She left the bedroom and he followed right behind, grateful that Cindy Whipple had sold him both types of bottles. If this worked, he'd have to go back and kiss her!

"So, everything's good and you're getting ready to leave with Lily?" Russ said to Sheriff Wilson as he and Coco headed for the kitchen. Russ sat on the sofa in the open living room, sipping on a drink, seemingly waiting for all this baby fuss to end so he could get on with his night.

"Not yet," Jet said, trying to dismiss the vision of Russ and that blonde, seeming so cozy.

"Lily won't take her bottle," Doctor Grant told him, sounding concerned.

"Maybe she's not hungry," Russ answered, as if he knew something about babies. "A hungry baby will eat."

"Where did you hear that?" Jet asked, but kept heading for the kitchen with Doctor Grant.

"I just made it up, but it sounds perfectly reasonable."

Jet couldn't help an eye roll. Fortunately, only Lily could see him, and when he gazed down at her, she seemed to appreciate the gesture as she sucked on her fist.

"Apparently you don't know much about babies. According to Sheriff Wilson, they're particular, especially if they've only been nursed. She may only accept a breast," Doctor Grant told him, as she rinsed the other bottle, the one with a nipple that looked more like a woman's breast.

"Then go find her one. There must be several women in this town who are nursing their babies."

Doctor Grant stopped what she was doing and stared at Russ. "You're kidding, right?"

"Well, what's the alternative?"

"We have another bottle. It has a different nipple," Jet said.

"And if that doesn't work?"

"Pray that it does," Doctor Grant said, her voice firm and filled with agitation. "Because if it doesn't, we're all in for a world of trouble."

Lily began wailing again, louder than ever. Doctor Grant took the bottle from Jet and sped up the procedure.

Russ abruptly stood. "Well, I can see that the two of you have this covered, so I'm going to be on my way," he shouted over Lily's protest. "If you need anything, anything at all, don't hesitate to call."

"You're leaving? Now?" Doctor Grant asked, as if

his departure took her by surprise. Jet's only surprise was that Russ hadn't left when Lily first arrived.

"Sorry, baby, but I've got a lot to do tomorrow, especially if the snow keeps falling like it is," Russ told Doctor Grant. "It proves my point that Sally Hickman isn't fit to be mayor. When I'm the mayor there will be more than enough snowplows to keep our roads cleared."

He shrugged into his coat that had hung on a hook by the door.

Doctor Grant handed Jet the new bottle, which she'd filled with the contents of the other bottle. Then she walked over to Russ. "But I thought we... I thought you and I..."

Then they disappeared out into her stairway, closing the door, leaving the sheriff to tend to the more important person in the room: baby Lily.

Once Russ Knightly made up his mind about something, he was the type of man who couldn't be budged...a trait that under normal circumstances, Coco admired... just not tonight.

He couldn't get out of there fast enough. He'd left in such a hurry, she hadn't even gotten the chance to kiss him goodbye before he was out the door and down the stairs.

"Are you sure you want to leave in all this snow? You might get stuck and have to walk back here, anyway," she called after him from the open doorway, having followed him down to the front door of her clinic.

Without even turning around, he said, "I've got four-wheel drive, and a snowplow on the front of my truck. I can get through anything."

And in the next few seconds he jumped into his oversize truck, turned over the ignition, lowered the plow and took off into the night.

She could have been upset as she closed the door, might have even thought that he'd been rude to leave so abruptly in the middle of things. She even could have decided that just maybe she might be dating the wrong man. But all she could focus on was the silence...the absolute and complete silence.

She quickly ascended the stairs to her apartment, wondering about baby Lily and worrying about the sheriff. Would he call the local hospital asking how to set up a volunteer nursing mom for Lily? Not that she knew exactly how that would work for an actual baby. She'd set it up for infant livestock before, but that was with the cooperation of local ranchers...

When she finally opened the door, somewhat out of breath from her rush to learn the truth, emotion gripped the back of her throat. She couldn't help the tears that cascaded down her cheeks.

"Oh, my gosh! She's taking it?" she whispered, fingers wiping her tears away. Seeing that tiny baby, eagerly drinking the bottle of formula, nestled in Sheriff Wilson's strong arms, while he took up all the space on her tan-colored overstuffed chair, was almost more than Coco could take in. For all his bluster, Coco now knew he was warm and fuzzy on the inside.

And as a bonus, Punky had curled up at Sheriff Wilson's feet, and aside from momentarily picking up his tiny head to watch Coco come back into the apartment, he seemed as though he wasn't about to budge.

"Hope you don't mind, but I let your dog out of the bathroom. I heard it whining so I figured it wanted out."

"Meet Punky. And he usually doesn't trust men. Did you give him a cookie or something?"

"Nope, just a little lovin'. He was lonely."

Punky normally didn't like strangers and tended to keep his distance. Heck, he didn't even like Russ, so this was some sort of miracle to say the least.

She almost couldn't believe what lay right before her eyes, and wondered if Russ could have been so gentle and loving with Lily if the sheriff hadn't shown up. Maybe that accounted for Russ's early retreat... He'd felt intimidated by the sheriff and would have been as compassionate if he'd only gotten the chance. Russ was a compassionate and caring man. He'd merely been in a hurry to beat the snow or he would be sitting in that very chair right now instead of the sheriff...who she had absolutely nothing in common with.

Except for baby Lily.

But other than that, they were as different as rain and sunshine.

"And what about Lily? Did you give her some lovin', as well?"

"It was just a matter of getting everything lined up right. The little sweetheart here was hungry. That tummy of hers probably hurt, plus I think it took her a while to settle into not having her mama feeding her. I don't want to speculate on why a woman gives up her baby, but whatever the reason, it sure is tough on the child."

"That goes for animals, as well. They get depressed, sometimes to the point of not wanting to eat. Plus, they cry a lot."

"Exactly like Lily."

"Well, she's not crying now."

"She's one content little girl who's getting sleepy. But I have to make sure she doesn't have any gas in that tummy of hers before she sleeps."

Coco watched as six feet four inches of muscled

alpha male expertly tucked tiny baby Lily onto his receiving blanket–covered shoulder and rubbed her back as she squirmed and fretted over the loss of her food. Within moments a couple of hearty burps erupted, and Sheriff Wilson once again cradled Lily in his arms to feed her the rest of her bottle.

"Seems like you've done this a few times before," Coco told him, amazed at his gentleness and ease with Lily. She was certain she'd be all nerves and frets if she had to feed her. Feeding a kitten or a baby goat or an abandoned foal was one thing, but a fragile baby was something entirely different.

"A few," he told her, but she could tell he didn't want to talk about it.

That never stopped her before. "Younger brothers and sisters?"

"None."

"Nieces and nephews?"

"No siblings of any age."

Coco perched herself on the edge of the sofa, intrigued now. "Then how…"

"One of the families I lived with consisted of a baby and a toddler, along with several other children. The older kids, like me, knew how to take care of themselves, but neither the baby nor the toddler got very much attention, which caused them to cry a lot. It was merely a matter of necessity. In order for me to get any of my homework done, I learned how to keep them content."

"Where were their parents?"

"Like me, and like Lily here, their parents, for whatever reason, had abandoned them."

Coco's heart instantly shattered. She'd had no idea. "So you grew up in foster care?"

"Yep. From the time I was six years old, but that's not anything to concern yourself with. What we need to think about now—" his voice spiraled down into a whisper "—is Lily."

"The snow hasn't let up at since you got here," she whispered, thankful that Lily had finally fallen asleep. "I know you want to get her to Child Welfare or maybe to Valley Hospital, but the roads look treacherous."

"What are you proposing?" He asked the question, but didn't take his eyes off Lily.

She knew the sheriff was a stickler for the law, but she was hopeful that maybe he could bend the rules if she framed her idea exactly right. Besides Lily, her menagerie of animals downstairs was definitely not legal within city limits. Maybe if she offered to keep Lily for the night, he wouldn't go snooping around her clinic, and even if he did, he'd let her slide without a fine... at least for now.

"Since it's not safe out there for either you or Lily, you both can stay here for the night...if you want. Of course, I'm not trying to step on your toes when it comes to your authority. All I'm saying is, it's a long way to Valley Hospital and then back to your apartment. Instead, I can put Lily down in her soft bassinet on my bed for the night and make up the sofa for you. I have a spare bedroom, but it's for storage."

He thought about it for a moment, as if his brain had to wrap itself around the idea that her proposal might come with illegal strings he couldn't see.

"While you think about that," she said, "can I get you anything to drink? Water? Coffee? Milk?"

"Actually, I'd take a shot of that scotch if I was going to stay. It's been one heck of a night on a lot of counts."

He stood. "But I can't stay. I tell you what. I'll leave Lily in your care for the night, but I should get going while I can still do that. I'll come by to pick her up in the morning once the roads are clear and I know for certain who will take her."

"You don't know that yet?"

"No. With the weather being what it is, the person I spoke to wasn't really sure how to handle it."

No way was Coco willing to let that baby go under those ambiguous circumstances.

"Then I'd be more than happy to take care of her tonight, and again, you're more than welcome to stay, as well."

"Thanks for the offer of your sofa." He gazed over at it, looking skeptical.

"Okay, so maybe you wouldn't be comfortable on my sofa. But if you slept on your side and bent your knees, five feet would be a perfectly acceptable fit."

"I appreciate the offer, but that SUV can get through just about anything. Now, let's get Lily settled in her bed."

Coco picked up Lily's cloth bassinet by the handles and made her way to the bedroom, where she placed it on the bed. Then, ever so carefully, the sheriff put Lily down on her back and expertly swaddled her with the blankets. Lily didn't even stir, but let out a long sigh.

Then he did something she'd seen her own dad do a million times to each of his children, always feeling the love her dad had for his family. The only difference now was what the sheriff said...

He leaned over and gently kissed baby Lily on the forehead, tenderly stroked the top of her head and whispered, "Sleep well, Lily. You're safe now."

Then he exited the room, leaving Coco to wonder: *Who are you and what have you done with by-the-book Sheriff Wilson?*

When Jet stepped back outside into the quiet night, leaving the warmth of Doctor Grant and baby Lily behind, the cold wind instantly sent a shiver down his spine. The thought of trying to drive through all this heavy snow only to get back to the drafty, lonely jail made him a combination of angry and sad.

Angry at himself for not taking the doctor up on her kind offer to sleep on her sofa, and sad that his life had come to sleeping inside a jail cell on a hard cot.

He shook his head as he made his way to his rig, which was somehow completely packed in snow. Still, he told himself if Russ could make it out of there, so could he.

One problem.

He would need a good-sized shovel to dig his way out. It looked as though a snowplow had purposely shoved snow all around his SUV, making it impossible for him to get out.

But who would do such an inconsiderate thing to the sheriff's rig?

At this point it didn't matter. What did matter was that he'd made a big deal about not spending the night with the doctor.

He corrected himself. Not *with* the doctor, but *at* the doctor's apartment. Was that the reason he didn't take her up on her offer of the sofa? Didn't he trust himself? Maybe he didn't trust her? If she and Russ had an "open relationship," would she try to seduce him?

He told himself that was plain silly.

He'd merely done the stand-up thing and left. Nothing more to it.

But now he was in a pickle, and had no choice but to take her up on that sofa offer.

"Fine," he said aloud as he trudged back to her front door, the snow and cold wind blasting his face and hands with its bitter sting. He hated nights like this, nights when Mother Nature reminded him of her power, and when memories of his childhood came crashing back. He wished he could talk to Lily's mom and tell her of the life that Lily more than likely would have. He'd like to somehow help Lily's mom with whatever reason brought her to abandoning her child. But most of all, he hated that Lily would now be a ward of the state and he would be the one to hand her over.

The irony was too real. By the time he'd graduated from high school he'd lived with twelve different families. Most of them were good people, but a few of them were borderline abusive or simply neglectful. Those were the kinds of households that he hoped Lily would never run across, but he knew the odds were stacked against her. Once she went into the system, there was no telling who would be her temporary parents.

Life sure could stink at times, he thought as he made his way back up the three steps to Doctor Grant's front porch, but before he was able to ring the bell for her apartment, she swung open the door and handed him that shot of scotch.

"Thanks," he said after he drank it down. "I really needed that."

"I figured as much," she said, her voice low and sultry, feet bare, pretty little toes painted a bright pink.

No doubt about it, he was in for it now.

Chapter 3

"I know these animals legally aren't supposed to be here, but there was nowhere else I could take them, especially after it started snowing," Coco told the sheriff as he helped her clean out their cages and pens.

Coco had slipped out of her lacy black dress, and instead donned jeans, rubber boots and an oversize red plaid shirt. She wore rubber gloves and had offered a pair of gloves to the sheriff, which he surprisingly took. She'd set up one of her many portable baby monitors, which she used for her animals, inside her bedroom, so she had baby Lily in her sights at all times.

As for the sheriff's part, he'd left his gun holstered and locked in a dresser drawer in the spare bedroom, his badge and cream-colored cowboy hat sat on a side table next to her sofa.

Medium-sized cages lined one wall of the room,

where sibling calico kittens played with a brown-and-white bulldog puppy, who eagerly rolled around with each of them, while a large tortoise watched the activities from the shelter of its hard shell. Fortunately, aside from the need of an occasional heat lamp and a meal of greens and maybe a strawberry or two, a tortoise was low maintenance. Unlike the rest of her critters, which required not only basic needs but some loving and human interaction. Otherwise they'd never be comfortable around people.

The area smelled of a combination of manure, fresh hay and animal fur, a scent that had lost its impact on Coco some time ago. Since her renovation, this part of the clinic was now separated from her apartment on the second floor of the original main building. This new clinic took up most of the empty lot that had been behind her house. She'd bought this property precisely because she knew she'd be able to expand her business. The closest house on her street was at least fifty yards away.

"I understand," the sheriff said as he scooped up goat dung and hay from the large pen at the end of the large room.

Those two words caught her by complete surprise as she stared at him and dumped the waste material into a big plastic trash can.

"Thanks," she told him, but she wanted to give him a big hug.

"Don't tell me you take care of all these guys by yourself?"

The piglet and all the other critters required time and care. She could never do it alone.

"Not exactly. One of my neighbors, Drew Gillian, helps out whenever she can. Normally she'll take in the cats and a couple dogs if we have them, but this time, she already has two pups and a kitten. I couldn't burden her with any more, so I'm keeping them here for a few days, at least until the weather clears up."

"You did what you had to do, Doctor Grant," he said, sounding official. This new attitude of his had to stop if they were going to make it through the night without her thinking that perhaps the sheriff was redeemable.

"Why don't you call me Coco," she told him, wanting to be on more friendly terms. After all, the man was helping her clean out the cages for animals that he knew being here were completely illegal.

He gazed over at her, a smile lighting up his normally stern-looking face. "And you can call me Jet, at least for tonight."

"And after tonight?" She stopped cleaning and looked over at him, grinning while the two goats kept rubbing up against him, wanting the bottles of milk she'd been warming in the large bottle warmer she kept in the other room.

"Protocol dictates the more formal name, and I wouldn't want you to think that just because we spent the night together…er, I mean, just because we slept… Yes, Jet will be fine."

She chuckled under her breath at the sheriff's— at Jet's—obvious awkwardness with the situation. It was almost as though he'd never spent the night with a woman before, at least not on a platonic basis. The thought caused her to snicker even more.

"Am I missing something?" he asked, obviously catching her hidden laughter.

"It's the llamas. They keep nipping at my shirt collar." Which they were.

The pen was fairly large, about fifteen by eighteen feet, but it wasn't enough room for them to run and play in, so she was getting all their extra energy. They kept rubbing up against her, then running around in a circle only to do it again. One was chocolate brown, the male, and the other almost pure white, a female.

"They seem kind of aggressive. Shouldn't they be in a barn somewhere, instead of cooped up in that pen?"

Jet was absolutely right, but she'd had no choice. They'd been left on her doorstep at a most inopportune time.

"They're not aggressive, more playful than anything else. Llamas are the sweetest animals you can ever have on a ranch. Plus, they're better protectors against coyotes or hawks or even possums. They only arrived this afternoon or I would have brought them out to my parents' ranch until I could find a home for them. Problem was, I couldn't risk driving all the way out there and getting stuck on my way back, so instead I decided to keep them here for a bit. I should be able to move them out tomorrow or the next day at most."

He gave one of the goats a pat on the head before it danced off, then loved up the other one when it nudged his leg. From all that she'd seen so far that night, Sheriff Jet Wilson was not the brute she had made him out to be. Jet Wilson seemed to be as soft and cuddly underneath that hard outer shell as any of her critters. A fact she would try to remember the next time he fined her for one of her forbidden country animals.

"No worries. Really. I understand."

Now she really didn't understand him, not even remotely. Who was this guy? How could she have misread him so badly?

"Why the change of heart? Why aren't you writing up a ticket? What changed?"

He turned to her and shrugged. "It's not your fault

the people of this town have decided to abandon their animals…and now their babies…on your doorstep. I guess I never understood what that meant before. These little guys deserve a break, deserve a new start, and apparently the townsfolk think you can give it to them. You're quite the protector, Doctor… I mean Coco…and everyone seems to know that."

"Does that mean you'll dismiss my pending fines?"

Now that he'd seemed to have a change of heart, she felt hopeful about asking for those dang fines to go away.

He stood up straight and looked directly into her eyes, wearing his official deadpan expression again. As if he could switch that authoritarian look on and off at will. "No," he said with certainty. "It just means I won't give you another fine for this group… That's contingent upon your finding a place for the goats and llamas as soon as the weather clears up. A place outside city limits."

She stuck a fist to her hip, somewhat peeved he couldn't let those fines go, but underneath all her hope, she was beginning to understand his tough position.

"Well, that's something. I guess."

"It's the least I can do seeing as how you've taken in Lily."

She didn't want him getting any ideas about her caring for Lily. Sure, she felt sorry for the poor little thing, and Lily had already made an inroad into Coco's heart, but she couldn't allow herself to spend too much time with the child or she would never want to let her go.

"Just for the night or until the weather clears up and the roads get plowed. With my schedule, I certainly can't take in a baby."

Which was true, so she latched onto that thought and held it close. It would allow her to hand Lily over to the authorities without breaking her heart. The abandoned animals were fine, but an abandoned baby caused her way too much internal grief, a grief she wasn't prepared to spill anytime soon…especially not in front of Jet Wilson. Sure, he had a softer side, but that outer shell was as hard as steel and she had no intention of going up against it.

"Nor are you qualified to take her."

Coco's internal antenna went up. Did he know something about her? Was there gossip going around that she didn't know about? "What's that supposed to mean?"

He stepped out of the goat pen, to the dismay of both goats, slipped off his gloves and headed for the next room that contained a refrigerator, a large bottle warmer and some supplies. "Not what you're thinking," he shouted back. She heard him open the lid on the bottle warmer. "Idaho has rules about who can be a temporary guardian for an abandoned baby, and you aren't certified. I checked."

She relaxed a bit. He'd merely been referring to some law she knew little about.

"And I suppose you are?"

He stepped back into the main room, holding a large bottle of warmed milk in each hand. Large nipples cupped the tops of the bottles.

"By default, yes. But I also had to take a few classes."

The goats bleated at the end of the pen, their heads hanging over the wire mesh, mouths open in anticipation.

"But I thought you said you knew all about caring for a baby from growing up in foster care?"

"I guess it's a combination of both."

He held both bottles down so the kids could nurse. They pulled down the milk as if they'd been starving, which they weren't. She'd fed them in the morning before she'd begun her day, and now before bed. Twice a day was sufficient for these little guys. The good thing about these two was that their owner had at least disbudded them well, so their horns wouldn't grow, a problem for domesticated goats.

"I wish I knew more about caring for babies. I only know animals," Coco told him.

The goats pushed and knocked their bottles, wanting the milk to come out faster, but Coco had given them the appropriate nipple with the appropriate slice in the top for a controlled flow. Anything more and they'd choke.

"It's the same thing. Neither a baby nor an animal can tell you what's wrong. You have to use your intuition and your expertise, and hope that you're right. I mean, look at these little guys. You manage to keep them all healthy, right?"

"Most of the time, but even with them, I can sometimes get it wrong."

"But you strike me as the type of doctor who keeps trying until you do get it right."

"Thanks. I like to think that I do. Yes."

She appreciated his confidence in her. Where he'd gotten it, she didn't know, but she sure liked it. Aside from her brother, Carson, her sisters, Kenzie, Callie and Kayla, her dad and mom, and a handful of the local ranchers, she didn't always get that kind of respect. There were times when she'd get outright skepticism. Not that she minded it, or resented it. She understood. Those animals meant thousands of dollars to the ranchers. Sometimes a healthy animal or a sick animal stood between a rancher and bankruptcy. A vet could, at times, make or break a ranch depending on his or her diagnosis. So it had better be the correct one.

"Have you always wanted to be a vet?"

She nodded. "I think for as long as I could remember. I love my job and I'm blessed that when Doctor Graham retired, he left his practice to me. What about you? Have you always wanted to be a sheriff?"

He chuckled. "Absolutely not. I wanted to be a bus driver, or a truck driver, then a fireman, a cowboy or a rodeo star, and for a short time I wanted to be a rock star. I play a mean guitar."

She smiled, envisioning Jet in tight black leather pants, no shirt and eyeliner. He clearly didn't fit the image. "Then how on earth did you end up being a sheriff?"

"When I got out of the military, I didn't know what to do with myself until I met Sheriff Perkins over in Chubbuck, who was looking for a deputy. The pay was good enough to keep me off the street, and I liked the sheriff, so I applied and got the job. He trained me, and a couple years ago when this job came up, he pushed me out of the nest and gave me a good reference. The rest, as they say, is history."

"So, does that mean you like it?"

"For the most part, it suits me."

"When doesn't it suit you?"

The baby goats emptied their bottles, their tails wagging like mad, indicating that their bellies were nice and full before Jet pulled the bottles away. They fussed for a minute, then went about bumping heads and playing.

He turned to her, looking sullen. "When I have to deal with an abandoned baby."

"That's exactly how I feel when someone abandons an animal on my doorstep. But a baby is a hundred times worse."

"So, it's safe to say, Lily is tough for us both."

"She's breaking my heart in more ways than I want to admit."

"Mine, too," he said, and in that moment, he took her breath away.

The snow had crept up above his knees, and he could no longer feel his feet or fingers. Every tree, rock and surface around him was covered in thick, heavy snow that continued to fall in great big lacy flakes, making visibility virtually impossible.

How he'd gotten out on a hillside, he didn't know.

With each breath, a billow of steam surrounded his face. His entire body shook from cold, but Jet couldn't stop moving forward. He knew he had to keep going, keep walking, one foot in front of the other. He had to keep going. Had to get to Doctor Grant's house.

He could barely make out a structure in the distance, a log cabin, blanketed in snow, with smoke swirling up out of the chimney and bright yellow lights glowing from the three windows, beckoning him forward.

In the distance he heard a baby cry, faint at first, then growing louder and louder with each step until the sound pierced his ears. He soon realized that he carried the screaming baby under his coat, held it tight against his chest. But why hadn't he known this before? What was wrong with him? How could he have not been aware? If he had known that the baby was his responsibility, he would have walked faster. He wouldn't have had that drink with the woman in the black lace dress at the bar. Was it her baby?

No. He seemed to know that for a fact.

But where did it come from? Who gave him a baby? The little darling screamed louder until his ears hurt, until he vibrated from the sound of the baby wrapped in a pink blanket. Then, suddenly, she began to slip from his grasp. He could no longer hold her. His hands were numb. He couldn't feel her, couldn't protect her. She kept slipping away...

"Noooo!" he yelled, jerking awake and immediately realizing it had been a dream—a really bad dream. But the crying had been real, and the cold he'd felt in the dream was also real. His blankets had all fallen on the floor, and his body ached from the weird position he'd been in trying to get comfortable on the mini sofa. When he flexed his fingers on his right hand, a thousand needles shot through his fingers telling him that he'd somehow cut off the circulation.

He sat up, taking in his unfamiliar surroundings. Someone flipped a light switch and his eyes stung for a moment as they adjusted to the bright light.

That's when he heard Punky yapping from somewhere off in the distance.

"Something's wrong with Lily," Coco said as she held Lily in her arms. "I took her temperature and it's one hundred and one. I made a bottle, but she won't take it."

"Did you examine her?"

Punky came running in, stopping at Coco's feet. His barking only adding to the noise factor already coming from Lily's intense wails.

"I was just about to."

Coco seemed levelheaded and cool, despite the squirming baby in her arms and the barking dog at her feet.

"Did you take an anal temperature? That's the only way to tell what's real with a baby this small."

"No, I took it under her arm."

"Let's put her on the table with a couple blankets under her," Jet suggested. He thought that would be the easiest way. "And take that temperature again."

Coco leaned over and spoke to Punky directly. "Stop. It's okay. Lily is okay. Sit."

At once the dog stopped barking and sat obediently on his haunches waiting for another command.

"How'd you do that?" Jet asked, amazed at how quickly the tiny dog obeyed.

"Training. Punky thinks he's a German shepherd and his bark means danger. I'm merely telling him that everything is okay."

"Wow. I wish I could get some ornery people to respond that way."

"It's all in the tone of voice."

"I'll keep that in mind the next time I'm trying to arrest someone."

She grinned. "I'll need a regular-sized stethoscope and an otoscope for her ears. I have small ones down in the clinic." She approached Jet with Lily in her arms. "Can you take her while I get a few things?"

"Sure. Just let me slip on my jeans," Jet told her, then he picked up his pants off the floor and slipped them on over his long tight black cotton underwear, then zipped them up. Normally he might have been a little hesitant about getting dressed in front of a woman he didn't know intimately, but there was something different about Coco, something easygoing about her that kept all his apprehensions at bay.

He wasn't wearing a shirt, which accounted for the dream of his being so cold—that and he'd been sleeping half-naked without a blanket. No wonder he felt like an icicle. He quickly slipped on his thermal undershirt as well, not bothering with anything else, like his shirt or socks or a belt. Lily needed quick attention, and his needs took a back seat to hers.

He settled Lily in his arms, shushing her as he did, and bouncing her to a rhythm in his head. Her little face was bright red, and her hands were fisted tight, her body tense and her mouth wide-open, screaming with everything she had.

"Hey there, sweet cakes, everything's fine. We're going to fix you right up. I promise. Shhh," he cooed, but Lily wasn't buying any of it and continued on her rampage. Coco returned with what she needed to examine Lily. Punky now paced on the sofa, obviously upset over the turmoil in his house.

"Let me get the blankets," Coco said and within moments she had everything set up on the table.

The first time she went to look inside Lily's ears, Jet noticed that her hands were shaking. "It's okay. You've done this a million times before. Lily isn't any different than any of your other patients. She's a baby in crisis. Take a breath, and slowly let it out. You know how to handle this."

Coco followed his instructions until her breathing became more regular and her hands stopped shaking.

"You're right," she told him with a slight grin. "I'm overreacting to something I know exactly how to do."

Jet held on to Lily, trying to soothe her with a lullaby as Coco listened to her lungs and heart, and checked inside her ears. Then she gently but expertly placed a hand on Lily's forehead, which caused her to cry even harder, if that was even possible.

Since the lullaby was no longer working, Jet rocked out on Michael Jackson's "Beat It." For whatever reason, that seemed to do the trick, along with baby Lily finding her own fist to suck on. Lily had exchanged crying for little slurping noises.

"She has a slight infection in one of her ears, and her temperature is elevated."

"What's our next step?" Jet asked as he slipped a fresh diaper on Lily and zipped up her sleeper gown.

"She's too young for any kind of drug. I think what we need to do is put a warm compress up to her ear and bathe her in tepid water with a cloth to bring down her fever."

"Whatever you think is best."

"I appreciate your confidence in me."

"Anytime," he told her with a nod and a grin, absolutely believing that she knew exactly what to do.

Forty-five minutes later, after working together, both of them singing most of Michael Jackson's hits, and after much screaming and fussing due to the wet cloth both on Lily's ear and on her tiny body, all his faith in Coco had been affirmed.

Lily had calmed down enough to take her bottle, and Jet was finally able to take a deep breath. The crisis had passed.

Now Coco leaned against the headboard on her bed as Lily happily suckled the formula. Her temperature had read ninety-nine the last time Coco had checked, and the inflammation in Lily's ear seemed to be subsiding.

Without giving it much thought, Jet climbed up on the bed beside Coco and leaned back on the headboard as Punky, who had used his little step stool to get up on the bed, curled up in a tight ball between them. As if on cue, he and Jet let out simultaneous loud sighs.

"Punky and I feel about the same," Jet said. "You were amazing, and I'm so glad Lily seems to be feeling better. I don't know what I would've done on my own. My expertise, if you could call it that, is limited to feeding and clothing and general, all-around care. Anything medical is out of my league. Although, I have been known to bring down a few fevers in my day, and I'm great with cuts and scraped knees." Jet crossed his long legs on her bed, slipping his cold bare feet under the mess of blankets and the comforter at the end of the bed.

"Thanks. Your patience and guidance were pretty amazing, too," Coco told him, grinning. "You'll make a great dad someday, if you ever want kids."

They both kept their voices to a calm whisper, cautious that their unfamiliar tones might stir Lily up again.

He turned his head to look at her, now only inches away from her lovely face, taking a second to notice the slope of her delicate nose, her full lips, the tiny laugh lines that seemed to embrace the corners of her mouth and the slight dimple in her right cheek as she stared down at Lily, who eagerly drank from the bottle.

"I do…someday, hopefully, but not while I'm in law enforcement. Too risky. I'm not about to leave my son or daughter without a father. I'd need a safe nine-to-five job first or a ranch to run or a snowplow to drive."

"So you're saying you won't have kids as long as you're the sheriff?"

"I will not."

"But I thought you said this job suits you?"

"It does, but not if I want to raise a family. Cops get killed or badly injured in the line of duty all the time. I won't do that to my child."

"Like your dad did to you? What happened to your parents? Was your dad in law enforcement?"

"He was a hotshot and lost his life fighting fire in Yellowstone."

"I'm so sorry. That must have been awful."

"I don't remember much about it, just that I missed him for a very long time. Still do, sometimes." He could barely remember his dad. All he had were glimpses of him laughing, or smiling down at him, not enough to know anything about the man behind the images.

"And your mom?"

Coco slipped the bottle out of Lily's rosebud mouth, put it down on the bedside table, then placed Lily on her shoulder. She fussed for a bit, but then burped a couple times. Soon Lily once again contentedly suckled her bottle.

Coco was a natural at this mother thing, unlike Jet's own mom, who never really got the hang of it.

"I don't blame my mom. She never had the temperament to raise a child on her own. It was only supposed to be temporary…leaving me in foster care…but weeks turned into months and months turned into years. She took me back when I was almost seventeen, but by then I was so used to being on my own that all we did was fight. We get along now, but the damage had already been done. She lives in Florida with her childhood sweetheart. I hate Florida. Way too hot and muggy for me.

"But I don't want to talk about me anymore. You're a natural at this, the way you handle Lily, the way you handled the emergency tonight. You'd make a great mom. I'm surprised you don't already have a house-ful of babies. Watching you with Lily, and the love you show to all your critters, any child would be lucky to have you as their mom."

He'd meant it as a compliment, not as an affront, but all of a sudden, Coco's eyes watered and big tears slipped down her beautiful cheeks. "No. What's wrong? Did I say something to offend you? I'm sorry if I did. Things come out of my mouth sometimes that I don't take time to think through. I didn't mean anything negative. Honest."

She wiped the tears away with her hand. "You didn't know. How could you? No one really knows, not even my family."

"Is it something you want to talk about? Because I'm like a priest in a confessional. Whatever you tell me is locked away...unless it's something illegal. Then don't tell me or I'll have to haul you off to jail, and I really wouldn't like that considering everything we just went through to get Lily to stop crying. And besides, the weather sucks."

He got her to smile again and his world lit up. "It's nothing illegal."

"Good, then what is it?"

She turned to look at him, her face streaked with tears. "Last year, I was diagnosed with moderate to severe endometrioses. It's when tissue that lines the inside of a woman's uterus grows outside the uterus. When it attacks the ovaries, cysts form. I have both of those issues and the chances of my getting pregnant without surgery or in vitro fertilization go down significantly with each passing year. That's why I wanted you to simply take Lily. I didn't want to be around her to remind me, and I certainly didn't want to give her my heart."

He couldn't help himself. He reached over and ran his finger down her cheek. "From looking at you now, both of those things have happened."

She gazed down at Lily, smiling and pulling her in tighter. She had fallen asleep, so Coco gently removed the nipple from her little mouth. Lily sighed and stretched, but never opened her eyes. Instead, she merely turned her head sideways, as if she was about to nurse on Coco's breast, and fell into a deep, comfortable sleep.

"Any man you marry will certainly love you enough to understand, and help you through any kind of surgery or procedure you want to do in order to get pregnant. And if that's not an option, then the two of you can adopt a baby just like Lily."

"I doubt there's another baby in the entire world like Lily. Look at how sweet she is, that little cherub face, and her deep blue eyes, and the way she seems to be smiling whenever she's content. And the way she coos when you talk to her, like she's trying to answer you. I tried so hard to keep my emotions out of this, but when Lily woke up with a fever under my watch, I couldn't help but fall in love with her. I know she has to leave me in the morning, and it's ripping me apart."

"You want to know something?"

She nodded.

"Giving her up is ripping me apart, as well."

Then, wanting to protect both Lily and Coco, he reached out and Coco scooted into his embrace, bringing sleeping Lily along with her. When they were both nestled in tight, with Coco's head leaning on his shoulder, a strong wave of compassion washed over him, causing his own eyes to well up with emotion. He could only imagine the grief Coco was feeling holding that tiny baby in her arms.

She continued, "I know I shouldn't question it, but

I can't even begin to imagine what could have drove Lily's mother to leave her child with strangers. The thought is inconceivable to me. I only wish I could talk to Lily's mom, meet her, get to know her reasons and maybe try to convince her to reconsider, but I know it's not my place to do any of those things. Still, I can't help but wonder if she's missing her baby on this cold snowy night, or if she's relieved she finally got rid of her. Either way, it breaks my heart."

He couldn't help but kiss her on her forehead, stroke her hair and pull her in tighter. In all his adult life, he'd never felt closer to a woman than he had just then.

He knew she was involved with Russ Knightly, a man he wouldn't drive across town to meet, and from what he saw earlier that night, Coco was probably in love with him, although Jet couldn't for the life of him understand why. Still, he knew he and Coco had shared something meaningful, and no matter what happened between them in the days to come, he'd always feel close to her.

He wanted to confess his own heartbreak about Lily's abandonment and about having to hand her over to strangers who would only be her caretakers and nothing more, but he changed his mind. In comforting Coco, he also comforted himself, and for now, that was all he needed. All that mattered.

Tomorrow, everything would be different, and for all they knew, Lily's mom might return, looking for her precious baby.

Chapter 4

Coco awoke slowly, wrapped up in Russ's arms, content as a kitten in the sun, only there was no sun, only a sort of darkness that a snowy sky can bring, and when she gazed up at her man, it wasn't Russ, but Sheriff Jet Wilson, sound asleep.

Punky stretched his front legs out, shook off sleep and jumped off the bed, waiting for her to let him out on the upstairs patio. He had a little area on the patio where he went and did his business when she couldn't take him out for a walk. This was one of those moments.

She quickly but ever so carefully slid out of Jet's embrace and panicked over the whereabouts of baby Lily. The last thing she remembered was holding Lily as she fell asleep in Coco's arms, while she fell asleep in Jet's arms.

"Oh, no," she whispered to herself. When she slid

out of bed, she nearly hit her shin on an open drawer, and before she could scold herself for being so absent-minded, she noticed that baby Lily lay all snuggled up on her back, sound asleep inside the drawer that had been lined with soft blankets.

Coco was ever so tempted to pick her up and hold her tight, but she stopped short as she fully realized that she'd spent the night in the same bed as Jet Wilson, wrapped in his arms.

She tried to remember if anything sexual took place during the night, but when her mind came up clean, she let out a thankful sigh. Although, looking at him now, his hair all messed up, the pillow scrunched under his head and that fabulous big muscled body taking up space on her bed, she wasn't sure if she would've minded if something sexual had taken place...at least a kiss or two.

She scolded herself for thinking such reckless thoughts as she led Punky through the kitchen, then opened the back door for him to go out. A blast of icy wind nearly froze her solid as she waited in the slightly open doorway. Snow blew in on her and covered her back patio in great big drifts that seemed higher than she was tall. Punky took two steps out the door and did his duty right there on the disposable mat, not wanting to go any farther. She always kept a thick paper mat close by for Punky in case of bad weather, and this ranked as some of the worst.

"I don't blame you, Punky," she told him as he came running back into the warmth of the kitchen.

When she headed back to the bedroom she reminded herself that she already had a boyfriend...kind of. Okay, so she and Russ hadn't slept together yet, but that was merely a matter of poor timing, she felt sure of it. She'd been in love with Russ for years now, albeit one-sided, but nevertheless, she cared for him. He was everything she'd ever wanted…aside from the fact that he didn't seem to like children…but then she couldn't have children, at least, not very easily.

She had wanted to assume that the man she would marry would love her enough to want to go through all the steps needed for her to carry their own baby, or that perhaps he would even consider adopting.

Maybe the assumption wasn't a fair one.

She hadn't been all that honest with Russ about her pregnancy issues really, insofar as she hadn't told him everything that she'd said to Jet last night.

And why she'd confided in Jet was beyond her. She'd kept that secret to herself for over a year now, and yet, there she was, blabbing like a schoolgirl.

Still scolding herself, she quickly showered, got dressed and added more makeup than she usually wore on a daily basis, telling herself that she wanted to look good if and when Russ stopped by. She also admitted that she wanted to look good for Jet, as well.

Oh, this was getting complicated and she didn't fully understand why. Russ was her man, not Jet Wilson, who couldn't even fully embrace being a sheriff. At least Russ knew exactly what career and future he wanted, and was willing to work really hard to get there. It sounded as if Jet had hardly worked at all to get his job; it was more or less handed to him.

While Jet and Lily both slept, she and Punky ambled downstairs to take care of the animals. Punky liked to check on the goats, and they liked to try to catch him. Punky believed he was a brute of a big dog, so nothing scared him, not even when the goats tried to butt him with their heads.

When the cages were cleaned and the goats, piglet, llamas, kittens and one lonely puppy were fed, along with the tortoise, Coco and Punky went back upstairs only to find Jet pouring batter onto her waffle iron, while baby Lily squirmed and cooed in her bassinet on the kitchen counter.

"Morning," Sheriff Jet Wilson said, a lilt in his voice that she'd never heard before.

"Good morning. Not only can you take care of an infant, but you can cook, as well?"

"Nothing too fancy, but yes. I make a mean waffle. How do you like your bacon?"

"Dry, just like my eggs, but let me help. What can I do?"

"You can play with Lily, who drank her entire bottle, I might add. She seems to be feeling better this morning, all thanks to you."

Coco went over and peeked in at Lily, who stared up at the ceiling lights, her little legs flexing and her tiny fingers spread out on her chest. A bright red streak crossed her right cheek.

"Aw, looks like her nails need clipping."

"Already taken care of."

Coco could hardly believe this guy. "Is there anything you can't do?"

His entire face lit up with a wide grin. "Several things."

"Name a few."

She went over to the stove and felt the kettle, already hot, so she made a cup of English Breakfast using a tea bag from her plentiful stash of teas.

"I can't ride a horse very well. Never really learned."

"I can teach you," she said without really thinking about what that meant. "We're all great riders in my family."

"If you live in Briggs, you know all about the riding skills of the Grant family. Seen your brother compete out at the fairgrounds, and your sisters Callie and Kenzie are expert riders."

She didn't want to brag, but... "I can rope a steer while on horseback faster than any of 'em. Just haven't done it in a while. You'd give me a reason to get back in the saddle, so to speak."

"I may take you up on that," he said as he plated their food. "One slice of bacon or two?"

"Three, if you made enough."

It was the first time in her entire adult life that a man other than her father or brother had made breakfast for her.

"I made plenty."

He piled her plate with scrambled eggs, a waffle and three slices of bacon. It looked yummy and she couldn't wait to dig in.

"Anything else you're not good at?"

"Are we still on me? How about you? I've seen you with Lily, and all your critters downstairs. You're amazing. And now you tell me you can rope a steer while on horseback. What can't you do?"

"Relationships."

He shook his head. "I can't believe that. You must have guys beating down your door."

Everything was cooked to perfection, the waffle crispy on the outside and light as air on the inside, the bacon dry and the eggs perfectly perfect.

"Just one guy at the moment, and after last night, I don't know if he'll come knocking anytime soon."

His eyebrow crooked up slightly, as if he was skeptical about something.

"He'll be back. I guarantee it. He's not going to let one little baby stand in his way. He strikes me as the kind of guy who always gets what he wants."

"Do I detect a little jealousy in that statement? I mean, isn't that good for someone who wants to be mayor?"

"Depends on who he has to step on to get there."

"So far, to my knowledge, he hasn't stepped on anyone."

"He may be good at hiding the bodies."

She detected more than jealousy. She detected a disdain for Russ, her knight in shining armor. "You don't like him very much, do you?"

He topped off his coffee, then added cream and a teaspoon of sugar. She couldn't remember the last time she saw anyone add real sugar to their beverage. The only reason she kept it around was occasionally she liked to bake something, but that hadn't happened in months.

"Can't say that I do."

"Why not?"

He hesitated, as if deciding how honest he wanted to be with his feelings. "My own personal reasons, but hey, if he's your man, then who am I to rain on your parade."

"I didn't know I was in a parade."

"Dating a prominent figure like Russ Knightly— every time you and he go out that door, you probably get a following."

She knew he was right, but still. "Sometimes, but maybe I like it."

"Don't you know?"

She hated that he tripped her up. "No. I mean yes. I mean, that's only temporary. Once he's elected, things will quiet down."

"He doesn't strike me as the kind of guy who does anything in a quiet fashion."

She suddenly didn't like where this conversation was going. "Okay. Enough about me and my relationship, which you obviously don't approve of. What about you and your relationships? I suppose you have women lining up at the jailhouse just dying for your attention?"

"If they are, I haven't noticed."

She liked how he suddenly tried to be coy... As if.

"Are you secretly dating anyone?"

"Why would it be a secret?"

She shrugged. "You strike me as a private sort of guy."

"I am, but not that private. I just keep picking the wrong kind of girl."

"And what kind is that?"

"The kind who can't seem to date one guy at a time."

"You mean like Dani Century?"

"How'd you know about her?"

"It's a small town."

Everyone knew he'd dated Dani, and that she dumped him for a rodeo rat.

"She said she wanted a steady guy and that she wanted to put down roots."

"You should've asked her how deep. That girl wasn't about to stick around long enough to break through the topsoil."

Jet chuckled softly as he took a bite of his eggs.

"Don't I know it. You have a way with words. Anybody ever tell you that?"

"You're the first, but thanks."

She took the last bite of her waffle, which was now swimming in maple syrup.

"How about another waffle? I still have enough batter for one more."

"Sure," she told him, wanting their breakfast to last a little longer. "Your waffles are amazing, crispy but light as a feather."

"Sally Crane's recipe, foster family number five when I was about ten. She got it from her mom who came from Sweden."

"But how did you learn it? Seems a little odd for a ten year old to want to know how to make a waffle."

"That's 'cause I was an odd kid. Whenever I liked something, whether it was something to eat, or build, or a skill I thought would be good to know, I watched the person carefully and wrote everything down in a journal. Then I'd memorize it, because keeping any kind of personal possessions in foster care wasn't always possible."

"That explains a lot about your ability to handle Lily. What a crafty kid you must have been."

"You could say that, but to me, it was more about survival. The more I knew, the more I thought adults would want to keep me around. But that didn't pan out the way I thought it would."

"I can't imagine how tough and confusing it must have been for you, or for that matter, for all the children who are in foster care. I'm so worried about Lily, and what her future will be like."

He gazed at her, warmth and concern all over his

face. "Maybe her mom will come back for her. I hope that's the case, but if she doesn't, Lily has a good chance of getting adopted fairly quickly. Babies and toddlers have the best chance of settling into a permanent home. It's the children five and over who have a harder time of it."

"My siblings and I are blessed. You and Lily have made that abundantly clear. I'll never take my childhood for granted again."

"Now, how about that second waffle?" he asked, while opening the lid on the waffle iron, steam pouring out.

Coco held up her plate. "Yes, please, and more of that great bacon, as well."

Jet filled her plate and she immediately poured on more syrup and took a big bite. She couldn't remember when she'd been so honest with a guy, and he'd been so honest with her. She held back with Russ, just as she was sure he did the same with her. But that would all change once they were a true couple.

As they sat there, sharing breakfast, listening to Lily's contented coos, she couldn't help the many thoughts that flitted through her mind on what it would be like to be married to Sheriff Jet Wilson. Not only had he cooked her a perfect breakfast, with perfectly crispy waffles, crispy bacon and soft scrambled eggs, but he'd showered, shaved with one of her plastic razors, no doubt, and gotten completely dressed in the jeans and long-sleeved dark-gray shirt he'd worn the previous night. She'd never noticed how good he looked in civilian clothes, but she sure did now.

Her mind wandered a bit, recalling how warm and safe she'd felt last night, resting her head on his shoulder, cuddling up against his strong chest, as he now talked about what the day might be like for him and who he needed to call first about baby Lily.

It was at that moment that her cell phone rang. The distinctive tune told her Russ, the man of her dreams, the man she wanted to spend the rest of her life with, the man she should have been sharing breakfast with this morning, was on the line.

But for some inexplicable reason, she didn't have those feelings exactly.

"Someone you're avoiding?" Jet asked as the tune played on and on.

She wished she'd switched her phone to vibrate.

"No. Of course not. Had to swallow my last bite first."

Jet stood when the bell went off on the waffle iron indicating that the next waffle was cooked, and he slipped it out onto a clean plate while she took the call...walking away from the table and into the living room for some privacy.

"Hey, Russ," she said into the phone, trying to sound excited.

"Hey, yourself. I take it that arrogant sheriff and the screaming baby are gone by now?"

"Um, sure," she said, flat-out lying. This was one time when she couldn't bear to tell Russ the truth. Besides, the sheriff and Lily would be gone for good once breakfast was over. She was sure of it.

"Unless you're walking, nobody's going anywhere," Drew Gillian told Jet as she stood in the kitchen drinking a supersize cup of coffee. "Even though I live down the street, getting here on foot wasn't easy, and driving anywhere would be next to impossible." Drew couldn't have been more than nineteen or twenty years old, had shoulder-length blond hair with purple steaks, a classic Roman nose, almond-shaped amber-colored eyes, cherub-formed lips with a beauty mark right above her top lip and a petite five-foot-two figure. Personality wise, she reminded Jet of Punky, a tiny bundle of roar.

"That's impossible," Jet countered, then took off down the stairs to check it out for himself. He'd looked out the window earlier that morning, before he'd sat down for breakfast, and he'd checked the weather report. Both had indicated that the city was coming back to life.

He opened the front door.

More snow had fallen in that hour or so he'd taken to enjoy breakfast, and it was still falling now. "Come on!"

His phone chirped in his pocket, and when he looked at the screen, he saw the deputy sheriff's smiling face from a picture he'd taken during the summer's Western Days festival. Nash had replaced Deputy Sheriff Hunter Sears, who'd gotten married and moved to Oregon soon thereafter.

"What's up?" Jet said into the phone after he accepted the call.

"A lot," Nash Young said. "Got several people stranded in their cars, a couple roofs collapsed, one on a business in town, but thankfully nobody was hurt, and what appears to be a break-in overnight at a house in the two hundred block of Main Street. Nothing is reported missing, though. I think whoever it was only wanted to get in out of the cold. Oh, yeah, and someone left you a note at the jail."

"Did you see who it was?"

"No. It was under the door when I opened up this morning. Where'd you get stranded last night? Looks like you left this place in a hurry. Your half-eaten dinner is still on your desk."

"Long story. An abandoned baby named Lily. I'm over here at Doctor Grant's clinic."

"A real baby? Not a foal or a calf or a puppy, but an actual human baby?"

"Yep, a two-week-old girl named Lily, according to the note."

"Well, in all this snow, I hope Doctor Grant can take care of Lily for a few days, 'cause there's no way you can drive her over to Idaho Falls to Child Protective Services, and from what I heard, the hospital is overrun with everything from a couple heart attacks to some nasty frostbite cases. This kind of weather brings out the worst."

"Thanks for the heads-up."

"You coming in today?"

"Not unless you drive over and pick me up. My rig is snowed in solid."

"Be there as soon as I can," Nash said, then Jet disconnected.

Nash Young's personal truck could get through anything. The tires alone were the size of a small person, and it was fitted with a supercharged engine good enough for any top-fueled drag race. Nothing could stop that vehicle, not even another car, which it could simply drive over. Deputy Sheriff Nash Young drove it for most of the winter months only because he'd designed it after the trucks he'd driven in Monster Jams across the country. He only gave up competing last year when he narrowly escaped an exploding rig and promised his mom he'd do so. Jet had a feeling that it was only a matter of time until he was competing again, but until that happened, Briggs was lucky to have Nash and his four-wheel monster truck to help evacuate stranded motorists almost anywhere across the valley.

When Jet walked back into the kitchen, Drew busied herself playing with Lily and asking way too many questions, questions that sounded more on the nosey, gossipy side rather than the friendly, getting-to-know-Lily side.

"So, Lily's name was written on the back of a receipt from Sammy's Smokehouse?" Drew asked Coco. "That's mighty curious."

"Yeah, and when I first took Lily out of her bassinet, she smelled of barbecue," Coco said.

"You told me about the receipt, but you never told me she smelled of barbecue. Why didn't you tell me this before?" Jet asked, miffed.

"I didn't think it was important."

"It's real important," Drew alleged. "This means whoever had Lily, probably the mom, ate at Sammy's right before she dumped Lily on your front porch. The curious element in all of this is why didn't this distressed mom leave her at the jail? Unless she knew how you take in strays, which would make the mom a resident of Briggs. Only a resident would know about your stray policy."

"For one thing, a baby is hardly a stray," Jet countered, then he turned to Coco. "You have a stray policy? And here I thought these folks left their animals on your doorstep because of convenience. The nearest pound is thirty miles away. If you have an actual policy for strays and didn't register it with the sheriff's department, your fines could be doubled."

"You would do that?"

"It's the law," Jet told her, expecting her to understand...although, from the acerbic look on her face, he didn't think that was the case.

"Fine. You just keep doing what you have to do or how else could you possibly sleep at night?"

"I don't, remember?"

"That's not what I saw last night."

"Sheriff Wilson spent the night?" Drew asked with a teasing grin.

"That's none of your business," both Coco and Jet said in unison.

Drew held up a hand. "Chill, I won't tell anyone."

"Jet didn't have anywhere else to go. The snow was too deep."

"Jet?" Drew asked. "You call the sheriff Jet?"

Jet stepped in front of Coco, facing Drew. He'd caught the look of anger on Coco's face and decided he needed to de-escalate this situation before she admitted that she and Jet had slept in the same bed together.

"Here's what happened, not that it's anybody's business, but just to get the record straight. Baby Lily was left on Doctor Grant's doorstep sometime right before ten last night. Soon thereafter, the doctor phoned me about an abandoned baby, and after stopping at Whipple's for supplies, I arrived to take the child. By the time we had her changed and fed, the snow inhibited me from leaving, so I spent the entire night on the sofa while Doctor Grant and Lily slept in her bed.

"As far as the mom or whoever left the baby on Doctor Grant's doorstep rather than mine goes, I can only speculate that Sammy's is on this side of town, and with all the snow that fell last night, driving any farther was next to impossible. And besides, I didn't get back to the jail until after ten thirty."

"Where were you?" Drew asked like she was trying to solve a mystery.

"On official business."

"No, you weren't. You were ahead of me in line at the pickup window at Sammy's."

Jet suddenly hated living in a small town.

Normally, Jet ate at Sammy's three times a week, and he always ate inside. He'd been worried about the snow buildup last night, so he'd decided on takeout instead. He wondered if he'd eaten inside the restaurant last night, would he have seen the mom or whoever had Lily? Things might be a lot different right now if he had…especially given the third degree by Drew Gillian.

"Look, we can't speculate on who left Lily or why. That's not our concern. All we can do now is keep her fed and safe until I can drive her over to Child Protective Services in Idaho Falls so the right people can take care of her. Thus far there's nothing coming in about a stolen baby, or a missing baby. The woman I spoke to is waiting for her, and will handle the case."

Drew shook her head. "Then she'll be a ward of the state?"

"Something like that, yes." He turned to Coco. "Deputy Sheriff Nash Young will be by soon to pick me up. Do you think you can take care of Lily until later today? By then, the roads should be open and I can drive her over. You're free to join me if you want to."

"Thanks, but I can't."

"I know how you feel about Lily, and this is tough

for both of us, but it's something we have to do. It might make you feel better if you can see where she'll be going."

Her face darkened, and Jet suspected something else troubled Coco other than just giving up Lily.

"Jet, it's not that I don't want to go with you... It's that... I have a date with Russ tonight."

Jet quickly took a step back, feeling as if she'd just slapped him. He should've realized that call from Russ earlier meant more than just a friendly good-morning greeting. "Oh, but I thought... Yes. Of course you do. Why wouldn't you? I simply assumed... But you know what they say about anyone who assumes. Anyway, I'll be going. I'll call you before I stop by to pick up Lily. By then I should have a car seat, as well. Okay, I guess I'll be heading out."

"Jet, I..."

"No. My mistake. We're good. All good." A horn sounded from outside, signaling that Nash had arrived. Jet faced Drew. "For Lily's sake, it might be best if you kept all this to yourself."

"Whatever you say, Sheriff," Drew told him, her phone only inches away from her arm as she sat in a kitchen chair with Lily resting on a soft pillow positioned carefully on Drew's lap.

Jet knew that gossip about Lily and most likely about his spending the night at the doctor's apartment would be all over town before Jet drove away from the front door.

He'd wager Drew's fingers were itching to start texting.

Infant supplies started coming in almost before Coco knew what was happening, and soon it looked like a baby shower had exploded inside her once modest single woman's apartment. Gone were the assortment of scented candles and silk throw pillows, and in their place were tiny coats, chew toys, boxes of diapers, blankets of all sizes and colors, onesies, tiny dresses, tights, itty-bitty shoes, handmade knit sweaters, caps and even mittens. A variety of bottles lined her kitchen counters, along with electric bottle warmers, blenders, plastic baby dishes and tiny spoons. There wasn't one flat surface that didn't have some sort of baby item on it, not one flat surface that even slightly resembled what was once her apartment, her home.

Now it was all about Lily, and no amount of reasoning could sway the good folks of Briggs, Idaho, not to contribute to this tiny abandoned baby. They made the trek through the heavy snow on snowshoes, by sled and by sheer willpower. Even when Coco would try to tell them that Sheriff Wilson would be taking Lily to Child Protective Services later that evening, no one seemed to listen. Even her sister-in-law, Zoe, had made the journey over to bring cloth diapers, which she explained had a myriad of uses. Kenzie was stuck on the ranch, so she couldn't stop by, and Kayla and Callie were snowed in on the other end of town…which was fine by Coco. All this fuss over a baby she couldn't keep seemed a bit silly.

But people just kept bringing gifts over. Mostly items that their babies had grown out of, but there was the occasional new item in the mix, as well.

"Really, Mrs. Walker, these blankets are lovely, but I already have several. You can bring them back to Hess's Department Store and get a refund," Coco told her, but

Mrs. Walker, wife to Mr. Walker, who owned Sole Man Shoe Repair, wouldn't hear of it.

"You can never have too many blankets. Go on and keep them," she said as she gazed over at a sleeping Lily all tucked into her bassinet that now sat on the sofa. "Poor darling. Her mom was probably passing through. Sammy has a couple of big signs out on the main road. I bet that's why her mom stopped."

"But how did she know to leave little Lily on Doc Grant's doorstep?" Kendra Myers asked. Kendra, a petite woman with long black hair and a ready smile, had six kids of her own, but still managed to work a couple shifts at Belly Up each week. She'd contributed more of the bottles that Lily liked, along with a cradle and several packages of baby wipes, which Coco truly appreciated considering she went through them like sand slipping through an hourglass.

"That's the puzzler," Amanda Gump said. Not only had Amanda brought over the infant car seat, but she'd brought an assortment of scones, muffins and cookies, as well as an entire chocolate cake from her bakery, Holy Rollers. "She either still lives in Briggs, or she used to live here. Beyond that, I can't imagine who it can be."

"Me, neither," Kitty Sullivan added. She had contributed onesies made of organic cotton, along with a couple of organic cotton receiving blankets. Everyone knew that Kitty Sullivan was into everything organic and wouldn't even consider anything artificial getting anywhere close to her. Last year she'd opened up her own organic shop, The Green Scene, which carried a bit of everything that had an organic source. "All the pregnant women I know are still pregnant."

"I wish we could figure this out," Cindy Whipple

said. "When the sheriff stopped by last night, he was being very tight-lipped about the whole thing."

"That's because Idaho has laws to guard the identity of the mother and protect her during the first thirty days," Coco warned, wanting everyone to leave now. "She has the right to full anonymity, and there's nothing we can do about it."

"Maybe so," Cindy said, "but wouldn't you like to know?"

"No," Coco told her. "It's the law."

"Oh, you sound just like Sheriff Wilson," Drew said, dismissing Coco, then going about speculating with the other women as they sat around Coco's dining room table, sipping on coffee and tea while enjoying the assortment of baked goods Amanda had contributed.

But for the first time since Coco had met the sheriff, she appreciated what his strict adherence to the law was all about and felt very protective of Lily's mom, whoever she might be.

"And speaking of the sheriff, Drew says he spent the night," Cindy said, just after she took another sip of tea.

"Did she happen to mention he slept on the sofa? He was trapped here because of the snow. Nothing we could do about it," Coco said.

Coco flashed on the warmth she'd felt cuddled up in Jet's arms, but that was no one's business.

"A good-looking man like that, and you let him sleep on the sofa?" Kendra chided.

"You all know I'm dating Russ Knightly," Coco told them.

"Does Russ know Sheriff Wilson spent the night?" Amanda asked. "'Cause snow or no snow, my Milo would be pacing the floor."

"Nothing happened," Coco said, knowing full well that was the honest truth.

"Well, why not?" Kendra asked, sounding put out. "You're not married...yet. And from what I hear, Russ ain't no saint."

Coco took offense. She knew that Russ had been out with a number of women, but all that had changed once they'd started dating...at least, that was the impression she had. "That's not... He... I..."

Kendra shrugged. "All I'm saying is keep your options open...at least until there's a ring on your finger... if that's something you really want."

"Is Russ going to propose?" Cindy Whipple asked, almost choking on her tea. "Who told you that?"

Then everyone started to speculate about Coco's pending engagement to Russ Knightly even before the search for baby Lily's mom had been settled. All Coco could do was sigh, while she hoped that Jet was having a better day than she was. Rescuing stranded motorists seemed like a much more useful way to spend the afternoon than gossiping about Coco's nonexistent love life...in front of her, no less.

Chapter 5

It had been a long, arduous day for both Sheriff Jet Wilson and Deputy Sheriff Nash Young. Not only had they dug out five cars and two pickups, but they'd helped the fire department rescue the entire senior center when the center lost their electricity from a downed power line due to the storm. He and Nash were able to use a couple generators to keep the heat going for the more immobile residents, but most everyone else had to be evacuated to St. Paul's church hall until that line was repaired. Needless to say, getting all those seniors comfortable on cots and folding chairs proved to be a real project.

Fortunately, Father Beau, along with several volunteer parishioners, were real lifesavers, distracting everyone with songs and games and hot liquids. Father Beau deserved a medal of some kind.

Then when the electricity was restored in the center,

everyone had to be transported back, which was helped out by Travis Granger and his sled pulled by his two magnificent Clydesdales.

All in all, it was one heck of a day, and it wasn't over yet. They both had to remain ready to act if there were more needed rescues that night, so Nash would try to get some shut-eye at the jail while Jet took care of Lily. At least, that was the plan. Jet made an appointment to meet with a Marsha Oberlin at eight o'clock in Idaho Falls. She'd agreed to be available whenever he was ready to drop off Lily, but on a night like this, everything could change in a heartbeat.

Both men stomped the caked snow off their boots right outside the front door of the station, then shrugged out of their coats and hung them on the coatrack next to the door. They each took their hats with them to their desks.

"Are you really going to make that hour's drive to Idaho Falls with Lily?" Nash asked once he sat in his wooden swivel chair and leaned back, the chair squeaking with his weight.

Nash's desk was located right outside Jet's office, and unless Jet shut his door, Nash could look right in, which he did. Normally, Nash was an easygoing guy, who stayed out of Jet's business and took to police work like a fish to water. Nash was young and had a backbone, which Jet appreciated a lot. He wore his brown hair extra short, his uniform pressed and his outlook positive.

"I don't have a choice. I can't impose on Doctor Grant for another night, and I certainly can't bring Lily here."

"Why not? You seem to like it here. Oh, there's that letter for you. It's on your desk."

But Jet didn't care about a letter, which was probably someone asking for some kind of favor. Right now, he was defending his logic concerning baby Lily and Doctor Grant.

"I don't like sleeping here, but for right now, with the water problems going on in my apartment building, it's been fine. But this is no place for a baby. There's no telling what can happen."

"This is Briggs, Idaho. Nothing ever happens."

Nash had a point. They ran a small Sheriff's department, one sheriff, one deputy and an answering service. There was one jail cell that so far had only held a handful of perps since Jet came to work there. One of them was Cindy Whipple's husband sleeping off a night of binge drinking. Another perp was a friend of Russ Knightly's, but he'd been in and out so quickly he'd hardly spent any time at all inside that jail cell.

"There's always a first time for everything. I don't want that first time to happen while there's a baby around. It's not safe."

"Want me to drive you? From what I hear, the roads still have some ice."

Jet could go a few miles in Nash's monster truck, but after that, the suspension bounced him around too much. Plus, all that bouncing wasn't safe for a fragile infant. "Thanks, but the SUV will be fine. I'll stop off and pick up a car seat somewhere first."

"Not much open, and besides, I understand that half the town stopped by Doctor Grant's place today with baby stuff. Somebody may have already donated a car seat."

Jet leaned on his desk and stared at Nash. "How do you always know everything that's going on and I don't?"

"I'm Facebook friends with Drew Gillian and she…"

"You can stop right there. I just met Drew this morning and I can tell she likes to keep everyone informed."

Nash smirked. "There's some stuff on there about you spending the night at Doctor Grant's. Now, if I didn't know you better, I'd say Russ Knightly might have a run for his money."

Jet instantly felt a pang of irritation that Drew had spread gossip about himself and the doctor, even though he'd known she would. Still, was there nothing sacred? No friendship that outweighed gossip?

Apparently not in Briggs.

"Nothing happened. I was stuck there because of the snow."

"Convenient, ain't it? I was stuck at Drew's house."

Somehow Jet didn't think that encounter had turned out the same as his. "How'd that go?"

"I was a complete gentleman. Besides, she lives with her parents, and her dad is about six foot four and probably weighs in at well over two hundred and sixty pounds. Believe me, I slept on the sofa. Where'd you sleep?"

"On the sofa," Jet said, but he wasn't very convincing.

"Huh, maybe I needed to send Brick Gillian over… that's his name, Brick, because he's as solid as a brick."

"Both the doctor and I are adults."

"Legally, so are Drew and I, but in Brick's mind, no one shares a bed unless they're married."

"I'll keep that in mind next time I'm snowbound over at Doctor Grant's."

Nash grinned. "Ha! Then you admit that you—"

Jet stood. "I don't admit anything. You're jumping to conclusions that can damage her reputation. She's in a relationship with Russ Knightly, soon to be our new mayor if he has anything to say about it, and come to think of it, they have a date tonight, so I better get going."

Jet had forgotten all about their date. He'd promised to be at Coco's apartment in plenty of time, and
he was already running late for both her date and dropping off Lily.

"I won't tell anybody if you admit the truth."

"Nothing happened, and even if it did, which it did
not, it's nobody's business."

"Tell that to Russ Knightly. I hear he's the jealous type."

Jet thought about Russ's likely lip-lock with that
blonde bombshell over in Jackson Hole. "Maybe so,
but he's got nothing to be jealous about between me
and his girl, Coco."

"On a first-name basis, huh?"

"I'm going." He secured his hat on his head, grabbed
his down parka off the hook and quickly slipped it on.

"Wait!" Nash said from behind Jet. "You forgot the
letter."

"What letter?" Jet asked, turning as he opened the
front door. An icy wind slammed against his body, causing him to instantly shiver with its force.

"The one I told you about earlier. The one I found
shoved under the door this morning when I came in."
Nash hustled over to Jet's desk, retrieved the letter,
walked it over and held it out for Jet. As soon as Jet
looked at it, he recognized the scratchy writing on the
front: *Dani Century*. What could she want?

Aside from all the fuss that afternoon over baby Lily,
it had been a relatively calm day for Doctor Grant. No
emergency out on a ranch was too dire that she couldn't
handle it over the phone, and nothing required her to
have to consider driving anywhere to take care of an
injured animal. She was grateful for that much.

Besides, she'd liked spending the day with Lily, surrounded with people who wanted to do well by her. Despite the speculation, and the gossip, the residents of Briggs had big hearts, as made apparent by all the clothes, toys and baby supplies scattered around her apartment.

All her orphaned animals had been fed, and their cages cleaned out, thanks to Drew's help. Coco had treated two dogs with bladder infections, prescribed medication for ear mites for three house cats and given yearly booster shots to two golden retrievers whose owners were determined to keep their pets on schedule, despite the weather. Coco didn't know what she would do without Drew to lean on. Drew had somehow managed to keep Coco's patients happy regardless of all the baby chaos.

Once again Coco had slipped into a provocative cocktail dress. This time she wore red lace with three-inch red velvet heels. Not quite as sexy as the previous night's ensemble, but it still clung to all the right places. She and Russ would be attending a dinner and dancing gala for all the business owners in Briggs, at Pauline's Inn on the edge of town. The roads were now somewhat cleared, so there shouldn't be a problem for the partygoers. A car would pick Coco up at eight, and whisk her and Russ to the event, and they would finish what they'd started the previous night. She'd worn her finest black lingerie for the occasion, and intended to end the evening with the sexy love affair they had begun the previous night, only this time, it would be at Russ's estate.

The problem was, she couldn't get Jet Wilson out of her head. Everything about him sent her heart racing and her skin tingling. He'd made her feel safe and relaxed, as if no matter what happened around her, he would handle it. He'd amazed her with his tenderness for Lily, and how adept he was with fulfilling all her needs. And even when Lily awoke in the middle of the night, he didn't shy away. Instead he was right there helping to make sure that whatever was bothering her could be resolved.

The man was simply too surprising to ignore.

Plus, the fact that she was giving up Lily really put a damper on her emotions. Getting out with Russ to a fancy event could only help put her in a better mood… but so far, she wasn't feeling it.

"You're kidding, right?" Drew said as she held Lily on her shoulder and walked her around the room with Punky following close behind, making sure the area was clear of any possible danger. Lily had been fussy while Coco was getting dressed, so she'd asked Drew for some help, which she seemed more than happy to give. "You're going out with Russ tonight? All of this—" she nodded her head and gave Coco the once-over "—is for Russ Knightly?"

Coco stood next to the dining room table, folding baby clothes into a pile, then placing them into a large paper bag with handles.

"He's the man that I'm dating, so yes, it's for Russ."

"And here I thought it was for the sheriff. Don't you like Sheriff Wilson?"

"He's bullheaded and a stickler for the law."

Drew rolled her big doe eyes, thick dark lashes only adding to the exaggerated reaction. "Um, duh. He's the sheriff."

"I'm aware of his job title, but you also know how many citations he's given me this past year, and how many fines I've had to pay. The man has no heart."

Not exactly true, especially in light of the previous night, but the more she thought about the sheriff, the more she realized last night may have simply been an anomaly brought on by extreme circumstances. Focusing on Sheriff Wilson's past aggressions seemed to help clear him from her heart.

That had always been her problem when it came to men. She couldn't see them for who they really were in the midst of being wooed by them...not that the sheriff was in any way wooing her...or was he?

Had last night been an elaborate scheme to win her affections so she'd let her guard down? But to what end? By all indications, he didn't like anything about her, especially her determination not to turn away stray barn animals when she knew they were outlawed within city limits.

"Maybe not for goats and pigs, but he sure does have a big heart when it comes to babies."

"That's beside the point. I deal in livestock and house pets, not babies, and if he's going to be my friend, he has to give me a break every now and then."

"So you're mad at him because last night he gave you a fine for your current menagerie?"

Coco wanted to tell her that she'd gotten a huge fine that would set her back a few months, but she hadn't gotten one. "Not exactly."

"I don't know what that means. Either he gave you a citation or he didn't."

Drew had a way of seeing things with extreme clarity, a trait Coco admired...most of the time.

"He did not give me a citation, but that doesn't mean he wasn't thinking about it. We were snowbound. What could I do about any of the animals then?"

Her face lit up, as if she'd stumbled onto the meaning of life. "So he bent the rules?"

"Kind of."

"More than just kind of. He could've still slapped you with a large fine, but he didn't. This says a lot."

Drew was jumping to conclusions that weren't grounded in anything other than wishful thinking. Truth be told, Coco knew that Drew wasn't a fan of Russ Knightly, either as a person or as a prospective mayor. Coco continually tried to change her mind, but so far all attempts had fallen on deaf ears.

"No, it doesn't."

"Yes, it does. It says that he's warming up to you. That he likes you. That he's willing to ignore his ethics for you. This is huge! I think you should cancel your date with Russ, and instead, when Sheriff Wilson shows up, you should invite him in for dinner before he takes baby Lily to wherever he has to take her. Besides, I know you're in no hurry to let this little sweetheart go."

With much care, Drew sat down on the sofa and moved Lily to her lap, laying her in the center of her legs so her tiny head was cradled between Drew's knees and her tiny feet rested against Drew's stomach. A position Lily seemed to love, and a position Coco had adopted for most of the day, both while everyone was there and once they'd left.

Punky jumped up and sat on the arm of the sofa…a perfect vantage point from which to guard the apartment.

The apartment, although rather large, could barely contain all the baby supplies that had been given to Coco for Lily. She only hoped everything would fit into Jet's SUV and they could donate it to Child Welfare when the time came.

That was if Sheriff Wilson was still planning on going through with his plan. She hadn't heard from him all day, and hadn't wanted to call him for fear he might come and take Lily sooner rather than later. But now it was getting late, and if the sheriff didn't show up in the next fifteen minutes, Coco was contemplating leaving Drew here to deal with him and with Lily.

"Don't be ridiculous. Certainly, I'm ready to let Lily go," Coco said, but in the same breath, she realized how sad she would be once Lily was out of her life.

She suddenly felt as if Lily understood her, especially when she let out a little series of complaints. Coco went over and sat down next to Drew, and she stroked Lily's perfect silky head. "Okay, yes, it's hard to let her go… extremely hard, but there's nothing I can do about it. She's not mine to keep, but I'm sure she'll be in good hands. Someone will take her into their heart very soon. I'm sure there are hundreds of wonderful people waiting to adopt a lovely baby like Lily. And no way do I want to make dinner for the sheriff. That would bring on way too many complications."

Although now that she thought of it, she would love to spend another night with Jet and Lily. She couldn't remember the last time she'd felt so at ease with a situation as she had last night, but she would never admit that to Drew or the entire town would have them engaged by morning.

"What kind of complications? That you actually like him? Which I can tell that you do. Every time you mention his name your face lights up."

Coco abruptly stood. "That's just my new dewy makeup. It's supposed to make my face glow."

"Whatever you say." Drew checked her phone for the umpteenth time. "Isn't the sheriff cutting it close? Shouldn't he be here by now?"

Drew was right. The sheriff was way overdue. Coco banked on her contingency plan.

"I was hoping you could stay with Lily until he gets here."

"I would love to, but I'm supposed to meet up with some friends in a half hour. We're going ice-skating at Skaits. The pond is open despite all the snow, and afterward, I'm meeting Nash for hot cocoa at Holy Rollers. Matter of fact—" she picked up Lily and handed her to Coco "—I have to leave now if I'm going to have enough time to walk over there."

"You're meeting the deputy sheriff? This is the third time in the last couple of weeks."

"I know a good guy when I see him, unlike someone else I'm best friends with."

But before Coco could put up any resistance, Drew had grabbed her coat and dashed down the stairs in less time than it took for Coco to adjust Lily in her arms. Punky barked in defiance, and suddenly, Coco was once again alone with baby Lily, the child who was stealing her heart.

Sheriff Jet Wilson's phone buzzed once again as he sat in his SUV parked across the street from Coco's place. He'd been sitting there for the past hour, in the cold, trying to wrap his head around what had to be the single most confusing news he'd ever gotten in his entire life. He'd wanted to go in and discuss it with Coco, who had called him at least four times in the past half hour, but he'd seen Drew up in her apartment through the windows and he didn't want to discuss anything either on the phone or in person while she was around. Not that he couldn't have simply asked her to leave, but that act alone would have spun some gossip, and frankly, he didn't need any more tongues wagging.

He watched as Drew exited out onto the front porch and then walked up the sidewalk to her house.

The coast was now clear.

Still, he hesitated.

He kept reading the letter over and over, not wanting to believe it, not wanting to accept it, not knowing how to accept it.

> …Lily is your daughter. I thought I could keep her and move on, but I've met someone and I can't look after a baby anymore…

When he'd first read those two sentences, he thought maybe he'd gotten the wrong letter, that perhaps it was meant for someone else…surely not for him.

Then when he read the name on the envelope again, and again, he knew Dani had written it for him. But it simply couldn't be true.

The thing was, he knew for a fact they'd never had unprotected sex, so unless Dani had purposely sabotaged one of the condoms, which he wouldn't put completely past her, or one of them was defective, which occasionally happened, Lily could not be his.

Or so he wanted desperately to believe.

He couldn't be a father. Not with his job, the state of his finances, his wacky sleep schedule. Heck, he didn't even have a place to live. And what of the townsfolk? They'd eat this stuff up and probably portray him as the bad guy. The dad was always the bad guy in these kinds of things.

At first he was angry over the letter. Why hadn't Dani confronted him in person? What kind of a mother left their baby on a cold, windy porch when the father, or who she thought was the father, lived right there in town?

But sometime during the past fifteen minutes, his attitude changed. He decided that Dani was lying, that the odds of him being the father were next to impossible. Besides, there was some doubt that she was loyal to him during the time they'd dated. He would proceed with his plans of dropping Lily off with Marsha Oberlin. He'd already called to tell her he would be late, and she was fine with it.

He felt certain that a loving family would adopt Lily. That there were probably three or four families right now waiting for her—all he had to do was drop her off with Ms. Oberlin.

Still, his mind raced with various scenarios, where Lily didn't get adopted and, just like him, she had to grow up in foster care.

And what if Dani was telling the truth? What if he was Lily's dad? How could he allow his own daughter to go into foster care? He exited his SUV just as a shiny black luxury vehicle pulled up in front of Coco's clinic. Jet knew it belonged to Russ from the custom license plate: NITE-HWK. When another man got out and walked over and rang Coco's bell, Jet knew Russ must have sent his driver to pick her up.

Undaunted, Jet made his way to the clinic just as Coco's apartment door opened. He quickly ascended the three steps to the front porch.

"Cutting it close," Coco told him as he stood behind Russ's driver, a short man with glasses, dressed in a black suit, trying to look official. "I called you several times, but you never picked up."

"You can wait in the car," Jet told the driver, who now turned, revealing a small gold name tag pinned to his jacket pocket. Jet caught the name. "Peter... Doctor Grant will be down in a few minutes."

But Peter didn't move until Coco assured him that it would be okay. "Give me about ten minutes to pass baby Lily over to the sheriff."

Peter nodded and went back to his SUV, turning over the engine, undoubtedly wanting to keep warm.

"Is Lily ready?" Jet asked as he forged his way through the open doorway. Coco, he noted right away, was wearing a lethal dress under her open coat.

He wanted this thing over with as soon as possible so everyone could get back to their separate lives.

"Yes, she just fell asleep. I put her in the car seat Amanda donated. It's for an infant, so she fits perfectly."

"Great," Jet told her, realizing he'd forgotten all about picking up a car seat. The letter had so thrown him that it was all he could do to concentrate on driving over to Coco's clinic, much less think about getting more baby supplies along the way.

As they got farther into the apartment, aside from Punky greeting him with a frantic tail wag and jumping in front of him until he gave the tiny dog a nod of recognition and a couple hardy scratches under his ears, he couldn't help but acknowledge the place looked like a warehouse for baby stuff.

"What happened here?" he asked looking around at the clothes, toys and other gear for infants.

"Drew told a few people, and they told more folks, and before I knew it, half the town stopped by to donate to Lily."

"Don't they know that she's not staying?"

"I tried to tell them, but they insisted on Lily having it. If not, they're hoping the stuff can be donated to a children's charity."

"Fair enough, but there's no time now to search for

a good outfit to donate to. I can do it tomorrow probably. For now, I just want Lily, a couple bottles of formula, a change of clothes and some diapers. I won't be
able to take any more than that, and I don't even know
if they'll let me give them that much."

He walked over and looked down at Lily, who was
fast asleep strapped into the car seat. She seemed so
helpless it about ripped out his heart just staring at her,
but he told himself it was for the best. He was only
doing what he had to do. There was no way he could
keep her even if she was his.

"But you know she won't take any other bottle. You
have to tell them about the bottle. I'd hate to have her
fuss all night and not eat."

Coco put a bag together with only the things he asked
for. While he waited, he tried not to look at Lily. If he
didn't look at her, he might be able to steel his emotions
so that he could go through with this.

Besides, what if Lily was his? What would it change?
Nothing.

This was for the best.

He kept telling himself that over and over, but he
didn't believe it for a moment.

"I will. I promise."

"And she doesn't like to sit when you burp her, she
likes it best when she's on your shoulder. Can you tell
them that, as well?"

"I think they know how to handle a baby," he said, but
he had no idea who would take care of Lily. He only knew
what it had been like when he'd lived with foster parents.
Most of them pretended to care for a little while, at least
while the representative came to check on things, but for
the most part he and any other child was on his or her own.

"From what you told me, I'm not so sure."

"Then come with us and tell them for yourself, or are you too busy with Russ to think about Lily's needs, and all you want to do is pile everything on me?"

Jet knew what he'd just said was mean, but he hadn't been able to stop himself.

"That's not fair. I'm only reminding you of *her* needs. You can do anything you want with the information."

This was going no place fast. "Is everything together? Because your driver is waiting and I'm already late. The sooner I get this over with the better for all of us."

"Except maybe for Lily," Coco spit out. Her irritation matched his.

He grabbed the handle on the car seat and swung Lily over to his side. When he went for the bag, Coco held on to it. "I'll carry this down the stairs. They're a little steep and I certainly don't want you falling while you're carrying Lily," she said.

"I won't fall." He reached for the bag, but she held it away from him, only adding to his impatience with the entire situation. "She's only an unfortunate outcome of someone's irresponsible behavior."

"You don't know that. How can you possibly know what went on with her mom? For all you know, maybe someone forced her to give up her baby, or maybe she's destitute, or maybe, just maybe, she had no other recourse."

"Or maybe Lily just didn't fit into her plans with her new boyfriend."

They stared at each other, their ire palpable between them.

"What is all of this?" Coco demanded. "Why all the anger? Did you learn something about Lily today that you're not sharing? Do you know who the mother is?"

A million reasons why he should walk out Coco's

door with Lily, deliver her to the authorities and not think twice about her or Coco ever again flooded his thoughts. But through it all, he remembered that Coco was the first woman he'd ever been completely honest with in his entire adult life. She'd been kind, compassionate and understanding, just as he'd been to her. They'd shared a moment, a time of complete honesty.

Was he willing to throw it all away on principle?

"Yes, but… I have to go."

He turned to leave.

"You can't do this. You can't leave and not tell me the truth about Lily. I deserve that much. It's only fair after everything we shared with her in the last twenty-four hours."

"That doesn't give you any rights, Doctor Grant." He couldn't bring himself to tell her the truth. If he did then it would be real, and he didn't know if he was ready for reality.

"So now I'm Doctor Grant again?" She folded her arms across her chest. "Is that how you want to end this? Maybe you should give me a citation for harboring a baby. After all, I'm not legally equipped to keep a child. I'm more the llama type."

That brought about a smile. "You don't give up, do you?"

"I can be quite scrappy. And you'll have to contend with Punky, as well."

He hadn't noticed it before, but Punky stood in front of the door, his teeth bared, looking as if he wanted to take a chunk out of the sheriff…a tiny chunk, but a chunk nonetheless.

"I can have you arrested for this, you know. Your dog is hindering my departure."

"He's only protecting Lily's best interests."

As crazy as this was, Jet refused to back down.

He went for the doorknob and Punky bit into his trousers, pulling on them with all his might. His small feet slid on the wooden floor—he'd lose traction and have to start all over again. Jet looked down at the dog, then up at Coco. "You're kidding, right?"

"Punky is a force to be reckoned with."

"Fine," Jet said, finally giving in to the absurdity of the situation. "I'll tell you, but call off your attack dog before he pulls out a tooth."

She gave Punky a command to sit and stay, and he followed her orders to the letter. Then Jet gently placed a still-sleeping Lily on the table, went over to the sofa and sat down.

"Do you have any more of that scotch?"

"I do," she told him.

"Then I think you should pour us both a glass."

"I have a feeling this is going to take a while. Maybe I should call Russ and tell him I'm going to be late."

"That's up to you."

"Before I do that, can you give me a hint as to what this is all about?"

"Lily might be my daughter," Jet said as Coco poured the scotch into two glasses. She drank hers down in one go and then picked up her phone.

"Russ, hi," she said in a strong, no-nonsense voice. "Something important has come up, and I'm sorry, but I'm going to have to cancel our date tonight."

Then she disconnected, poured herself another scotch, walked over to the sofa and sat down next to Jet, tucking her feet under her bottom.

"So start at the beginning. I've got all night."

Chapter 6

"I keep causing you to break your dates with Russ," Jet told Coco as he sat next to her on the sofa, his legs stretched out in front of him. Boots, coat and hat all had been placed near the front door.

"No worries," Coco told him, now much more comfortable in checkered red-and-gray tights and a bright red oversize sweatshirt. They shared a plate of assorted cheese, sliced pears, apples and chunks of French bread that Coco had put together for a light dinner. "Russ understands. Heaven knows he's broken his share of dates with me."

She thought about last Saturday night when she'd raced home from a ranch almost thirty miles outside town so she could meet him at Belly Up, only to be told he'd forgotten about a fund-raiser in Jackson Hole that he needed to attend. When she questioned him on it, he'd blamed the mix-up on his assistant, who he always seemed to use as an excuse. Sometimes it made her wonder if there was something else going on.

"Not to be nosey, but how close are you and Russ? I mean, this is the second night you've canceled because of me. If we were dating, I'd be concerned."

She didn't know how honest she wanted to be about Russ, but she also knew Jet wouldn't go spreading the truth around town. Coco liked the fact that everyone seemed to be thinking they were more serious than they actually were.

"We're just getting to know each other, in the early stages of dating. No real commitments, yet."

She wanted him to know that the potential was still there, even if they hadn't taken that next step, which was none of his business, anyway.

"Ah, now it makes sense."

"What makes sense?"

She took a little offense. Did he know more than he was letting on?

Jet fidgeted, as if something was bothering him. "Nothing. I just thought you two were in a serious relationship. You know how this town likes to talk."

"I do, and this whole thing with you and Lily could rip through our town like wildfire on dry grass. So, tell me, since we're talking relationships, are you still in love with or have feelings for Lily's mother? I mean, maybe the two of you should try to work this out. For Lily's sake."

An important fact, considering her earlier thoughts about the sheriff...not that she was actually pondering having any kind of committed relationship with Sheriff Wilson. Still, she wanted to know where he stood, emotionally.

He shook his head. "Not possible. That ended a long time ago."

"You don't have to tell me who she is, but is it someone I'm going to bump into around town?"

The thought of running into the woman who gave up Lily made her pause.

"It's Dani Century, and as you probably know, she moved away months ago. I have no intention of working anything out with her. Besides, according to her note, she's with somebody else. Thing is, I don't see how any of this is possible. We always used protection."

Dani Century had breezed back into Briggs for about three months, then left one afternoon in a hurry. If memory served Coco right, she'd taken off with a cowboy who was busy learning the rodeo circuit and wanted Coco's brother, Carson, to teach him how to ride a bronc. Carson knew right off he wasn't serious and told him so up front. They both departed shortly after that.

"You know there's always a slight chance…" She didn't feel comfortable finishing the thought. "Well, sometimes there's a fault in the… I'm only saying."

With all her veterinary training, and all the foals and calves and kids she'd delivered, talking about sex still made her uncomfortable.

"Yeah, but come on…that's so rare."

"Apparently not rare enough," she chided. "But if you feel as though she's lying, you and Lily can always take a DNA test, just to be certain. The results can be had in a few days. That way you'll know for certain."

"That's true, but what do I do while I'm waiting? And, if I could help it, I really don't want anyone to know about this." He raked his hand through his hair and she noticed how his upper arm bulged under his shirt. The thought of his ripped chest sent her mind racing with sinful thoughts and she had to force herself to reel her mind back to the present problem.

"Well, if there's even a remote chance she's yours, you can't turn her over to Child Protective Services. There's no telling what would happen if you did. I'm sorry, but it seems like you're going to have to keep her until you can get the results of the test."

Coco felt as though she was making perfect sense, even for the stubborn, by-the-book sheriff.

"That's the problem. Actually, it's a twofold problem. I don't have anywhere to live. I've been sleeping at the jail while my landlord fixes a broken water pipe, which was supposed to have been taken care of early this week. With all this snow, who knows when it'll get fixed? The pipe is under the house.

"Plus, with my schedule, how the heck am I supposed to take care of an infant? She requires constant care and most of my day is spent out of the office. This will never work."

Coco thought for a moment, desperately wanting to help Jet and baby Lily, who she'd fallen completely in love with.

"My parents always taught me that all problems have solutions, you just have to dig deep enough to find them."

He drank down his scotch, then looked over at her. His deep brown eyes appeared almost completely black in the low lighting of her apartment.

"I can appreciate the sentiment, but my upbringing serves as the perfect example of how that theory doesn't work."

"On the contrary, it's the perfect example of how it

did work. Maybe not for your ideal way of thinking, but you weren't homeless or starving. The solution was to put you in foster care."

"So, after all that I've told you, you believe I should still turn Lily over? Is that what you're saying? I thought you were opposed to that."

"I am. We're not digging deep enough, but I may have a temporary solution, at least until your apartment is livable again and you can learn the truth about Lily. You and Lily can stay here!"

He smirked and looked down at the floor for a moment, obviously contemplating what she'd just suggested.

"As much as I appreciate the generous offer, this sofa is by far one of the most uncomfortable pieces of furniture I've ever sat on, much less tried to sleep on. And, even though we haven't discussed it, I can't keep sleeping with you. Besides, I don't think Russ would like it."

The thought of waking up every morning lying next to Jet Wilson was more than she wanted to contemplate.

She immediately told him her idea. "Obviously neither of those will work. However, I have a spare bedroom that I use for some storage and for my office, but you could buy one of those super air mattresses—they're exactly the size of a queen-size bed—and I can move my laptop anywhere. Lily can continue to sleep with me. I love having her share my room, so that's not a problem."

"Do you understand all the ramifications of that arrangement? It's one thing for me to have a scandal, but if Lily and I move in for a few days, that scandal will grow to epic proportions. Are you ready to take that on?"

She knew it was risky, but it seemed like the best idea for everyone involved. Russ was a tolerant man.

She felt certain he'd understand. Besides, it gave her more time with Lily, and that alone made her happy.

"Let them talk. It gives them something to do other than focus on the weather."

"It could hurt your relationship with Russ."

"I can take care of Russ. He's an open-minded man. He'll understand."

Jet looked skeptical. "There are a lot of words I would use to describe Russ Knightly, but *open-minded* isn't on the list."

"You don't know him like I do," she said, defending Russ. She truly believed that tolerance was one of his best qualities. Jet simply had the wrong opinion of him.

"If you say so, but let's not forget that Lily wakes up a lot during the night. I don't care about my sleep, but it's not fair to you."

"I don't mind. I'm used to it with all the emergency calls I get. Some of the animals are sick and require medication in the middle of the night. Besides, you and I can take turns feeding Lily."

His face began to soften, and she could see that his entire body was beginning to relax.

"Okay, I can see how this might work, for a while, but we both have outdoor day jobs. What do we do with Lily while we're running around the valley?"

"I can take her with me when I know my day won't be too intense. She's not a burden. And if I can't, I know Drew would love to babysit her. And maybe Nash can take on more of the outdoor problems, and you can take Lily with you to the jail for a few hours."

Shaking his head, he pushed himself up on the sofa. "I don't like children in a police station, much less near a jail cell. You never know what might happen."

"Well, then, maybe you can work from here for a few hours a day. Transfer any phone calls to your personal phone instead of an answering service."

He folded his arms on his chest, showing his last bits of resistance to the idea.

"I don't know," he said with a slight crack in his voice. "It's a lot to put on you. Why would you do this?"

"Because Lily deserves the best possible chance at life."

"And you think I can give it to her?"

"I do," she told him, looking straight into his eyes. "You'll be a great father to Lily."

He looked away. "I'm the last person she needs as her father. Lily deserves two parents who love her, who can raise her together. She should have a father who doesn't have a dangerous job, and a mom who won't run out on her for another guy."

"She does, but for now, you're all she has, and after that DNA test comes in, she may not even have you. But for the next few days I'm willing to give her all the love I have…if you are."

"Either way, this is a tough decision."

Lily started to fuss, with little groans and complaints.

"It's either my solution or you should be packing Lily up soon, because it's a long drive with a screaming baby."

Lily began to wail, and they both jumped up to take care of her at the same time. Coco unfastened her from the seat and picked her up to love her.

"I'll make the bottle," Jet said, a wide grin warming his face.

"I'll take care of her diaper," Coco told him, satisfied she'd changed his mind.

It was then that Coco realized that for the next sev-

eral days, she, Lily and Sheriff Wilson would be playing family. She only hoped she hadn't just set herself
up for a huge heartbreak…with Russ.

Bright and early the next morning, after Jet had
showered, dressed, changed and fed Lily, then left for
the day, Coco cleared out the boxes in the spare bedroom. Lily slept as Coco stored what items she could in
her walk-in closet, and the rest of the containers downstairs in the clinic. Though, as soon as the animals heard
her rattling around, they all started clamoring for food
and attention, which she gladly gave them. She let the
kittens, the piglet and the puppy out of their respective
cages for some much-needed playtime. They'd have to
be adopted out soon, she realized. She didn't have the
heart to keep them penned up all day.

Funny thing about baby animals, they all got along
usually once they'd given each other a good sniff. Even
the llamas enjoyed playing with the puppy that at once
tried to show his dominance, only to be shot down by
a couple strong nudges.

Coco checked her messages and learned that her sister Kenzie, who managed the Grant family ranch, would
be able to stop by this week to pick up the farm animals.

Then she checked on her appointments. She had
three, but was able to push them off until tomorrow,
when she knew all the back roads would be cleared
enough to navigate safely. Fortunately, she only had
a couple of appointments in her clinic that afternoon,
so keeping Lily with her wasn't going to be a problem.

She thought she'd spend part of the morning getting
everything ready for Jet and then manage a late breakfast with Russ at Holy Rollers, the local bakery. Next

to her mom's cookies and cakes, the items in this place were her absolute favorite.

Russ and Coco took a private table inside the bakery, which prided itself on offering almost any kind of baked good a patron could want.

"How long did you say Lily and the sheriff would be staying at your apartment?" Russ asked for the second time.

Coco sipped on a mocha latte while Russ drank a cup of iced black coffee. They shared a plain oatmeal muffin, not exactly Coco's first choice, but Russ had ordered it before she'd had a say in the matter. She'd gone back and ordered a dozen assorted doughnuts to go, and had already stuffed the box in her SUV for later. She now knew Jet liked doughnuts, especially the custard-filled kind that she enjoyed, with thick chocolate frosting. They both liked chocolate frosting. The owner of Holy Rollers, Amanda Gump, who had generously donated the car seat to Lily, who always had a good word for everyone she knew, had offered up all this doughnut information without Coco having to tell her why she wanted to know.

The cozy shop buzzed with the usual morning rush, as customers hovered over the glass display counters waiting for their morning shot of sugar and caffeine. Holy Rollers was *the* morning hangout for all ages. Coco couldn't get through a week without stopping in at least three times for a latte and her usual cream-filled, chocolate-covered doughnut, a treat she was anxious to get to once she got back home.

"Only for about three or four days," Coco told him, trying her best to convince him that this was a good idea and truly believing that once Russ knew all the

facts, he'd be on her side. After all, Russ was a reasonable man, a man of virtue. Why else would he be
running for mayor and doing so well in the polls? The
good people of Briggs would never elect someone who
didn't exemplify their moral code. "Just until his apartment is livable again. Right now, there's no water due
to a broken pipe."

Baby Lily slept in her donated car seat on a chair next
to Coco. Outside, the sun tried its best to melt the snow,
but the cold temperature wouldn't cooperate.

"So, let me get this straight. Tilly might be the sheriff's baby?"

"It's Lily, and yes. Dani Century is the mom, but we
really shouldn't be talking about this here." She looked
around to see if anyone was close enough to listen in
on their conversation. "Sheriff Wilson doesn't want this
news to get out."

"Huh. And he claims he had no idea about any of
this?"

"He's not even certain that Lily is his. He's getting a
DNA test to prove it one way or the other."

Russ snickered and shook his head as he drank his
coffee. "Gotta hand it to the sheriff. Never thought he'd
be a part of something like this. A reckless scandal of
the year for ol' Briggs, Idaho."

"It's not a scandal, at least not yet. No one knows
about it but you and me, and I only told you because I
know I can trust you. And I wanted to make sure you
understood all the facts of why Jet's staying with me.
But it has no bearing on our relationship. Matter of fact,
I hope our date is still on for tonight."

"Of course it is. My only concern is how this might
look to the good people of Briggs...the sheriff moving

in with my girl. Might cause a lot of speculation, a lot of unnecessary gossip."

"Not if we don't tell anyone. It we play it right, by the time the gossip leaks, Sheriff Wilson and Lily will have already moved out."

"Yes, but I…"

Russ kept getting distracted by friends and acquaintances who wanted to wish him a good morning or talk to him about anything from extending the Western Days festival to adding a streetlight on Main and First.

"Excuse me, Mr. Knightly, but we sure could'a used those extra plows in the last couple'a days," Marty Bean, owner of Moo's Creamery, said in a loud voice. "You've got my vote, that's for sure."

"Thanks," Russ told him, turning to shake his hand. "I appreciate it. There's so many more community improvements I want to make. You're going to be amazed at how efficient this town runs after I'm elected."

"Looking forward to it," Kerry Walker, the local cobbler, told him, holding on to a paper cup filled with a hot beverage and carrying a pink box of pastries.

It had been like that ever since she and Russ sat down. People kept coming up to their table to wish him well with the election that was less than two weeks away. Great for Russ, but not so great for a serious conversation with him.

"Is this Lily?" Betty Hastings, an older woman, asked. "I heard all about her from Amanda Gump. Poor little dear. Glad you're both taking such good care of her."

"It's our pleasure, especially while the sheriff is so busy," Russ told her.

Coco's stomach did a flip and her throat tightened. She gave Russ a look, but he seemed to ignore her.

"Our sheriff has enough on his plate without having to look for Lily's mom," Kerry Walker said. "Poor darlin' needs her mom."

"She sure does," Russ announced, as he gazed lovingly over at Lily. It was the first time he'd really looked at her since she and Coco had arrived almost an hour ago. "And her dad."

Panic tightened Coco's chest and she could feel her eyes go wide. Hadn't she been clear enough that Jet's paternity was a secret?

"Whoever that is," seventysomething Phyllis Gabaur added. Phyllis was by far the town's biggest and best gossip. If anyone wanted to spread a rumor, they could just say something in front of Phyllis and it would travel faster than if it had been written in the sky.

"Didn't you know?" Russ began, looking over at Coco, who shook her head. "Oh, wait, that information might be a secret. Is it private and confidential, darling?"

Coco hated this.

"Actually…"

"I love secrets," Phyllis said.

I bet you do, Coco thought. "We're all simply waiting to learn information about Lily like everyone else. There's no secret," Coco said, trying her best to quell the storm and not pique anyone's interest. If Phyllis thought there was a secret, she would be relentless until she learned its origin.

Russ turned, set his focus squarely on Coco and with a reassuring voice said, "Oh, well, in that case, if it's not a secret that Sheriff Wilson is the father—"

"*Might* be the father," Coco said, leaping to the sheriff's defense. "Wait…no… We can't be…" She clammed up, but she couldn't take back the words.

"*Our* sheriff is the father? Well, I'll be," Phyllis said, and slipped away like dust in the wind. One minute she was there, ogling baby Lily, and once she had her tidbit of gossip, she vanished.

Coco's heart raced, and as if on cue, Lily stretched her arms and legs, and opened her eyes.

"Wow, Sheriff Wilson has a baby," Betty said. "That's wonderful news!"

And with that, questions came rapid-fire, but Lily wanted no part of it. Her wails permeated the shop, and soon everyone in it, including the staff, stared at Lily. Coco wanted to get out of there. Fast. The damage was more than done.

She slipped on her coat and collected Lily, and without Russ even noticing, she stepped out of Holy Rollers. She needed to find somewhere to feed Lily, and then she wanted to meet up with Jet and explain what had just happened before he heard it from almost anyone.

Coco picked up her pace.

"Why didn't you tell me you were the father?" Cindy Whipple asked as she rung up Jet's only item—earplugs. Several customers walked up and down the aisles collecting items in their baskets, but Jet knew they were doing their best to listen to the conversation he was having with Mrs. Whipple.

"Excuse me?" He wasn't sure he'd heard her correctly. The register was making too much noise. He knew she'd said something about a father, but he wasn't sure in what context.

"Baby Lily… The other night when you stopped by for all those baby things…why didn't you tell me you were her father?"

He did a mental shudder, almost in disbelief that she already knew about the letter, and he wondered how that was even possible. It was barely noon. How in the devil could it have gotten out and spread so quickly? He'd only told Coco and from the way she'd talked last night, there was no chance she would have passed that information around. She knew how he felt about it. How unsure he was that Lily was actually his. She wouldn't do that to him.

Would she?

"There's more to the story," he told Cindy while handing her a five-dollar bill.

She made change. "Like what? I'd love to hear it. And I was right about the mom being one of them Century girls, wasn't I? I'm pretty good when it comes to these kinds of things. Got a sixth sense. Should have been one of them fortune-tellers. Might have made a lot more money reading tarot cards than opening a corner market. Although I still can't figure out why a man like you ever got mixed up with the likes of one of those girls. Makes me wonder who you really are under that badge you wear on your chest every day."

"I'm just a man, Mrs. Whipple, like every other man in this valley."

She handed him his change and nodded, a knowing look in her eyes. "You mean you're a horny toad?"

By now everyone in the store was standing around, listening to them talk.

He took his change and grabbed the earplugs off the counter. "Good day to you then, Mrs. Whipple."

"Well, now that you're living with Doctor Grant, don't you go gettin' her in a family way, as well. She's a proper veterinary doctor, she'll be wise to your seducin' ways. Besides, she's dating Russ Knightly and if things keep going the way they are, she could be our first lady. Everybody knows that."

"I'll keep that in mind and try to keep myself in check," he said and stalked out of the store, with everyone snickering as they stared at him.

"Is that a promise?" Cindy Whipple hollered after him.

Never turning around, he hotfooted it out of the store.

Once he stepped outside, he suddenly noticed how some of the townsfolk were staring at him, smirking with each hello. He hadn't thought anything of it earlier when he'd gone into Holy Rollers for coffee and a cream-filled doughnut. He figured everyone was merely being nice after all he and his deputy had done during the past couple of days, what with the big snowstorm.

But now he knew the truth. They were gossiping about his connection to Lily.

Coco had probably spilled his secret to someone, maybe Drew, and it had spread exactly like he had predicted. He wanted to lash out at Coco for spilling the information. He thought for sure she would hold it close at least for a couple days.

Apparently, she hadn't.

He couldn't figure her out. When they were together, he thought for sure there were some embers burning, if nothing else, at least the embers of a solid friendship. Then, as soon as she was out on her own, she'd turned on him. Betrayed his trust. But maybe there never was any trust. Maybe he'd been played for some crazy reason he couldn't quite understand. Maybe it had something to do with the election. With Russ. With her inner desire for power.

He knew he was probably thinking off the deep end.

It didn't make any sense, especially since he'd loaded up his SUV with enough of his things for several days, and he'd found an air bed at Hess's Department Store like she'd told him about, bought it, and he was just about to bring it over to Coco's apartment and set it up in that spare bedroom she'd talked about.

But now he wasn't sure that he should.

Why would she invite him in, appear as if she had his back, if she was simply going to stick a knife in it?

He couldn't begin to imagine her motives.

For a man who valued his privacy...treasured his privacy...all the details of his now scandalous affair had instantly become fodder for the town's busybodies.

As he hurried back to his vehicle down the now cleaned sidewalks, past the open-for-business shops on Main Street, trying to get a handle on all of this, total confusion muddied up his thoughts.

He'd known this would happen eventually, just not the first day.

He beeped open the SUV and jumped inside, shutting out the town around him, trying his best to understand what this all meant.

Chapter 7

For the next couple of days, Jet and Coco were polite and mindful of each other's privacy, circumstances that Jet appreciated. Circumstances that he knew were only temporary. He went about his business, and she went about hers, meeting only at night for dinner, a situation he didn't fully understand, given how, until recently, Russ had buzzed around her like a bee to a flower.

Not that he was complaining about the situation. He wasn't. Matter of fact, he truly enjoyed their dinners, and was looking forward to one tonight, but he found it curious nonetheless and continued to keep his distance.

They hadn't discussed how the town had learned about his letter from Dani, because it never came up in conversation. Every time something even remotely close to that subject was mentioned, one of them would quickly change the subject. And for the time being, Jet could live with that just fine.

Plus, he didn't press his luck. He tried to be gone when Coco woke up in the morning, dropping Lily off with Drew and her folks whenever possible. Sometimes, like yesterday, Coco had packed up and left with Lily before he'd stepped out of his room, which was okay with him. He had also learned how to pack up Lily with everything she needed and take her with him when all he had to do was attend a council meeting or participate in a school function.

He even managed to set up a DNA test with Lily without anyone, even Coco, knowing what he was up to. He wanted to keep the test a secret for as long as possible. Not that everyone didn't already think he was the father—he just didn't want them betting on the results, which he knew for a fact they would do.

He'd made the appointment with Doctor Bradley Starr, the town's general practitioner, for a Saturday afternoon, when he knew Coco would be out tending to two new stallions on one of the outlying ranches and couldn't take Lily along. There were virtually no internet or phone signals out there, and Coco didn't want to put Lily in that kind of situation, especially while out in the pastures.

The doctor agreed to have them come into the office when no one, not even his nurse, would be around. They could meet in complete privacy.

"From all indications, Lily is about three weeks old, maybe closer to four," Doctor Starr said. "Her weight is right on target, and in general, she's in very good health. We should get the results of the DNA test in about five to ten business days."

Jet did up Lily's pink jumper, then slipped on her warm funny monkey outer jumper and zipped it up.

When she was all nice and toasty, hood fastened, hands completely covered, Jet secured her in her car seat.

"There you go, sweet cakes. You're all set." He looked over at the doctor. "That's great news on all fronts, Doc. Thanks."

Lily had barely fussed during the exam, and now she was busy looking around at all the bright pictures and mobiles that dominated the small examination room. Even though Doctor Starr was a GP, he treated most of the babies and children in the town, so he kept one of his examination rooms dedicated to those patients.

"I'll send the results over to the station when they come in. Will that be okay?"

"Yes. Thanks. And if it's possible, I would so like it if you could keep all of this to yourself."

"Sure thing, but how are you coping with the possibility, Jet? Everything okay?"

Jet and Doctor Starr had been building a friendship of sorts ever since Jet had first come to town. Not only was the doctor his personal physician, but on the first Friday of every month some of the guys in town would play poker at Belly Up. Although no money would ever change hands in any of the games the sheriff participated in, at least.

"Doing fine, just fine. No worries there."

"Have you thought about what you're going to do if Lily is yours? And what kind of relationship you'll have with her mother?"

"I'll cross that bridge when I come to it, but for now, Dani has moved on. We won't be having a relationship."

Jet shrugged on his coat and secured his hat on his head. He was in no mood to discuss the scenario with the doctor or anyone, for that matter.

"Then have you thought about how you'll take care of Lily? Raising a child is a big responsibility, Jet."

"Believe me, I'm fully aware of that."

"It would mean moving to a bigger place. That thimble of an apartment you live in now won't cut it. And you'll need to hire a full-time nanny. Admittedly the city doesn't pay you very much, so that expense alone will be tough, not to mention all the other costs of raising a child."

He picked up Lily's car seat. "Doc, I appreciate everything you're saying. Really, I do. But in my line of work, I can't afford the luxury of 'what if.' I only deal in the facts, and right now, there are no facts supporting Dani's claim. And until paternity is proven, one way or the other, all I can do is provide Lily with a safe and loving environment."

The doctor rested his hand on Jet's shoulder. "All well and good, Sheriff Wilson, but I can see that Lily has already stolen your heart. I'm thinking if it's proven that she's not your child that will be harder on you than if she is."

Jet hated the fact that Doctor Starr might be right. No matter how hard he tried to steel his feelings for Lily, whenever she did something new, or reacted to his voice, she stole a piece of him that would always be hers.

"Either way, I'm fine."

Jet shook hands with the doctor and snuck out of the office through the back door, knowing perfectly well that someone might see him coming out of the front door, which was right on Main Street.

Before he stepped one foot outside, he was about to toss a blanket over the top of the car seat to shield Lily from the cold wind, but that sweet little baby seemed to be looking right at him, making him sigh on the spot.

Not only was he falling for Lily, but despite himself, he was falling for Coco just as hard.

"These little guys are perfect," Kenzie told her sister Coco as they loaded the baby llamas onto Kenzie's horse trailer.

Coco was thrilled her sister had driven in to get them, but she had a hard time concentrating on what her sister was saying. Ever since Russ had betrayed her secret about the sheriff and Lily—if it was a betrayal—she hadn't been able to think about him in the same light. That question had her thoughts in such a tangle that she had a hard time concentrating on anything else.

"That's nice," Coco mumbled without hearing everything that Kenzie had said.

"I've been thinking about getting a couple llamas to add to our livestock," Kenzie continued. "The coyote population is getting mighty restless and encroaching on the ranch at a steady pace. These little guys will help ward them off. They just need a couple more months to grow, and they'll be a formidable deterrent."

"Good idea," Coco told her.

"Are you actually listening to me?"

The sisters stood behind Coco's clinic in the clearing they'd made through the snow. For her part, Kenzie backed up that trailer like a pro, only requiring a minimal amount of direction. Something Coco could never do. She could barely back up her SUV, let alone an entire trailer.

"Of course I am. The llamas are a formidable deterrent."

Kenzie looked all warm and cozy in a hooded, deep red down-filled parka, jeans and her usual tan-colored cowgirl boots. Even in the dead of winter, with several feet of snow on the ground, Kenzie never wore anything but a sturdy pair of boots. Her makeup was minimal, and her long, almost black hair was clipped up. Thick work gloves covered her hands, and a black scarf encircled her neck.

"Is everything okay? You seem very distracted. For one thing, it's colder than a cave out here and you're wearing a summer jacket."

Without thinking about it, Coco had slipped on the thin jacket that always hung on a hook next to the back door. No scarf, no gloves, but she did manage to step into her favorite black lace-up, calf-high boots. No cowgirl boots for her. She found them completely uncomfortable and useless for the kind of work she did.

"I'm fine. Just didn't feel like running back upstairs for my coat, is all. We're almost done here, anyway."

Unfortunately, this move was taking longer than Coco had anticipated. The cold had wrapped around her like a vise and chilled her to her very bones. Despite feeling frigid, she helped to load the animals, imagining it would only take a few more minutes, so she could stand the frosty conditions. Besides, she couldn't stop thinking about Russ's attitude the other morning at Holy Rollers. What was that all about? Had she somehow misjudged him?

She kept knocking that hour at Holy Rollers around in her mind, sure that she'd told him to keep the sheriff's information a secret.

Or maybe she hadn't made herself clear? Why else could he have gotten so confused and told everyone the details?

Her mind fogged up like a mirror in a steamy bathroom every time she thought about it. She couldn't see past the betrayal, his eagerness to tell the group all the details surrounding the sheriff and baby Lily. It was almost as though he'd delighted in having something scandalous to share about the sheriff.

How could that possibly be true? She'd wanted to talk to him about it, but whenever she'd called, he'd been too busy to discuss it. Fortunately, they had a date that night. She was hoping to clear the air so they could get on with their relationship, because as it stood now, she could hardly think of him without getting completely frustrated.

The goats' bleating brought her back to the present and she noticed that Kenzie was giving the kids a healthy snack.

"Sure you don't want to adopt those fellas, as well?" Coco asked, hoping her sister would change her mind and say yes. Finding a forever home for goats at this time of year was tough. They ate like crazy, and with no grazing land available due to the weather, most ranchers didn't want two more mouths to feed.

"At this point, despite them being adorably sweet, they're a liability. It's a shame. I'll take them for now, though, to get them out of your clinic so Sheriff Wilson doesn't give you another fine, but it's a temporary situation…for a few weeks max. You'll have to find them and the piglet a permanent home after that."

Coco's teeth chattered from the bitter cold.

"There's one more thing I should tell you before you go, and I'm surprised you haven't heard about it already. Maybe you should come inside for this. It's complicated, and I'm really freezing."

Coco wanted to get warm. Her ears felt a bit numb, and her insides couldn't stop shaking. She crossed her arms over her chest and hugged herself for warmth.

"Sorry, sis." Kenzie fished out the key for her truck from her pocket. "We've been snowed in until today, remember? We've been so busy, it's a wonder I had time to drive into town for the animals. As it is, I can't even sit for a visit. I need to turn right around and drive back. The heavy snow destroyed one of our hay sheds. Everyone's working hard to repair it. I need to get home and help. Can you give me the short version?"

Coco took in a deep breath, wanting to get it all out in one big push. The bitter wind stung as she breathed. "Sheriff Wilson might be the father to a three-week-old baby that was left on my doorstep a few nights ago, and because he doesn't have anywhere else to stay, he's moved into my spare room. It's completely platonic, I can assure you. Oh, and somehow Russ thought I said it wasn't a secret, and now the entire town knows all the details, but I haven't told Jet how that happened yet."

"Jet? You're on a first-name basis with the sheriff?"

"After all I said, that's what you're most interested in?"

"It's the most important part of the story. Last I heard, you and Russ were an item. If I know anything about Russ Knightly and his swollen ego, he can't be good with this situation. Is it any wonder he blabbed it all over town?"

"He didn't blab it all over town, exactly. It just came out when Phyllis and a few other people happened to be standing around our table, meeting Lily."

"Who's Lily?"

"Pay attention, would you?" Coco's hands ached

from the cold. She needed to go inside. "Lily is Jet's baby."

"I thought you said he didn't know if the baby is his?"

"He doesn't."

"Then why did you just tell me that Lily is Jet's baby?"

"I don't know what I'm saying. I'm too cold to think. And this is a potential crisis. I'm having a relationship meltdown. I need your input."

"This thing with Jet sounds complicated. Especially when you bring Russ into the equation. Everybody knows there's no love lost between those two men."

Coco shivered. "Russ has been nothing but a gentleman."

"I wish I could help you out more." Kenzie walked to the front of her truck with Coco following close behind, amazed that her feet still held up her freezing body. "A gentleman wouldn't spread all those private details about the sheriff." Kenzie stopped, shrugged and gave her sister a hug. "Maybe you should talk to Mom, or Carson might be better. He's always good at sorting out these kinds of things. And get indoors. You feel like a popsicle." She glanced back at the house, gesturing with her eyes. "And speaking of Sheriff Jet Wilson, isn't that him standing in your doorway?"

Coco whirled around, and sure enough, there was the sheriff looking as handsome as ever. Lately, every time she saw him, her knees went a little weak.

"What's he doing here?" Coco asked out loud. "He's not due until later tonight."

"Last I heard, he lives here, Doctor Grant. Now go on before you freeze to death. And call Mom or Carson…

On second thought, why not talk it over with Jet? The way he's looking at you, there might be more to this platonic living arrangement of yours than you realize."

"What's that supposed to mean?"

But Kenzie didn't answer and instead stepped up inside the cab, slammed her door shut, turned over the ignition and drove away, leaving Coco to her own devices. Truly a situation she didn't want to be in.

Kenzie had driven off before Jet even had a chance to say hello. Somehow, by her quick departure, Jet had the feeling she knew about all the stories floating around town concerning Lily, and Dani. Probably not a situation she wanted to get involved in.

Smart woman.

By the time Coco slowly made her way back inside, closed the door, then didn't move, Jet knew something was wrong. She wasn't wearing a hat or gloves, and her coat looked like something you'd put on for a mild spring day, not for a winter cold snap in Idaho.

"Are you all right?" he asked, trying to get a look at her face.

She turned to him. "I… I'm…"

He took her hand in his and immediately knew what was wrong. She was colder than a calf caught in a snowdrift.

Without giving it another thought, he pulled her in tight against his body and wrapped her in his arms.

He expected some kind of resistance, but instead she immediately tucked herself in even closer, apparently starved for warmth.

He checked her pulse… It seemed too slow.

"The Fitzpatrick family taught me all about symptoms of hypothermia and how to treat someone who might be suffering from it. Dan Fitzpatrick, the dad, was part of a mountain rescue team. From what I learned, I'd say you were in the beginning stages."

"I'm… I'm…so cold," she said in a whisper, her entire body quivering. "I…should've come inside, but… I'm so tired."

He rubbed his hands up and down her back. "Don't try to talk. Just lean into me." He pulled his wool parka up around her. "This coat you're wearing wouldn't keep a kitten warm, much less a grown woman. What were you thinking?"

"That's just it… I haven't been…thinking. I'm… sorry about…"

But she couldn't finish her sentence. She was shaking so hard he thought she might break, but the shaking was a good sign. Her body's heat regulation system was still working. "It's fine, just let me take care of you."

"Okay," she said and collapsed into him. He picked her up and carried her upstairs, her head resting on his shoulder. "You can't be…"

"Hush for a minute, we need to get you warm before hypothermia sets in, remember? You can say whatever you want once your temperature comes back up to normal."

She felt as light as a feather in his arms, and being this close only raised his awareness of how much he genuinely cared for her. Sure he was mad as a bull standing in front of a red cape now that the entire town knew his personal business, but that didn't mean he wasn't attracted to her like all get-out.

She smelled clean, like fresh snow, with a hint of flowers, maybe roses. He liked being this close to her, just as he had liked her falling asleep on his shoulder the other night. She was a woman who brought up all sorts of emotions in him, and most of them had to do with making love to her.

But he didn't have time to dwell on any of those feelings. He needed to get her temperature up because it seemed to be falling fast.

She tucked her hands inside his open coat for relief. They felt like little icicles against his chest. Her entire body was icy.

Not good.

He took the stairs two at a time. When he walked into her apartment, with Punky at his heels, he headed straight for her bed and set her down, covering her with the comforter and every other blanket he could find. The tips of her ears were pure white. He tucked her in good and tight, making sure her shoulders and neck were covered. Then he reached under the blankets, unlaced her boots and slipped them off.

Punky used his step stool to jump up on the bed and licked her face. Then he cuddled up next to her, as if he knew something was wrong.

"Thanks," Coco said. "But...you don't have to make such a...fuss. I'll be fine."

She seemed so small and helpless, when he knew she was anything but. It always struck him how vulnerable a person looked when their health was compromised. They could be the toughest person around, attitude off the charts with bulging muscles, but when they were hurting, everything changed. All their human frailties took over, and that person was as vulnerable as those baby goats Kenzie had just carted away.

"It's no problem. Are you warming up?" he asked. "Or are you still cold?"

He figured she was finally getting warm, the shivering had subsided substantially, but he wanted to know for sure.

"Much better," she told him with a half smile. He noticed that her ears were beginning to get a rosy glow once again, and he relaxed thinking he'd caught her in time. He'd seen firsthand what hypothermia could do to a person. Not a pretty sight. Dan Fitzpatrick had taken him on one of the team's training rescue missions. He'd learned a lot. A person could die or lose limbs because of hypothermia, or just be sick for quite some time. Not that she had been close to having hypothermia, but certainly another ten or fifteen minutes out there, and she would have been a prime candidate.

Once he got a fire going in the fireplace, he put the kettle on, and by the time she could sit up and have her first sip of hot tea with honey, the shaking had completely stopped. She was able now to speak and pet Punky, who seemed to love the attention.

"Thanks for all of this. No one has done so much for me since my mom took care of me when I was living at home, and that was a lot of years ago."

He tugged off his coat and tossed it over a wicker rocking chair in the corner of the room, along with his hat. He had already locked his weapon away. Then he sat on the bed next to her, gave Punky some loving and leaned back on the headboard.

"You're welcome, but you shouldn't have let yourself get so cold. Being a doctor, you know better than that."

She nodded, holding her cup with both hands. "My fingers are actually tingling."

The blanket slipped from her shoulder and he reached over and gently covered her again. It was then that he caught the look in her eyes and for a moment he wanted to lean in and kiss her, but he didn't and settled into a pillow.

"You're really a kind man under all that bluster," she said after drinking down some tea. "Especially given what happened at Holy Rollers the other morning. It's been the elephant in the room every time you and I have been together. I don't know why we can't seem to talk about it."

He wasn't good at handling compliments of any kind. One of his teachers in high school had taught him to simply thank the person and let it go, but still, he never could get used to it.

"Don't tell anyone that I can be a nice guy or they won't respect my mad-dog authority anymore. What happened at Holy Rollers?"

Her forehead furrowed. "I, um… We, um… That's when it came out about your connection with Lily."

"Oh, that." He wasn't angry anymore, not since he'd seen Coco shivering and thought about her with hypothermia. Now, that was serious. Everything else could be dealt with.

She stared at him hard. "*Oh, that?* This is your opportunity to lay into me. Why aren't you?"

"Lay into you for what?"

"Don't pretend that everyone in town isn't talking about you being Lily's dad."

"I *might* be her dad. We don't know that for sure. There's a good possibility Dani might be lying."

"Is that what everybody is saying? That you *might* be her dad?"

He sipped on his own cup of hot tea that he'd picked up from the nightstand and fought off the last remnants of irritation still swelling below the surface. He was no longer angry at Coco, but rather angry with this darn town and how the people in it loved to spread gossip.

"No. They're saying that I *am* Lily's father. Cindy Whipple even knew that Dani is Lily's mom."

"I can explain," she said, her face contorted in a deep frown. He didn't like seeing her look so sad, not on his account.

"I'm more worried about you getting warm again than how the gossip got started. Besides, folks were bound to find out sooner or later, anyway."

"Yeah, but this was way sooner than either one of us had anticipated."

"More tea?" he asked, not wanting to talk about it anymore. He would have to learn how to deal with it on his own terms, and so would she, for that matter. This affected both of them as long as he was living in her spare room.

"No, thanks," she told him. "I still have some."

He went into the kitchen, bringing his things along with him, hanging his coat out on the hook along with his hat. The way he had it figured, the cow had already left the barn. No putting her back now.

He made himself another cup of tea. Checked his text messages—nothing that Nash wasn't already handling—and went back and sat on the bed next to Coco. Color had returned to her face, and she had pushed the blanket down to her chest.

"Where's Lily?" he asked, missing the sweet little darling.

"She's with Drew and her parents. Turns out her

parents love babies as much as Drew does, so getting Lily away from them will be a challenge. They'd like to move her right in."

"They're doing me a tremendous favor, and I'm grateful. So are you. Thanks again."

"But aren't you angry about all of this?"

He turned so he could see her, one leg bent for comfort. "I have to admit, there were moments in the last couple of days when I was seeing red, but I'm okay with it now, if you are."

She put her cup down on the old trunk she used as a nightstand on her side of the bed and stared at him, obviously building up the courage to say something he probably didn't want to hear.

"I'd like to explain what happened. It was my fault… Russ and I had a bit of a miscommunication when I told him what was going on. He thought I said…"

He held up a hand. "You don't have to go any further. It wasn't your fault. I know exactly what happened and why."

Jet had forgotten the bond Coco still had with Russ. He never thought she would tell Russ so soon about the details of Jet's recent discovery. Jet knew couples told each other everything, but he simply didn't realize the speed with which "everything" flowed.

Well, maybe not everything. He had a hunch, from the way Coco talked about her relationship with Russ, that she didn't know about the blonde in Jackson Hole, but Russ seemed to know everything about Coco. She was more like an open book, whereas Russ only told her what she needed to know.

Jet decided he would have to keep that in mind while they were still living together. He could understand why Coco liked to keep the channels of communication open with Russ, and Russ was apparently like a conduit to the folks in town, especially when it came to gossip about the sheriff, who he seemed to dislike almost as much as his rival, Mayor Sally Hickman, one of Jet's few personal friends.

"In Russ's defense, I wasn't as clear as I should have been."

"You should know up front, in my view, there is no defense for Russ Knightly's actions. I'm not fond of the man, and I'm sure the feeling is mutual. If that's a problem, I can take Lily and get a room in a hotel."

She didn't respond right away, and Jet braced himself for a negative reply. He thought for sure she'd tell him that it might be better if he did just that.

"That's not necessary. I would like you and Lily to stay. I'm sure this was simply a misunderstanding that Russ and I will sort through. In the meantime, you and Lily will always be welcome to stay right here... not here in my bed, but in my apartment."

He liked her response and how she got all flustered qualifying her invitation. "Hmm. I liked the first offer better, but I'll take the second. Thanks."

She glanced at the clock and threw off her comforter. "Is that the time?"

It was going on six o'clock.

"Yes. Why?"

She slid out of bed and stood, a little shaky at first, but then she put her hands on her hips, looking determined.

"I have a date with Russ that I intend to keep."

"You're kidding, right? Just ten minutes ago you were near death."

"Ten minutes ago I thought you were mad at me."

"I didn't say I wasn't. Exactly."

"Well, then, how about I simply move forward with my plans?"

"Are you saying you weren't as cold as I thought you were? That you were playing me to keep me from giving you a piece of my mind?"

"And what piece was that?"

"The angry piece."

"Didn't we just cover that? Keep that anger for your criminals and speeders and whoever else you have to arrest. Right now I need to get dressed before Drew brings Lily back."

"And when will that be?"

The doorbell rang. "That's probably her. Or it could be that Russ is early."

"I can't believe you're still going out with that guy."

"In case you didn't notice, Russ is my boyfriend."

"You mean the man who betrayed your trust? That man is your boyfriend?"

"It was a mistake, I'm sure. The Knightlys have done a lot for this town and for my brother. I refuse to believe Russ would purposely do anything that might hurt me or you or an innocent baby. Russ is a hero."

"By whose standards?"

"Just about everyone's in this town, including mine."

Jet had heard about Russ saving those trapped mustangs in the mountains, but he'd also heard that it was in fact Coco's brother, Carson, who got those horses out. Apparently, for some reason, Carson had given all the credit to Russ, who couldn't even make it up the mountain.

But the sheriff couldn't validate that rumor because Carson wasn't the type of guy to blow his own horn, nor was he the kind of guy who would try to undermine someone else's glory.

She went to take a step and staggered.

He bolted out of the bed and gathered her up in his arms. She willingly went along with it.

"Jet, I…" she began, then stopped.

This time when he looked into her eyes he saw something more than mere gratitude. He saw affection, and as soon as he recognized it, she pulled back.

"It's okay. I understand," he said. "But you're in no shape to go anywhere or do anything. In fact, you've been doing too much. Maybe you should take a break for tonight. I'll care for Lily and those remaining critters downstairs. You get some rest. There's nothing pressing me to go back into work. I can stay right here."

He gently put her down on the bed and covered her up again, but with fewer blankets this time.

She didn't argue.

"I'd like that," she told him, smiling.

The thing about it was, whenever she smiled at him his whole world lit up. He had it bad for Doctor Coco Grant, who just happened to be in love with another man. That was the story of his life. Why should this woman, this situation, be any different?

The doorbell rang again and Jet went to answer it. He assumed it was Drew. He hadn't seen Lily all day, and found that he missed the little darlin'. He knew he shouldn't allow himself to get attached to her or to Coco, but he couldn't help it.

"But what do I tell Russ?" Coco shouted from the bedroom, fracturing Jet's pleasant thoughts. Just the mention of Russ's name soured his stomach.

"That you're sick," he shouted back over his shoulder as he opened the apartment door.

"This will be the third date I've broken with him. He's going to think I'm avoiding him."

Jet liked that scenario, but he didn't want to make waves between himself and Coco. He descended the stairs and swung open the door as he quickly turned back to say, "I'm sure Russ will understand."

"Understand what?" Russ asked, standing in the doorway, carrying a dozen red roses and a bottle of wine.

"That Coco isn't feeling up to going out with you tonight."

"What are you, her doctor now?" Russ gave Jet a dismissive look, then brushed past him and hustled upstairs.

Jet followed close behind the arrogant sneak, wishing he would simply go away, but knowing the man was probably here to stay.

"Hey, babe, where are you?" Russ shouted while standing in the living room. Jet walked up next to him and gathered up his things off the hook next to the door.

"In here." Coco's voice echoed through the apartment. She sounded as if she was feeling much better. Still, Jet wanted to make sure. He trailed Russ back to Coco's bedroom.

As soon as he saw the blissful look on her face when she saw Russ, Jet knew he was the odd man out in this situation.

Russ entered the bedroom. "Oh, babe. We've got all night to make you well again," he said, shutting the door in Jet's face.

Chapter 8

"You're early," Coco said as Russ sat down on the bed next to her.

"What are you doing under the covers?" he asked.

"I got a little too much cold weather and Jet... I'm going to have to break our date tonight. Again. I know you had a fund-raiser for us to attend, but I can't go."

"No worries. The fund-raiser was canceled because of the weather. They're forecasting more snow. We can order in and watch a movie, or..." He leaned over to kiss her and for the very first time, she pulled away from his kiss.

"I'm sorry, I really don't feel well, and I don't want you to catch anything. But maybe if I eat something, I might feel better. I'm in the mood for some hot soup from Sammy's. What about you?"

"I'm in the mood, all right, but it's not for soup." He crawled up on the bed after he put the roses and the wine down on the trunk. As strange as it now seemed, all she could think of was how much she didn't want him to be there.

She wanted Jet, not Russ.

She tried to laugh off his advance. "I am sorry, but we need to wait on this. I want to be at my best."

He stared at her for a moment and then moved away. "Okay. I understand. I'll order soup for you, and some ribs for me. We'll have a picnic in bed."

Truth be told, she didn't want Russ in her bed, or in her apartment, for that matter. And she especially didn't want him there with Jet in the other room.

The doorbell rang again. A second later she heard Drew's voice.

"I haven't seen Lily since this morning. Do you think you could ask Drew to bring her in here?" Coco asked, hoping he would at least do that much. What if Jet was going out for the evening?

"Babe, I haven't seen *you* for way too long. Can't we have some time to ourselves?"

Coco knew he was right. They needed their own time alone. To talk about their relationship and about what had happened at Holy Rollers when he'd revealed the news about the sheriff.

She'd reacted to what Russ had done more strongly than she would have thought possible…but still, they needed to discuss it. Yet, the more she heard Drew and Jet laughing in the other room, the more she wanted to be out there, instead of in the bedroom with Russ.

She slipped out of bed. Russ got up and said, "I thought you didn't feel well."

"I don't, but I want to see Lily."

She entered the living room just as Jet left.

"Where's the sheriff going?" she asked Drew, who stood, holding Lily comfortably in a sling resting on her chest.

"He went over to the station. I have a date with Nash, and my parents have a dinner party to go to at my cousin's house, so if you want them to take Lily along, they will, but I thought I should ask you first."

"Yes!" Russ said without hesitation, leaning on the bedroom doorjamb.

Coco looked at Russ. "Um, I haven't spent any time with Lily since this morning and I'd love for us to keep her right here."

"But Sheriff Wilson said that you and Mr. Knightly might want to be alone," Drew countered.

"And we do," Russ chimed in, grinning.

"Actually, what Mr. Knightly really means is that he and I would be happy to have some alone time with Lily."

"You would?" Drew asked Russ. "Even now, when you know that Lily might be Sheriff Wilson's daughter? Wow! You *are* a great man. What other guy would want to do that? I wasn't going to vote for you, but now that I know you're so nice, I may change my mind."

Russ smiled and Coco knew Drew had caught him by complete surprise. He needed every vote that he could get. "Certainly I want to spend time with the sweetheart. Little Millie means the world to me."

"Lily," Drew corrected.

"That's what I said. Lily."

Then he went over and tried to take a sleeping Lily from Drew, who wouldn't let him. "I fed her about a half hour ago and finally got her to sleep. We shouldn't wake her up just yet. She'll be mad."

"Let's put her in her bassinet, Drew. It's on the floor

in my bedroom. Please pick it up and put it in the middle of the bed before you put her down. Thanks so much."

"You got it," Drew said cheerily and went off to take care of Lily.

"Did you mean that? That you do want to spend time with Lily?"

Russ busied himself playing with his phone. "Sure, but I just got a text from Ben Cartwright and he has some news that he can only tell me in person. So I have to jump, babe." Ben was Russ's campaign manager and best friend. The two of them were like brothers.

Russ gave Coco one of those air kisses and rushed for the door. "Tell you what, babe. You call me when you're free for a real date. I have a lot going on, and this, whatever *this* is, can't work right now. Once the campaign is over and I'm the mayor, things will calm down, but for the time being, with the sheriff moving in with you, it doesn't look too good. Besides, I don't like the guy and I'm not crazy that you asked him to move in without asking me first. You know how this town is. The rumors are already flying about you and the sheriff having an affair."

Wait. She couldn't believe that he just told her she needed his permission to ask someone to stay in her own apartment. She wanted to tell him what she thought of his small-minded opinion, but Drew was close by in the other room.

Instead, she held back and said, "You know none of those rumors are true."

"I know and you know the truth, but the townsfolk only know what they perceive to be the truth. So until it's just you and me again, we should cool it."

His words swirled around in her head until she landed on a thought that caused her irritation to escalate.

"Are you breaking up with me?"

"Absolutely not, but you can't have it both ways. It's either him or me. This town and clearly this apartment aren't big enough for the both of us. I gotta run."

And with that, he left, slamming the door behind him. Lily immediately woke up and had no problem wailing her disgust at Russ Knightly's ultimatum.

It had been more than three days since Russ had walked out and Coco still didn't know exactly how she felt about the situation.

She'd started to call him a couple of times, to try to sort out the situation between them, but then never went through with the call. Something always stopped her. She didn't like ultimatums and she especially didn't like Russ's temper…a side of him she'd never seen before, and hoped to never see again.

Her feelings for Russ were all jumbled up, she knew that much, so rather than make any sort of decision about their relationship, she decided to let it be.

In the meantime, she, Jet, Lily, Punky and the critters that needed homes who still lived in her clinic had all become good friends. She'd been too busy during the day at the clinic to spend much time with anyone. On the days when he could, Jet volunteered to take Lily with him, assuring Coco that her instincts about the sheriff were good. He'd make a fine dad. So it was the evenings when she and Jet were able to spend time together with not only Lily, but the entire group of friends from downstairs.

On her ranch rounds she'd managed to get the piglet adopted by Travis Granger, and the puppy, Mister Wiggles, seemed to love his new home with old Mr. McGregor, who'd been looking for a companion pet. That left Tortie the tortoise, and the two kittens, Garth and Reba, who rolled around on the kitchen floor while Jet tried his best not to step on a tail or a paw as he finished frying the chicken. He'd already whipped up a pot of Idaho's finest Yukon Gold potatoes along with boiling some frozen sweet corn. Tortie wanted nothing to do with the kittens and instead made his way back and forth through the apartment, trying to find a good hiding place.

Coco had put together a mixed green salad about an hour earlier, before Lily had needed a bottle and a diaper change.

Garth and Reba no longer lived down in the clinic once Coco closed up shop for the day. She couldn't seem to get them or Tortie adopted out, despite the cute posts she'd left on Cindy Whipple's community bulletin board in her store. Coco took the critters up to the apartment, and of course, just like Lily, into her heart, a vice she knew she needed to work on.

"Sorry about these little guys having to be with us at night, but I just don't have the heart to leave them down in their cages. They need to be around people."

The problem was, the more time she spent with Jet, the more he made inroads into her heart, as well. Ever since Russ had left her place, she found she hadn't really given him much thought...which told her a lot about her own emotions.

How could she have gone from thinking Russ Knightly was the man she wanted to marry, the man she loved, to having feelings for Jet Wilson, a man who annoyed her so much? A man who did everything by the book...or at least he used to.

She couldn't figure out how one tiny baby could have changed him so quickly.

Jet, who had told her that he wasn't used to kittens or puppies or critters of any kind, had apparently decided to simply go along with all of it.

And the thing that truly set her mind spinning was that he seemed to enjoy coming home to the chaos.

"Not a problem," he'd told her as the kittens ran between his feet. "I'm sure you'll find permanent homes for them soon."

"I'm trying, but finding somewhere for two kittens at once can be a challenge. I don't want to break them up. They love each other and it would be traumatic for them to be separated. And finding a home for a tortiose is next to impossible, although the 4-H Club might have a few members who may be interested. Tortie certainly qualifies as an interesting pet."

"I don't know why I didn't think of this before, but you can petition the town council to change the law. They can make it so if any kind of livestock is abandoned on your doorstep, you have a predetermined length of time to find homes for them outside city limits. That way, you can avoid all the fines."

"That's a great idea. Sounds like a win-win."

Just then, the kittens and Punky ran past Coco. Barking ensued, startling Lily, who began to wail in Coco's arms. Coco gently bounced her, telling her that everything was all right. It didn't take long for Lily to begin to settle again, almost as if she was beginning to adjust to Coco's voice, and her touch. Coco tried not to think about Lily's future, and instead concentrated on giving her all the love she could right now. She'd learned to move past her emotions when it came to all the animals that had been left on her doorstep, but doing the same for Lily seemed impossible. Whatever happened, she knew she was headed for heartache, but she couldn't help herself. She'd fallen in love with baby Lily and all her nuances. Especially the way she looked up at Coco, eyes bright, little fists punching the air, and the sweetest of smiles creasing her delicate lips whenever Coco sang to her.

Not long ago, she could never have imagined that she'd be falling for such a darling baby or that Sheriff Jet Wilson would be standing in her kitchen, cooking up dinner in the midst of so much noise and traffic. But there he was, flannel shirtsleeves rolled up, well-worn, torn jeans hitting his bare feet, thick dark hair tousled— a man looking as though he was enjoying himself.

She'd never known a man who seemed more at home with complete bedlam going on around him than Jet Wilson. Even her dad, who loved to help out in the kitchen like Jet, had his limits.

This man broke all the rules, and she couldn't help but like it…a lot.

"Dinner smells wonderful," Coco said as she stood in the kitchen doorway, trying to soothe Lily to sleep.

"I hope it tastes as good as it smells," Jet said over the mayhem all around him. "What's up with Lily?"

"She's just tired and doesn't want to give up the fight."

The kittens nudged Coco's legs, wanting her affection.

"Hey, guys," Jet said. "Let's play in your pen." He then picked up the two squirming kittens and put them down in their plastic snap-together toddler play yard in the middle of the living room, along with Punky, who tried his best to wiggle from Jet's strong hands. Kendra Myers had given the play yard to Coco for Lily, but it turned out to be perfect for the menagerie and all their toys.

Soon Punky and the kittens attacked each other affectionately, rolling around in friendly playful bliss, all making sweet guttural noises.

"Where'd you learn to cook?" Coco whispered once Lily began closing her eyes and soothing herself as she sucked on her closed fist.

"I picked up a love of cooking from one of the families I lived with, the Garcias," Jet told her as he served them dinner, bringing the steaming plates over to the dining table. "Mr. Garcia did all the cooking and I'd lend a hand. I loved it. Then he lost his job and they had to move to another town and couldn't take me. I was with them for almost two years."

"That must have been tough to lose all of that."

"I think that one hurt me the most, but I toughed it out. I was sixteen and used to moving around by then."

"Still, the disappointment had to stick with you. You were only a kid."

"Well, shortly after that I went to live with my mom. If we hadn't fought so much, and I hadn't been so rebellious, it probably would have been a decent time in my life. Sometimes I just can't tell when I have it good."

Like now, she thought, but couldn't say it out loud. There was always an edge to Jet Wilson, like he couldn't completely relax even when he had no reason not to. It seemed to Coco as if the man was always anticipating the rug slipping out from under his feet. She wished for once, for one night even, that he could find peace within himself. But from what she'd seen so far, it seemed impossible.

Still, she liked to think her place gave him some solace for the time being.

He walked over to Coco while holding tongs in one hand and a yellow dishtowel draped over his shoulder, peeking in at Lily. "She's sound asleep."

"Perfect timing. I'll put her down," Coco murmured, as she moved into the living room, the menagerie beginning to tire as they curled up on each other for a nap. The sight of those happy kittens, along with Punky, feeling safe and comfy pulled at Coco's heartstrings. But she wasn't going to focus on all that now.

Coco just wanted to get Lily down as soon as possible. Once she was in dreamland, the sweet baby could sleep through almost anything, but getting her to fall asleep had always been the challenge. She smiled down at the little girl, now snoring softly.

Coco put Lily on the sofa, rolled up a pink receiving blanket and placed it next to her. Not that Lily could possibly tumble off, but Coco would never be too careful when it came to Lily's safety.

With Lily secure, Coco walked back to the kitchen. "Can I do anything?"

She caught Jet's intense gaze as he turned to her. For a brief moment, she wanted to melt into his arms and have him hold her close, feel his strong body embracing hers, knowing she would feel safe and comforted, too. She could tell he was feeling some of the same emotions…as if he wanted to kiss her. He leaned in.

But she took a step back. "Jet, I…"

He stood up straight again and nodded toward the dining room. "Everything is done and on the table. Let's eat before Lily wakes up."

Coco didn't argue as Jet poured each of them a glass of red wine. "By the way, Doc Starr said I should have the results of that DNA test any day now."

The back of Coco's neck tightened as she took a seat across from him at the table. "Are you nervous?"

"I'd like everything settled," he said, avoiding her glance and taking a few sips of wine.

"So it doesn't bother you that you may have to give up Lily?"

"I wouldn't say that, exactly."

He poked two pieces of chicken with a fork and carefully placed them on his plate. She searched his face for any tells that this whole subject tortured his soul, but she didn't see any emotion at all.

"What if she's yours? Will you keep her?"

He finally looked at her, his face solemn, guarding any emotion. "No matter what the outcome, I'll do what's best for Lily."

"I don't know what that means."

He put his fork down and stared into her eyes. "It means that I can't allow my feelings to get the best of me. At this point, I have no idea whether or not I'm Lily's father. If I am, then my life may have to change. If I'm not, there are different options for her that can happen." His face softened as he quickly peered over at Lily, then focused again on Coco. "I've had years of practice at shoring up what I'm feeling. This time it's especially difficult because of…well, because of you. You've shown Lily and me nothing but kindness and support, and we're both thankful for that. Problem is, I'm in law enforcement, and as such, I can't allow my emotions to sway me one way or the other. I hope you can understand that."

Coco's throat tightened as tears burned the corners of her eyes. She could tell that Jet was trying his best to keep his distance until he knew the truth. He certainly didn't need her to get all mushy on him by crying.

"I understand," Coco said, holding back her tears. She drank down some of the delicious wine with the cherry undertones. It was the bottle that Russ had brought over the other night, but never got a chance to open. She knew he wouldn't like the idea of the sheriff drinking a bottle of wine intended for himself and Coco, but she was in a feisty mood ever since Russ had given her his ultimatum.

"This looks great. Almost as good as my mom's cooking, which you're going to love tomorrow night."

Every Sunday, Coco's parents hosted a family dinner that also included several guests. Coco had invited Jet just that morning, before they both went off to work.

"Looking forward to it," he said, breaking into a grin. Still, Coco detected apprehension. "But shouldn't it be Russ going to a traditional Sunday dinner with the Grant family?"

"Actually, there's something I should tell you about my relationship with Russ," she began.

Just then, her phone chirped, and as if he knew she'd been talking about him, Russ's picture appeared on her screen.

She stared in disbelief. Eventually, Russ had relented and finally called her. She didn't know how to react, how she felt, if she, in fact, felt anything at all for him anymore.

"Aren't you going to answer that?" Jet asked, breaking her trance.

"No," she told him with conviction. "This is our time, and I don't want anything or anyone getting in the way of that."

Jet held up his glass. "To us."

"To us," she echoed, clinking his glass, and for the next couple of hours, she and Jet enjoyed their dinner and each other with absolutely no distractions.

* * *

Coco agreed to meet Russ at the pancake breakfast over at St. Paul's hall, and had dressed for the occasion in a gray sweater dress and her best lace-up black boots. She'd even applied the full spectrum of makeup, including a shiny pink lipstick. Lily had been cooperative that morning, and not only allowed her a complete shower, but also didn't make one peep while she dressed. It was a miracle of sorts, so Coco was ready for whatever came her way.

Whatever the result, she and Russ needed to come to terms.

This was the third year for the pancake event, which was held around Thanksgiving. The sweet breakfast was a fund-raiser for Spuds and Turkeys Across Idaho. Each year, various places of worship of all religions would hold a pancake breakfast and the money would be pooled to buy turkeys and a sack of Idaho potatoes for anyone who couldn't afford to put Thanksgiving dinner on their table. Last year, the breakfasts brought in over two hundred thousand dollars. This year, they expected to reach over three hundred thousand dollars, which amounted to one heck of a lot of spuds and turkeys.

"This isn't exactly conducive to us having a conversation," Coco said to Russ as she poured batter onto one of several hot pancake griddles. She hadn't been planning to pour batter this year, but somehow had gotten talked into it by her cousin, Father Beau, who was also one of the cooks, along with Doc Granger, the only pediatric dentist in town, and Milo Gump, Amanda's husband and owner of Belly Up Tavern, along with Spud Drive-In. Several other town residents helped prepare the batter, and kept up with cooking the sides, and plat-

ing the food. It was a group effort of mega proportions
that the good people of Briggs loved to participate in
each year. Coco's entire family had already been served
and were seated somewhere inside the hall. She had intended to sit with them, until Father Beau along with
Russ had commandeered her.

The hall was meant to hold over two hundred people,
and from what Coco could tell, at least two hundred
and fifty had squeezed inside, with another hundred or
so braving the cold to stand in line outside. For fifteen
dollars, each person received a full stack of pancakes,
sausage, bacon, hash browns and all the coffee, tea or
milk they could drink. Kids five and under ate for free,
which always brought out most of the young families in
town and in the surrounding ranch community.

The batter was donated, along with all of the sides;
so 90 percent of that fifteen dollars went to buy the turkeys and potatoes for the less fortunate.

Coco normally loved to volunteer her time to help,
but this year, standing in Russ's shadow wasn't very
much fun. He was supposed to be handing out the
plated pancakes, which was simple enough, but instead he seemed more interested in securing endorse-
ments from the last remaining uncommitted holdouts
in town, which slowed everything down.

"What's to talk about?" Russ told her under his
breath while wearing a fake smile for everyone he
passed a plate to. He looked his usual handsome self in
a crisp white shirt, sleeves rolled up like he was working hard in the kitchen, black dress pants and black spit-
shined, handmade cowboy boots. "I was wrong. You
were right. Besides, everybody in town knows you and

I are a couple, and that Sheriff Wilson and his baby are simply a temporary inconvenience."

Coco spoke with her back to the hall filled with people, facing the griddles and a makeshift blue cloth wall behind them. "They aren't an inconvenience at all, and we don't know if Lily is the sheriff's baby. The DNA test hasn't come in yet."

"Oh, please," Russ whispered, still maintaining his smile. "As if there's even a question. He's just shirking his responsibility and trying to hone in on the good thing we've got going on. It's as clear as the pretty little nose on your face. He's making a play for you. Everybody in town knows it. You seem to think it's all about Lily. Believe me, babe, he's playing you."

She resented his calling her *babe*. As if they were still in a relationship, which they most certainly were not.

Coco turned to correct what Russ had said, just as he handed Marty Bean and his family plates filled with pancakes. Marty's dad and Coco's went way back, having served in Vietnam together. "Remember, a vote for Russ Knightly is a vote for a brighter future." He leaned in closer to Marty. "Plus, I can help expedite those permits for the expansion you want to make to Moo's Creamery."

Moo's was the family-owned ice-cream parlor in town. Marty wanted to expand it into a chocolateria as well, and was having a few problems getting his permits approved, but if Coco knew anything about Marty, he was completely against insider favors of any kind.

Marty and his family smiled and kept right on walking toward Mayor Sally Hickman's stand. She and a few of her supporters were serving up the sides. Coco knew for a fact that Marty and his family preferred the incumbent mayor, and from what Russ had just told him, there would be no doubt who Marty and his family would be voting for.

Coco switched back to her griddle and poured out more batter. "Not only did you just alienate the entire Bean family, but I believe you just referred to *us* as in a couple."

"Marty is a businessman. He'll come around. And I would think you'd be happy that I refer to you as my girl, considering the messy circumstances."

Coco flipped a dozen pancakes that were now bubbling on her griddle, desperately trying to control the anger that was building inside her. That anger only intensified when Russ slid his arm around her waist and pulled her in close, as if everything was fine between them.

She instantly shifted away.

Fortunately for Russ no one was paying attention. He and the other volunteers had set out enough plates with pancakes that everyone just took a plate and continued down the row.

She leaned into him so that he was the only one who could hear what she had to say. "Here's the thing. I'm not *your girl* or *your babe*. Nor have I ever really been *your girl*. We dated briefly and that's it."

"You're overreacting to what I'm saying. Let's wait until later to talk about this, when we're not so in public. I can't afford any more gossip when it comes to our relationship. The townsfolk need to believe we're solid."

She wanted to yell it out, but she restrained herself. "Solid? Is that why you asked me here? So everyone thinks we're still a couple? You're the one who gave me an ultimatum and told me I had to choose between you and Sheriff Wilson."

His face softened as a smile stretched his tight, thin lips. "I was wrong to put you in that position and I'm sorry. But you have to understand where I'm coming from. It doesn't look good that my girl is sharing her apartment with another man. It's bad for my image."

"Your image?"

"Yes. I'm running for mayor against an incumbent who seems to have the morals of a saint. I can't have anyone associated with me who isn't held to those same high standards." He spoke under his breath. A tone so low she could barely hear him with all the loud voices and laughter bouncing off the walls.

"Let me get this straight. You're worried that I might lose the election for you because I've taken in a helpless baby and Sheriff Wilson, who needed a place to stay while his apartment is being repaired. Since when is that immoral?"

He greeted a few more people, and gave them his vote-for-me pitch while Coco waited for an answer. After the folks walked on past, he turned his attention back to Coco, still wearing a charming smile.

"You're twisting what I'm saying," he whispered, his voice sounding sharp and curt.

That was the last straw.

"I'm not twisting anything except maybe this so-called relationship. I'm hereby announcing that I'm breaking up with you," she said and handed him the spatula as she peeled off the white apron she'd slipped on earlier.

"You can't be serious."

"As serious as a war."

"Don't do this. The election is only a couple days away. You know how much it means to me and how many great things I have planned for this town, and for you, for that matter. It will no longer be illegal for you to take in abandoned livestock within city limits. That one change will be a benefit to you and to those unfortunate animals. If you have any feelings left for me at all, you won't make this public. Not now. Not when your brother, Carson, is set to officially endorse me during this breakfast."

"I don't need you to change the law for me. I can petition the town council myself. You don't care one bit for those abandoned animals. You only care about winning at any cost."

Their relationship suddenly became crystal clear. It was all about getting the town hero, Carson's endorsement. What a fool she'd been.

"Let's not jump to any conclusions. Our relationship shouldn't be a factor in this election. It's not fair to the good people of Briggs."

Okay. He had a point. She didn't want to be personally responsible for changing anyone's vote. This was between her and Russ. No one else needed to know the truth about their nonrelationship until after the election.

"Fine. I won't tell anyone. At least not yet. But make no mistake, this thing we had is over." She'd whispered it with a great big smile on her face, as if she was telling him a sweet story. Then she kissed him on the cheek, put her apron down on the table next to the griddle and made her way to the door. Feeling as though she'd finally taken the blinders off and the road ahead of her was now clear.

The last time Jet had been to the Grant ranch, their horse barn had been on fire. It had been one of those nights he'd rather forget, especially the sounds of the horses that were trapped inside. Fortunately, all the horses had made it out in time, and the brand-new barn that now stood directly in front of him was a sight to behold.

Jet hadn't liked to talk about the fire much, probably because it gave him his own nightmares. One of the families he'd lived with had lost everything when their roof had caught on fire on Christmas Eve from hot ash in the fireplace. Everyone was safe in the end, but all their things, including the gifts under the tree, went up in flames. In the aftermath, Jet had lost one of his first families. They were the only ones who had filed to adopt him, but after the fire, they couldn't afford to keep him. It had been his first real disappointment in a long line of many to come.

Never had he reflected on his life so much as he had since Lily arrived. And even now, being around her only reminded him of what her future would be like if she wasn't his baby.

Even if she were his baby, how could he possibly be an attentive father with his particular job? If something happened to him, she'd end up in foster care. Just because Briggs was an easygoing town, with virtually no crime, didn't mean someone couldn't come in and put his and someone else's life in jeopardy. Anything was possible.

"That's some great barn," Jet told Coco as they leisurely strolled toward it after dinner. Jet carried Lily in a sling as she slept all warm and cozy up against his chest, while little Punky followed on a red leash. It was a clear night with a full moon bright in a cloudless sky, a night without any wind to chill the already crisp air. The Teton Mountain Range loomed in the distance, reminding Jet how much he loved this valley.

"It can hold twenty-five horses, and was built to the

strictest fire codes. Nothing short of cannon fire can bring it down now. I still can't believe it sometimes. Half the town pitched in both with the supplies and with muscle thanks to Jake Scott putting out the word. He really came through for our family and I'm so proud to have him as a brother-in-law. He's a true hero in my book."

"In anyone's book, to be sure."

"That barn serves as a constant reminder of how quickly life can change in a heartbeat."

Lily squirmed against his chest, tiny knees and elbows poking at him. "I know something about life-changing moments."

"Unfortunately so does Lily. Whatever happens to her, I feel lucky that she was dropped off on my doorstep and I've been able to be part of her life."

Almost on instinct, he took Coco's hand in his. "I am, too. You've been wonderful to both of us. Thank you for that."

They were inside the warmth of the dimly lit barn now. A few of the horses nickered and scraped the bottom of their stalls. The familiar smells that Jet actually liked filled his head with some good memories and some not-so-good memories. Regardless, they made up the fabric of his life, and this night only added to it.

"My pleasure. I'd do it again in a heartbeat."

He turned to her. "I only hope Lily can grow up with all the love I felt around your dinner table tonight. Your parents are a delight, and the banter between Carson, his wife, Zoe, and your sisters, Callie, Kayla and Kenzie, is a riot. Not to mention the seemingly tight friendship between their spouses. I don't think I've ever witnessed anything like it. Thank you for inviting me. But again, shouldn't it have been Russ?"

"That's what I wanted to talk to you about, away from my family. I promised Russ I wouldn't tell anyone until after the election, even though I rarely keep anything from my family. Still, I thought I should tell you first. I broke up with Russ today."

Jet could hardly believe what she'd just said. "Is this for good? I mean, are you sure? He might be the new mayor and you'd be, well, maybe one day, be the town's first lady."

Although he doubted that Russ could settle for any one woman, even someone as truly wonderful as Coco Grant. The man was a complete fool to let her go.

"It's not a title that suits me."

"What does suit you?"

"Doctor Coco Grant, the woman dating Sheriff Jet Wilson."

He let out the breath he'd been holding. "Are you sure about that?"

"Been sure for a while now…that is, if you'll consider…"

But before she could utter another word, he leaned in, raked his hands through her thick hair and kissed her, hard, wanting her to know how much he'd been wanting her since that first night they'd spent together on her bed.

Of course, Lily picked that exact moment to start squirming and then let out one of her ear-shattering wails that scared some of the horses. Soon the entire barn erupted with angry whinnies that only grew louder with a crying baby.

"Let's pick this up later," Jet told her.

"Uh-huh," she whispered as they held hands and quickly walked back to the house.

Chapter 9

The very next night, despite the fact that Coco had promised Russ that she would keep their breakup a secret, Jet decided to ask Coco out on a proper date. He wasn't planning on announcing anything to anyone, nor was he planning on kissing her in public. However, he thought the breakup was cause for a celebration away from Lily where they might get some time alone. And if anything sparked after that, they'd just have to find somewhere private to ignite that fire.

Drew was babysitting at Coco's place where Deputy Sheriff Nash Young was planning to stop by, according to Drew, who had a crush on Nash a mile wide.

In truth, all Jet wanted was a relaxing meal that neither he nor Coco had to cook and that wouldn't be interrupted by a needy baby...not that he in the least bit minded taking care of Lily. He found that he truly enjoyed it, but tonight was all about spending time with Coco. He even wore a suit for the occasion.

Hot Tomato, one of the oldest and the only upscale restaurant in Briggs, was owned by two generations of the Salerno family. Everyone in the family worked or helped in the restaurant, including little Mary Salerno, who couldn't be more than ten or eleven years old. She sometimes greeted the patrons as they arrived.

Tonight was no exception. Coco and Jet had decided they would meet each other at the restaurant due to their schedules. They figured since they were already living together temporarily no one would be the wiser.

"Good evening and welcome to Hot Tomato," Mary told Jet as he walked through the front door. Mary wore a pretty hunter green velvet dress, white tights, black patent shoes and a matching green satin bow in her long dark hair, which was neatly parted on her right side.

She reminded Jet of what Lily might look like when she was Mary's age, and it made him wonder if he would still be a part of Lily's life by then. Funny thing was, for the first time in his entire life, he allowed himself to hope for something that was a long way off, and it scared him.

He pushed that thought out of his head. Tonight was all about Coco and he didn't want anything to get in the way of that. He was getting ready to enter a relationship with a woman who was unlike anyone he'd ever dated before, a woman he'd lusted over for months, a woman who was by far the kindest person he'd ever known.

For one thing, she had roots, real roots that bore down deep into Briggs, and he liked that concept. He'd grown weary of living a "temporary" life where he couldn't or wouldn't commit to anything or anyone for the long term. Even his position of sheriff in Briggs was subject to the pleasure or displeasure of the mayor, and if Russ won the election, Jet's job could end on Russ's first day.

"So nice to see you, Mary. That's a very pretty dress."

"Thank you, Sheriff Wilson," Mary said with a smile. Then she held out her hand, pointing to the podium. "Right this way to check in with the hostess."

Jet followed directions. It was still fairly early, only six thirty, so the restaurant wasn't very busy. He was hoping for a table in the back of the restaurant where he and Coco could have some privacy.

As soon as he checked in with the hostess, Mary's seventeen-year-old sister, with whom he exchanged quick hugs and double kisses, she escorted him to the absolute perfect table where Coco was already seated.

A great big welcoming smile lit up her beautiful face, then she stood and kissed him on each check, Italian style, and he willingly reciprocated.

"I could get used to this real easy-like," he said, wanting to pull her in closer before she backed away from his embrace.

"It's the official Salerno greeting," she told him, her face showing a slight blush.

"We should adopt it."

"Done," she said, chuckling then sitting back down in her wooden chair across from him.

It was the first he'd seen of her alone since they'd kissed the previous night. Lily had needed immediate attention after that, and they'd gone back to the house to feed her. Then they'd given Father Beau, who had also attended the dinner, a ride to St. Paul's, and by the time they walked into Coco's apartment, Lily needed feeding and changing again. Of course, after all the excitement, Lily wouldn't fall back to sleep, so Jet stayed up with her until she finally drifted off around two in the morning, only to wake back up again at five.

Needless to say he was dog-tired, but nothing was going to stop this dinner.

"You look beautiful...stunning actually," Jet told Coco, as his gaze gently caressed her lovely curves.

She'd worn a very low-cut navy blue cocktail dress that only increased his intense desire for her.

"I haven't worn this dress since a friend's wedding in Boise a couple of years ago. It's a bit risqué for Briggs."

He wanted to devour her.

"It's perfect," he said, knowing his voice had gone down an octave. The excitement that rushed through his body made him wonder if he was going to be able to get through this dinner without kissing her. He felt grateful they weren't in a booth sitting side by side, but instead in chairs directly across from each other.

"You don't look so bad yourself," she said. "I don't think I've ever seen you in an actual suit."

"That's because I've never owned one until today. Never had the need."

"You bought a suit for me? For our date?"

"I did." If he were the blushing kind, he knew his face would be bright red.

"Jet Wilson, you do something to amaze me almost every day."

"I hope that's a good thing."

Her full lips stretched into a big smile. "A very good thing."

Just then Mama Salerno, a short, plump, classically Old World–looking woman in her midseventies walked up to the table with an open bottle of wine and two stemmed glasses. "This is a wonderful thing to see you two in my restaurant. Tonight, the wine, she is on me."

Mama Salerno poured two glasses, then gave each of them a hug and double kisses.

"Thank you," both Jet and Coco said almost in unison.

Mama took a couple steps back, holding her hands together just under her ample chest. "So, tell me, how is that baby of yours? I hear she's a little doll. You're gonna have to bring her in so I can bless her. Nothing bad will happen once I bless her. I have the power. It's been passed down to me through the generations. It's the tradition in my family." She held up a hand, waving to indicate a very long time.

"I will," Jet told her to Coco's surprised look. "Anything to keep her safe."

"I always knew you was a good man," Mama Salerno said, squeezing his shoulder. Then she gazed over at Coco. "That Russ Knightly ain't the man for you. Trust me. I know the truth."

Then she turned and strolled back to the kitchen.

"She's right, you know," Jet told Coco. "I have it from a reliable source that Mama is always spot on with her advice."

"Oh, yeah? And who's your source?"

"I can't say or they'll put a curse on me."

"And you believe in curses?"

"Only when they benefit me."

"And this does, I take it."

"One hundred percent."

Coco laughed and Jet's entire world brightened. This night was off to a great start and it could only get better from here on out.

* * *

"Are you sure it's okay that we're in here?" Coco asked as she followed Jet inside the dark police station.

Coco had to admit it was perhaps the craziest place she'd ever made love…not that she had much experience with making love in crazy places. That trophy would probably have to go to her sister Kayla, who was caught kissing Wade Porter when they were budding teens inside the bull pen. Fortunately, Carson had spotted them and pulled them out before their bull was able to charge.

Jet took her hands in his and squeezed. "I'm pretty sure the sheriff said it would be fine," he teased. He gently kissed her while unbuttoning her coat. "Your skin, it's so soft."

She slipped her arms out of her coat, he did the same with his, allowing both jackets to fall to the floor. "Sheriff, you say the sweetest things."

"I'm sure I'll have more to say, once you're not wearing that dress," he mumbled into her ear as he kissed around the edges of it, which caused her to feel a combination of anticipation and excitement.

She ducked away from him and began to unzip her dress. "Then maybe I should get out of this."

He shrugged out of his suit coat, then started on his tie. "Oh, sweetheart, I can't think of anything better."

Her dress slipped from her, landing by their coats in a puddle of fabric, revealing the deep crimson lace lingerie ensemble she'd picked up that afternoon at Hess's Department Store. She'd decided Jet was more of a hot red man.

"How's this?"

She'd never been so bold in her life, and she liked

how it made her feel. Powerful. Seductive. Confident. Happy.

He pulled his shirt off over his head, revealing muscles she'd seen before but couldn't touch. The man was ripped, with a fine dusting of hair on a gorgeous, defined chest.

"You're driving me wild, Coco. You're all I can think about right now."

He swooped in and pulled her tight to him, one hand stroking and cupping her breasts, stirring feelings deep inside her. His kiss was tempting her lips as their tongues gently played the rhythm of desire, causing Coco's knees to go weak.

"Let's just make this easier on both of us," he said as he picked her up and carried her to the one cell in the back of the jail.

"Am I under arrest?" she asked, playing it up, while wearing a wide grin.

"You sure are. You're my prisoner and I'm locking you in for the night."

"But what have I done?"

"It's what you're about to do," he said, his voice deep and raspy. His eyes had gone almost black, and his skin seemed hot against hers.

He laid her down on the bed in the corner, the bed with the bright blue quilt that the Ladies of Blue Spuds had made last year to perk up the jail. There was even a matching pillowcase. She knew this because she'd contributed a couple squares for the cause. Little had she known that she'd be making love on that very quilt with the sheriff who, at the time, thought the quilt was silly.

She chuckled, warmed by how fast Jet was trying to

ditch the rest of his clothes. "But, Sheriff, I'm a good girl."

He quirked his mouth into a smile and quickly slipped out of his dress shoes, pants and briefs, then eased on top of her. Slowly he ran his hands up the sides of her body, then back down again, slipping his thumbs under the corners of her panties. Within moments they were off, along with her bra. She felt free, desired and full of passion for this complicated man.

"You're so beautiful," he said, his hands skimming her body, as if he was exploring every nuance. "I'm so lucky to be here, like this, with you." She arched into his touch, and he gently suckled each breast, caressing her and loving on her.

Her hands roamed over his body, stopping on his manhood until his moans filled her ears with his passion for her.

"Sheriff Wilson, I do believe you've captured my heart."

"Doctor Grant, you've had mine since the first day we met."

"But you were giving me a ticket when we first met."

"I know."

Then his lips came down on hers again, and this time the sensations were too much for her. Emotions ripped through her body as he made it his own, taking her to places she never thought possible.

When he slipped on protection and carefully entered her, she ran her hands up and down his strong back, feeling every muscle as he moved inside her. Feeling him on top of her, inside her, only heightened her ecstasy until they both fell over the edge together in a flurry of delicious whispers that wrapped her in his love.

* * *

Jet opened his eyes sometime in the middle of the night, and realized they were both still in the jail cell. Drew would be waiting for them, or at the very least worried about where they'd gotten to.

But first, he had to take a moment to gaze over at Coco, who was fast asleep next to him. She looked even more beautiful when she slept, a pert nose, and beautiful full lips. He gently ran his thumb over her lips. They felt like silk.

She instantly opened her eyes and smiled. Then she turned on her back, exposing those gorgeous breasts of hers, stretching with her arms above her head. He couldn't help himself, he had to taste those breasts again, causing her to giggle.

"Breasts are sensitive, you know. You can't just go kissing them without a chain reaction," she quipped.

He stopped and perched himself up on one elbow so he could stare at her. "What kind of chain reaction?"

"The best kind."

"What if I touched them and caressed each nipple between my fingers?"

She slid down under the covers, letting out a breath. "Only if you want more of what happened last night."

"Is that a promise?" he asked, throwing the covers off her. He hoped they had time for more lovemaking before they had to leave.

As the colorful quilt fell from the bed, he noticed that the cell door was shut. "Wait a minute. When did that door close?"

"What door?"

"The cell door?"

"I don't really know. Why?"

"It has an automatic lock on it."

She leaned over him. "Does that mean we're locked in, Sheriff?"

"It might, if I left my keys in my coat pocket."

She paused and looked at him. "Wait. Is this sexual banter or are you really saying we might be locked in?"

"As much as I would like this to be sexual banter, I'm saying we might be locked in."

She sat up.

Jet sat up.

"Maybe it just looks like we're locked in," she said, almost pleading.

Jet stood, hoping against hope that she was right. The jail suddenly felt freezing cold and he remembered that the temperature in the station was set to lower to sixty-two at night. He reached out for the metal door.

Solid.

He raked a hand through his hair. "Okay, but one of us has a phone, right?"

"Mine's in my purse out on the desk."

"And mine is in my coat pocket along with my keys."

Coco stared at him and then burst out laughing.

"This isn't funny," Jet said, trying to think of how they might get out of there. Looking around he realized there wasn't even a barred window they could scream out of for help.

"Oh, come on, this is very funny. The town sheriff has locked himself and his lover in the one and only jail cell and they can't get out."

Feeling the absurdity of it now, he allowed his barriers to come down and play with the moment. After all, here he was, locked in for the night with Coco Grant. Could life get any better?

"You planned this, didn't you? Getting back at me for all those tickets I've given you?"

Soon he was loving her once again. Nash would just have to let them out later in the morning when he came in.

Still, a pesky notion poked at his thoughts, and he hoped that tomorrow wasn't the morning when the members of the Briggs Historical Restoration Association were scheduled to visit the station. He never could keep those kinds of things straight unless he wrote them down, which he had, on his phone. But his phone wasn't at hand and at the moment, smothering himself in the delights of this fine woman, he had a hard time focusing on anything else.

"This place could use a complete overhaul," Coco heard a voice say. It sounded like Deputy Sheriff Nash Young, but she couldn't be sure. Her mind was still a little foggy as she slowly opened her eyes. There was the sound of footsteps fast approaching the jail...many sets of footsteps.

"It hasn't been upgraded in well over fifteen years," a woman said. Coco knew the voice, but couldn't quite put a face to it, probably because shock had crept under her skin and threatened to shut her brain down completely.

She stared over at Jet, wide-eyed.

"Oh, boy," Jet said in a whisper, as he leaped off the bed and tugged on his pants. "Cover up."

"You knew about this?"

He handed her the panties and bra from the floor and she quickly slipped them on under the quilt. Then she pulled the blanket tight up to her chin. A myriad of voices suddenly erupted inside the jail, laughing and talking in fast-paced clips.

"Um, I didn't know when they were stopping by exactly, and I didn't want to needlessly panic you last night. I didn't have my phone to check on the actual date and time."

"So this is better? I'm beyond panicked, I'm mortified!"

Bile crept up her throat. This couldn't be happening.

"I'm so sorry. I never thought—"

"Is that the sheriff?" Coco heard a woman ask.

"And Doctor Grant?" a male voice confirmed with a snicker.

"Well, I'll be doggoned," a husky male voice chided. This time Coco recognized the speaker as Hank Marsh, owner of From The Ground Up Building Supply.

"But, Russ, I thought you and the doctor were a couple?" Sammy Hastings's baritone voice bellowed through the jail. Sammy owned Sammy's Smokehouse and was on several town committees. Darn that Sammy for being so civic-minded.

She winced.

Yep, Coco felt completely and utterly mortified down to her bright pink toenails, which were now sticking out of the bottom of the quilt.

She quickly pulled her feet under the colorful blanket, wishing she could simply disappear…or die. At this point, she'd welcome either one.

"Apparently not anymore," Russ Knightly said loud and clear. "It seems our sheriff has no morals when it comes to wrecking other folks' relationships. What does that say about him doing his job…using the jail as his own private motel?"

Yep, death would be welcomed, Coco mused. Swift and absolute.

"Now, hold on! I can explain," Jet said, standing, wearing his pants but still shirtless. "Nash, can you grab a key and let us out of here, please?" Deputy Sheriff Young didn't move at first, the deer-in-the-headlights phenomenon, Coco assumed. "Nash! The keys!" Jet shouted.

Coco wasn't ready to leave the cell, she realized. If she remembered correctly, her dress was on the other side of the jail…on the floor…with her coat…and possibly her shoes.

"Yes. Sure. Keys," the deputy repeated, pulling an overloaded key chain from his pocket, unlocking the door and swinging it open.

Jet bolted out of the cell, and frantically picked up the trail of clothes as he went, trying his best to slip on his shirt and button it. From what Coco could see, everyone followed him, except for Cindy Whipple. She stepped forward with Coco's much-needed dress.

"You might want to put this on, dear," she said, handing Coco her missing clothing. "Huh. There's not much privacy in these cells, is there, dear?" She leaned over to whisper to Coco, "The mister and me did it in a public place once. We were outed by a real busybody, we thought we'd never live it down, but we did. So don't feel bad. These things happen…although, we were smart enough not to get ourselves locked in overnight. But hey, who am I to judge? It still makes me blush, though. Must have been pretty exciting being locked in." Cindy nudged Coco in the arm, as if they were old friends.

"Thanks for bringing in my dress," Coco said without acknowledging Cindy's sisterly comment. She was simply too embarrassed to see the humor at the moment.

"Figured you might be needing it. I put your coat and purse over by the back door if you want to sneak out before all the questions start."

"I can't leave the sheriff to take all the heat. And for the record, I'd broken up with Russ before last night happened."

"He's a brave man, our sheriff. I'm sure he can handle the situation and I'm also sure he wouldn't want you to stick around. Okay, you've broken up with Russ, but his ego must not have gotten the message. He's madder than a hornet caught in a net. No telling who he's gonna sting next."

"He's been humiliated. I can't really blame him."

"I can. He's just a blowhard. Nothing coming out of that mouth of his but wind. I don't think you two were ever meant to be together. You're much too smart for him. Never could see the attraction, but then I never liked the man, myself. Too uppity for his britches. Likes to look down on people, especially if they don't agree with him. The sheriff's a good man, a little too reclusive sometimes, but I suspect that's due to his upbringing. Raising Lily will change all that, believe you me."

"But we don't know for sure if Lily's his baby."

"Either way, I know he'll do the right thing by her, and by you."

"How can I ever thank you?"

"You brought back a memory I had long since forgotten. That's thanks enough in my book. Now skedaddle before Phyllis shows up and starts asking questions you don't want to answer."

Coco gave Cindy a tight hug and left out the back door, feeling as if she'd done something wrong, and secretly happy she had.

* * *

"Got word that my apartment is livable again," Jet said as he stood in Coco's living room. He'd packed up most of his things, except for the air mattress, while she'd been out with Lily. He hadn't been able to face her all day, so he'd waited until she'd gone out to collect his belongings. He had hoped to have left by the time she returned, but she'd come back sooner than he'd expected. "Under the circumstances I should be moving back into my place."

Coco stood by the open doorway to her apartment, carrying Lily in her car seat.

"Now? Tonight? Shouldn't we talk first?" Coco asked, her voice breaking. He had the distinct feeling that she was about to lose it emotionally, and he didn't want that to happen. He'd made a huge mistake, several to be honest, and he didn't want to compound the issue.

"There's nothing to talk about. I should have never brought you to the station. There was no excuse for it. I'm sorry, and I'm sorry about this morning with the town council and Russ."

"Thanks. I accept your apology, but I'm a grown woman and I knew exactly what I was doing last night. It was an unfortunate accident to have gotten locked in. That wasn't anyone's fault. Now, can we sit down and talk about what this all means? Besides, I wouldn't change anything about last night, and I can't believe that you would, either."

"What happened between us probably shouldn't have. We come from two different worlds. I don't stay in one place for very long. It never works out for me, and if Russ gets elected the first thing he'll do is take my badge. Heck, after this morning, I wouldn't be surprised if Mayor Hickman asked me to resign."

"She would never do that. I know she thinks the world of you, and so do most of the people in this town. Don't leave. Let's talk."

But if Jet had learned anything in his life, it was when it was time to cut his losses and move on. He only wished he hadn't fallen so hard for Coco Grant. Then his leaving would be easy.

"If you could, please take care of Lily for a few more days until someone from Child Protective Services can pick her up. It might be easier for them to collect her, rather than me driving her over there. I can't seem to get around to doing that."

"But you still don't know if she's yours. You wouldn't put her in foster care if she's yours. I know you couldn't do that."

"You don't know what I'm capable of doing."

It was tearing him apart to be so cold, so seemingly uncaring, but it was for Coco's own good, and it was especially for Lily's own good. He'd make a lousy dad, and obviously he wasn't very dependable or they would never have been locked in that jail cell. He deserved to be fired, and if he wasn't, he was thinking of handing in his resignation.

"Yes, I do. I know you're a loving man with a heart that's probably breaking right now, but you're also a stubborn man. I wish there was something I could say to change your mind."

"There isn't. Thanks for taking care of Lily. It would be better if she stayed with you. No telling what might befall her if she stays with me."

Secretly, he knew it would kill him to give her to the

authorities, so he would do anything to avoid participating in that transfer.

He picked up his bag and backpack, and headed for the door.

As he came closer to Coco, she said, "Sure, I'll take care of Lily. But, Jet, you need to know one thing. In that jail, I fell in love with you, and for what it's worth, I've had more fun with you in the last few days than I've had with any man in my entire life. If you want to throw all of that away because of some misguided notion that you don't belong anywhere, let me say that you belong with me and with Lily. We want you to stay."

His throat tightened, and for a second or two he thought about dropping his bags and taking her in his arms.

But then he remembered the humiliation he'd caused her that morning, and the retaliation from Russ and possibly the entire town that was bound to come his way, and hers, for that matter.

"I can't," he told her, moisture filling his eyes.

He walked right past her, and Lily, then he was out the door, once again leaving behind everything he loved.

Chapter 10

Of all the complaints Sheriff Wilson could get, he certainly didn't want to hear about the disturbing noise level coming from the Knightly estate. He thought he could merely call over to Russ's mansion and remind him that Briggs had a noise level ordinance after midnight, and this would be his second violation in six months. He hoped that phone call would be the end of it, but no. It was now almost 1:30 a.m. and it seemed as if the neighbors were upset en masse now.

He'd had his fill of Russ Knightly and for the past day and a half had been brooding about the embarrassment at the jail. He and Coco had exchanged a few text messages about Lily, but other than that, they'd kept their distance. He simply didn't know what his next move should be, and apparently, neither did she.

He and Nash would have no choice but to drive themselves over to the estate, a task he dreaded.

"Look at it this way," Nash told him as the two men hiked up to the front door of the sprawling estate. "This may be your very last duty as sheriff."

The estate sat on several acres of good open ranch land, with a view of the Teton Mountain Range. The house itself was a modern two-story gray-and-white brick-and-mortar monster that never fit into the surrounding landscape. No doubt purposely constructed to stand out in a town of mostly redwood-cabin-type homes and a few late-nineteenth-century Victorians. Although Jet had never seen the inside of the Knightly mansion or been on the property, he knew it had both an outdoor and an indoor swimming pool, six bedrooms, a full-size bar, a movie theater that sat fifty people and a two-lane bowling alley.

The only good thing about the place was that its black metal fence only went around the back of the property. The front door had access to the street, so Jet and Nash didn't have to wait for some massive gate to open before they went in.

"Is that supposed to make me feel better?" Jet asked, obviously missing the irony of the situation that apparently Nash could see.

"Yeah, gives you that short-timer's attitude. By tomorrow night, we'll know who the new mayor will be, and if it's Russ, we can both probably kiss our jobs goodbye."

He had a point, but Jet wasn't in the mood to adopt it.

"Believe me, I know all about that attitude and all it does is get you into trouble," Jet said.

Nash chewed on that notion. "Okay, let's change this up. Are you committed to the town of Briggs and all those who live here? And as such, do you want to hang on to this job?"

"Yes," Jet responded without giving it any thought, an honest reaction that came from his very soul. He really did want to keep his job and stay right here in Briggs.

"Even if Russ wins?"

"I don't want him to win. I'm hoping this town comes to its collective senses and votes for Mayor Hickman."

"Then you need a new strategy."

"What's that?"

"What's that adage? If you give someone enough rope he'll hang himself? I'm thinking we need to take that approach tonight. Russ is arrogant enough to do his own hanging if we provide the rope. He won't see it coming."

Jet stared at Nash for a few seconds, thinking that this young man might be on to something.

"Follow my lead," Jet told him.

"I'm right with you," Nash said, adjusting his cowboy hat on his head as if he was getting ready for a physical battle and didn't want to worry about the hat falling off.

The two men were decked out in their dark brown uniforms, but both wore black cowboy boots and their own favorite hats. Nash had his black cowboy hat with the blue beaded band, and Jet wore his chocolate-colored handmade hat, one of the very first ones he'd purchased once he was on his own and making money. The hat symbolized his independence, and never was that more important to him than right now.

After ringing the bell several times, the door finally opened and the blonde Jet had seen kissing Russ while he was over in Jackson Hole stood on the other side. She wore a short, slinky purple dress and no shoes, her long hair draped her shoulders, and bright red lipstick accentuated her thin lips. "Can I help you?"

The music was deafening now that the door had been opened.

Jet nodded. "Got a call from the neighbors. Is Mr. Knightly in? We'd like to talk to him."

"He sure is. Come on in!" she said, her voice high with excitement. From what he could see, the Russ Knightly for Mayor gang was already celebrating the man's victory. Signs and banners were everywhere. A hundred or so people mulled around the big open room that soared in front of Jet, decorated with modern white furniture against pure white walls.

At the far end of the room, standing next to the floor-to-ceiling bank of windows, was the man of the hour, Russ Knightly, looking ready for bear when the Jackson Hole blonde was whispering news of the sheriff's visit.

Russ, dressed in a striped brown shirt and brown dress pants, immediately made his way to the door, after he scooped up a woman on either side of him. The Jackson Hole blonde being one of them. The other woman looked like a carbon copy of the blonde only with auburn hair.

Russ began talking as he approached. "If you've come to wish me well on the election tomorrow to try to butter me up so you can keep your job, Sheriff Wilson, you're too late. I'm already drawing up the paperwork to terminate you. I have several candidates in mind to take your place, candidates who I know for certain will do a much better job than you ever could."

Jet knew Russ was trying to get a rise out of him, but Jet knew how to curb his emotions in situations like these. He never flinched and never backed down.

"We're here because your neighbors are upset about the noise. It's going on 2:00 a.m., well past the midnight deadline for the local ordinance. I'm officially asking you to turn the volume down," Jet told him succinctly.

Russ smirked while still holding on to the women. "I'm going to change that stupid law so they should start getting used to it."

"Whether or not you'll change it has yet to be determined. Right now, the law requires you to cease and desist. And because this is your second notice in the last six months, I can confiscate your equipment and put you under arrest for disturbing the peace."

That was a bit of a stretch, but Jet wasn't in the mood for games. He was tired, and had had it with Russ's belligerent attitude.

"Ha!" Russ turned to his group and shouted, "The sheriff and his deputy here say we have to turn down the music or he can arrest me."

The music instantly stopped. Suddenly all eyes were on Jet Wilson and his deputy.

Russ turned back to the sheriff. "Is that better?"

"Yes, thank you, and please don't turn it on again tonight. We don't want to come back here."

"Well, I certainly wouldn't want to do anything to cause any trouble."

Nash said, "That's probably a wise decision on your part."

"Is that some kind of threat?"

"We would never threaten you, Mr. Knightly," Jet told him. "We're simply doing our job."

"What's with the Mr. Knightly crap?" Russ asked, resentment spilling over everything he said.

"Just showing you respect."

Russ laughed out loud, big deep belly laughs, so much so everyone in the room quit talking and paid close attention to what was going on at the door. Some of them pointed their phones at them, no doubt taking pictures and videos of the escalating situation. Russ let go of the two women and continued to laugh. "Respect? Oh, that's rich, after what happened yesterday morning at the jail."

Jet readied himself for what would likely happen next.

"That was an unfortunate circumstance that had nothing to do with you," Jet said.

And in the blink of an eye, Russ pulled back and threw a punch at Sheriff Jet Wilson. Jet ducked, and Russ socked Nash in the chin, causing him to fall back on his butt.

Within seconds almost everyone at the party had pulled out their phones, capturing the events in videos and pictures as Sheriff Wilson cuffed the potential mayor in front of all his potential voters.

"What was that you said about enough rope?" Jet said to Nash under his breath as the two men escorted Russ to their official SUV. Nash read Russ his rights, then they showed Russ the back seat. All the while the mayoral candidate was yelling about how his lawyer would bring them both down and how they were finished in this town.

Jet shut the back door, blocking out Russ's explosive diatribe of hateful rhetoric.

"Just wish you hadn't been so quick to duck, Sheriff. The guy packs a solid punch!" Nash rubbed his jaw, which was already turning bright red. "Have to admit I didn't think *following your lead* would land me on my backside."

"Frankly, neither did I. But it's a good reminder of

how dangerous our job is. His fist could just as easily have been a hidden weapon that he attacked us with."

Nash said something else, but Jet was imagining a much darker scenario...one where it wasn't a fist that had hit Nash in the jaw, but something much more deadly.

Without further hesitation, Jet immediately called Marsha Oberlin at Child Protective Services and left her a message to come and get Lily. It was time to end this thing. Lily deserved a decision.

As Coco arrived at the Briggs Community Center to cast her vote for the new mayor, rumors were flying. Coco thought she'd be the topic of those rumors, along with Sheriff Jet Wilson and how they'd gotten trapped inside the jail cell. She expected that the talk of the town would be filled with snickering, scoffing and possible insults about how she and the sheriff had not only humiliated themselves, but humiliated Russ Knightly, who would most certainly be the new mayor by now.

She braced herself when the biggest town gossip came right for her as she entered the building. Even holding on to Lily in her cozy sling wouldn't protect her, nor would walking in with her hero brother, Carson, by her side. She'd called and asked him to join her.

Nope, Phyllis Gabaur was headed straight at her with a look of absolute disgust on her face...of course, Phyllis was always wearing that expression, even when she was happy, but it seemed intensified just then.

"Hang on to me," Coco whispered to her brother, who looked like his usual handsome self in a brown cowboy hat, a black wool parka, jeans and dusty work boots. He'd been over at M&M Riding School, teaching kids how to ride, a job he loved.

"I'm right here to run interference. Let me handle this," Carson said as Coco threaded her arm through his. She could always depend on Carson to get her through whatever came her way...all her sisters could. He had always been their fearless champion, defending them against anyone and anything that tried to bring them down.

"Mrs. Gabaur, nice to see you again," Carson said, tipping his hat in her direction.

She ignored him and looked at Coco, as if he wasn't even there. "I hope you're not voting for that scoundrel Russ Knightly. Serves him right if nobody voted for him given how he treated our sheriff last night for simply doing his job. And what of Deputy Sheriff Young? They're saying he lost two teeth over the matter. That Knightly shouldn't be mayor of anything, much less of our fair city of Briggs. We deserve better. We deserve another four years of Mayor Sally Hickman, an upstanding, honest mayor who abides by the laws and doesn't flaunt them. A vote for Sally Hickman is a vote for Idaho values."

Then she handed both Carson and Coco large buttons that featured Mayor Hickman's smiling face and walked to the next voter behind Coco, beginning the same speech all over again.

"What was that all about?" Carson asked in a hushed voice.

"I don't have a clue," she replied, scanning the center.

Carson and Coco needed to get their ballots. They walked over to Hank Marsh and his wife. There were a few other proposed laws on the ballot that the townsfolk were voting on. Like whether or not the city should add another holiday to the already packed roster. There was a petition for an official Spud Day to coincide with all the Spud events that happened over at the fairgrounds every year in the early fall.

Still, in spite of the other issues that the good people of Briggs would be voting on, deciding who would be mayor of the city was the biggest.

"Mornin', Carson. Doctor Grant," Hank said as he handed each of them a ballot.

"How's that little baby doing?" Dottie Marsh asked.

"Just fine. Thanks for asking," she said.

"Can I get a peek at her?" Dottie wanted to know.

"Sure, but can you tell me what's going on with Russ? Did something happen?"

"You don't know? I thought for sure…because of the sheriff…and you. Mr. Knightly spent the night in jail for punching Deputy Sheriff Nash Young in the face. Apparently, it was pretty bad. I don't like to gossip, but I heard the deputy might have to get dentures."

"What? I don't believe that."

"It's what everybody's talking about. People even videoed it on their phones."

Hank and the others filled Coco and Carson in on the rest of the details. It seemed everyone's focus was squarely on Russ's shoulders and his wild punch.

And not only that, if Russ thought he had the title of mayor locked up, he was wrong. Sally Hickman was going to give him a real run for his money, which meant that Jet would probably be able to keep his job…if he wanted it.

The problem was, after everything Jet had told her the last time he was at her house, Coco didn't know if staying in Briggs was something Jet Wilson would ever truly consider.

* * *

When Jet spotted Coco and Carson exiting the community center, everything in him had to be forced to shut down. He could barely keep his eyes off her, the soft curve of her features, the way her hair framed her face, the way she walked with a confident step, which made her hips sway sweetly, the way the corners of her mouth tilted up as if she were always happy, the way she loved to carry Lily around in that sling that swept across her chest, keeping Lily warm and safe next to Coco's body.

He took in a deep breath and slowly let it out, thinking about the curves and edges that made Coco Grant. Heck, he even loved her pretty toes painted a soft pink. There wasn't one thing about her—her great disposition, how smart she was, how considerately she treated Lily and all those critters she took in without giving it a second thought—that he didn't love.

He had it bad for Doctor Coco Grant and just seeing her again broke his heart. He truly didn't know how he would ever get over her or Lily, who he'd also fallen in love with that very first night.

"She's under your skin, and for the life of me, I can't see what's keeping you from settling down with that fine woman. I know she's all about wanting to be with you, but you're suddenly playing hard to get. You want to talk about it?" Nash asked as they both jumped into the SUV. Fortunately, they'd missed out on crossing paths with Coco after they voted—for Sally Hickman, of course.

"I don't want to talk about it," Jet said as he stuck the key into the ignition, backed out of the parking space and drove away.

"Well, I do. I want to know what's going on with you."

"None of your business."

Jet's phone vibrated as it sat on the dashboard, where he could see who was calling. It was Marsha Oberlin from Child Protective Services. He'd already received a couple calls from her, but in the light of day, he had decided he wasn't ready to speak to her, after all.

"But it is my business after I've taken a punch for you. You owe me big-time and this is how you can pay me back. Tell me what's going on in that ornery head of yours and why you're not talking to your girlfriend."

"She's not my girlfriend."

"Oh? You could'a fooled me. She sure looked like your girlfriend yesterday morning inside that jail cell. Yes, siree…she was absolutely no longer Russ Knightly's girlfriend, that's for sure."

Jet hated when Nash wouldn't give up on a subject.

"I don't want to talk about it."

"You said that already and obviously it has no effect on me. I'm here to listen. I'm a good listener. Even Drew says I am, and she should know, she's one of the best listeners in town."

Jet drove them the next couple of miles in silence until they reached the station. Russ had long since gone home after his lawyer had him released bright and early that morning.

He and Nash sat at their respective desks before Jet said another word. "Doctor Grant deserves better than me. I'm not the kind of man who can remain in one spot. Something always happens to mess it up. I don't want to get her hopes up. Heck, I don't want to get my hopes up. Every time I do…well, it never works out."

Nash let out a slow breath. "You're kidding, right?"

Jet gazed at him. "No. I'm not kidding."

Nash sat back in his chair, stuck his feet up on his desk and slipped his hat over his face. "Tell you what. When you've got something to say that makes sense, wake me up, 'cause right now you're so full of nonsense, it's—"

"I'm spilling my guts to you and you're going to sleep?"

"You sound like you're still a kid trapped in the system," Nash murmured from under his hat. "Wake up, Jet Wilson. Those days are over. Just like last night with Russ. You were in control, not him. You get to choose your next move, and if you want Coco Grant, and that little baby that's probably yours, you have to fight for both of them. As it is you're not looking like much of a fighter. Didn't all those years, good and bad, teach you anything? Listen, my dad was an alcoholic for most of my childhood. We all have our own stuff to deal with. But the secret is to deal with it. Not sweep it under the rug, and not use it to shield us when something is tough. At least, that's what my mom would tell me, and believe me, she dealt with a lot from me and my four brothers."

"You have four brothers?"

Nash sat up a bit, taking his hat off and resting it brim up on his desk. "Yep, and each one was worse than the last."

"My heart goes out to your mom for having to deal with the likes of you, and your brothers," Jet said. He rose from his desk and pushed Nash's feet off his as he walked over to the small basket that caught all their mail next to the door. "You make a lot of sense for a man who doesn't know when to duck."

Nash grinned. "That was all your fault. You should've

stopped him with your manly shoulders and mean sheriff ways."

"I told you to follow my lead," Jet said. "You saw me duck."

Jet rifled through the mail until he stopped on a letter addressed to him from the lab in Boise. His heart raced as he stared at what had to be the results of his DNA test. Of all the days for it to arrive, this had to be the worst.

"I'll keep that in mind next time."

Suddenly, Jet's entire focus narrowed to that letter and what it could mean for him, Lily…and Coco, too.

Then, as if he'd been hit by lightning, or a light had gone on inside his head, he knew exactly what he wanted to do…what he needed to do…and nothing else mattered.

"Good idea, Nash, and, hey, thanks for the advice. I knew there was a reason I was keeping your sorry self on the payroll."

"Anytime."

"Don't let it go to your head. You're still only a deputy."

"That's for dang sure," Nash said, cupping his very bruised chin.

Jet's phone vibrated in his pocket. Everything seemed to be coming at him at warp speed and he didn't know if he was completely ready for the onslaught as he contemplated his future.

When he looked at the screen he saw that it was from Coco. For a second, he didn't want to answer and instead wanted to speak to her in person, but then something told him he should take the call.

"Coco? Are you home? I want to stop by."

"Hi, Jet. Yes, and you better get over to my place fast.

Marsha Oberlin is here from Child Protective Services and she wants to take Lily. I don't think I can stop her. She said she's called you several times, but you're not picking up. What's going on? Jet?"

"Stall her. Whatever you do, don't let her take Lily."

The good thing about living in a small town was that whenever you needed the townsfolk to help, it only required a couple calls and everyone for miles circled their wagons to support you.

That was what happened once Coco called Drew. Within what Coco could only describe as minutes, a bevy of people, the same ones who had donated all the baby things days before, along with a few more, showed up at her clinic to waylay Ms. Oberlin as best they could. Their arsenal? Cakes, cookies, more baby supplies and a barrage of questions about fostering and what Lily could expect.

Not that Coco believed that anything they put forward would deter this woman from doing her job. But it helped, for instance, when Amanda Gump offered to send the woman home with several dozen tasty treats from Holy Rollers for the kids in her charge in Idaho Falls. Fortunately, Ms. Oberlin couldn't turn down the offer and followed Amanda out the front door. Amanda also told a little lie about how Sheriff Wilson and Lily were at Holy Rollers then, taking a much-needed break.

Actually, baby Lily was fast asleep in her bassinet on Coco's bed.

The crowd trooped after Amanda and Marsha Oberlin. Just in the nick of time, too, because the very next moment, Lily woke up with a start, protesting all the commotion. Before Coco went into the bedroom to get her, she slipped one of the premade bottles in the electric warmer so it would be ready for Lily once she was fully awake. Lily didn't like to wait when she was hungry.

Coco then went to her bedroom to hold that little darling, wondering if this would be the last time she ever cradled her. As soon as she picked up Lily, she stopped crying.

"There's my big girl," Coco purred, then hummed "Happy Birthday" to her.

Coco carefully placed her on her shoulder, her little head bobbing as Lily tried to lift it. She had that sweet baby smell, and her skin felt like silk. Coco's love for her was all-consuming, and having to give her up was tearing her apart.

Lily began cooing with the sound of Coco's voice and her touch. "Did you have a good sleep, my darling? I bet you did, and now you're hungry. Well, I've got a bottle warming just for you."

Coco loved holding Lily, and fussing over her. She loved how she felt in her arms and how her little eyes were beginning to focus and how Lily would try to talk whenever Coco played with her. They had a rhythm going, the two of them, and having Marsha Oberlin close by bothered her more than she could have anticipated.

She had no idea how she was ever going to let Lily go and had even thought about maybe adopting her, or start out by being her foster parent. Coco had already begun the paperwork online. Just because Jet could let her go, didn't mean that Coco would, as well. Lily meant so much to her now, no way would she allow some stranger to take her.

"Not on my watch," Coco told Lily as she stroked her silky round head.

"Nor on mine," Jet said from behind her. Coco whirled around to see Jet standing in her bedroom doorway, his hat in his hand, still wearing his overcoat.

"You came."

"Did you doubt that I would?"

"Not this time. They want to take Lily. The woman said that you called her."

"I was confused. Calling her was a mistake that I deeply regret."

"What do we do now? I don't want to give her up."

"Neither do I."

Coco's eyes watered. "But what if she's not yours? Will you still fight to keep her?"

"Yes."

Coco couldn't help but smile .

"Why the change of heart?" she asked.

"I realized that I love her and I love you. I was scared to admit it. Scared that you didn't feel the same way and once again I'd have to steel my emotions."

"What's giving you the courage to say all of this now?"

"Because I know what I want, and it's you and Lily and I'm willing to fight for you both. I'm so very sorry for what I said yesterday and how I acted. I was such a fool. Can you ever forgive me?"

Coco could no longer stop the tears that spilled down her cheeks. She loved Jet Wilson more than she could put into words.

"I forgave you as soon as I heard your voice," she said.

They fell into each other's arms, and kissed while Lily cooed on Coco's shoulder.

Drew entered the room, clearing her throat, announcing that she'd arrived. "We tried our best to keep Ms.

Oberlin away," she said, "but as soon as she realized you and the baby weren't at Holy Rollers, she marched right back here. She'll be here any second."

"Well, tell her she can't have Lily," Jet said, pulling an envelope out of his coat pocket then handing it to Coco. "She's mine."

She stared at the envelope. "But this isn't even open. How do you know what it says?"

"I always knew, but couldn't face it. Now I can. Open it."

Coco hesitated. "I...can't."

Jet took it back and ripped open the envelope, and there in no uncertain terms were the results. Baby Lily and Jet Wilson shared the same DNA.

"Sheriff Wilson, I do believe you're a father," Coco said after looking at the letter and handing it to Drew, who left the room with it.

Jet smiled and opened his arms. "But will you be her mother?"

Coco nodded. "Yes. A thousand times yes."

Lily began to fuss, and Jet held them, stroking the baby's head. "It's okay, sweetheart," he told her. "You're safe now."

And with that, they would each swear for years to come that baby Lily giggled.

Epilogue

Three weeks later

Jet Wilson pulled his SUV to a stop outside the Grants' ranch house knowing perfectly well this was the beginning of many Sunday family dinners that would now be a welcome part of his life. It was something he'd dreamed about and longed for, and to think that it was becoming a reality after all this time was almost more than he could bear.

He was going to get the full, honest-to-goodness family experience—and he hoped it would be a forever one—where members stuck around, no matter what. And he could put down roots knowing he wouldn't be "moving on" like he had his whole life.

"It's going to be okay," Coco told him as she squeezed his shoulder, glancing into the back seat to see that Lily was waking up, her big eyes looking around as though trying to figure out exactly where she was. "I know you're nervous about telling my family we're engaged, but don't be. They already love you as the town sheriff, Jet, and I know they're going to love you and welcome you and Lily as part of the family."

"That's what scares me the most. Me, big tough sheriff, and look at me, I'm scared of having your family reject me. That I might say or do something wrong… that it won't be true, that it won't be what I'd always dreamed… It's just weird for me, that's all." Again, he had the thought of how grateful he was that he could be totally honest with this woman and how reassuring that was.

"It's Thanksgiving. There'll be so many people at dinner, even if you did say or do something silly, not that you will…but if you did, nobody would notice. I promise you. And besides, Lily and I are your family now, and we'll always be here for you. And we know you'll always be here for us, too."

He turned to look at her. In the fading light she was even more beautiful than he ever thought possible. "Do you know how much I love you?"

She nodded. "As much as I love you. Now let's go in and enjoy the evening. Dinner won't start until everyone is seated. Rules of the house."

Just then Mayor Sally Hickman and her husband parked next to them. Sally had won the mayor's race by a landslide, shutting Russ out completely. Last thing Jet had heard about Russ Knightly was that he'd put his estate up for sale and moved to Jackson Hole for good.

"The mayor is here?"

"Longtime friend of the family."

"I had no idea."

"There's a lot you don't know about the Grants."

"And now I have all the time in the world to learn."

"Yes, you do. Shall we go in?"

"Not before we kiss."

He leaned over and pressed his lips to hers. Warm and inviting. It always amazed him how each time they kissed he felt her love and passion race through his body, matching a surge of happiness and that unmistakable feeling of completeness. He had a hunch…one so strong that he didn't doubt it…that it would always be like this between them. His wish, his dream, had come true—a woman who loved him, a child to cherish forever and an extended family to welcome him into their folds.

When he and Coco pulled apart, she said, "I love you, Sheriff Jet Wilson, and I can't wait to be your wife."

"Maybe we should elope."

"Can't. My family hates to miss a wedding…and speaking of weddings, we should probably have a small one. Something always goes wrong when my family plans for a big wedding. It never seems to go off right the first time."

"Well, we already have the license and isn't Father Beau coming to dinner?"

"What are you saying?"

Jet knew it was a crazy idea. One that he could never have imagined just a few weeks ago, but it was an idea that made perfect sense now. Why not?

"In order to make sure nothing goes awry at our wedding, Doctor Coco Grant, will you marry me now? Tonight? Before dinner? All your family and, from what you've told me about your parents, most of your friends are probably already inside. Why don't we use this night to officially start our lives together? I have a feeling Lily would like it if we did, and I know for certain that I would. So, my love, will you marry me, right here, right now?"

A wide grin spread across her lovely face. "Why, Sheriff Wilson, you couldn't have made me any happier. Yes, I will marry you right here and right now."

"You will?"

"I will. Everything about our relationship has been spontaneous from the beginning. Why should we change it?"

"Okay then. But how do you think your family will take to this?"

"Are you kidding?" She beamed at him.

So, in the hour that followed, while the turkey browned in the oven, and those good Idaho potatoes boiled in a pot, he, Jet Wilson and Coco Grant exchanged wedding vows in front of her entire family, many friends, including Drew—who instantly became Coco's maid of honor—Drew's parents and Nash Young—who stepped up, of course, to play the part as best man. All the while baby Lily stared wide-eyed at the loving couple from Mildred Grant's arms.

"I now pronounce you husband and wife," Father Beau said. "You may kiss the bride."

And with that, the group erupted with hoots and good wishes, as baby Lily tried her best to add her own voice to the resounding glee in the room.

* * * * *

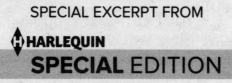
*Rancher Jack Hollister travels to Arizona to discover
if the family on Three Rivers Ranch might possibly be
a long-lost relation. He isn't looking for love—until
he sees Vanessa Richardson.*

Read on for a sneak peek at
The Other Hollister Man,
part of New York Times *bestselling author
Stella Bagwell's beloved Men of the West miniseries!*

"The Joshua trees and saguaros sure are pretty," Jack
said reflectively. "This sort of looks like the land west
of the Three Rivers Ranch house. Where you showed
me the North Star, remember?"

Remember? Those moments had been burned into
Vanessa's memory. Even if she never saw him again
for the rest of her life, she'd always have those special
moments to relive in her mind.

The thought unexpectedly caused her throat to
tighten, and she wished the waitress would get back
with their drinks. She didn't want Jack to think she was
getting emotional. Especially because she could feel
their time together winding to a close.

"I do. And I just happen to know a place not too far
west of here where there's another special view of the
evening star."

His eyelids lowered ever so slightly as he looked across the table at her. "After we eat, you should show me."

Did he expect her to look at him in the moonlight and not feel the urge to kiss him? Or maybe she'd get lucky, Vanessa thought, and the moon would be in a new phase and the light would be too weak to illuminate his face.

Damn it, Vanessa. Who are you fooling? You could find Jack's lips in the darkest of nights.

Thankfully, a waitress suddenly approached their table, and the distraction pushed the mocking voice from her head…but not the idea of being in Jack's arms again. She was beginning to fear she'd never rid herself of that longing.

Don't miss
The Other Hollister Man *by Stella Bagwell,*
available August 2022 wherever
Harlequin books and ebooks are sold.

Harlequin.com

Love Harlequin romance?

DISCOVER.

Be the first to find out about promotions,
news and exclusive content!

Facebook.com/HarlequinBooks

Twitter.com/HarlequinBooks

Instagram.com/HarlequinBooks

Pinterest.com/HarlequinBooks

YouTube.com/HarlequinBooks

ReaderService.com

EXPLORE.

Sign up for the Harlequin e-newsletter and
download a free book from any series at
TryHarlequin.com

CONNECT.

Join our Harlequin community to
share your thoughts and connect
with other romance readers!
Facebook.com/groups/HarlequinConnection

HARLEQUIN

Heartfelt or thrilling, passionate or uplifting—Harlequin is more than just happily-ever-after.

With twelve different series to choose from and new books available every month, you are sure to find stories that will move you, uplift you, inspire and delight you.

SIGN UP FOR THE HARLEQUIN NEWSLETTER

Be the first to hear about great new reads and exciting offers!

Harlequin.com/newsletters